Lost Shadow

Neverwood Chronicles
Book 3

Chanda Hahn

LOST SHADOW
Copyright © 2018 by Chanda Hahn
ISBN: 9781791707750

Cover design by Steve Hahn
Edited by Carolina Valdez Schneider

All rights reserved. Except for use in any review, the reproduction or utilization of this work in whole or in part in any form is forbidden without written permission of the author.

www.chandahahn.com

Also by CHANDA HAHN

Daughters of Eville
OF BEAST AND BEAUTY
OF GLASS AND GLAMOUR

The Neverwood Chronicles
LOST GIRL
LOST BOY
LOST SHADOW

Underland Chronicles
UNDERLAND
UNDERLORD

Unfortunate Fairy Tale Series
UNENCHANTED
FAIREST
FABLE
REIGN
FOREVER

The Iron Butterfly Series
THE IRON BUTTERFLY
THE STEELE WOLF
THE SILVER SIREN

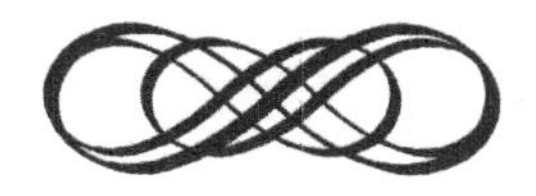

For my Dittos- The Twins
You are my greatest adventure

-1-

A TWIG SNAPPED IN the darkness. Wendy froze, her eyes scanning the trees, searching for shadows and the source of the noise. Nerves were frayed, as everyone waited on bated breath for the signal to continue. Tootles reached for her hand, his small body shivering from the cold and fear. Wendy squeezed his hand back reassuringly.

They had been traveling through the night—sore, beat up, and exhausted— having abandoned the van off of an old logging trail early on to walk most of the way on foot. After Neverwood was destroyed, and the Red Skulls captured the lost boys, they'd had no choice but to leave their home and head to Neverfalls, the safe house, a secret location that Dr. Barrie had built in the mountains. No one had been there since it was constructed years ago, and there was never a road, just an overgrown path. The moonlight gave them enough light to see a few feet in front, but not much else as they worked their way up the mountain.

Wendy observed their small band of eight, ranging from the youngest—Tootles, who was shivering and wide eyed—to the oldest—Jax, who was grim, focused on the tree line and shadows, his hands clenched, ready to fight. John, her brother, was acting as the pack mule, carrying the largest pack filled with his and Michael's belongings as well as Tink's many computers and gadgets.

Standing in the middle of the moonlit path, Wendy shivered, each breath releasing a white puff of air, as she waited for Tink and Jax to tell them what to do. Tink and Jax were leading their group through the treacherous trail. Ditto and Slightly were pulling up the rear, keeping the youngest and the most vulnerable in the middle—Wendy, John, Tootles, and Michael, who was blindfolded to keep Neverland from hacking into his brain and seeing their location. While Peter's shadow hung back following them at a safe distance.

When no other noises came from the woods, Tink motioned for them to keep moving but adjusted her direction to lead away from the snapping sound. They'd already adjusted their course twice before because of mysterious noises.

They'd only walked another hundred feet when an audible crash came from the left, startling a crow into the air. Jax cussed under his breath. Wendy turned to the woods in alarm.

"We're being hunted, aren't we?" she whispered to Jax.

His jaw clenched. "No, we're being herded." He nodded to Tink, the young computer and weapons genius.

Kneeling on the ground, Tink motioned for John to bring his backpack to her. She untied the bag, dug inside and went to work distributing their small arsenal. At the tail end of their ragged convoy, Slightly and Ditto shook off all traces of fatigue and turned to Jax for direction. After a few silent hand motions, they spread out in a protective circle around John, Tootles, and Michael.

Tink pulled on her specs, special goggles that let her see the shadows, or lost souls. When enough of these shadows gathered together, they attracted morphlings, shadow monsters that fed on the lost souls, which would pose a serious problem for Wendy and the lost boys. Morphlings were rapacious hunters, controlled and sent out by Neverland, that could emerge and shift through shadows, searching for prey. But after searching the immediate area, she lifted the goggles and shook her head.

"Do you see anything?" Tink asked Wendy as she handed specs to Jax and Ditto.

Wendy didn't need the specs to see the shadows, and she had the ability to call and send them away.

"There hasn't been a shadow for miles other than Peter." Wendy glanced behind her down the trail and her heart ached seeing Peter's shadow as he hung back, staying far enough away to not attract morphlings, but close enough to keep her in his sight. It pained her to see his soul lost in this shadow form, his body imprisoned somewhere in Neverland Corporation's hidden base. Peter was sulking, hanging back, then his shadow stilled and he became alert.

Their moonlight faded as a cloud passed overhead, sending them into darkness.

"Something's out there," Jax growled.

"It's too dark to see any—holy cow!" Ditto was cut off as a dark shadow sprang out of the woods. It was Peter rushing them, trying to warn them as more crashing sounds erupted from behind him.

In that instant, Ditto replicated into two Dittos and everyone armed their braces with light swords, preparing for potential battle.

"Morphling!" Slightly yelled, his voice deepening into a roar as his slim body ripped through his jersey and grew to four times his normal size, into what Tootles nicknamed The Bulk. He didn't turn colors or gain any extra appendages, but Slightly could put any wrestler or movie hero to shame. He shifted seconds before a morphling launched from the shadow of a tree, then grabbed its oversized jaw as it lunged at Michael and tried to swallow him in one bite.

"GAAHH!" Slightly yelled as he flipped the eel-like shadow monster onto the path near Ditto. In a frenzied blur of punches and kicks, Ditto attacked the morphling.

"Watch out!" John grabbed Michael and Tootles and pulled them out of the way as a second morphling arose from the ground under the boys' feet. Its tongue shot out of its mouth and latched onto Michael's leg. Jax was quick to react and shot a blast from his bracer, severing the morphling's tongue clean from its mouth as the shadow monster's tongue burned into a pile of ash.

The morphling squealed in pain and tried to back away into the shadowy hole it had passed through, but Jax was prepared, lighting up the ground with light.

Tink whipped out the light gun from the holster on her hip and launched a spray of fiery light beams into the darkness in front of her and heard a squeal of pain.

"How many are there?" she cried out.

Ditto, whole again, pulled his light swords, and took off running deeper into the dark woods after the retreating morphling.

"This is for Fox!" he bellowed in a war cry.

"No! Don't, Ditto! Stop!" Tink cried out, but he didn't heed her warning. Ditto was angry, filled with determination and a vengeful wrath as he disappeared into the dark.

Tink and the others waited breathless and paralyzed with worry in the middle of the path as more screams of pain echoed; some were Ditto's, others the morphling's.

"Go after him!" Wendy screamed at Jax, who looked grim as he shook his head.

"No! It's complete darkness in there. It's a suicide mission. He knew better than to abandon his post for a personal vendetta. I will not leave my charges and risk your lives because he risked his."

Wendy looked to Tink for help, but she was already shaking her head at her.

"Don't be stupid," Tink said, though without any bite.

"We can't just leave him to die!"

"We don't stand a chance off the path. It's just too dark, and they have the advantage there—"

Training or no training, she wasn't letting him face a morphling in the dark alone.

"John," she called out sharply, turning to her brother, and he tossed her the light brace out of the bags he was carrying.

Wendy twisted the small bracelet on her wrist and it powered up. "If no one will go after him, then I will."

Shadow-Peter flew at her and tried desperately to grab her arm and prevent her from going after Ditto, but his shadow hand would just pass through her, causing chills and goose bumps to rise on her flesh. He gestured frantically at the others to try and get them to stop her, but unlike Wendy, they could not see him, and she said nothing about him. She ran where she'd seen Ditto disappear and halted when she saw movement coming toward her. A silhouette, silent and slow-moving.

Wendy's brace hummed, and she gathered a ball of light into her palm and readied herself to destroy the morphling. Then the clouds parted and revealed the moon once again, and in its light, the silhouette became solid.

Ditto stepped into the moonlight, his face colorless, his chest heaving from exertion.

"Ditto, are you okay?" Wendy asked.

He opened his mouth to speak and fell to his knees, his hand going to his side, where a dark stain was spreading on his shirt. He smiled, his teeth, once bright, now covered with blood.

"I'll be with you soon, Fox," he promised, collapsing to the ground.

-2-

"DITTO!" WENDY CRIED, rushing to his aid. Flipping him over to his side, she pressed her hand over the wound, staunching the flow of warm blood. She didn't want to lose him. Couldn't lose another boy.

Tink and Slightly came to help. Slightly narrowed down into his normal body, and his smaller, nimble fingers made quick work of opening the medical bag and reaching for supplies. If there was anyone from Neverwood that could help Ditto, it would be Slightly, their in-house medical wonder.

He studied the injuries in front of him and his face paled. "This isn't good."

"What do you need?" Tink asked, she slipped her bag off her shoulders and unzipped it.

"More than what I have in the kit," he said gravely. "I can't stop the bleeding here, and if I don't, he will die before we reach Neverfalls."

"We're still hours away on foot," Tink estimated. "Slower now that we have to carry him."

"What about me?" Wendy spoke up. "What if I walked through the shadow realm with him?"

"The morphlings would get a whiff of blood and hunt you down in seconds in their world. You wouldn't make it," Jax answered.

She knew he was probably right. "What about Tootles?" Wendy asked.

"If he could have done it, don't you think we would've had Tootles teleport us to Neverfalls instead of walking?" Tink snapped. "I'm not walking all these miles for my health. Tootles was too young to remember Neverfalls. It was still under construction when he visited with Dr. Barrie. There's no way he can poss—"

"I can do it," Tootles huffed, pushing through John and Michael to stand in front of Tink, his hands on his hips. "I can remember."

Tink kneeled, placing her hand on his cheek. "It's okay. You were only a toddler; your formative memories wouldn't have kept enough collection points to make the jump safely."

Tootles was getting frustrated, tears pouring down his eyes. "Then help me remember. Please!"

She leaned back on her heels, her own eyes welling with tears. "I don't know how."

Peter's shadow drew near Wendy, and she could feel his presence tickling along her skin. His shadowy hand reached out and touched Wendy's palm, and he spoke to her using images. A house built into a waterfall.

Wendy gasped aloud. She ran to kneel next to Tootles. "Give me your hand," she commanded. "Maybe I can help you."

Tootles reached for Wendy, and she clasped his hands between hers and gave them a quick kiss. "Okay, this may not even work, but I'm going to try. It might feel strange. Cold even, but I'm right here with you, and so is Peter. We will help you remember, okay?"

He nodded, his bottom lip protruding in stubbornness.

Wendy looked at Peter's shadow and signaled to him. Peter placed his shadowy hands over the top and bottom of Wendy's as she wrapped hers around Tootles', sandwiching the boy's between her palms. He shared his memories with her, and she hoped Tootles picked up glimmers, flecks of any image that would spark his own memory. At first nothing happened. His face scrunched up in concentration, and she didn't see any change in his expression.

It must not have worked.

It was a long shot, she supposed. She was about to pull her hands away when Tootles gasped, his mouth opening in surprise. "Oh, I see," he whispered. A few seconds later, a smile appeared. "Yes, yes. I see it."

"Good job, Tootles." Wendy beamed, cupping his face and pressing her forehead to his. "Do you have enough? Can you see it now?"

He nodded, his tears drying.

"Go," she whispered encouragingly, giving him a slight nudge.

He pulled away and ran straight toward Tink, who was cradling Ditto in her lap. Tootles leaped toward Ditto and grabbed his arm, and with his left hand, grabbed Slightly's wrist.

All four disappeared in a flash of light, teleporting them to the house in the waterfall.

Jax turned and gave Wendy a wry smile. "Do you think he'd remember to come back for us?"

"I hope so?" Wendy said, but when the flash of light didn't reappear, her hope dwindled.

Twenty minutes came and went as they paced and waited for Tootles to return and teleport them to Neverfalls. If they left this spot, Tootles wouldn't be able to find them. Or they could try finding their way on their own.

"Do you happen to know where the house is?" Wendy asked Jax hopefully.

"Nope, only Tink does." He never took his eyes off the surrounding forest. "And apparently Tootles."

"Great," John groaned sarcastically. "We're going to die. Bunch of teens lost in the woods. Enter madman in a hockey mask. And based on the numbers of all the blockbuster algorithms, I would be the first to go."

"He'll come back for us," Wendy said firmly. "He's just distracted because of Ditto. I'm sure as soon as he's stable, they'll remember where we are."

"I don't even know where we are." John threw his hands in the air, and addressing no one in particular, he yelled, "I'm over here, axe murderer. Pick off nerdy white guy number one."

"Stop being so dramatic," Jax snapped.

Her brother and Jax bickered like old ladies. Wendy knew that whenever her brother would get overly stressed or anxious he would act out. She wasn't worried about his hysterics, though. If anyone deserved a moment to vent about the world, it was her brother.

She looked back at Peter, needing to reassure herself that he was still there. He raised a hand when he saw her looking at him, and for a moment, his shadow appeared to flicker. Then, it almost appeared as if his shadow was lighter. Like he was waning. "Peter?" Wendy walked down the path to where he'd retreated to keep the morphlings away again. He was trying to speak to her, but she couldn't "hear" him unless they touched. But it was clear something was wrong. He was diminishing, his shadow filling with light and becoming translucent.

She ran to him and his misty hand reached for hers, but she knew she wouldn't make it. In a last-ditch effort, she jumped, reaching for him. Her fingers brushed the cold tip of his shadow just as he dissolved into nothing.

"No!" She fell to ground, her elbow and her face buried in the wet, muddy leaves. "Peter!"

In the midst of her grief, Wendy remembered she was not helpless here. Not even close. She had power at her fingertips—no, on her arms. There within the tattoos hidden beneath her sleeves, she had the power to call and control the shadows—the souls—and they would do her bidding. This was her gift, and with it, maybe she could get Peter back. Damp earth caked on her face as she rose to her feet using her powers over shadows to summon them, not caring whether the influx of shadows brought ten morphlings down on her. She would deal with them later. The hidden tattoos glowed and rose on her arm, and the shadows came in droves.

Wendy walked among them as she searched her shadow subjects, but the one she sought never came. If he was in the shadow world, he would have come. They touched her arm tentatively and communicated to her with images. Peter was no longer in the shadow realm.

He was gone.

-3-

HE GASPED AS air painfully filled his lungs. A huge weight crushed his chest, but thankfully it wore off as his lungs remembered how to operate.

Breathe in.

Breathe out.

His eyes were stiff, heavy, and no matter how many times he blinked, he only saw white. *Was he blind? What happened?*

Turning his head, the white sheet covering his body slipped, revealing colors. His fingers and arms were tingling, a sensation akin to a hundred little prickly spiders dancing across his skin. He pulled the sheet farther down to his waist and blinked at the sterile gray room that could either be a prison or a hospital.

"So you *do* have nine lives," spoke a female voice through an intercom.

Across the room, on the other side of a glass window, a young woman with messy hair and floral-colored glasses sat behind a computer monitor.

"Wh—where am I?" he asked, his voice raspy and dry from disuse.

She didn't answer, her fingers clicking and tapping on the keyboard. "Nowhere that concerns you."

"What happened?" He rolled onto his side and sat up, only to realize the sheet covering him was the only covering he had. Underneath he was bare as a newborn baby.

"You've been dead twenty-four hours." She shrugged and gave him a matter-of-fact look. "And now you're not."

Wrapping the sheet around his waist, he stepped off the cold metal table. When his feet touched the tile, his unused body betrayed him and he lurched, trying to regain his balance. His steps were tentative but became steadier the closer he came to the glass partition. He leaned on the window and tapped the glass, hoping she would acknowledge him.

The woman looked up at him, her eyes owl-like in appearance through her thick glasses.

"Help me," he begged, knowing he looked a mess, half naked, covered in a sheet.

She chewed on her lip and shook her head. "Sorry, I'm not in any position to help you leave."

Leaning his forehead against the glass, he closed his eyes and sighed hopelessly. "I can't remember—I don't know . . . anything."

Her hand moved the mouse and a few clicks later, she read off the screen. "Your name is Peter. You're nineteen years old and are an original in the D.U.S.T program. You've been discovered to carry the Lazarus gene. Your lack of memories after a resurrection is called panning. And let me tell you, you sent Hook into quite uproar when you didn't immediately come back to life after you died." The last bit he knew she added for his benefit.

"Who are you?" he asked. Confused and a bit shocked by the information she was telling him. It seemed like she was spinning a fairytale. Maybe if he waited, he would wake up and realize it was a dream.

She exhaled reluctantly. "Candace, but just because you know my name doesn't mean we're friends. We're not. I've been assigned to monitor you and help get you back into peak physical health. And that's just what I'm going to do."

"Candace," Peter echoed testing the name on his tongue. "Thank you." Her name felt like a lifeline to him in these cold and turbulent surroundings.

That was two things he was now sure of, his name and that of the woman on the other side of the glass. Each new bit of information gathered helped him put order into his very blank mind.

When he turned his head just right, he could catch his reflection in the glass. He backed up to study himself, running his hand over his face, turning it this way and that. His hair, unruly and auburn, some might say reddish tones. Eyes that were too green. The person he was staring at was a stranger to him.

"When can I leave?" Peter asked.

"You can't. You belong to Neverland."

A buzzer sounded through the room. Then the door opened and a tall man with a slightly crooked nose marched into the room and addressed him with much disdain. "I had thought that was it, boy." He said the word boy with derision. "Thought you'd given up on me. Glad to see that we have you for a few more rounds of tests."

"Who are you?" Peter asked, alarmed by the word test. Immediately taking a dislike to the strange man before him who wore a black military uniform with a red skull and crossbones patch on his arm.

Hook ignored him, directing his question to Candace. "This is a tiresome annoyance with his memories being the way they are. Anything you can do about it?"

Candace flicked a Bic pen against her chin in thought. "There's something I want to try. It might take adjusting and some trial and error but it might be worth a shot."

"Do it," Hook snapped. "I want to find out what he's hiding from me."

"Yes, Captain Hook," Candace answered. "But what about the one who controls minds—Curly is it? If I had his help, I could retrieve it faster . . ."

Hook's face turned downright furious. "Gone. He walked right out the front door, right past the guards after he got his payment. They're still clucking like chickens from his mind control." Hook snarled, "If I ever see him again, I'll—" His hands pantomimed wringing a neck.

After a few seconds, he seemed to remember Peter and stormed toward the glass partition, coming to a stop just inches from him.

"Look closely at my face, boy, and pray you'll never forget it again. For I tire of this game."

Peter tried to recall how he knew Captain Hook, but there was nothing but emptiness. Wary, he locked the man's features into his brain, but wasn't sure if he was friend or foe?

Hook gave Candace a nod as he turned to leave. Then he punched the code on the door and headed out.

Hook made Peter nervous. There was something sinister about him. He wanted nothing to do with the captain and didn't trust his intentions. The sooner he could get his memories back the better.

"Did you say you can help me get my memories back?" Peter asked tapping on the glass.

"In theory. Before you panned you were in a . . . well, you wouldn't understand, not yet. But because of where you were, I happened to be able to record your memories and was able to get snapshots of your life from them. "I'm going to upload them to you like you would a computer."

"You can do that?" he stammered pressing a hand to his head, wondering if it would hurt.

"I'm going to try."

"Please . . ." Peter turned, still holding the sheet around his waist, pressing his palm against the glass. "I'll do anything."

"Anything?" Candace grinned. "I thought I was going to have to talk you into it. I see that I was wrong. But first things first." Her eyes dropped to the sheet, the corner of her mouth rising in a crooked smile. "You need to get some pants on."

-4-

THE STARCHED MILITARY clothes given to Peter to wear were black with a red skull on the arm, like Hook's. The boots, like the rest of the uniform, were spotless, stiff and clearly brand new.

He tied the laces on his boot and stood up to present himself to Candace, but she had turned around to give him privacy, so he cleared his throat to give her the all clear.

Candace swiveled back around to face him and leaned forward to speak into the intercom. "Good, now sit your butt down in the chair and strap your arms into the restraints."

There was only one chair in the room by the far wall, and over each of the armrests were leather bands with metal buckles. He didn't like the look of the chair and he refused to budge.

"It's the rules. I can't enter the room unless you're restrained," she explained over the com.

Peter darted frantic looks around the room, looking for an escape route, even though he knew there was no way out. There was only a single exit—the door he'd been led through to enter this room not ten minutes before, through the observation room, where Candace now sat behind a glass partition watching him with a bored expression. The door had no handle on his side, only a keypad to open it from his end, and he didn't think he would be able to figure out the code.

When he didn't move toward the chair, Candace spoke up again. "Fine. You can live your life as an empty shell with no memories."

Peter gave her a heated look and threw himself into the chair, then used his right hand to secure his left with the leather strap. He couldn't get his right hand strapped down, but he didn't have to wait long. The door buzzed and Candace wheeled into his room. It was then he took note of her wheelchair, which her desk had hidden from his view.

She made quick work of his other restraint and then moved to a table and lifted a helmet covered with various tubes and electrodes and wires. Because of the difference in their heights, she struggled to reach his head, but with a grunt a determined lunge, she succeeded and fastened the buckle under his chin.

Next, she pulled out a syringe and tested his arm, searching for veins to see what arm would be the best.

"What is it?" he asked.

"I'd rather not say."

"Will it hurt?"

"No, just a pinch for the shot. Now let me explain. What I've been doing for the last eight years is observing, recording, and processing what I learn. I started because of a special case we have here. And though you weren't my primary—"

"Special case?"

"It doesn't matter. Pay attention. The important thing is that when you arrived, I was already in the habit of recording all subjects. Including your dreams, thoughts, and projections, etcetera are recorded in my computer. You weren't in the pod long before you died, but it was enough, I believe, to jump-start your brain."

"Pod?" he asked.

"Yeah, um . . . you'll learn quickly. Don't worry."

"How is it going to work?"

"Pretty much, I'd be doing an info dump into your brain. Just imagine me knocking over five boxes of photos from your life and some would land face up and others wouldn't. The ones that didn't turn up—you'd never recover those. But of the ones that did, you would have something to rebuild your life with. It's better than no—"

"It's okay," he said, anxious to begin. "Some memories are better than none." Peter's fingers curled around the armrest. His foot kept tapping the ground in nervousness.

"You seem in a hurry?" she asked, as she flipped a few buttons and prepped the machine on a table beside him. Peter heard the whine of the machine turning on.

"I can't explain it, other than an underlying feeling of having to be somewhere."

"Like I said before, Peter. You're not going anywhere," she said sadly and flipped the switch.

Peter's head snapped back as a current shot through his brain. His body seized up, his eyes rolled back into his head, and all he could do was scream.

-5-

"WE NEED TO KEEP going," Jax argued, pointing up the mountain path. It had been an hour since Tootles and the others had teleported, and it was obvious that no one was coming back for them. Or at least not right away.

"Not yet," Wendy said from her position on the ground, her hands wrapped around her knees. She hadn't moved from the spot where she had last seen Peter. She wasn't in a hurry to leave in case he came back.

"We should stay," John said, then sat on a rock and began leisurely cleaning his glasses to emphasize his point. He wasn't in any hurry to scurry off in the woods. "You said so yourself, that you don't know where you're going. It's dark and we're tired. It's better to stay and wait for help than to wander around in the dark, stumbling into who knows what."

"I'll protect us," Jax turned, his eyes flashing in frustration. Wendy recognized that look. Of the lost boys at Neverwood, he had the shortest fuse, along with the strongest and most destructive power. He was the one who'd trained all of them in hand-to-hand combat. "But we need to move to a more secure location where I can do that. We are out in the open."

"If we move, Tootles won't be able to find us," Michael piped up, his teeth chattering. He was shivering from the cold, his fingers trembling as he messed with the blindfold that was irritating his eyes. "He'll come back. I know he will."

Wendy finally left her spot on the ground and moved nearer to Michael, wrapping her arm around him, trying to keep him warm.

"And when he does, we could have hundreds of morphlings on our tail," Jax snapped. "Tink is smart. She'll track my light brace." He held up his wrist, displaying the brace, which by all appearances was little more than a silver band about two inches wide. When activated, the bands gathered energy and, with a small three-inch wand tool that slid into a palm, could fling light orbs. Some of the lost boys had special braces that created light swords and axes.

Jax began to pace and stopped in front of Wendy. "Wendy, surely you can be reasonable. It's freezing out here. Just look at your brother."

Wendy squeezed her arm tighter around Michael and glared up at Jax. She could feel the tears welling up in her eyes. Too much had happened, and the loss of Peter was still just so fresh. She felt wholly unequipped to cope with Jax at the moment and just wanted to mourn in peace. But she could feel Michael trembling beneath her arm, and she could no longer justify sticking around.

"Jax is right, we should keep moving. But I'd feel better if we found a place where we could stop for the night and start again come morning."

Jax sighed and ran his hands through his dark hair. "Thank you."

He leaned down and picked up the extra bags their companions had left behind. Wendy nodded to John, and he collected his backpacks. Wendy grabbed her own, and Michael stuck to her side like glue.

After a half mile of walking, Michael was lagging, his steps slowing, his head drooping. Wendy slipped off his blindfold, pushed her backpack around to her front, and kneeled in front of her brother, urging him onto her back, all under the watchful eye of Jax. It was evident from his furrowed brow and frown that he was not pleased with the young boy and former Neverland soldier.

Wendy had no idea that Michael was her blood brother when they stumbled upon him—only to realize later that he was a Trojan horse, implanted with a computer virus that accessed Neverland's mainframe and shut down their defense systems. Which led to the Red Skulls infiltrating their home and kidnapping most of the students. Michael had done what he could to try to fight them, and had successfully kept them at bay for days, but his young mind could only do so much.

Jax's steps slowed, and he waited for Wendy to catch up with him. "This is a mistake," he said.

"Following you? Always," Wendy grumbled, keeping her focus on the ground, trying to not trip or fumble and send them both to the dirt.

"Bringing him with us. Neverland accessed him once, they can do it again."

"And I blame myself!" she hissed.

Jax was caught off guard by her statement. He swallowed and motioned to the bandana. "You should put it back on."

"Give me a break. He's asleep. He needed a breather from being treated like a prisoner. Can you even imagine how terrified he was during the attack to not be able to see anything? And he didn't once budge the blindfold or complain, for fear of putting us in danger. I know grown men that wouldn't be able to handle what he's been through, much less a young boy."

"Still, he's—"

"My brother," Wendy interrupted. "That's all I'm going to say about it." Carrying on the heated argument and carrying Michael was making it difficult for Wendy to catch her breath.

Jax's lip curled in disapproval, but then he sighed and made a move to take Michael from her.

"No!" she snapped, backing away. "Stay away from him."

"I won't harm him. You're being slow and dragging the whole group down. Hand him to me, and you can get him back when you catch your breath," he whispered, careful to not wake the sleeping boy, but the look on his face left no room for argument.

John had paused farther up the trail and was observing the power struggle between the two of them with interest.

"Fine, but only until I catch my breath," Wendy agreed.

"Then hurry up and you can have him back," Jax remarked while adjusting Michael's arm around his neck. He lifted him in his arms and picked up the pace.

Even carrying multiple bags and a boy, Jax's pace was relentless. Wendy still had to take double steps to keep up with his much longer legs.

John dropped back to walk with his sister. "You doing okay?" he asked.

She shook her head, tears threatening to spill forth, but she took a deep breath and held it in.

"Not really," she said for his ears only. "I would do better if I knew where Peter is." Rubbing her arms, she glanced back over her shoulders, praying to see him.

He wasn't there.

"We don't know what happened, Wendy. Maybe he is here and we just can't see him."

"I know you're trying to help, but I would know if he's still out there. He's gone. I can't see him, and the thought that he is gone for good . . . and not coming back terrifies me."

"Wendy, he'll find a way to come back."

"I hope you're right."

"Of course I am."

"I found a place to stop for the night," Jax announced, coming down the path. Still carrying Michael, he didn't even look winded or to have worked up a sweat.

"Thank God," John murmured and followed Jax to a small rock outcropping that had created a natural shelter from the wind and cold. It wasn't deep enough to cast shadows but enough for four people to lie next to each other.

John used the packs to shape a makeshift pillow for Michael as Jax set him down next to him. John slipped a pack behind his back and propped himself up, leaning against it while he stretched his long legs out in front of him. He dug through a second pack looking for snacks. Wendy carefully set hers down on the other side of Michael. The only space left for Jax was next to Wendy, but he didn't sit, choosing instead to stand outside the makeshift shelter. He kept his arms crossed as he stared into the night, his face grim, as if his determination alone could chase away the monsters.

Wendy was about to say something to him, but John gave her a look.

"Leave him." He yawned and laid his head back. "If he wants to guard us, that's his prerogative. Truthfully, I'll sleep better knowing that one of us is on guard. Get some shut-eye. We don't know when we'll stop next."

Wendy followed suit, curling up on her side, her hand under her head. Within minutes, she could hear soft snores coming from John's exhausted body. She was just as tired as Michael and John, but in the quiet darkness, the loss of Peter's shadow came rushing back, dominating her thoughts with grief and worry that kept her wide awake.

Silent tears slipped down her cheeks, and she tried to wipe them away. She believed she had kept her sniffles quiet enough, but Jax leaned down and gave her a solemn look.

Wendy ignored him, until he sat down, legs extended out in front of him. There wasn't a lot of room, and his thigh was touching hers. Leaning back against the wall, he crossed his arms over his chest and looked at her expectantly.

"What are you doing?" she asked.

"I'm trying to be a good friend," he answered. "You're hurting."

Wendy looked over at him, squinting to see his expression in the dim light. "Are we, though? Friends, I mean."

A moment passed before he murmured, "I guess that's up to you." He paused. "But Peter was my friend." The silence became weighted with guilt.

"I know." She did know. Even though she had probably loved Peter since they were kids, she hadn't grown up with him like Jax. They were as close as brothers.

"And . . ." He cleared his throat and turned to look her in the eyes. "It's not your fault. Peter or your brother."

"If I hadn't died back at Neverland, I wouldn't have panned and forgotten that he even existed. I would never have left him that night. I would have brought him with me."

"It's not your fault, and you know it."

"I brought the shadows to Neverwood." She buried her head in her knees. "They followed me after we walked through the shadow realm. They brought the morph—"

"Stop," Jax interrupted, placing his hand on Wendy's back. "Neverland was always coming. We knew that they would find us one day. We've been training for years. You didn't bring them to our doorstep. I did."

She turned to hide her tear-stained cheeks from him and whispered, her voice filled with sadness, "I wish I had never met you."

"Believe me, I feel the same about you. You complicate things. When I'm around you, things aren't so black and white. I see gray areas, lines I shouldn't cross, but I'm tempted. I don't know how to—forget it." He shook his head.

Her breath caught in her throat at his admission. Was he talking about double-crossing them again or something else? He was hard to read and understand.

With the hand still resting on her back, he gave her a few awkward pats, and she stiffened.

"Relax, you need to get some beauty rest."

"Are you saying I'm ugly?" she tried to joke.

"On a scale of one to ten, with the crying, the red nose and the tears . . . yeah, you're a four."

"I never was a pretty crier," she mused, reminded of her friend Brittney who could cry full out without ever turning blotchy or getting swollen eyes.

"Doesn't matter. Your tears are from the heart, and that makes you beautiful."

"You just said I'm a four?" she corrected, feeling her mood lighten.

"Yeah, to me. Peter obviously thinks you're a ten when you cry."

At the mention of Peter, the mood plummeted. They both stopped talking and Wendy lay down and turned on her side, giving Jax her back, tentatively putting her arm over her young brother. She took a deep breath and tried not to think of the horrible things that had happened and focused instead on building a new future with her long-lost brother and her adopted one.

A light sprinkle fell along the rocks and forest floor. The sprinkle evolved into bigger drops and with the rain came a sudden chill to the air. While John and Michael never stirred, Wendy shivered and curled into a ball, burying her head into Michael's shoulder. It wasn't helping. The constant chill became a plague and her teeth chattered when she inhaled.

Despite the cold, she still found herself drifting off, and somewhere between sleep and awake, she thought she felt a slight pressure on her arm, maybe the start of a dream, and she welcomed it and its heat, which slowly replaced the chill. She sighed and nuzzled into the warmth.

Birds chirping in the early daylight stirred her awake. Opening her eyes, she felt the brush of denim against her cheek. It was Jax. Sometime in the night she had turned over and burrowed her head into his chest for warmth. It was his arm wrapped around her shoulders, keeping her close.

Startled, she looked up and discovered Jax staring down at her. "Shh, you'll wake them," he whispered.

Wendy turned her head only to see John sprawled out; his glasses had slid down his face, his mouth wide open.

Michael had rolled over to him and was sleeping with his back against John's side.

Feeling extremely self-conscious at being so near Jax, she moved away and he groaned.

"What's the matter?" she asked. It sounded like he was in pain.

"My arm's asleep. It's been stuck in that position for hours." He flexed his fingers and rotated his shoulder to bring the blood pumping back into his arm.

"You didn't have to do that," she accused, her face going red with embarrassment.

"Wasn't planning on it, until you rolled over and helped yourself to my body heat. I can't help it if my power makes me a living furnace. It wasn't harming anyone, so why should I let you freeze?" His matter-of-fact way of stating that it was no big deal helped relieve her mind.

"Thank you," she said, looking away, unwilling to make eye contact.

"I did it for Peter," he said. "I failed him in so many ways. It's the least I can do."

"Peter?" Wendy turned back to face him, feeling uncertain. Jax was a mystery to her, full of contradictions. He could seem so hard and unyielding, with such a temper, but then he said things like this and she realized Jax was not someone she could easily sum up.

She studied Jax's gray eyes, which were a tad red. Was it from crying or lack of sleep?

He didn't look her way again as he dug into his bag and handed her a chocolate chip granola bar. They tapped them together amicably and tore them open. It was a tenuous friendship, one they seem to have come to an understanding about. Even if he had just tried to kidnap her for Neverland a few days ago, he'd risked his life fighting to protect the boys. That had to count for something. For that alone, she could respect him and be grateful to him. Still, he had broken her trust, and she didn't think he would ever fully gain it back.

They ate in silence as the sunrise crested the hill.

"It's beautiful," Wendy said in awe.

"It sure is," Jax agreed.

"Do you think he's okay?" Wendy asked, fidgeting with her granola wrapper.

"Yes," Jax said confidently.

"How can you be sure?" She hated sounding weak, but she needed affirmation that Peter was alive, that Neverland hadn't destroyed him, that he could come back from being a shadow, that his soul wasn't gone forever.

"Because if I was Peter"—he looked over at Wendy, his voice growing husky—"nothing would keep me from the girl I love. Not even death." He spoke with such grit and passion that she knew his words rang true. Jax had never spoken a word about a great love, but there was no doubt he had one.

"Who is she?" Wendy asked.

This time it was Jax who dropped his head and fidgeted like a middle schooler with his granola wrapper. "I don't even know her name. Just the number on a pod. My friend nicknamed her Alice."

"How—" Wendy began.

"Neverland," Jax answered. "One day I stumbled into an area I wasn't supposed to be in and I saw her. She was beautiful, floating, sleeping, dreaming. I wanted to stay, to try to find a way to free her from their grasp, but Candace says she can't survive outside of the pod. That the machine she is hooked up to is the only thing keeping her alive."

"That's horrible," Wendy added. "That's why you kept going back, isn't it? For her. For Alice."

"Yes." Jax nodded his head. "Even now I feel like I've abandoned her. And the sad part is she doesn't even know that I exist. Stupid, isn't it, to care for someone and have it be one-sided. I have a bad habit of loving people who don't love me back."

"No, not at all. I think to not care is stupid." This time it was Wendy who extended her hand and gave Jax the awkward pat on the shoulder. His breathing evened out, and he sighed. "I'm sorry, Wendy. About everything. Neverwood, Peter, and—"

"Don't . . . please," she begged. The wall around her heart began to break down and crumble and with it, her resilience. The flood of painful memories came whipping back to tear at her heart.

"Your parents."

"Stop," she commanded. She wasn't ready to bring everything up when she had so carefully put her feelings in a box and mourned her parents already. It was too soon.

"It's just that, I should have stopped them. I—"

"I said stop it," Wendy hissed vehemently and stood up. "I can't do this right now." She needed to get away.

Wendy ran haphazardly down the path and followed the sound of water until she came to a stream. She kneeled beside it, wrapping her arms around her knees, and there with no one around, she let the tears fall. Deep sobs came forth, and she let the sound of the stream comfort her. When she had cried herself dry, and her heart was numb, she finally stood up, then realized she wasn't alone. Jax had followed her. He reached out a hand as a peace offering, and she evaded it, giving him a wide berth. "I'm sorry. I just need a moment."

Wiping at her eyes, she climbed the path back up toward John and Michael, who were awake and already going through their bags and eating all the food. Jax followed at a slower pace.

The hum of an engine could be heard in the distance, and Wendy and Jax stood in front of the outcropping, putting themselves as a barrier between Michael and John. The hum grew louder as the engine drew closer.

Jax muttered, "Four-wheeler."

Twenty seconds later, a red four-wheeler crested the top of the hill and the driver hit the brake. With the sun shining behind the motorist, it was impossible to tell the gender of the driver—until she took off her helmet. Tink waved at them, and pointed to the black electronic box she had strapped to the four-wheeler.

"Found you!" she chanted enthusiastically. "Now, I'll hide and you seek."

John pushed his way between Wendy and Jax and ran up the hill to give Tink a huge hug, lifting her physically off the four-wheeler and spinning her around. "I've never been so excited to see you," he said.

"I bet. Sorry we didn't come sooner. Teleporting three full-sized adults that distance was rough on Tootles, and he was already emotionally beat. He collapsed after he brought us there, and we were busy trying to save Ditto."

"How is he?" Michael asked.

"He's stable, resting for now."

"Oh, thank goodness," Wendy sighed.

Tink grinned like the Cheshire cat hiding a secret. "But let's stop talking and get you to Neverfalls. I can't take you all at once, so we will have to do this in turns. John, Michael, you first. Wendy and Jax, I'll see you in an hour and a half, okay?"

"We'll be fine," Jax said.

"Wendy," Tink whispered. "Watch out for him. Make sure he doesn't try to run away or go back to Neverland. I still don't trust him."

"You got it," Wendy agreed. "I'll keep him in line."

Jax gave her an incredulous look and snorted. "As if you could stop me."

"I did it before. And I'll do it again, but this time drop you in the shadow plane for good," she warned him gently.

"Touché," he chuckled. "I remember. You won't have to worry about me. I'll be good." Jax helped Michael secure his pack to the back of the four-wheeler. Wendy walked over and pulled the blindfold down over his eyes, and he gave her a reassuring grin, telling her it was okay, he understood.

"Just a little longer, I promise."

"I know." Michael reached for Wendy's arm, but missed and hit her back. "You'll find a way to fix me. I know it."

The engine started, Tink driving, John sitting on the basket, and Michael wedged between them. She cut off up the hill she'd come down, and Wendy listened until she could no longer make out the roar of the engine.

She looked over at Jax and tried to judge the progress they had made in their friendship. He was trying to build a bridge, she just wasn't sure if there was a troll lurking under it.

Wendy decided to head back to the outcropping and sit underneath it for shade. Tink said it would be an hour and a half. Well, she was pretty sure she could sleep for the same amount of time. She closed her eyes and Peter's face flashed across her mind. Forget sleeping—she would focus on ways to bring him back. She had to.

-6-

HIS HEAD WAS exploding with pain. Flashing images burned into his subconscious. Fire, guns shooting, boys running for their lives. A beautiful girl, with flowing blonde hair, eyes of the palest blue—her hand reached for him, he reached back, and then she was gone.

Peter jerked in his chair as the current through his head stopped and the pain lessened, though his finger still twitched uncontrollably under the wrist restraint. What had he just seen? *Who was the girl?*

Hands pulled at his head—Candace was loosening the chin strap to remove the helmet. His neck muscles were jelly, his head rolling and bobbing like a lure in the ocean.

"What was that?" he mumbled through numb lips.

"Memories, although from when or from what, I couldn't tell you. That is for you to figure out."

"I saw someone. A girl." Peter paused, unsure of how to continue. How much was he supposed to tell this stranger?

Candace's eyebrows rose. "Really. Tell me about her."

Peter became quiet. "Nothing, that's all that I remember."

"Old? Young? Pretty?" she continued to press, and Peter's lips pinched into a thin line.

"I don't know." His slipped his right hand out of its restraint and he pulled the helmet off of her lap and put it back on his head. "But I'm going to find out." He smiled at her look of utter surprise at seeing him slip from the restraint so easily. "I think it's too soon," she said, shaking her head as he struggled with the buckle on the chin strap of the helmet. She was shocked at his willingness to undergo more pain. "The damage it could do, and we've only started testing it out. I would hate to overdo it and—"

"Kill me," Peter finished for her. "If what you said was correct, that's not the end of the world for me. But I need to find out who she is."

"Peter . . ." Candace's voice lowered in warning. "You may not like the answers you find."

"I have to find her. The answers are in there. I'll do whatever it takes." It was difficult to tighten the chin strap using only his right hand, and when he was finished, he slid it back under the all too lose wrist strap. "I'm ready."

Candace chewed the inside of her cheek as she debated whether to help him or not.

He slipped his right hand out of the restraint and grabbed her hand. "Please, help me."

She took a deep breath and sighed. "Okay, but be careful."

"They're my memories. What is so dangerous about what happened in the past?"

Candace didn't seem convinced. "Memories can be a dangerous thing. What I wouldn't give to wake up with a second chance at life without the weight of my past haunting me at every turn."

"I'd trade places with you in a heartbeat." Peter leaned his head back and closed his eyes. "I'd do anything to get rid of this empty and hollow feeling I have."

He waited, as Candace buzzed the door and moved to her computer. He knew pain would come, and he was preparing himself mentally. He tensed.

The shock was worse the second time. His head snapped back hard into the headrest, his toes curled in pain. He tried to search the bits and pieces and flashes of memories, searching for her, but they didn't come in a neat and concise timeline. He recognized Hook, saw the mercenaries in their uniforms that matched the one he was wearing. He saw a mansion, or what could be a boarding school filled with boys with special powers. He began to remember some of their names. Ditto, Slightly, and another girl with white-blonde hair—Tink. None of them were her.

"W—where are you?" he ground out between gritted teeth.

Flying through clouds of memory, he searched for her. And there she was, in some sort of sterile room. No—a hospital room. He instantly recognized her as a young child. He was there too—they were playing board games together. His heart beat faster with anticipation. He saw her again at a high school in a cheerleading uniform with her friend Brittney. Then Wendy and him were together on a rooftop. His heart was exploding with love. They kissed. And then he was flying above her, lighter than air and euphoric. He had done it. He found her. Found his Wendy.

But in the next moment—

Bang! A gun was fired, and Wendy dropped to the ground. Blood spread slowly from her stomach. He held her in his arms and watched her die. "NO!" Peter screamed in anguish, his breathing ragged, and he tried to hold on to her image, but the memory floated away and was gone. He ripped the headgear off. The machine stopped, and he opened his eyes. His head was brushing the ceiling of the room.

He was levitating, flying in the air, with the chair firmly secured to his backside, his arms still locked in the restraints.

"You're flying," she said in awe over the intercom, her eyes wide with shock. He looked down and his heart dropped—and so did the chair, crashing to the floor and breaking into pieces with Peter in it. He could have pulled himself up, but instead he crumpled on the ground and cried.

She was gone.

Dead. And he might as well be too. He thought he was empty before . . . now there was only a darkness that was spreading.

In those few moments, he had felt a love stronger than any other. He knew from the very first glimpse of her, she was his, his soul mate. But she was dead. No wonder he seemed so hollow.

He wiped his face and let his anger build as he looked around the room, at the machines, at Candace behind the glass partition. It was too much, the weight of this place, of being trapped like a prisoner, of being abused by these adults. His grief turned to rage.

The leather straps with broken wood were still attached to his arms. He flung them at the glass partition, then stormed to the door and pounded on it.

Candace jerked at Peter's violent pounding. Warily, she leaned forward and hit the intercom.

"Yes?" she said, trembling.

"You said you record memories?"

"Yes."

"And you uploaded them, so you have them on record. Show me!"

"I don't know if I can help you," she said, flustered. "There are so many."

"Just show me the last few minutes of my own memories."

The blank screen in the corner of the room clicked on. Candace began scrubbing the video, fast-forwarding through his memories. On the screen, it wasn't as clear as it was in his head. It was like watching a video in a snowstorm. He searched and searched.

"Stop!" he commanded. "Go back . . . There."

He studied her smile in the blurry screen and felt his soul tear in two, committing her image to memory.

"Who is she?" Peter asked.

"They killed her, Peter."

"Who?"

"The boys from Neverwood. Your so-called friends. They turned on you, betrayed you, killed your one true love, and then killed you. She's gone, but we're here. We're your new family. We will give you a chance to fight for her honor."

"What is it that you do here?" he demanded.

"I can't say exactly. It's top secret," she deflected. "But we will make you stronger, train you to fight, and you can put your anger to good use."

"There's nothing for you in your past," spoke a deeper voice from behind the partition. Hook, who had been observing in a dark corner, stepped forward and leaned over the desk so he could speak into the intercom more easily.

Peter had seen enough of the past, and what he'd seen gave him pause. Maybe it was time to give Hook and this program a chance. They gave him back his past, and now he had a chance to have a future.

"There's nothing for me now." Peter's face curled into one of fury. His knuckles turned white as he clenched his fist. His jaw ticked with anger.

"I think we can help with giving you a new purpose." Hook's cruel face turned upward into a smile. He clicked off the intercom and spoke only for Candace's ears.

"You uploaded only what I told you . . . yes?"

"Yes, the image of the girl dying."

"Good, good. Let's do everything we can to bury his past with hate. I need him to want to stay here, and if it takes filling his head with lies, so be it." He clicked on the intercom. "Welcome to Neverland."

-7-

PETER WAS PLACED in a bunk room with two other teenagers—Wu Zan and Leroy, who by the sound of his thick accent was a good old Southern boy. Both boys had occupied the lower bunks in the four-person room, leaving the top two open for the taking.

Peter stepped in and tossed his bug out bag on the top bunk above Wu Zan's.

"I think you have the wrong room," Wu Zan stated, spying Peter's uniform. He crawled out of his own bed and, standing beside the bunks with his arms crossed, looked Peter square in the eye. "Newbs come in on the lower level through basic training. I've never seen you before."

"I've never seen you either," Peter answered, moving to the locker that now had his name on it. He opened the gray metal door and peered inside at the meager but usable items. A mirror, deodorant, toothbrush and paste, and comb still in the packages. There was an extra uniform and street clothes folded neatly. He closed the door and turned to find Wu Zan standing directly behind him, closer than he was comfortable with. At five-nine, he stood eye to eye with Peter.

"He looks familiar to me," Leroy said in his Southern drawl. He lay flat on his back, hands tucked behind his head, on his lower bunk on the right side of the room.

"We don't want you in our unit dragging our scores down," Wu Zan snapped.

Peter eyed both of his roommates. Wu Zan was fit, athletic, his hair dark and slicked back. There was an air of barely controlled rage about him. He reminded him of someone but wasn't sure who. Leroy was built like a tank; his white shirt barely contained his muscles. His eyes were hazel and his skin a warm brown. He hadn't moved, seeming content to recline on his bunk. Where Wu Zan bounded around like a jackrabbit, Leroy was the opposite, slow to engage, but Peter didn't doubt that if he ever did, those hammer-like fists would be deadly.

"I won't drag your score down. It's you who will probably drag down mine."

"Why I ought to—" Wu Zan pulled his fist back.

"Zan." Leroy stood faster than Peter had thought possible, his large hand gripping his shorter friend's shoulder in warning. "Leave him be. There must be a reason the captain put him with us. Besides, like I said, he looks familiar."

"All the newbies look the same to me. I can't tell them apart . . . or care to," Wu Zan grumbled, shrugging off Leroy's arm and returning to his bunk to pout.

"That's a joke. It will be fine. You'll see," Leroy said. "It takes Wu Zan time to warm up to new members of our team. Most of them come up from the lower ranks, so it was surprising that you were placed with us, without any prior knowledge.

But I have a good feeling about you. Yes, I think you'll fit in just fine."

"Watch your six!" Wu Zan yelled, coming from around the corner. He sped up, his body a blur of super speed as he knocked the attacker back into the wall, protecting Leroy's back. Leroy was engaged with an army of soldiers marching down the street. With inhuman strength, he grabbed a pickup truck and with ease tossed it like a bouncing ball into the mass of them. The truck exploded in a ball of fire.

"Peter, don't just stand there!" Wu Zan screeched at the top of his lungs. "Do something."

Peter had become distracted by his surroundings. His hands seemed clumsy, and he struggled to get in sync with the other two boys. He heard the whiz of a rocket and looked up to see the streak in the sky. He was going to die. He couldn't stop it. Or could he?

With a running jump, he was off and flying, meeting the rocket midair. He pushed the nose, trying to steer it off course, and it wobbled but then corrected itself, auto-locked on a target. He tried again, but it was no use. He didn't have the strength to move the rocket. He pulled open the hatch and saw the timer, the controls, and the wires. What to do? Did he cut the wires? Hit a switch?

He pulled the wires, and it didn't do anything.

Seconds later. It exploded and with it, Peter.

"Nooo!" Wu Zan screamed, throwing the controller on the ground. "I told you, you'd mess with our scores. On the rockets, you can't pull the wires. They're heat seeking. It wouldn't have hit us. That's why Leroy created the explosion. If you had let me take the lead, we would have been miles away. But no, you had to play the hero."

Peter pulled off the VR headset and watched as Wu Zan had a hissy fit in the training room.

Leroy smirked, giving him a thumbs-up. "You'll do better next time."

"Next time, I'll have his head on a platter," Wu Zan grumbled.

The boys had taken Peter to the training room, where they were hooked up to a virtual reality simulator exploring the virtual world of Hollow City in the video game Warfare 8. Neverland had supplied them all with the games as a way of training their minds for the scenarios that could happen, but their version of the game was different. Instead of creating a modified character, the VR glasses scanned them and inserted them into the game—powers and all.

Peter never guessed the amount of money people could spend on VR stuff. It felt real. All too real.

"Hey, what the—" Wu Zan mumbled, still wearing the VR headset. "Are you seeing this, Leroy?"

Leroy leaned forward in interest. "I see it."

Peter quickly put his own headset back on to see his dead avatar floating in the middle of the screen. But the life gauge, which had once read zero, was filling back up to one hundred percent and a golden halo now encircled his character. His avatar did a flip in the air and came back to life, giving everyone a thumbs-up.

"I've never seen that happen," Wu Zan exclaimed.

"We've never had a soldier do that before. We only get one life." Leroy lifted his VR goggles, his eyes wide as he stared at Peter.

Wu Zan tossed his to the bed, his face breaking into a huge smile. "You have unlimited lives?"

"I guess. I'm told it's called panning. When I die, I can come back, but my memories are wiped."

"Well, Peter Pan, you're going to be very popular around here. What else can you do?" Wu Zan leaned forward eagerly.

-8-

NEVERFALLS WAS A HOUSE straight out of an architect's magazine. It was built into a cliff, hidden on all sides as well as from the air, with the entrance covered by a rushing waterfall. Wendy never wanted to leave.

Tink drove up a rocky path and as they neared the waterfall, she hit a button on a remote, which opened a garage door tucked into the hill, carefully camouflaged with vines, rocks and moss. She pulled in, parking the four-by-four by three others, leaving the key in the ignition. Stepping back outside, Tink closed the door and started heading down a path that led behind the waterfall. Jax and Wendy followed.

"Dad built this place as a sanctuary, a last resort in case we needed to disappear for a while from the public eye," Tink said, walking just steps ahead of Wendy and Jax. "The contractor who built it did it in stages, and everything was flown in and built on site. There are no roads or easy access out, unless you have a boat. I only wish he could be here with us now." Trailing right behind Tink, Wendy stepped down the rocky slope. Distracted by the beauty of the waterfall, she slipped and almost toppled forward, but Jax grabbed her arm, keeping her from falling.

"Thanks," Wendy gasped, her heart racing as she took in the drop and the rocks at the bottom. A bit farther down, the path became even more treacherous, but there was a chain attached to the rocky wall, and Wendy gripped it tight as they began to pass under the waterfall itself.

Tink turned and yelled back at them, but her words were lost to the thunder of the falls.

"What?" Wendy called.

Jax leaned forward to yell in her ear, "She said, 'Careful, it's slick.'"

"No kidding," Wendy muttered and her shoe slipped. This time she caught herself on the chain.

The farther under the falls they stepped, the darker it became, until Tink stopped in front of a metal door. She punched a code in the keypad and the door swung open.

"Welcome to Neverfalls!" she said happily, her arms open wide, greeting them into their new home.

Never before had a place felt more like home than here. She expected a house hidden under the waterfall to be dark and gloomy, but it wasn't. Skylights placed throughout lit the room, and the light pine and white décor made it seem even brighter and much bigger than it was. They entered a foyer and beyond was a sunken living room with a white fireplace. An open concept house, there was a clear path between the kitchen and the dining room. Wendy turned and saw there was indeed a window, but it looked out into the blue and white rushing water of the falls cascading down the side of the house. Mesmerized by the view, she could hardly look away, then gasped when the dark shadow of a fish swam past the window.

"Bedrooms are upstairs," Tink said, turning their attention back to her. "We'll have to double up as this place isn't as big as Neverwood. It would never hold all the lost boys, but maybe he knew that for us to have to fall back on Neverfalls, we wouldn't all make it." Her shoulders dropped, and she scuffed her shoe on the floor.

"It's beautiful," Wendy encouraged.

"It's a house," Jax seemed unimpressed and headed up the stairs passing Tootles.

"WENDY!" A joyous cry came from the young boy. Then Tootles teleported down the steps and wrapped his arms around her waist. He looked up at her like an adoring child looking at a parent. "You're here! I'm sorry I couldn't come for you. I just woke up." The state of his ruffled hair and sleep-ridden eyes spoke to the truthfulness of his statement.

"It's okay, you saved Ditto. That's all that matters." She gave him a squeeze. "I'm proud of you."

"Ah, thanks! Hey, guess what? Ditto woke up. He's doing better."

"That's fantastic news." She smiled, letting out a sigh of relief. Until this moment, she hadn't realized how worried she still was about him. "Tink told us he was stable, but . . . well, I'm so glad he's awake now."

John came down the stairs, his face in awe. "Have you seen this place? It's amazing."

"Not all of it, but from what I can see, it is pretty incredible." Wendy headed to the kitchen and opened the fridge. Empty other than bottled water. What did she expect? Fresh food? The cupboards fared better results. Lots of canned food, boxed food, and dehydrated meals. So at least they wouldn't starve. She added the rest of her granola bars and junk food to the cupboard, then headed up the stairs to the bedrooms.

Passing an opened door, she couldn't help but glance in, and she saw Jax unloading his bag on one of the two twin beds in the room. She kept just out of sight as he took out his clothes and put them in the bottom drawer of a small two-drawer dresser, leaving the top empty. A picture frame came out next, and he put it on the nightstand between the beds. Even from this distance, she could see it was a picture of Dr. Barrie, his arms around a young Jax and Peter.

Wendy was about to step into the room and ask about the picture, but Tootles teleported onto the empty bed and began to jump up and down on it.

"Hey, I get this bed," Tootles called out.

"No, you don't, pip-squeak," Jax laughed, and with a gentle shove, knocked the kid off-balance and he tumbled onto the mattress.

"Yeah, I do. I claimed it by farting on it," Tootles squealed in delight as only a boy obsessed with bodily functions could.

"Well, then I will leave it to you to tell Peter why you farted on his bed."

Tootles' eyebrows rose, his mouth dropped open in surprise. "Nope, you're right. It's his. I'll share with Michael. You're not going to tell Peter I tooted on his pillow, are you?"

"No. It doesn't matter."

"Good, because I farted on your bed too." Tootles jumped up in the air again and laughed.

"Get over here!" Jax lunged for Tootles and pulled him down onto the mattress, and grabbing the pillow, he swatted him with it playfully. Tootles never stayed in one spot long, so it wasn't a surprise when he disappeared and moved to Jax's bed, and grabbing his pillow, he plopped on his mattress.

"Just did it again. Mmm, smell the aroma!" He waved the pillow, and Wendy couldn't hold back her laughter from the threshold.

Jax's face was mortified at being caught, and a sly smile crossed his face. "Hey, Tootles."

"Yeah, Jax?"

"Have you christened all the bedrooms yet?"

"No," he said, his voice rising, and he looked over at Wendy, his grin curling up to rival the Grinch's.

"Don't even think about it," Wendy warned.

Tootles disappeared, and she heard his giggle and a door slam in the next room over. A few seconds later, the door slammed across the hall. She could only imagine Tootles teleporting into each room and slamming the door to keep her out while he did what he does best. Be a stinker.

Wendy smiled wryly as Jax fluffed the pillow and put it back on Peter's bed.

"You're really saving it for him?"

"You may not believe it, but we've been through thick and thin. We're a lot alike, but nothing ever comes between our friendship. He'll be back. I promise."

"You better keep that promise," she said wistfully.

Wendy moved down the hall, knocking on all the closed doors, peeking in until she found a room that wasn't occupied. Like Jax's room, it had two twin beds with a nightstand between them and a single dresser. She took her pack and put it on the bed, then immediately grabbed her soap and shampoo and headed for the shower.

She was covered with dirt and grime and Ditto's dried blood. At the end of the hall, there was a communal shower, but Wendy locked the door. Savoring the time spent alone, she let the hot water run over her scalp and back. Placing her forehead against the tile, she tried to forge a plan to get to Neverland.

How could they, a group of six teenagers—one of them injured—and two children take on a corporation with its own hired mercenary group and monsters plus their secret weapon, the Dusters? It didn't seem possible. It was a lose-lose situation. No matter how she looked at it, declaring war and going to Neverland would mean more death. More than likely theirs.

After her hot shower, Wendy towel-dried her hair, got dressed and walked barefoot through the tiled house, searching for Ditto and Slightly.

She found Ditto in a bedroom that had been turned into a makeshift hospital and recovery room. He was sitting up in bed, shirtless, his stomach still wrapped in bandages.

"Hey," she whispered and moved to sit on the edge of his bed. "How are you doing?"

He sighed and leaned back on the pillows. "Thanks to Slightly's mad medical skills and the antivenom you gave to him to counteract the morphling poison, I guess you can say I'm fine."

"Fine as in good? Or fine as in, 'I don't want to tell you I'm miserable'?" She helped fluff the pillows to give him better support.

"No, I really am fine. I'm just—" He tried to sit up and winced. "It was stupid, what I did. I wasn't thinking clearly. I was angry. I left the group, endangered everyone, and now I'm paying the price." When she was done, he leaned back and wore a relieved smile.

"Why did you do it?" she asked.

"I blame myself for not stopping the Red Skulls, for not being strong enough. If I could just replicate myself more, I could be the only army we would ever need. No one would have to sacrifice themselves in the war against Neverland. I could be an army of one."

"That's a heavy burden to carry alone. Neverland isn't just your enemy. It's the enemy of all of us. Don't try to rob us of our retribution, Ditto. We fight together, or not at all. Do you hear me?"

"Yes, Wendy," he smirked.

She understood she sounded motherly in that moment, but he didn't seem to mind. She did seem to mother the boys since they didn't have one.

The door opened and John came in with Ditto's backpack. Ditto visibly brightened, and despite the pain, he sat up. "Did you bring my bag?"

"Of course I did. It's extremely heavy. What's in it?" John asked, placing the large pack on Ditto's bed.

"Tink said bring only the necessities." He unzipped the bag and held up the Xbox console and the green video game case.

"Warfare 8? All right!" John said. "I heard they're coming out with a new live update that's only available for the top gamers."

"Yeah, I heard about it." Clutching the cord, Ditto considered the distance he'd have to travel from his bed to the TV on the wall to plug it in. "Do you mind helping a brother out?" he asked sheepishly.

"Only if I get first dibs on battle royale," John answered.

"Sounds good to me." Ditto pulled out the rest of the cords while John set up the system.

-9-

JEREMY WAS THRIVING in the Red Skulls. Never before had he understood the need or the drive to succeed. He'd just floated through his classes, picking up cute girls and partying on weekends. Essentially passing time until he could graduate and pick a four-year college where he would do the minimum to get a bachelor's degree and then work for his dad's company.

The high he got from the PX drug they gave him was better than any street candy he could find. Though the greatest thrill he'd had thus far came from when he showed his allegiance to Captain Hook by hitting the button to kill his rival—the one called Peter.

He grinned just thinking about the look in Peter's eyes when he slapped the button and he went deathly still. It didn't even seem to faze Hook. He just nodded his head in approval, then took him down to the bunks, and Jeremy was quickly assimilated into the group. They would wake up every morning for breakfast, and then train in weapons and hand-to-hand combat. They would line up after lunch for their shots, where they were given the PX drug. A few of the soldiers had their own injector pens they kept in their pockets; he was told he would get one down the line, that his first few weeks of injections needed to be closely monitored.

The one thing that he didn't like, finding it to be very similar to high school, were the obvious factions that had already formed within the ranks. There were the general hired guns, or mercenaries that made up the Red Skulls, who taught the classes and led the combat fighting. These tended to be older men in their thirties and forties and were there to keep the recruits in line. The younger teens, some having been recruited, others forcibly kidnapped, were called the Dusters. With enough treatments, they developed gifts, powers akin to any comic book hero sans spider bites or toxic waste spills.

He heard the talk, about how the drug only worked on kids who had a special PX gene, also nicknamed the Darwin gene. PX gene allows the genetic code to be altered by the PX drug to gain super powers.

Jeremy squeezed his fists and felt the burning sensation in his veins and he just knew that he was a special one. He had to be, needed to believe that it was so. Because on his second day here, he saw what happened to those whose bodies didn't adapt. Burn out, it was called. When the drugs didn't work anymore and the soldier's internal organs would just shut down.

No, he was a special one. He would survive.

He grabbed a tray and stepped in the food line behind his bunkmate, Brillo, nicknamed because his skin could turn to steel and his crazy curls looked like a Brillo pad whenever he changed. Very carefully, Jeremy stalled and reached behind another duster, pretending to grab a muffin, but with his nimble fingers, he stole an injector out of the other soldier's pocket. He tucked it under his tray, then slipped it into his own pocket. He then proceeded to fill his tray full of scrambled eggs, bacon, and pancakes and followed his bunkmate to their table, but he passed a familiar brown-haired girl, who looked to be drowning her sorrows and pancakes in syrup.

"Brittney?" Jeremy paused and looked at the former cheerleader who was from his school.

"Jeremy?" She blinked up at him in confusion. Then her eyes flew wide in panic and she stood up, grabbing his shirt. "You've got to help me. I don't know what's going on or how I got here."

"Shh, chill." Jeremy put his tray down and grasped both of her wrists in his hands, forcibly removing them from his uniform. "Everything will be fine."

Her head swung side to side, her brown ponytail half fallen out; she looked to have barely touched her makeup in ages. The old Brittney would never have let anyone see her without her makeup on.

"N—no, I'm not fine. The injections. It hurts. I shouldn't be here." Her hands were trembling, and she tried to wrap them around her waist in an attempt to comfort herself.

Jeremy didn't have time for this. He leaned forward, picked up her fork full of pancake, and held it out to her. "Eat and you'll feel better."

"No, I don't want to eat. It makes me feel weird," she hissed, smacking his hand away. The fork flew across the room, leaving a trail of pancake and syrup. Heads turned their way at the commotion, and Jeremy saw a few of the Red Skulls move away from the wall in their direction.

Frustrated and letting his temper get the best of him, he grabbed her by the elbow, pulled her out the door and into the hall.

"Listen here, Brit. I've got a good thing going here, and I won't have you spoiling it with your whining."

"Wendy," she said, not paying him any attention. "Is she here? Have you seen her? I was in the library with her, and this monster came out of nowhere and attacked me. I woke up here, and no one will tell me where here is, or if I can go home."

Jeremy's irritation rose at being reminded of Wendy—the cute blonde he had hoped to score with until Peter sabotaged their date. But he couldn't be too upset about it. It's because of that sabotage that he'd ended up chasing Wendy into an alley, where, like Brittney, he'd met a scary monster and woke up here, but they clearly had different reactions. She hated it here, but he loved it—and the drugs they continually gave him for free.

"Relax Brittney, you have a chance to be a part of something great. If you just give it a try."

"Give it a try?" she scoffed. "What's wrong with you? We've been kidnapped. Shanghaied."

"Yes, but I don't want to leave."

"You have Stockholm syndrome bad. Do you not see what kind of place this is? It's a—"

He needed her to stop yammering. Instinctively, he grasped her around the throat. He didn't even realize he was choking her until she started turning red and clawing at his hand. A powerful thrill coursed through his body as he watched her squirm. He barely applied any pressure, and he knew with a flick of his wrist he could kill her. His grin grew wider.

"I know exactly what kind of place this is, and so do you. If you know what's good for you, you will stop your complaining or you will never see your home again. I have two pieces of advice for you. Are you listening?"

Brittney's eyes grew wide, her mouth opening and closing like a beached fish. She attempted to nod her head yes.

"Adapt or die." He thrust her away from him, her head smacking hard into the wall, but he didn't care. He left her there shivering and shaking in the middle of the hall while he headed back into the dining area to finish his morning meal.

He knew she wouldn't last long. He could tell already that she wasn't like him; she wasn't taking well to the drugs. She wasn't one of the special ones.

Brillo looked up from his oatmeal. "Problem?"

"Nah," Jeremy answered. "Not anymore."

"Today you get to meet the Primes," Brillo informed him, shoving a bite of eggs into his mouth and chewing.

"Finally," Jeremy replied with enthusiasm. He had heard of them but hadn't seen any so far. Primes were what the recruits called the original PX-1 group, those chosen years ago and who had grown up in the program. They were the elite of the Dusters—the strongest and the toughest. Most were girls—pity. But there were a few boys that had slowly been added into the mix. He didn't mind fighting girls; he liked being in control and showing them who's boss.

"I wouldn't be excited. They're going to mop the floor with you," Brillo said with a mouth full of food.

"I'd like to see them try," Jeremy said confidently.

"That's because you never had your body rearranged in pieces and handed back to you on a silver platter. They're not a joke."

"Do you see me laughing?" Jeremy said, growing irritated. Brillo acted like he couldn't take care of himself and that he was going to be beaten. Just wait until he showed them. He would show them all. He just needed an extra push.

After cleaning up his tray, he avoided his roommate and headed to the restrooms, locking himself in a stall. He pulled out the stolen injector and gave himself an illegal dose. He knew he could handle more than they were giving him. He would become stronger and faster than anyone else. He would prove them all wrong.

Jeremy's eyes rolled back in his head in pleasure. He sighed and looked at his hands, and he could see his veins, normally blue, glow red and pulse with his heartbeat before settling down again. He grasped the metal toilet paper dispenser and crushed it like it was tinfoil.

He wouldn't lose today. He very well might kill a Prime just to prove that he was a force to be reckoned with. Yes, he would do that. Kill one of them. Jeremy almost felt sorry for the unlucky Prime who was about to be paired with him.

-IO-

PETER WAS DISTRACTED as he lined up in the training room with his roommates. This was a big deal, a real sparring session between the newer recruits and the more experienced ones. Everything in him was screaming to run and save himself from getting beaten to a pulp—or killed. But even without the threat of inevitable pain, he had a thousand other reasons to not want to be here, wherever here was.

Wu Zan seemed anxious too; his fingers kept flickering in and out of view as he tapped them against his thigh in super speed.

"Is something wrong?" Peter asked him.

"I'm just going to meet my maker. Literally."

At Peter's blank stare, Leroy leaned back and explained before Wu Zan could, "The Primes."

"Primes?"

"It's the nickname for the first generation of Dusters. The injections we get are built from their DNA, and most of the time we develop the same traits. Wu Zan's injections of super speed, come from a Prime named Pilot. He just returned from a successful mission where he helped rescue a bunch of the kids from the enemy."

"We have enemies?" Peter asked.

"Yeah, didn't you know? Years ago, one of the doctors kidnapped a bunch of sick kids that were part of the D.U.S.T. program. Barrie and his team have been hiding them for years and brainwashing them into believing we're the enemy. When in fact, they were sick and Neverland was treating them."

"So Pilot rescued these kids?" This Barrie must be involved with the people that killed Wendy. Peter could feel his fists clenching as he listened.

"They retrieved most of them. They're in the freezer going through testing, to make sure they're healthy. Once they come around, they'll join us."

"I take it Pilot had super speed like you?"

"You got it. By the way, I'd kill for a taste of whatever Prime gave you your DNA. So we now are matched up to fight the Primes, and Hook doesn't like it when we lose to them," Wu Zan said.

"But someone has to lose," Peter said.

"Yeah, but losing doesn't mean death. Your best chance is to kick your opponent's butt and try not to die in the process. Winning means you start the next round of injections from a different Prime."

"More injections?" Peter prompted but Leroy didn't have a chance to respond before the room became hushed and everyone looked across the empty room to the double doors.

Hook was first through the doors and on his heels were two female Primes; one tall with tiger-like eyes and one petite with curly red hair and freckles. A few other boys entered, led by a slim boy with an air of confidence so thick Peter could almost feel it. The boy had a cocky smile that bore even white teeth, and though his eyes hardly strayed from Hook, who stood directly ahead of him, Peter was quick to notice the boy crook his head subtly at Wu Zan.

Wu Zan's fidgeting became worse, and Peter knew the cocky boy must be Pilot.

"Greeting, recruits," Hook announced. "I have some news. Our testing has almost reached a pivotal goal, and we are done recruiting. From among you, our future will be determined, but there is only room for the best. Our buyers only want the strongest. So it is time for another culling."

Peter didn't like the sound of that word at all. He wasn't nervous before, but now he was . . . terrified. The Primes didn't look any different from the recruits. Like the recruits, the Primes, all looked to be between the ages sixteen and twenty-two. Except the Primes had an air of confidence and seemed to enjoy flaunting their power at the recruits. Winking, nodding and smiling.

He hung back and watched as Hook pointed to one of the Primes.

"Amber, you first," Hook said to a redheaded girl about seventeen. She stepped forward, her arms crossed over her chest, a smug smile on her face. Then he motioned at two of the recruits—a male with long hair touching his collar, a nose a little too long for his face, and glasses, and a female with a tight black ponytail and bright green eyes. They both stepped up to the mat, stopping just short of a line drawn on the floor in chalk and began to stretch and jump up and down in place.

Hook's hand pointed at the ground and he lifted his arm in the air, signaling the start of the first fight.

Amber shifted, her body becoming a blur and remolding first into a short woman with shoulder-length hair and bangs that covered her face. The other two recruits quickly shifted to look just like the same short woman as Amber.

Peter didn't recognize the woman the three combatants had shifted into, and he nudged Leroy. "Who?"

"She's a famous singer. The shifter battles are always the coolest to watch because the fighters try to mimic celebrities. Dude, that's Ed Sheeran!" Leroy exclaimed in excitement, his hand covering his mouth.

Peter turned and saw three redheaded men with glasses shift, one into a man in a suit, another into a tall muscular man in a jersey.

"No, you don't mix basketball with politicians," Leroy hissed and booed.

The battle continued as LeBron James, Ariana Grande, Tom Cruise, three American presidents, two senators, and a plethora of other famous musicians crossed the mat. Peter had gotten so involved that he quickly lost track of who was who, but he could see that one of them was slowing down, unable to keep up with the other two.

A sheen of sweat banded across the brow of two of the shifters. Finally, one collapsed on the ground, holding his chest. Not able to keep the form anymore, the famous late-night host shifted back into the boy with glasses. It was down to two.

The battle didn't slow, and it quickly altered. One of the two remaining fighters changed into an elephant. Their trumpet raising in the air, blasting a call of triumph, the other fighter followed suit, but just as quickly, the Prime, had shrunk down into a furry white rabbit.

"They can't keep this up," Leroy whispered. "Shifting takes a lot energy but going from an elephant down to something that small is a killer on the nervous system. They're asking for a burnout."

Fascinated, Peter couldn't tear his eyes away as the second fighter became a rabbit and they hopped toward each other. A flash of light and the recruit with the tight black ponytail was on her knees in her own form. Sweat was dripping from her forehead, and she stumbled as she tried to get to her feet.

The other rabbit, the Prime known as Amber, didn't move. She hopped around, her nose twitching and squealing a high-pitched cry. Never had he heard such a noise from a rabbit.

The ponytailed recruit kneeled in front of the rabbit. "Can't change back, can you? Too bad, you should have practiced and studied zoology harder."

She grabbed the rabbit by the scruff of the neck and held it up in the air like a trophy.

Scattered applause traveled through the room, the loudest from the recruits.

The tiger-eyed Prime stormed over to the recruit. "Give me Amber," she demanded.

"Yes, Sgt. Lily," the ponytailed recruit said, handing over the animal. Sgt. Lily, spun on her heels then disappeared out the double doors. Peter wondered briefly where she was taking her.

"Very good . . . er." Hook waited for the winner to announce her name.

"They call me Slip." She grinned.

"Because . . . ?"

"I slip my skin so easily."

Hook made a notation on his clipboard and gestured for her to take the spot on the other side of the room with the Primes. "Welcome."

Slip took Amber's vacated spot, and with it her title.

The room hushed and Wu Zan was vibrating in place. It looked like Pilot was about to step forward onto the mat, but one of the new recruits on the other side of the gym pushed through the ranks and stepped up to the line.

Hook motioned for Pilot to step back, then gave the eager recruit a rare smile. "So soon? You think you're ready, Jeremy?"

"Yes," Jeremy answered, his fists clenched. "I need this."

Snapping his pocket open, Hook pulled out an injector. "You mean this, this drug?"

"No, I need to prove myself to you, that I belong here." Jeremy stared at Hook, and the captain rubbed his chin thoughtfully, his eyes scanning the crowd before coming to rest on Peter.

Peter's mouth ran dry.

"You." Hook pointed right to him and beckoned.

He didn't move. Couldn't.

Hook's lip curled in impatience, and he beckoned a second time.

Leroy shoved him forward onto the mat. "Don't blow it, man," his bunkmate whispered.

Peter stood facing the young recruit and was unsure what to do. The fights were supposed to be between a recruit and a Prime. Oh, wait. Candace had said he was one of the originals. Did that make him a Prime?

The once sure and cocky recruit paled as Peter stepped forward. "No way." Jeremy's hands shook, and he took a step back. "No, you're dead. I killed you myself." Jeremy looked to Hook for confirmation, but the Captain only shrugged his shoulders. This momentarily deflated the teen, but he recovered, his eyes narrowing, his jaw clenched. "Doesn't matter. I will kill you now."

Jeremy didn't wait, but rushed Peter, his fist aiming for his jaw— and stumbled when his fist went flying through dead air. Peter hadn't waited for the man to punch him but rather floated out of the way.

"Wha—?" He was surprised, but not for long. He aimed a roundhouse kick at Peter, but Peter caught his foot midair, and gripping it tightly, he lifted him into the air. The recruit was now being dangled upside down in midair as Peter flew him higher and higher to the ceiling of the warehouse thirty feet in the air.

Peter grinned as the cocky recruit squirmed like a fish on a hook. He was about to bring him down to the mat again when he felt a sharp pain in his leg that made him cry out. He looked down at Jeremy's evil grin, then at Jeremy's hand wrapped around an empty injector; he had thrust a needle deep into his leg. Jeremy wrenched it out and stabbed him two more times. Instinctively, Peter let go to grab at the painful needle in his leg and inadvertently dropped the recruit, who fell to the mat thirty feet down and didn't move.

Peter grunted as he pulled the bloody needle and let it slip through his fingers. He slowly descended to the ground but couldn't look at the mangled body on the mat. He didn't wait for Hook to congratulate him or to pat him on the shoulder, just limped through the crowd and headed toward the exit.

As he pushed the door open, he heard Hook announce behind him, "Now that, recruits, is a *Prime* example of a perfect kill."

Jeremy blinked, pain rushing through his body. His brain was on fire. Groaning, he stretched his leg, which was bent at a weird angle, and slowly pulled himself off the floor.

Audible gasps came from around the room. Jeremy looked up into the shocked faces of the other recruits. He turned his head, his neck aching, and heard a snap as something popped back into place. A few recruits looked squeamish, and one ran for the garbage can. He didn't care. He searched the gym ceiling for Peter, then scanned the room, but he didn't see him anywhere. A low growl came from his throat and he stood up, ready to continue the fight. It wasn't over. He wasn't going to lose like that.

"Whoa, there." Hook grabbed his shoulder, and Jeremy spun around, ready to throw a punch until he realized who stood before him. "Looks like you've acclimated to your treatments. Unbelievable you picked up his power, and so quick too." Hook took Jeremy aside.

"What power?" Jeremy said. He was angry and frustrated at losing in front of so many. "I couldn't fly."

"No, you didn't. You died."

"Died?" Jeremy scoffed.

"Your PX injections came from Peter's DNA strain. It seemed almost poetic in the way you obeyed my order to kill him when you were the first to receive the injections made from his DNA. Like a son killing his father. You can thank him later."

"Thank him, but why? I lost."

"Did you? Not the way I see it. You're both still alive. Your recovery time was remarkable, and you don't seem to have the same side effect as him either. You know who I am?"

"Captain Hook, sir," Jeremy answered.

Hook's grin widened, displaying his molars. "Excellent." He waved away the recruits. "That will be all for today. No more matches until I have some time to talk with this young man." Hook rested a hand on Jeremy's shoulder, giving it a squeeze.

Grumbles filled the air.

Pilot glared, his jaw clenching, as he watched Hook lead Jeremy into the hall.

Brittney trembled near the back, holding onto a pillar for support, her eyes skirting the room and landing on the door that Peter had left through.

-11-

"I KILLED HIM." PETER gazed at his reflection, wishing his own image was familiar. Lifting his hands, he stared at his palms, imagining blood covering them. "I'm a murderer."

Is this who he was? Is this what his future entailed? He hadn't meant to drop the recruit, but he was unprepared for the painful attack and he instinctively released his grip. The memory of him falling to his death would haunt him.

He sighed, closed his locker, and moved over to his bunk. Leaning against the top, he pressed his forehead into his arm. "You are better than this," he mumbled to himself. "Don't become something you hate."

The door burst open and his roommates stormed in. Wu Zan kicked over a trash can before plopping down on the lower bunk, forcing Peter to step aside. Leroy closed the door and leaned against it.

"You all right?" Leroy asked, nodding to Peter. "You cut out of there pretty fast."

Peter shook his head. "Yeah, I'll be fine. I just wasn't expecting to kill someone so soon."

"You didn't," Wu Zan mumbled from below, resentment filling his voice as he tossed a red ball against the underside of his bunk. "He's like you. He's got multiple lives."

"Really?" A rush of relief passed through Peter. He hadn't killed anyone. At least not permanently.

"Don't be like that, Wu Zan," Leroy soothed with a calm voice. "You'll get your chance against Pilot soon. You can look at this as an opportunity—now you get more time to prepare.

As Wu Zan's anger rose, the ball bounced faster and faster against the bunk.

"I have to stay here. There's nothing for me out there."

"You will," Leroy said.

"Not if I can't beat Pilot. You heard Hook. They only want the best, and you—" Wu Zan leaned up and his expression changed to one of shocked realization. "Hook paired you with a new recruit. Why would he do that, unless . . . ?"

A streak like lighting shot from the bed, and then Wu Zan was pulling on Peter's collar, looking at the mark, the small white brand with his subject number 1-00.

"You're a Prime? Man, why didn't you tell us? Not only that. You're the first."

Peter sighed. "I don't know. I only just put it together myself. I don't remember everything."

With a huff, Wu Zan let loose of Peter and backed away, looking sheepish.

"Remember, every time I'm killed"—Peter gestured to his head—"I forget."

"That sucks," Wu Zan admitted. "Maybe I don't want to be like you."

"I wouldn't recommend it." Peter chuckled.

There was a soft knock at their door, and Peter answered it. A girl with long brown hair, eyes red from crying, stood before him, her hands clasped to her chest.

"Peter?" she whispered. "You're Peter, right?" She stepped into the room.

Peter moved back. "Yeah?"

"I'm Brittney. You came to my school. We met in the gym." She pressed on with her interrogation, and Peter tripped over the overturned garbage can.

"No, I didn't. What school? Where?"

His answer didn't persuade her. "I saw you, and you weren't alone—you had friends. You were looking for my best friend Wendy."

"Wendy?" An image of a smiling girl flittered across his mind and disappeared as fast as it came.

Brittney's hopeful face fell. "Please"—she grasped the front of his uniform—"You have to help me escape from here. You can fly. You can get me far away."

A quick intake of breath came from Leroy, and Peter glanced his way. Both Leroy and Wu Zan were shaking their heads, a subtle warning.

His view of the program was drastically changing by the minute. He didn't like having killed someone after being forced to fight. Then here was Brittney begging to escape, and he was now reconsidering what he had been told about Dr. Barrie and Wendy being killed by his enemies.

He gently pried Brittney's hands off, and was surprised by the feel of them. They seemed so slim, so fragile. "I'm sorry, I don't think I can help you." He pressed his hand into the small of her back and escorted her out the room, closing the door behind them.

Her shoulders shook and small sobs escaped her lips.

"Shh, just give me time and I'll help you escape," he whispered.

Her teary eyes brightened and her lips trembled as a smile came to her face. "Oh, thank you, thank you."

"But don't tell anyone and don't approach me in public. I'll find you when I have a plan. Do you understand?"

Brittney nodded and scurried away, her footsteps a little lighter than before. Peter sighed and stepped back into his room.

"Man, that girl is bad news," Wu Zan said, deciding to weigh in.

"What do you mean?" Peter asked.

"She's going to get you killed," he finished. "If you try to escape, the Red Skulls shoot you on sight."

Peter wasn't worried about dying. That seemed like a chance he was willing to take if he could help someone.

"She's a wild card. I can tell from the way she was shaking. She's either going to adjust to the injections or she'll burn out," Wu Zan said.

"Burn out?" Peter hadn't been forced to take any injections yet.

"Die," Leroy said sadly. "It happens to some."

"How long does she have?" Peter asked worriedly.

"With how bad she's jonesing? Days at most," Wu Zan answered.

Peter's lips pinched into a thin line, and he hid his balled fist in his pocket.

He would only have days to find a way to escape the D.U.S.T program. But he would find a way.

Hook sat behind his desk in his office, staring at his inbox. He frowned and scrolled down the messages, refusing to open most and sending them to his trash bin. They all said the same thing from Helix. Helix was the man behind the curtain, the one who had the most shares in the corporation, the one currently holding the reins—and the noose around Hook's neck

When will they be ready?

Buyers are getting anxious.

The launch date is here.

He'd always thought it had been about training soldiers for hire. It wasn't until they were two years in that he'd learned the true vision behind Helix's plan. All because his investors saw money to be made. Money that would line his own pockets. Everyone wanted to have their hands on the next big thing, and Helix was going to bring it to them. His only regret was not getting his hands on Wendy. There was something about her, he could tell, but he was out of time.

Hook stretched his arms above his head and leaned back in his chair, placing one large boot on the desk. He had gotten ahold of Peter, which was a feat in itself, and now the test results from Peter's DNA sample had been surprising to say the least. After only a few days, a recruit receiving injections made from Peter's DNA had been able to come back to life. Remarkable.

Hook opened a drawer and fingered the colored vials—one, a cure for morphling poison, and another, for wiping memories. He wondered if it was because they'd used these memory suppression drugs on the kids during the experiments when they were younger that Peter developed the undesirable side effect of memory loss.

Closing the top drawer back, Hook then pulled out the second drawer and looked at the other vials of PX drugs, each recently created from the stock of new boys brought in from Neverwood. Hook pulled out the one vials made from Peter DNA and held it up to the light. It sparkled softly, catching the light from his desk lamp.

"Immortality in a bottle." He smiled, loading it into the injector gun, and rolled up his sleeve. Closing his eyes and taking a deep breath, he pulled the trigger and felt the prick and then the coolness of the serum entering his bloodstream.

No sooner had the rush begun to fade when his computer screen beeped, warning him of an incoming video call.

He pushed the answer button, being careful to stow away the injector out of sight.

"Hook!" a voice barked on the screen. A man in his fifties with short white hair and a fitted suit sat behind a desk.

"Yes, President Helix," he answered, keeping his face neutral to hide his secret from the caller.

"You're avoiding me," President Helix accused.

"No, I just don't have anything new to report."

"Nothing at all? That seems suspicious considering our last report was that your mission was a success."

"And like I said, we retrieved them, and they're undergoing harvesting, but we haven't tested the newest serum," Hook lied, not ready to share the secret of immortality... yet. "When I have something more to report, you'll be the first to know."

"What about adults? Have you found a way for the serum to work on full-grown adults?"

"No, but I have high hopes for one," Hook said, meaning himself.

"Was this in your report?"

"No," Hook answered uncomfortably. "So far it's only speculation."

"I can't sell speculation. I need cold hard facts, and I need it for the announcement."

His teeth were grinding, and he used all of his control to not curse at the president of the Neverland Corp. "We will get you the results you want."

"Do it. Because you are replaceable. The D.U.S.T program isn't."

The screen went blank, and Hook slammed the laptop closed.

He sighed. It was time to launch with what they had. Make as much serum as they could from the new boys and then get them ready to leave. It didn't leave them much room for error. They would have to start shipment soon. He picked up the phone and dialed a familiar number.

"Yeah, it's a go. We need to go mobile again. This site is done. Sweep it. Leave no trace."

He hung up the phone with a click and pulled out his tactical knife, searching the map attached to the wall. His keen eyes scanned the massive blue area and with aim that only came from years of practice, he flung the knife and it sunk an inch into the wall, the point perforating the map at the exact location of the launch.

A mass of blue in the middle of nowhere.

His mind traveled back twenty years ago to when he was younger, a helicopter pilot in the military. After he was discharged, he ran a private business chartering flights for entertainment and corporate purposes. Currently, he was chartered to fly two rich investors into the middle of the Pacific Ocean. The older investor had his own private yacht with a heli pad and he was searching for something. Each day the older investor would demand Hook fly him out to coordinates his friend had mapped out. Most days the coordinates were a bust, just miles of blue ocean.

"What you searching for, Atlantis?" Hook had joked at one point to the man he mentally nicknamed Polo, as he crossed off another line of coordinates in his book. He never made it his affair to try and learn his client's names.

"Something like that," Polo mumbled absently and circled another set of latitude and longitude coordinates and held the book up to Hook. "Can you take me here?"

Hook looked at his instruments and did the calculations in his head. "Negative, not without refueling. It's just past our point of no return. It wouldn't be safe."

Polo crumpled up the paper and tossed his book on the ground. "I had a good feeling about this one." Leaning back in the seat, he looked up at the pilot and adjusted his headset. "Just like I have a good feeling about you."

Hook looked over his shoulder. Polo slipped his Rolex off his wrist and leaned forward, dangling the timepiece like a carrot. "Take me there and this is yours."

Hook grinned, snatching the Rolex from the air and slipped it into his uniform pocket. "We will arrive at those coordinates at nineteen hundred hours."

When they flew near the location, Polo kept shifting in his seat funny, craning his neck, searching the horizon.

There wasn't anything there. Hook knew it was a wild-goose chase because there was nothing on the map. He had lied about the fuel levels, because he wasn't about to tell the man that he was getting bored spending every day flying him around the ocean. At least at the yacht, he had his own room, plenty of alcohol, and food. But then he had to offer him a Rolex, which was too good to pass up.

But now that they were out here, he knew they couldn't stick around much longer. He was close to the point of no return, and he didn't want to be crashing into the water anytime soon.

"There!" the Polo yelled excitedly. "Go there!"

Hook turned his head and saw just north of their location a speck of black. "What is it?"

"A phantom island. My island," he said smugly.

Hook had heard of phantom islands, but he'd never seen one. They were islands of lore, and myths. Islands that had over the centuries, slowly sunk into the ocean, never to be seen or heard from again.

"I've been documenting these islands for years. My father's research had pinpointed the most famous of these mythical sunken islands and it stood to reason that if they could disappear like magic, then one day they might just as easily reappear. And if an island were to reappear without the government having any record of it, then all the more reason to try and find it?"

Hook could understand now why the investor had chosen to do his search out here. They were nowhere near any shipping or plane routes. If something would appear and be undocumented, it would be here.

In a few minutes the rocky island came into view. The palm trees and vegetation were young but abundant, the beach almost nonexistent along the rocky shoreline. From their altitude, Hook could see the coral reefs that made it almost impossible for a ship to come near the shore, except for one small slip.

"Can you land?" the investor yelled.

"Are you kidding me?" Hook spoke into the com. "This bird will never land. The island is too rocky."

"Twenty thousand!" he eagerly offered. "If you can get us down."

Hook quickly scanned the island, then nodded his agreement. His eagle eye had spotted a cliff clear enough to land, but there was a chance the blades would skim the trees. He was going to try. Approaching at an impossible angle, he swung the chopper and landed with barely a foot to spare. He powered down the engine, and his investor was out of the chopper like a hound after a jackrabbit. Hook stepped out and the investor whooped and laughed.

"Never land?" he scoffed. "You said it couldn't be done. It's because you're small-minded; you have no vision. But me, I have a vision. That's it." He waved his hand in an arc. "You, Hook—you refuse to live on the edge, so you can't see what's possible."

The whole time he was spouting off at Hook, he was dancing on the edge of the cliff. Oblivious to the bluff.

"Not until you were properly motivated did you even attempt the impossi—whoa!" The man lost his footing on the edge and slid down the side of the cliff.

Hook rushed to the side and kneeled down, looking down as the investor was clinging to the edge. "Help me!" he cried out.

"Well, I don't know about that," Hook replied. "For you see, I'm not properly motivated to help. It must be because of my small mind, you see." Hook tapped the side of his skull.

"Fifty thousand!" the investor screamed.

Hook leaned forward. "Come on, live on the edge. Take a chance."

"What do you want?" he whimpered.

"I want in on your vision." Hook grinned, then glanced toward the back seat of the chopper, ignoring the man hanging over the cliff.

"Okay!" the dangling man screamed.

Hook reached down to pull the investor up by the jacket. Just as he lifted the man's body over the edge and his foot found purchase, Polo swung wildly with a pocketknife, slicing just under Hook's chin.

"I will never work with scum like you," Polo bellowed.

Warm blood spilled down his neck, but Hook didn't have time for petty grievances. With a quick twist of his wrist, he trapped the man's arm in a wristlock, disarmed him, tossed the knife down the cliff, and with another crack, broke his neck. He took the man's cell phone and wallet out of his pockets and dumped his body over the cliff.

He turned back to the second passenger, the silent investor who was sitting in the helicopter, ankle crossed over his knee, watching him with interest.

"I'll give you the same offer, and I want it in writing," Hook demanded. "Or I'll leave your corpse to rot next to his. Because only two of us know where the island is, and only one knows how to fly a helicopter."

The man with silver-touched hair nodded slowly. "How did you know?"

"That you're the one calling the shots? Nobody talks this freely about a top-secret project. He was a loose end. You were going to cut him loose anyway as soon as you had what you wanted. The island. Am I correct? What are you planning on hiding here?"

The second investor's eyes narrowed. "You are very perceptive. I could use someone like you in my company."

"How deep are your pockets?" Hook asked.

"Very." The man pulled out a pen from the inside pocket of his jacket and began to write out a contract. Hook's eyes gleamed with greed.

"I'm yours," Hook answered truthfully and eyed the man's name, Thomas Helix. "So what is your company exactly?"

President Helix's eyes glinted mischievously. "I've got my fingers in many ventures. Heard of Wonderland games? No? We haven't quite decided on a name for our new venture to be built here, on this island. But I have one now, based on your conversation actually."

"All right" Hook nodded, distracted, focusing on stopping the bleeding on his face with a handkerchief.

President Helix looked out along the rocky coastline. "Neverland."

Hook fingered the years' old hidden scar under his chin that had developed from that fateful incident. Helix had given him his own Red Skull army, made him a rich man in his own right, but there was something missing. He still wasn't satisfied. He wanted more power. And he knew just what he needed to do to get it.

-12-

WENDY LISTENED TO the rushing of the waterfall, lost in her thoughts. She wandered the halls, staring into each room, searching for Peter even though she knew he wouldn't be there. She was becoming restless from waiting. She'd thought that once they made it to the new hideout, they would immediately head out and go after the boys that were taken. Instead, they were licking their wounds. Well, not literally, but lying low while Ditto recuperated. To go after Hook, they would need every able body available.

John and Tink had become inseparable, brought together by the tragedies of the last few days. The normally abrasive girl had started to show her softer side to her brother, and John was smitten. Tink had set up her laptop on the kitchen table and, under the fluorescent light, was furiously working on something.

Wendy paused, curious and maybe a little leery, when she noticed John hunch over the table as well, pulling a lamp over so Tink could see better as she soldered wires together. He gave her a shove to move over. She shoved him playfully back, giggling. Tink's censor box activated, its bells tinkling softly, drowning out her cuss. She must have called him a name, though it was obvious from the look on her face she was just teasing him.

A flash of anger hit Wendy in the stomach like a rock when she saw them flirting. There wasn't time for games. They should be preparing to attack Neverland. She stormed over to the table and was about to snap at them, but as she neared them, a small spiral of smoke floated through the air and Tink leaned back on her stool. John handed her a towel, and she wiped the sweat off her brow.

"Do you think that did it?" he asked.

"Think?" Tink scoffed. "If Neverland can do it, I can too."

"Do what?" Wendy asked, leaning over John's shoulder to look at what lay upon the table. She was expecting weapons, a newfangled bracer. She frowned. It was just a pair of specs, the goggles they used to see the shadows. They were messing around.

John must have read the disappointment in her expression because he held them up. "They're for Michael. Tink's genius idea, actually."

Tink blushed and tucked a strand of her white-blonde hair behind her ear. Normally her hair was pulled back in a messy bun or multiple braids in a stodgy no-nonsense style, but today she wore it down and it flowed over her shoulder like silk. She looked pretty and young. Wendy had forgotten how young she was, how young they all were.

"I don't think it's right to keep him imprisoned in the dark, so I came up with a plan. Er, uh—we came up with a plan." She smiled at John, who straightened his shoulders. "Neverland was using Michael as a Trojan horse to infect our systems and spy on us. I've altered a pair of specs that we used to see the shadows to work on a different signal. Michael can see with them, but when the specs detect any outside signal trying to access his brain, it will send a stronger signal, bypassing Michael's, supplanting it to show an infinite loop of a *Sesame Street* episode.

"That was my idea," John said.

"That is genius." Wendy grinned, trying to show her excitement, but inwardly she was berating herself for having thought that they were wasting time, when they were using it to try to better the quality of life for her real brother. Her heart folded in on itself and tears began to gather at the corner of her eyes.

She was hurting, from burying the death of her adoptive parents and Fox, from hiding her misery at Peter's disappearance, from knowing that she had seen an angel in the form of her real mother at the lake. She kept pushing it all down, but it was always there, waiting to bubble up and run out.

"Good job." Wendy's lips curled although the smile didn't reach her eyes. "He'll like it."

She turned abruptly and headed out of the kitchen passing Jax in the hall. Then she made her way to the front door and out. Following the chain-link path, she exited from under the waterfall to the top of the cliff. Running farther into the woods, she stopped when she came to a clearing and collapsed to her knees.

She didn't cry, just screamed in anger at herself, at the world. She could feel power building around her and the wind began to pick up. Shadows swirled around her fingers and she could feel them waiting for her to call them. She would go, without them. Use the shadows to pass through the realm where the monsters lived and find Neverland. Once there, she would . . . she would . . . save them.

"Don't," Jax's voice came from behind.

Wendy spun in place, the smoky shadows dissipating into nothingness, her arms free from their murky bands. Jax stood by a tree farther up the path, his hands tucked into the pockets of his jacket.

"I know what you're thinking. Hell, even I'm thinking it, but rushing headlong into the enemies' camp without a plan is suicide."

"You don't know that."

"Worked real well for Ditto." His voice tapered off as he slowly made his way down the path to where she was. "Unless that's your goal . . . suicide. That'd be a real shame then, because when Peter comes back, I'd have to explain to him how I let his girl run headlong into danger. But of course I couldn't do that, so I'd have to go with you and then we'd both probably be dead, so there really wouldn't be anyone to explain our stupidity to Peter. Except for Tink, and then she'd probably get the story all wrong, cause she hates me, and then we would live forever in utter infamy. And that's not how I would want Tootles to remember me."

"You sure know how to wreck a revenge plot."

"I've spent years scheming my own. Trying to figure out how to get out of there with Alice."

"Jax." Wendy stood next to him, looking up into his face, and saw the worry in his gray eyes and the stubble across his face. "We'll find a way to save her. We'll save them all."

His mouth moved, forming a small smile. "You're unbelievable."

She was taken aback. "What?"

"I don't expect my own words to come back at me. It's my job to reassure you, but here you are, being a good friend to me. We're both messed up."

"Pardon me?" She was becoming indignant.

"We're both in love with someone else. And are *obviously* only enduring each day on the slim chance that we can find them again." He turned and gave her a pat on the head. "Too bad we can't learn to tolerate each other. We'd have a better chance of a happy ending that way."

Wendy's brows rose and she elbowed Jax in the stomach playfully.

"There you go!" he wheezed out, grabbing his gut. He stood to leave. "That's the Wendy I know. But take some advice—your anger will work as armor for only so long. You'll need to address the deeper issues before facing your enemy." Jax's voice grew distant as he stepped away. "Otherwise, your vulnerability will be our downfall."

His boots crunched along the leaves as he left her staring into the woods alone. Her only solace came from the chattering of the birds, and cool breeze that soothed her.

She hated that he'd called her out. That he could see past her exterior to the struggles beneath. That even though she was putting on a brave front, she felt as brittle as a dry leaf. Ready to crumble at the slightest breeze of adversity.

"Oh, Peter," Wendy whispered. "Come back to me. I need to know if you're okay."

-13-

PETER WAS EATING dinner with his bunkmates when he heard the two of them talking about sneaking into the freezer.

"Freezer?" Peter asked, pushing the food around on his plate. He didn't have an appetite since he was too worried about trying to break out of the facility. Red Skulls heavily guarded most of the hallways he had been in, but maybe this freezer room had another exit.

Wu Zan's legs were bouncing under the table with excitement. "Yeah, it's where they brought in the others from the raid. They're in containment pods down the restricted hall. We're thinking about taking a look. You in?" He raised his eyebrow expectantly at Peter.

"Yeah, count me in," he readily agreed, knowing he would have to check every crevice and cranny if he was going to help Brittney escape. Peter stood to clear his tray, but on his way to the trash bin, he could feel someone watching him. Keeping his focus on dumping his food, he looked out across the table and saw Brittney, her own food untouched, her face pale, body tense. Was she waiting for a signal? He slowly shook his head, and she picked up her fork, her face turning down in disappointment.

He exhaled in relief. She was very high-strung and he half expected her to run over to him.

Peter slapped the tray once in the bin and was laying it on a cart waiting to head back to the kitchen when he could feel a smack of resentment through the air, directed his way. He didn't have to look to know that it came from the one named Jeremy. Having spotted him earlier, he'd made sure to sit with his back facing the unstable teen. No good would ever come from any encounter with him, he was sure of that.

Leroy and Wu Zan were huddled together as they whispered excitedly. Peter pulled his chair over and listened.

"We go at night, when the girl in the wheelchair—"

"Candace," Peter interrupted, seeming pleased he knew her name and could contribute.

"Candace, right," Wu Zan wasn't fazed, "is not on duty. I haven't seen her late at night when I've done my runs." At Peter's confused look, Wu Zan added, "I've been sneaking out and running around the facility. Relax, I'm so fast no one sees anything, unless they have reason to pause a security camera."

Leroy pointed to Peter. "You'll fly up and shift the cameras to the left. Not enough to alert the watchers."

"Watchers?" Peter felt like a child needing to be retaught everything.

Wu Zan rolled his eyes. "You don't expect them to give us full run of a facility. We're walking weapons. They have people assigned to watch treatment facilities, including ours, to make sure we don't escape. Why else do you think there are so many cameras?"

Peter didn't answer but kept his composure chill. "What about the keypad?" he added.

"Got the password already. I timed a run just right and caught the last three digits."

"You need four," Leroy spoke softly.

"Yeah, but we will just have to guess. I mean, there's only nine numbers." Wu Zan didn't seem worried.

"And how many incorrect code entries before we set off the alarm?" Leroy chuckled.

"Bah!" Wu Zan waved him off. "They won't catch me. I'll be nowhere near the lab when the guards come. Can't help it if you are both slow."

With a plan in place, they headed to their mandatory class. Each day there was one class taught by a different Red Skull, on fighting techniques, weapons, and working as a team. Wu Zan, Leroy, and Peter took seats near the back so they could talk quietly and hash out the rest of their plans. It seemed that the boys had no other agenda than to just break in and look at the teens in the pods to ease their curiosity, because they knew that from them, their next set of gifts would originate, and that one day on the mat, they may very well meet them in combat.

An older instructor in a lab coat came in and told the room to hush. He flipped the lights off and turned on a projector, and the room full of teenagers chattered in excitement at a film lesson. Peter was only halfway paying attention when a scientist on screen began to drone on about different planes and what exists on the physical plane. His mind was tuning it out until he heard the scientist say one word that made every muscle in his body seize. Morphling.

Shadow monsters were controlled by Neverland and were used to hunt down those with the gene Neverland favored. Peter watched on the screen as the creature pulled its body out from a shadow of a tree and then launched itself at an unsuspecting jogger. The scream of terror from the jogger echoed in the room, and a few of the boys clapped and hollered at the attack, but not Peter or his roommates. Peter knew he had fought this beast before. His wrist flicked out, and he instinctively stood, knocking his chair over, readying to fight the monster.

Heads turned his way. Peter's blood was pumping and his breathing was coming hard. He didn't notice Leroy trying to help him until he physically pulled him back down into an empty seat.

Coming out of his fog, Peter realized that he had acted out of instinct, and that most of the recruits in the room hadn't had an encounter with one before. It took a few more minutes before Peter and his roommates returned their focus to the projector and the scientist on the screen, describing the morphling's deadly venom and that a scratch would give them horrible hallucinations; a deeper cut could kill them without the antidote that each of them will be carrying. He held up a gold vial and showed them how to load the injector gun.

"You've seen one?" Wu Zan asked excitedly.

"I believe so," Peter answered.

"Sweet. You know our old roommate had been sent out a few times with the morphlings. I think you would have liked him if you met him," Wu Zan whispered.

"I bet," Peter said, not in the mood for small talk but willing to appease his friend.

"Yeah, he was cool. He was a trainer here. His name was Jax."

Peter looked at Wu Zan and shrugged. "That's cool."

"I wonder whatever happened to him?" Leroy mused. "He was the one we learned about the pods from. We watched him sneak out enough times at night to go there. So we had to see for ourselves what the fuss was about."

A clearing of the throat from their instructor silenced their discussion. Peter didn't pay any more attention to the lecture on the morphlings. Instead, his mind kept picturing an imaginary brace around his wrist. If he closed his eyes, he could almost feel the weight of it. *What was it? Why did he remember it?*

The video ended, and the recruits filed out of the room, some heading to the gym to spar, others heading to the lounge room. Peter and his group headed back to their rooms, the whole while Peter silently counting every security camera and locked door. When he got to twenty, he realized that they weren't as free as they let on. The security wasn't to keep the enemy out, but to also keep them in.

All of them were in bed well before lights out, and the anticipation of their escapade kept them alert and on edge.

"Now?" Wu Zan would whisper, only to be hushed by Leroy.

"No."

Twenty minutes later, "Now?"

"No, Zan," Leroy would mumble.

"Geez, man, I want to go see them," Wu Zan would whine.

Another hour passed and finally Leroy sat up in his bed. "Now."

Leroy led the way and pointed to the cameras. Peter flew to each, adjusting them with the slightest of increments until Leroy nodded in approval. They moved down the halls, working slowly, listening quietly and flashing each other boyish grins full of mischief. Peter himself felt the thrill at rebelling against the rules. When they finally came to the keypad-locked door, they paused to confront the final challenge.

Wu Zan's fingers hovered over the keypad. "You ready to run if I get it wrong?"

"No," Leroy chuckled. "My body isn't made for running." He patted his stomach for show.

Wu Zan sucked in his breath and started at 9 on the keypad and then entered 9-8-5-1. A red error code flashed.

Peter and Leroy were on edge as Wu Zan began again 9-8-5-2. Another error code.

"C'mon, man," Leroy muttered. "You going to walk your way through the numeric system? This is it. Your last chance."

"Stop messing with me," Wu Zan hissed. "I need to focus, get my Tom Cruise on."

"This isn't *Mission: Impossible.*"

Peter scanned the hallway, looking for signs of intruders, because no matter how much they whispered, they were still loud. Then he spotted movement around the corner. He froze, studying the darkness, expecting a morphling to appear. Instead, a shadow slipped out and waited, watching, not approaching.

Peter tapped Leroy's back, but he didn't notice as he was in too deep of a discussion with Wu Zan about the best *Mission: Impossible* movie.

"G—ghost!" Peter whispered, unsure what to call the apparition.

"Nah, man, the original was better than *Ghost Protocol.*"

"Doesn't matter, you're not Tom Cruise if you can't get through the lock."

Neither of his roommates seemed to see the shadow.

"If you remember, it wasn't him who hacked. He had outside help," Wu Zan snapped and began to punch in the numbers slower, starting with the 9.

The shadow didn't move but shook his head and held up his hand telling him to wait.

Wu Zan entered 8, and they each held their breath in anticipation.

"You're sure that the first three are right?" Leroy asked.

"Of course I'm sure. It's just the last one I didn't catch."

The shadow closed its hand into a fist and then flashed its palm, gesturing for them to stop.

Wu Zan pushed 5 and then moved his finger toward the top of the keypad, aiming for the number 3.

The shadow that only Peter seemed to see was now shaking its hand back and forth.

It was then Peter understood what the shadow was telling him. Wu Zan's finger barely brushed the three when Peter knocked it out of the way and pushed 5 a second time. The light turned green and the door unlocked.

Wu Zan's mouth dropped open in disbelief. "How did you know?"

"Yeah," Leroy accused. "How did you know?"

Peter scanned the hall for the shadow, but it was gone. Would they believe him if he told them?

"I didn't." Peter opened the door and beckoned for them to precede him. "It just made sense. If Wu Zan only saw three numbers keyed in, it was probably because the last number was a double."

"Ah!" Wu Zan announced. "I knew that."

"No, you didn't," Leroy huffed, and they tumbled into the room, closing the door behind them.

A second door opened, and they entered the lab.

Chills raced up and down Peter's arm, making the hairs on his flesh stand on end. There was a definite aura of weirdness about the room.

"It's like something out of the movies," Leroy declared.

"If they made this into a movie, I'd ask them to make me taller," Wu Zan said as he turned in a full circle, taking in the rows of pods. Most had numbers stenciled onto the side, but inside each pod was a sleeping person entombed in water, with a breathing apparatus over their mouths.

Peter had no desire to go near them. He was having a serious case of déjà vu, but he didn't know what exactly. What he did know was that something bad happened here.

"I wouldn't worry about it. Our characters would just be whitewashed. It happens to all the good books-turned-movies," Leroy said sadly. "I'd probably even lose my Southern accent."

"The movie would be better without your Southern accent." Wu Zan choked on his own laughter.

"This isn't right," Leroy said, noticing a young brown haired girl—maybe fourteen or fifteen—floating in the pod. "This is wrong. What they're doing is wrong."

Even Wu Zan mellowed as he took in all the rows of pods spread out around the single one with the girl. "I never expected this." He looked over at Peter and became worried. "Hey, earth to Peter. Are you okay?"

Peter was now shaking physically with anger. He gathered the courage to approach one of the pods, which held a young man who appeared to be in slumber. Except that Peter's approach startled him. His eyes opened, and they focused on Peter before widening in surprise.

The young man tried to speak, bubbles escaping out of his mask. He pounded on the glass, kicked his legs, and began to fight, working himself up as Leroy and Wu Zan came to stand next to Peter. The two of them in their uniforms alarmed the young man even more. His eyes turned black as gems, and Peter could see the pod begin to vibrate with power.

"Look away!" Peter warned instinctively. Without a second's thought, he covered his roommates' eyes and closed his own until the throb of power passed.

"What just happened?" Wu Zan yelled in alarm as Peter pulled them both out of view of the stranger in the pod.

"Stay here. Don't let him see you," Peter commanded.

"Did he just try to kill us?" Wu Zan was becoming angry.

"He's scared, and to him you're the enemy."

"And you're not?" Leroy asked.

"No. I'm not."

Peter walked to the front of the pod and pressed his palm to the glass. The young man inside with the glittering black eyes matched him, meeting his hand on the glass. The pod's sensors turned on, registering the occupant's vitals as being awake. The computer on the side clicked on, and he could see a dose of medication being administered through a tube and into the young man's arm.

His eyes became sleepy, and his muscles relaxed, but he fought to keep his hand on the glass next to Peter's. His arm slid down, and a frustrated moan came from behind the young man's mask and he kept blinking.

"E-d-e-r," he wailed, crying out Peter's name, begging him to save him. The young man moaned and slapped his hand against the glass, although it was lower, struggling to stay conscious against the drugs pumping into his system.

Peter absorbed the young man's grief as if it was his own and slid his own hand to keep it pressed against his. He would not abandon him.

-14-

"PETER, WE NEED TO go!" Wu Zan pulled on his shoulder.

Peter shrugged it off forcefully, turning to inspect each of the pods more closely. There was no doubt in his mind that the drugged teen had said his name—which meant that he knew them and probably the others in here as well.

He rushed to another pod and pounded on the glass, trying to wake up the boy inside.

"Stop it!" Wu Zan hissed. "You're going to get us caught!"

"We need to help them," Peter snapped before moving to the next pod, where another boy floated inside the drugged-laced tube.

"We can't, Peter," Leroy said regretfully.

"You heard him." Peter pointed to the tube where the drugged teen slept. "He said my name. He knows me. And I think I know him."

"You can't be sure that he said your name," Wu Zan said.

"It was my name," Peter insisted.

"How? Tell me how in the world, then, do you know him?"

"I, uh, I don't know."

"Then you don't—"

"I just do," Peter interrupted Wu Zan, silently pleading with him to believe the unexplainable. "His name is Onyx. And if he was one taken from Dr. Barrie, then maybe I was too?"

"I believe you," Leroy said, pulling Wu Zan away from Peter and placing his large form between them as a barrier. "But we can't help them now."

"But—" Peter began but was silenced by Leroy's pointed look.

Peter turned and regarded at the boys in the room as Wu Zan ran to the door and punched the code to exit. Leroy took a few steps and called over his shoulder for him.

He didn't budge, his heart growing heavy with a weighty decision. Despite his promise to Brittney, he couldn't leave now. Not without them. He could feel their fear, their uncertainty, as he pressed his hand to the glass. They were so lost.

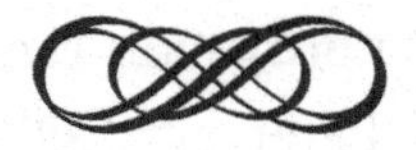

Peter was the last to clamber into bed, climbing onto the top bunk. Wu Zan and Leroy were both silent as they processed what they had seen and discovered. No one slept, each of them tossing and turning in their bunks, shifting restlessly.

Leroy finally spoke aloud. "It's wrong."

Peter held his breath, not wanting to be the one to steer the direction of the conversation. He wanted them to be on his side willingly.

"Did you see the tubes in their arms?" Wu Zan whispered. "I knew that it was being harvested from them, but in my head, I just saw it as a simple blood donation. You know, one prick and it's done."

"They're imprisoned, like animals." Leroy's voice became gravelly with emotion. "Is that what happened with the first group, the ones we call Primes? Do you think they were ever in those machines?"

"Yes," Peter said emphatically. "I'd bet my life on it."

"And you?" Leroy asked.

Peter closed his eyes and tried to search his sketchy memories, his mind swimming through the darkness . . . and there it was, just a hint of recollection, a vague memory of the weight of the mask over his mouth. He brushed his hand against his face, recalling the pressure. Then he remembered someone walking in front of his pod—the recruit named Jeremy, and Hook was with him.

With each blink of his eyes, a flash of a memory came back to him, and he mentally replayed the moment when Jeremy had hit the button to sever his life support and Hook grinned. He remembered the instant he died.

"Yes, that is where Jeremy executed me." He took a deep breath and tried to calm his anger.

"Whoa!" Wu Zan said, sitting up so fast he whacked his forehead into the bunk with a soft *oomph,* but quickly dismissed the pain. "You mean to tell us you were in one of those pod things and that meathead executed you?"

Leroy propped himself up in bed. "Was that the first time it happened to you?"

"Dying and coming back?" He thought about it and shook his head. "I don't think it's the first time. What about you? Do you remember anything at all from before you came here?"

"Of course," Wu Zan stated. "I lived in . . ." He paused in thought. "I mean, I told Leroy the story of how I was recruited, right? Leroy will remember."

Leroy shook his head no. "I don't recall you ever telling me how you came to be here. And all I remember is Neverland."

"What about your mother?" Peter pressed. "Your father."

"Oh, yeah," Leroy chuckled. "I had those. How else could I be here?"

"What are their names?" Peter asked.

"Mom and Dad," Leroy said, but he didn't sound sure.

"Siblings?" Peter added.

Now Leroy's face blanched as fear slowly appeared on his face. "Wu? I talked about my siblings, right? I think I had them."

"Nah, man. I mean, I think you did, but that was months ago."

"We're forgetting?" Leroy looked up at Peter, a look of terror filling his eyes.

"I think they're drugging us with more than PX, something to suppress our memories," Peter answered. "Who wants homesick soldiers?"

Wu Zan and Leroy seemed disturbed by this news. Peter could only speculate about how often, they were administering the drugs to make them forget where they came from.

"Jax knew," Wu Zan said angrily. "He kept asking us about our families, making us tell stories of the past. Why else would he do that? He probably convinced himself he was actually helping us," he scoffed, "all while keeping the truth about this place from us!"

Peter's fist curled again at the mention of their last bunkmate. He didn't know why he had such a strong desire to punch him, but the thought wouldn't diminish.

An alarm sounded and a white light flashed on and off in the room. It wasn't an ear-piercing wail, or a sound that might signal an emergency. This one had more of a somber tone.

"What is that?" Peter asked.

"Evacuation," Leroy said, moving to his locker and throwing his belongings into a bug-out bag. "This site is being decommissioned."

"Decommissioned?" Peter jumped off his bunk and followed suit as the two others left their bedding and only grabbed the few items in their lockers.

"Yeah, we don't stay in one spot long. We move every few weeks and always at night."

"What will happen to the lab?"

"Don't worry. It gets broken down and comes with us. Didn't you see the rooms and how they're assembled?"

Peter hadn't been paying attention. But then he thought back on the lab he'd woken up in with Candace. The brick walls were solid, but not every wall. Some were made of reinforced glass and bolted to the ground. Even the computers were built into metal desks on wheels that could be closed up and moved. Neverland was portable.

This was the chance he needed. He could escape, grab Brittney, and ensure a mass escape of everyone in the pods while in transport. It was a brilliant idea. He tried to hide the smile that came too eagerly to his lips.

Wu Zan and Leroy lined up at the door but didn't open it. Peter didn't understand why they weren't moving until a knock came on the door from the hall. Wu Zan opened the door to a Red Skull standing there with a fully automated gun.

"Don't move," he growled. "Wait." The Red Skull guarded their door, and Peter could see movement in the halls as the other recruits were herded out of their rooms and down the hall. When the room before theirs emptied, the Red Skull barked out an order for them to follow.

It seemed this wasn't anything unusual to his roommates. Wu Zan picked up his step and followed in line behind the other room. There were Red Skulls lining the halls, hands on their guns, as the recruits were herded like cattle.

The girls' bunks were emptied, and he saw a terrified Brittney jump into the line a few feet in front of him. Her eyes wide, she craned her neck until she saw him, her eyes pleading.

He gave a slight nod, and her brows rose in understanding. They were going to escape tonight. She spun back around, her head down as she followed the three other girls from her room.

Peter didn't have a plan. He just knew that if they were going to escape, it would be during the transport.

Double doors opened at the end of the hall, and the chill of night air hit him. It was still dark out, and he could smell gasoline in the air. But they wouldn't be outside for long because before them was a loading dock and a ramp into a semitrailer. Inside the semi were rows of benches. To his right and left, Peter saw more semis and soldiers loading up large crates. This was it.

He began counting down in his head, the paces to the semitrailer, gauging how small of a window of opportunity they might have.

Brittney slowed her footsteps and dropped back until she was right in front of him. Wu Zan and Leroy stepped into the trailer of the semi.

Peter stepped through the outer doors and grabbed Brittney's hand, pulling her back. He heard her sharp intake of breath, but there was no time to explain. Focusing on the open sky above, he began to float up, Brittney along with him, but his feet had only left the ground a few inches before he was smashed in the face with the butt of a rifle. Brittney screamed as Peter collapsed to the ground, pain radiating from his temple. The ground felt like it was shifting beneath him.

"Going somewhere?" Hook sneered.

At the sound of his voice, Peter stared up into heated eyes of Captain Hook.

Hook motioned and two Red Skulls grabbed Brittney and dragged her into the back of the semi. "I knew that if you were going to try an escape, it would be during our relocation. But you even went so far as to try to take another recruit with you."

Brittney whimpered and Peter tried to defend her. "No, she didn't know. I surprised her."

"Nevertheless, she will be dealt with—but you, my son. It seems that you need a bit more reprogramming. Maybe let's try again from the beginning. Another reboot."

Fear raced through Peter's body. He tried to rise to his knees. "No!" He reached for Hook.

Hook raised his gun, and the butt came down onto Peter's face.

-15-

"THIS SHOULD DO IT," Dr. Mee murmured to herself as she made more notes in her journal, which was littered with ideas and formulas, all in different handwritings, each one like a timeline of her thoughts and how she was slowly losing them. Each idea was attached to a string of a kite, and as she aged, more strings were cut. But Dr. Mee was smart. She left herself notes of her work along with numerous tape recordings—all of it an attempt to counteract the side effect of the memory loss drug Neverland had given to them. A drug that had been administered to all the techs, aids, and personnel that had worked for Neverland Corporation.

It was Neverland's dastardly insurance policy. Their way of ensuring their confidentiality if someone ever left the company. Without the daily antidote, Dr. Mee and other former Neverland employees would slowly lose their minds; she had witnessed it with her oldest and dearest friend Dr. Barrie, had seen what it had done to his once-sharp mind. The horrifying truth of Neverland had been reduced to children's bedtime stories.

"Think . . . think . . . think." She tapped her head, trying to force her thoughts into a more cohesive train of thought. "You've studied the parameters. Tested it on Peter and Wendy. It worked on memories lost short term. But is it enough . . . for him? For me?"

Dr. Mee stared up at the mirror in her small basement apartment and held up the small needle, her hands shaking as she pushed it into the vial and filled the syringe. That day so many years ago, she had stolen a few days of the antidote, and as soon as she had touched foot on land after escaping the island, she had begun to run tests to find the chemical makeup of the medicine, trying to determine the exact recipe. Except, there was a chemical ingredient she couldn't identify, that didn't appear in any textbooks, one that she could not duplicate. She had been experimenting for years to try to find a substitute for the unidentifiable chemical. Like searching for a sugar substitute when you can't use sugar.

She had made enough progress that she had been able to keep her mind stable for longer than anyone else, by using small doses of the fake versions of the antidote on herself. But she had done it, discovered it worked fine on Peter if he'd recently panned. But to bring back someone's mind that had been gone for years, she needed something stronger. A super drug.

And she believed she had it, but now to test it.

Dr. Mee slipped the cap on the needle and reached for her overcoat. She tried to smooth her ruffled black hair, and pinched her tired cheeks. It didn't matter, though. If it didn't work, he wouldn't recognize her anyway.

Herding her German shepherds into their kennels, she gave them a treat and checked their water before locking up and exiting her building. The landlord would look after them while she was gone.

Dr. Mee took the bus, and after two bus transfers, ended up outside of a large park with a clock tower, winding bike paths and open green spaces. Finding a well-placed park bench she settled in and opened a book to look inconspicuous, while she watched the small two-story bookstore across the street. It was near closing time and she hadn't seen any customers come in or out in the last thirty minutes. She also hadn't seen the bookstore owner through the window.

She was going to have to go in and find him. Opening the door, the bell rang softly announcing her arrival. A giant Saint Bernard padded out of a back office and came to sniff her pant leg. Deeming her friendly, Nana leaned on Dr. Mee's leg, giving it all the weight of an attention-starved dog.

"Hello, Nana," Dr. Mee greeted warmly, bending over to give the dog an affectionate pet. She was the one who had given the dog to her old friend. She knew he would need someone to look out for him. Dr. Mee squatted down and looked into the dog's eyes. "Where's Barrie?"

Nana's big head swung and huffed at the back office, where she could see through a partially open door, an obstructed view of a very cluttered desk illuminated by a lamp.

"Let's go, girl," she coaxed.

Nana took off running, her tail thumping into every bookcase and table between the door and the back room. Dr. Mee followed after the dog into the office and found Dr. Barrie slumped over his desk.

Her breath caught in her throat. She was too late. He never got a chance to remember before he passed.

Nana whined, nuzzling Dr. Barrie under the arm, and a soft snore came from his mouth. Dr. Mee sighed in relief. He was only sleeping. She tiptoed around the desk and saw the scattered notes and drawings depicting an island. Careful to not disturb him, she read over his shoulder, and saw the truth and evil of Neverland sanitized and disguised, retold as a child's fairytale. He had been trying to record his memories before he forgot them, but it all came out as doodles and stories.

"Oh, Dr. Barrie, what have they done to you?" She pushed his gray hair off of his forehead and gave him a small peck on the back of his head. Pulling the syringe out of her pocket, she uncapped it and felt along his arm. "I pray this restores what was lost to you. I hope it brings you back to your daughter."

She injected the experimental antidote into his arm and moved away to sit in the chair across from him, waiting for the drug to take effect—hoping that it could restore years of memories, like it had for Peter and Wendy.

Nana moved away from her sleeping owner and pushed her head into Dr. Mee's lap, demanding attention and scratches. As she gave the dog plenty of affection and kisses, she encountered a bump along the collar. Curious, Dr. Mee unstrapped the collar and discovered a tracking bug sewn with an untrained hand into the thick braided cord.

"Isabelle," Dr. Mee mused aloud and smiled, proud that even though Dr. Barrie was nowhere near his daughter, she was in fact keeping tabs on him.

Her inquisitive mind piqued, she studied each of Nana's tags: one for her rabies vaccine, another with her address, and then a silver heart with nothing inscribed. Dr. Mee held it up to the light and made out the smallest indent in the tag. Using a nail file from her purse, she wedged the silver tag open, and gasped. Inside of the tag, there was some kind of circuit. Dread filled her as she realized what it was.

It was another tracking device, much more sophisticated and advanced than Tink's hand sewn tracker. Neverland. They have been tracking Dr. Barrie. She looked around in a panic, wondering if there could be hidden listening devices in addition to the tracker. Did they know she was here? Her hands shook as she removed it from the collar.

She did find a listening device under Dr. Barrie's desk and one in the potted palm by his office door. Grabbing the heaviest book she could find, she smashed the tracker into pieces, and then flushed it down the toilet, knowing it would be quickly swept into the city's sewer system.

Now terrified, she pulled out a chair and carefully ran her hands along the bookshelves, then searched the register areas and even the back hall, but didn't find any bugs in the store. It seemed that whoever planted them didn't really have any interest in the book business, but more on Dr. Barrie himself.

Dr. Mee made quick work of the other two bugs she found and discarded them like the first. She began to tidy his desk when she noticed he began to stir.

Dr. Barrie blinked, slowly sat up, and stretched. He noticed Nana first and reached down to pat his companion, whispering, "Good girl."

His alert eyes scanned his office with renewed interest as if he was seeing it all for the first time. When his eyes alit on Dr. Mee standing to his right, he smiled. "Why, hello."

Her heartbeat picked up with anticipation. "Y—you remember me?" she stammered.

"Yes, I think I do. He paused in thought, scratching his head. "Your name is . . . just on the tip of my tongue." Dr. Barrie stood and looked down at his drawings and notes, his expression changing as he processed what he saw. His memories slowly coming back to him. "Yes. Yes. That's right. Neverland. The research." He looked up his eyes glassy. "My daughter. I have a daughter."

"That's right Dr. Barrie," she encouraged.

"And you're Susan." He stood and pulled her into a warm hug.

"Oh, Dr. Barrie, how I've missed you." Tears fell freely from her eyes.

"I suppose I have you to thank for this?"

She nodded. "I've been trying to find a cure for years. But it's only temporary. You have to keep taking these. She handed him an orange medicine container full of liquid gel pills. "Just like we did at Neverland. I'm still working on improving it, but now with your help, I can make it stronger."

"We will, don't worry. We will. All will be right now. Don't cry." He wiped the tears away from her cheeks.

He gave her arm a squeeze, then headed out of the office and searched up and down the aisles of the bookstore, before returning to the office. "You haven't happened to have seen my daughter anywhere, have you?"

Dr. Mee crumpled into the chair. "Something terrible has happened to the children."

"But they have Neverwood. The school, the teachers, I put people in place to take care of them in my absence.

"The school was attacked." Her lips trembled anew. "They took them."

"What?" He grabbed on to the doorframe for support. "Isabelle is gone?"

"I don't know. I was hiding from them for so long, and I knew I shouldn't. Not when two of the children kept panning. So I went to Neverwood to drop off a supply of the drug and to check on them, and the school was . . . so much damage. I can't even fathom what had happened. I don't know where they fled. I don't know where the children are," she cried, her shoulders shaking in fear. "If Neverland took them, then everything we've done is for naught."

"I can't accept that," he said. "Some would have escaped . . . and if they did, I know where they would have gone."

Dr. Mee wiped her eyes as Dr. Barrie grabbed his coat off the coat hook. Nana, sensing the change in the room, barked in excitement and ran to the front door.

"Come on, they need us."

"Where?" she asked.

"Neverfalls."

-16-

"WHOOP, THERE IT is!" John crowed at the video screen. Having taken down the enemy, he stood and did a little dance around the room, then high-fived Tootles and Michael. Michael's grin was huge and his face owlish as he looked around the room wearing his new and improved specs, thanks to Tink and John.

Tink was sitting in the chair next to Ditto's and speaking quietly with him, her face grim. Wendy noticed the change in the atmosphere between the two old friends and made her way to Ditto's bedside.

"Don't, Ditto," Tink admonished. "Don't try it when you're injured."

"Tink, I'm done hanging around here. We need to get the others back."

"You're not well enough."

"I am. I'm stronger than you think." Ditto pulled the blanket off his lap, exposing the bandaged wound, and Wendy winced at seeing the damage the gauze was hiding. It's much easier to convince yourself your friend is well when he's just sitting in bed playing video games than when he pulls back the sheet to reveal his wound. "I'm healing fine."

"We will go," Tink said. "But you will not be coming with us."

Ditto's face turned dark. "You can't do that. I'm one of you. I need to help save the others."

Tink's chin jutted out, her mouth pinched in a firm line, eyes narrowed stubbornly. "It's been decided. We can't take you. You will stay with Tootles and watch over him while the rest of us go."

Ditto's head shook in disbelief, his voice hitched with emotion. "You can't leave me behind."

"You leave us no choice. If you hadn't acted so foolishly, we could have left sooner. We had only planned to come here to get supplies and recoup before heading out, but then you had to go and get yourself hurt, and we obviously couldn't leave you until you were on the mend. But now that you're at least out of the woods and mobile, we can't delay any longer. You're able to take care of yourself if something happens to us, but you'd only slow us down if you came with us."

Ditto's eyes turned dark, and he turned away from Tink. "You don't get to make the decision for me."

"It wasn't her decision," Jax spoke up from the doorway.

"You don't get to make the decision either. Traitor," Ditto mumbled under his breath.

"With Peter gone, I'm in charge," Jax retorted.

"If Peter were here, he would let me come."

"I beg to differ," Jax said. "He absolutely would not."

Ditto struggled to get up, and when his feet touched the wood floor, he dipped and had to catch himself on the edge of bed. His legs wobbled, his teeth gritted in pain, but he pulled himself up to stand face-to-face with Jax. His nostrils flared and his breathing was ragged, but Ditto clenched his fists at his sides and stuck his chest out, threatening one of the strongest leaders of Neverwood.

"Don't, Ditto," Jax warned. "It's not the time nor the place."

John and Michael had long stopped playing and were watching the power struggle on the other side of the room.

"It is, especially if you are talking about leaving me behind. I'm a soldier. A lost boy, like you. I deserve to fight."

Jax seemed to be thinking it over, but Tink shook her head. "Jax, no."

He considered Tink and started to nod, but then he caught the pleading look in Ditto's face. "I don't know, Tink. You're probably right. He could be a liability." Then turning to Ditto, he said meaningfully, "But I think he has a right . . .He has a right to prove himself. You'd want the same for yourself, Tink."

Tink's censor box went off and ringing bells filled the air as her mouth moved, but no audible words came out.

"You can come—" Jax began.

"Thank you, Jax," Ditto said, his face beaming. "I won't let you down."

"If you can replicate into four right now," Jax finished.

Ditto's face paled. "W—what?"

"You heard me," Jax said. "Replicate right now. Prove that you're strong enough to do that and you can come."

A heavy silence befell the room and all eyes gazed upon a pale Ditto.

"That's not fair," Wendy said. She had thought Jax had changed, but it seemed that he was setting Ditto up for failure. Or he knew more about the situation and Neverland and was trying to protect Ditto.

"Jax," Tink said. "He's never been able to go past two."

"If he wants to go with us, he has to prove he's fit," Jax said stubbornly, his jaw set, though there was a slight twitch to his mouth. "If he's not fit, he stays." When no reply came from him, Jax nodded his head. "Okay, he'll stay behind with the young ones."

"No, I'll do it," Ditto murmured.

"No, don't," Wendy said. "You could get hurt."

"It's not worth it," Tink called out.

Ditto's head dropped, and he blurred for a second as his body tried to separate. A scream came from his lips at the pain of being torn in two. He flickered between one body and two and then solidified again into a single Ditto. He tried again, with another scream of pain being ripped from his lips.

Tink's hands went to her mouth in horror. "Jax, if he replicates now, he not only doubles himself, but the pain from his injury is amplified."

"I know," he said regretfully.

"Ditto," Wendy pleaded, wishing with all her heart that she could help ebb his hurt. Over and over again he would try to replicate, but the pain would double and you could see him trying to control both bodies through the agony.

"If he can't control himself here, then he won't be able to once we get to Neverland. We can't allow Ditto to be captured. You don't understand what they would do if they had access to his ability. It's bad enough they got Peter. But a whole army that can replicate would be disastrous. We have to know he can control himself. Defend himself," he said callously.

Another cry echoed, followed by a shout of triumph, as Ditto split himself into two. The two Dittos blurred again as he attempted to replicate again.

Wendy struggled to focus as the Dittos both were blurring and separating again. Ditto was going for four.

"I don't believe it," Tink said as Ditto attempted what had never been done before.

"He doesn't want to be left behind." Tootles cheered him on. "Go, Ditto!"

For a split second, Wendy saw it. Four individual Dittos, hands in fists, raised above their heads. Then four mouths screamed and collapsed on the floor in a single heap. Grabbing his side, Ditto groaned and tried to rise to his feet before sliding to the ground and passing out cold.

"Jax," Wendy pleaded. "He did it."

"No, he didn't. You saw him. He couldn't hold it. He can't go."

"Well, maybe if he wasn't injured, he could have," Wendy insisted, stepping in front of Jax as he tried to leave the room.

Jax's body went still, his eyes narrowing, and Wendy felt the full force of his stony gaze. "Don't make excuses for him. I set the bar, he didn't pass." He pushed past her.

Wendy followed him down the hall. "The bar was too high," she snapped at him.

Jax spun on his heel, his face coming inches from her, his voice softened as he pleaded with her, "Maybe I didn't set it high enough. We're too few, Wendy, to take on Neverland. We'd neve—"

"Peter!" Wendy breathed out, interrupting Jax. She saw him, recognized his shadow at the end of the hall, behind Jax's tall form.

Jax followed her gaze, his eyes squinting, seeing nothing.

"Peter?" he called out.

She stepped around Jax and slowly approached the dark shadow that was waiting for her.

"Where did you go?" she whispered, her voice shaking. "You left me alone. You left me." Her voice rose in anguish. "You promised you wouldn't leave me."

Peter's shadow rushed closer to her and reached out, and she eagerly pressed her hand into his presence and closed her eyes. Images scattered into her mind as she tried to make sense of what he was showing her. Soldiers, a training room, a semi. His urgency caused him to ambush her with his fear, and the images hit her like a sledgehammer. It was too much, too fast.

She felt herself slipping to the ground, heard Jax cry out her name in alarm, and Peter's shadow flickered out of view as her eyelids closed.

-17-

Her head wouldn't stop throbbing. With each beat of her heart, a stabbing pain hit her in the temple. Wendy struggled to open her eyes and found Jax standing guard at the foot of her bed. He was tense, his focus aimed at her door, his arm outstretched, his brace armed and ready to fire.

"What's happening?" Wendy cried, alarmed by his stance.

Jax gave her the briefest glance, and Wendy took note of the specs on his eyes that allowed him to see the shadows. Was he protecting her from Peter?

"I don't know. You called his name and then collapsed. When I touched you, your body was ice cold. If Peter did this to you, I'll kill him," he growled out.

"Jax, he already is—"

"I know," he snapped. "I'll kill him again. He had no right to assault you like that."

Wendy attempted to lean over the side of the bed to glance into the hall, but Jax's body made a better wall than a window. She couldn't see if Peter's shadow was out there.

"Where is he?" she asked, hoping that he was still here, and that Jax hadn't destroyed him.

"Down the hall on the left," Jax mumbled and shifted his weight. Peter must have made another attempt to move closer because Jax raised the brace again. "Don't even try it, Peter. You want to see how many times you can regenerate?"

Wendy slipped her feet off the bed and tried to stand. Her head weighing a million tons, she felt like a weighted blow-up clown balloon, and with each step, she wobbled back and forth.

"Stay back, Wendy," Jax warned. "He attacked you. I'm not sure what is going on, but he can't hurt you like that. I won't allow it."

She gently touched his right arm, pushing the brace down to aim at the floor. "He's scared, Jax," Wendy soothed. "He didn't mean to harm me, but something scared him and he tried to tell me all at once, and it was too much for my system. Perhaps if we try it again." She stepped past Jax.

Once Wendy was in view, Peter rushed forward and Jax moved like lightning. He raced and pushed Wendy behind him, his brace aimed at the shadow. "No man, I'm not going to let you hurt your girl. Move toward her again, and I will send you where the sun don't shine."

"Jax, we need to figure out what's going on. We must communicate with him. See what he can tell us about Neverland and the boys. Unless this has been your plan all along," she accused, her suspicions coming back to the surface. Suspicions she suppressed as she started to grow closer to him. "To weaken us. First you demand Ditto and the younger boys stay behind, and now you won't let Peter help us."

"No! I wouldn't do that. I'm just trying to protect them . . . and you." Jax dropped his head, and a deep sigh resonated from his lips. He very deliberately stepped aside and waved her toward Peter. Wendy slid past him into the hall, and Jax grabbed her elbow. "Listen, I so much as sense that you're in danger, it's over."

She nodded and paused in front of Peter as his shadow floated in front of her. He was milky black; at the right angle she could see through him to the stairs. His form was always moving, shifting but discernable to her. She would recognize his shadow anywhere now. Her heart would always lead her to him.

She didn't reach for him as eagerly as she had before. It took a minute of gathering her nerve, as if to extend a hand to a dog that had bitten her. Her fingers trembled as she reached her palm out.

Jax took another step forward, and she felt reassured by his presence. Peter's hand froze inches above her palm, not moving down to connect or pass through hers. She could see him contemplating the exchange himself, could sense his hesitation. He was afraid to hurt her. Peter's shadowy gaze turned to Jax in question and he withdrew his hand.

"No, Peter," Wendy gasped. "I can take it. It will be fine. I've done this before, we've done this before. You won't hurt me a second time. It was just a fluke. You were scared, that's all."

Peter's shadow didn't acknowledge her. Instead, he beckoned with his chin toward Jax, and Jax crooked his head in thought.

A silent exchange passed between them, a bond born of brotherhood and battles, and Wendy would never be able to fathom what they were conspiring.

Jax's shoulders stiffened. His wrist and brace lowered, and he looked at Peter through the goggles. "Do it."

"Do what?" Wendy asked unnecessarily as Peter's shadow rushed past Wendy and dove into Jax's body.

Jax gasped as the momentum of Peter's soul entered him and thrust him against the wall, his head thudding loudly.

"Jax!" Wendy screamed, rushing to aid him as his legs folded under him and he crumpled to the ground.

Wendy grabbed Jax's shoulders, steadying him, calling his name as she scanned the hall for Peter's shadow. Unlike before, when the shadows would pass through a person and out the other side, Peter's didn't. He was gone.

"Jax, answer me," Wendy pleaded.

Jax's eyelashes fluttered open. His gray eyes met hers and he flashed a cocky grin at her. "Told you, Wendy girl, nothing would separate us," he teased jovially.

Her hands dropped from Jax's shoulders and she fell onto her backside in shock.

"Peter? Is that you?"

Jax regained his balance and helped Wendy off the floor before patting his chest and rubbing his hands along his jaw. "Yes, and no. It seems that Jax and I are cohabitating at the moment. But I don't know for how long. He was never very good at sharing things." He grinned at her.

Wendy's heart danced at having Peter back, and she wrapped her arms around him. Peter's hug was a lifeline in the stormy waters. His presence calmed her spirit, even if he was in the wrong packaging, and she couldn't stop the sniffles and the tears of happiness that trailed down her face.

"Now, now, there's nothing to cry over. I'm here. Well, I was here before, but now I can talk to you easier," he soothed and headed down the stairs to the living room. Wendy followed in disbelief.

"What happened to you?" she sniffed.

She felt him shudder under her palms. "I died."

"Oh, Peter," she began, but he cut her off.

"I stayed as long as I could. But I can't be away from my body too long or I may not be able to come back, and that would be a tragedy."

"Please always come back to me," she whispered and closed her eyes. It was easier to believe that it was Peter with her eyes closed.

"I will, Wendy. I promise." He nuzzled her head with his chin.

They stayed locked in that embrace, taking comfort from each other, but then a loud cough came from behind them. Jax and Wendy looked up into the very shocked face of Tink at the top of the stairs.

Her pinched mouth and red-tinged cheeks were enough of an indicator that volcano Tink was about to erupt with her opinion. Her mouth opened and Wendy prepared herself for the onslaught of bells, since she knew how much Tink distrusted Jax.

"Hey, Tinker Bell," Peter-Jax quipped, and Tink's mouth went slack in confusion at the nickname that only Peter knew.

Her mouth opened and closed multiple times, and no bells or horns sounded. Finally, after a few false tries, she managed, "Jax. No, he wouldn't. How . . . Peter?"

Peter-Jax grinned and nodded, then stepped away from Wendy, opening his arms wide.

"It's me, Tink, back from the dead."

Tink squealed and ran to Peter, jumping into the air and wrapping her arms around his neck. Peter-Jax swung her around, her legs flying in a circle and taking out the lamp off an end table. Wendy felt a little hurt by the overly friendly greeting between them. When her feet finally found purchase on the wood floor, Tink bopped him on the back of the head.

"What took you so long? And do you get to keep the Jax meat suit?"

Peter-Jax chuckled. "Ah, Tink, you don't mean that."

She huffed. "Maybe I do. Although, he's not necessarily an upgrade."

"Upgrade. You still don't trust him after he fought with us at Neverwood?"

Tink shook her head.

Peter-Jax frowned and shook his head. "Tink, we need him. Something bad is happening at Neverland."

"What's going on, Peter?"

"The boys, I've seen them. They're being harvested. Their DNA is being used to upgrade Hook's crop of new recruits, his Dusters."

"Well, then show us where they are and we'll bust them out," Tink declared palming her fist.

"I can't. I don't know where they're going. They were shutting down their operation and moving. Loading everyone into shipping containers. I get the impression this happens a lot. By the time we got there, they'd be gone. I tried to escape with your friend." Peter-Jax turned to Wendy.

"My friend?"

"Yeah, the cheerleader . . . um, Brittney. It was during my escape attempt that Hook—" Peter drew his finger across his throat and Wendy winced.

She didn't need it spelled out how Hook killed him. "What about Brittney?"

"I don't know. I didn't get to see what happened or where we were going when he . . ." He trailed off.

"How do we find them?" Tink asked. "If they keep moving their base, how are we ever going to find them?"

"The shadows could take us?" Wendy said. "I'm sure if we asked, they could."

"I'm sure with all the morphlings, the shadows have all been taken care of within twenty miles of Neverland," Tink said.

"True, I hadn't thought of that." She forgot that Neverland was also the home of the morphlings, which hunted down the shadows and devoured them eagerly. It seemed that the shadows also gravitated toward anyone with a hint of supernatural gifts, anyone who had the PX gene, hoping that someone could see them. It was the shadows that had led the morphlings and Red Skulls to the victims that would be forced into becoming recruits in their horrible program.

"Don't worry, Tink. We'll find our boys and bring them home," he said confidently.

Tink's blonde head lowered, and she nodded, surreptitiously wiping a tear away. "Okay, Peter. Just tell us what to do."

He scanned the living room and made a beeline for the stairs to the rooms, popping into each one until he saw Ditto slumped over his bed in despair.

It was odd to see Peter's confident swagger in Jax's body—Jax, who was always so stiff and formal. "You ready, Tweedledum?"

Ditto lifted his head from the pillow and gave Jax the most confused expression. If his eyebrows rose any higher, they'd turn into a butterfly and fly away.

"What? Jax, you said I couldn't go?"

"Nonsense, I need my left lieutenant, and my right. I said you're going and it's final." Peter-Jax put his hands on his hips and grinned.

Ditto put his hand to his mouth in shock. "It can't be—can it?" He looked to Wendy and Tink who nodded in affirmation. Ditto rushed to hug Peter. "I'm sorry I failed you, Peter."

"Never, Ditto. You're alive. That's all that matters. If you died, then I am the one who failed you, by not protecting you. But I'm not going to keep you from your destiny. It's time we go back. All of us that are left. We will go and take back Neverland."

"It really is you, Peter," Ditto breathed out and leaned back, giving his leader the grandest salute and cheekiest grin he could muster.

Peter's answering smile on Jax's face made Ditto grimace in fear. "Don't do that."

"Do what?" Peter asked, confusion filling his voice.

"Jax never smiles like that. You look like a serial killer."

A deep, gut-busting laugh filled the air, and he turned to look at Tink and Wendy whose faces held a similar look of revulsion.

"Really? It can't look that creepy when Jax smiles."

They both nodded their head. "It is."

Peter-Jax sighed, his brows furrowed, and they both lit up.

"Aw, there's Jax." Tink chuckled.

"Yes, much better," Wendy agreed.

"Yep, it's better if you just stay surly until you get your own body back," Ditto said.

"Well, now we know why Jax is always angry. When he's actually happy, you accuse him of being a psychopath," Peter-Jax said.

"Sociopath," Tink corrected. "But he's *our* sociopath."

Peter-Jax sighed and patted his heart, or Jax's heart, in an attempt to be nearer to his friend. "Yes, he is ours."

-18-

"HOW ARE WE GOING to find them now?" Tink asked, sitting cross-legged on the floor. Wendy, John, and Michael had taken the couch, Ditto the lone armchair, and Slightly leaned on the armrest. Other than Peter-Jax, Tootles was the only one not sitting as he kept teleporting to the kitchen for snacks.

Peter-Jax walked back and forth, his gait looking unnatural in Jax's body. "I can only tell you what I saw before I was taken out. But the bigger problem will be when I come back to life. I will have panned again. Only while I'm dead do I have any memories of what happened before."

John pushed his glasses up his nose. "Do you remember having been a shadow before? I mean, it's not the first time you've panned, but why are you a shadow right now?"

"That's an excellent question." Tink smiled at John and Wendy's brother blushed.

"Yeah, Peter, why now? How come you aren't panning right away and coming to? What's with the delay?" Ditto asked.

"I wish I had those answers. Although I suspect that it has something to do with where I died."

"You mean Neverland?" Slightly crossed his arms appearing to do calculations in his head. "It can't be the place, because their base of operations is continually moving, never in one spot long. There must be something or someone that is causing the shadows. I mean, this is only an assumption."

"But a valid one," Tink answered. "He's right, we need to assume that there is something—an item, a machine—something that is causing the souls to separate. Because you've panned at Neverwood and never had an outcome like this."

Peter-Jax shook his head. "No, I haven't. But truthfully, I'm worried. I'm slower. I'm not coming back as fast as I used to."

"What do you mean?' Wendy asked worriedly, her heart already fluttering between nervousness that she was about to lose Peter any second and joy because he was back.

He gave her a gaze filled with yearning and loss. "We were never meant to be immortal. No one should live forever, that's just the way of it. And if by chance we could, I don't know if I would want to. Our time will eventually run out. I have a feeling that mine will before yours. I've been fighting Hook for years, taken risks that I would never allow any of the other lost boys to take, because I could. Every time I died, I knew I was taking the place of one of the boys. I was saving them."

It was Tootles who spoke up from the kitchen. "Go back, Peter. Go back and find them. Then as a shadow come tell us where they are."

Peter-Jax's head snapped in the direction of their youngest boy. "It could work, if I kept my memories and could purposefully end my life."

A heavy silence fell on the room, as everyone contemplated what he had just spoken aloud.

"No," Wendy jumped up getting emotional. "Anything but that. No one should have to go through that. You're talking suicide."

Peter-Jax met her eyes and her heart began to weep at the thought of what they were asking him. "Please don't do it," she whispered.

Peter-Jax nodded. "Then, we need Dr. Mee. Find a way to get her memory antidote, or if she knows of a way I can restart my memories at Neverland."

"It would take a few days to track her down and find her," Slightly added. "There's a chance she could have taken off again. But if you want, I will go in search of her. Except, what if you're not here when I get back? What if you're"—he made a *poof!* gesture with his hands—"gone?"

"Then I get a reboot, Neverland style, and it won't give me all my memories back."

"And we're sure that Jax can't help us?" John spoke up. "I find it very hard to believe that he was in league with the Devil for so long and can't take us there or give us more information."

Peter-Jax rubbed the back of his neck and went to stare into the fireplace. "I have considered the same thing multiple times and multiple ways. Always believed that he was keeping stuff from me, but even being in the program for a few days and meeting soldiers that have been there a lot longer than me, let's just say they thrive on secrets and orders, so it's quite possible there was a lot Jax never knew. I finally understand what Jax meant when he said he couldn't tell us where they were, and I understand a bit more fully what he went through and the sacrifice he made to keep them off our trail."

The room became silent and Peter-Jax scratched his arms, a sign that he was uncomfortable cohabitating with Jax.

"So what do we do now?" Ditto asked. "Do we wait to try to find Dr. Mee? Grab some candles and holy water and do an exorcism to get him out of Jax's body? I mean, Peter, how long can you exist in Jax?"

"I don't think very long." He scratched his arm again. "I can feel the pull of my body and I haven't much time left. I'd like to spend it with you." Peter-Jax looked at Wendy and motioned for her to follow him. He headed out the main door, away from prying eyes. The rushing of the waterfall made speaking almost impossible without yelling near each other's ear.

"Wendy, I'm sorry," Peter-Jax said, and tried to pull her into a hug, but she resisted. She didn't want to be in Jax's arms. "Close your eyes," he commanded.

She took a deep breath, closed her eyes, and listened to the waterfall. Over the turbulent waters, his voice sounded different and she could believe it was him. Peter. She raised her arms, and he pulled her into his embrace.

He spoke into her ear, his voice husky with emotion. "I never meant to leave you, or for this to happen. I promise I will come back . . . somehow."

"No, Peter. Don't do it." She knew it was selfish pleading with him. "Find another way. Don't die just to help us find the boys. What if it's the last time? What if you can't pan again? It's not worth risking your life. I don't want to lose you. Wait for us to find you."

He pulled away. "Death will never separate us. I've proven that. Trust me."

With her eyes still squeezed shut, her trembling began. She could tell he was going to leave her. "No," she begged again.

He embraced her again and pressed his cheek to hers. He whispered encouragement and sighed. When her trembling didn't cease, he turned his head and sought her lips. She wrapped her hands around his neck, keeping her eyes pressed closed. In desperation he deepened the kiss. Wendy in turn locked her arms around his neck as if to hold him forever to her.

The kiss changed, becoming more demanding as his mouth crushed into hers. He lifted her a few inches off the ground, his hands wrapped around her waist. She broke apart first and sighed. "I love you."

When he didn't respond to her declaration, she opened her eyes and gazed into the heated and fully cognizant gaze of Jax.

"Jax!" Wendy gasped and struggled to be released from his grip, but she couldn't find purchase on the ground. "Put me down."

He wasn't in any hurry to obey, continuing to hold her close to him.

Wendy's cheek's burned in embarrassment. She hadn't meant to—she never expected Peter to kiss her using Jax. In fact, she's pretty sure he wouldn't have. But then she had to wonder if it was Peter that had kissed her or Jax?

"Now, Jax," she demanded and pushed against his shoulder. There was a hint of disappointment in his eyes before his face turned to a familiar unreadable stone.

"As you wish." He dropped her suddenly.

She was unprepared for his sudden release. With her own momentum from pushing away from him and the angle at which her feet hit the wet stone, Wendy slipped backward into the rushing falls.

Wendy gasped as the thundering barrage hit her full force in the face as she was swept over the side of the fifty-foot cliff. A roaring din and a million hammers dragged across her chest as she fell. There was a moment under the weight of the water when she felt like she was weightless and flying instead of falling down the waterfall.

Then she remembered the rocks.

-19-

HE COULDN'T FIND HER. When he saw her fall over the safety chain, he was seconds behind her. The mass of water, pulling him so hard, it knocked the air from his lungs, and he forgot to breathe. It felt like an eternity, but was only seconds later, when he crashed into the pool below, the pounding of the falls turning him over and over, worse than being tumbled in a washing machine as he struggled to find up. Feeling the pull of the river, he kicked his feet, and an agonizing minute later, he crested the water and breathed.

Jax scanned the water, searching for Wendy's strawberry blonde head to appear, but it never surfaced.

"No!" he cried out in terror and with large strokes swam closer to the falls. Taking a deep breath, he dived under and searched for her. Nothing. He kept up his pursuit until his lungs screamed for oxygen, only surfacing when he felt close to blacking out. It wouldn't do him any good if he passed out before he found her.

Fear fueled his desperate search, and he puffed out his cheeks, taking three more deep breaths before diving under again. His desperation made him reckless and he wouldn't give up, even though it was hard to see and he felt himself start to cramp. No! He saw her, or at least what looked like could be a piece of her shirt. Using all the strength he had left, he pulled himself through the water, his hand grasping clothing. It was Wendy.

He had her. Kicking downward, he pulled her up, his hand locked under her chin. Both of their heads broke the surface, and he turned to Wendy with a grin. Except, Wendy's face was pale, and she wasn't breathing.

Instead of fighting the current, he used it to help him get to the riverbank. Pulling her onto the shore, he checked her pulse and swore.

"Sorry, Wendy," Jax muttered, then checked her airway and began to perform CPR. Over and over, breathed into her mouth, following it with chest compressions, even praying to God. When she didn't respond, he knew it was because of his curse. He always hurt those closest to him. First his best friend Peter, the lost boys, and now Wendy.

Jax collapsed on the bank. Pulling Wendy into his lap, he wrapped his arms around her and sobbed. She was so pure, so good. Too good for him, and she was gone.

He had known the moment Peter had left his body, had felt his friend leave. In his mind, he'd seen Peter nod his thanks for letting him share his body. But Jax was angry at Peter. When Peter left, he hadn't felt jovial at all, but a loss. The very next moment when he regained his full senses, he had Peter's girl, Wendy, in his embrace.

Out of spite. Out of bitterness toward them both, for having a happiness that he could never achieve, he had kissed her. Once before, when he was training her, he had stolen a kiss out of anger, to catch her off guard and to fight him. This time it was purely selfish. He wanted a kiss, and when she responded, it about undid him. It sent him reeling, wishing for something he couldn't have and wouldn't dare take. To pursue Wendy for himself, he would be forever damning his soul. He would never forgive himself and neither would Peter.

Never before had he seen lovers as fated to be together as Peter and Wendy. Even as children, amongst the most trying times of their lives at Neverland, they had gravitated to each other, seeking shelter from the other's company. When apart, they were solemn, quiet. But once together, their matching grins could light up a room, freeing the atmosphere of worry and fear, their laughter and spontaneous giggles drawing crowds of kids. They were two halves of one soul, and when Peter lost her that night on the boat years ago, he saw his best friend break. The next seven years were filled with him learning to live without her. Peter had hidden the pain of his loss behind a fake charm, always keeping a smile plastered on his face for the boys at the school. Only Jax ever saw the real him.

He was a fool for trying to become part of their world. Because no matter how much he tried to deny it, she had stolen a piece of his heart. And from the looks most of the others gave her, it was clear they adored her as well.

He sighed, but each intake of breath became harder than the last. He looked one last time into her lifeless face and began to sob again.

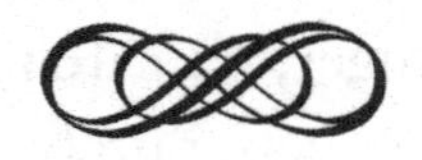

Her teeth hurt and began to chatter. Warmth surrounded her like a blanket, banishing the cold to be replaced by an almost unbearable burning heat. The heat was better than the bitter bite of the chill and she snuggled closer. But the heat was moving, shaking, and when she opened her eyes, she stared into the sobbing face of Jax.

Water dripped from his wet hair, running down into her face. They were sitting on the bank; behind him a majestic waterfall rose up like a throne. She was curled up in his lap, his arms wrapped around her, his forehead pressed close as he rocked her.

"I'm so sorry," he whispered. Great heavy sobs wracked his body as he cried hard, shaking them both.

Unsure, Wendy blinked up at Jax, at his tan face and deep black hair. Why was he sad? Why was he holding her like she was his long-lost love?

Feeling an unmistakable need to comfort him, she reached out and touched his cheek. His eyes opened and Wendy was hit with eyes as gray as a foggy morning.

"Wendy?" His breath sucked in and hope filled his eyes.

"Peter or Jax?" she muttered, wishing it was Peter.

His hard face broke into a smile. "Jax. I'm so glad you are okay." He pulled her closer and buried his face into her neck in a hug. "I thought you had died. I'm sorry. I didn't mean to have set you down so hard that you fell over the falls."

The falls? Wendy was trying to make sense of his words.

She looked up and over his shoulder at the rushing waterfall. She had fallen over that and survived? It seemed impossible and mighty unlikely.

"That's right, I fell," she said in awe.

He nodded. "I jumped after you into the falls and was washed downstream. But you, you never surfaced, so I kept diving until I found you. I thought I was too late."

He hugged her again and she let him. Until she remembered why she fell, and then she shoved him away from her and glowered at him.

"You kissed me," she cried in accusation.

Shocked by her sudden burst of temper and change of mood, he laughed, which only fueled her anger.

"You kissed me back," he laughed.

"No, no, no!" Wendy shook her head and struggled to get out of his arms. "I was hugging Peter, but then he kissed me. I mean—you kissed me. I mean, he wasn't you at the time, or was he?" She looked at Jax suspiciously. "How much of that kiss was you?"

He leaned back, a crooked smile of enjoyment splayed across his handsome face. "You may never know."

"Ooh!" Wendy growled out angrily. Gathering all of her strength, she pushed him in the chest. "That's for kissing me and then letting me fall off a waterfall," she snapped.

"Technically, you slipped," he grumbled, rubbing his chest. "But I did save you."

"Did you? Well, who is going to save you from me?" Wendy took a threatening step toward him and watched as Jax tried to back away. Tripping over his own feet, he landed on the ground.

Wendy smirked. It felt good to have gotten the upper hand with him for once. With a sigh, she reached out her palm in a peace offering to help him up. Jax took it and then he purposefully used all of his strength to pull her back with him into a pile of leaves.

Wendy howled as she landed in a heap atop his chest, dried leaves tangling in her blonde hair.

She looked over at Jax, and he whistled cheerfully before offering her his hand. "Truce?"

"Truce," she sighed and took it, both of them awkwardly trying to get out of the leaves.

"Jax, do you know what happened to Peter?" Wendy asked softly, looking down at the ground.

"He's gone. I felt him slipping away and I tried to hold onto him, but there was a sharp pain, like a shock and he was gone."

"Do you think—?"

"He's fine. I promise. C'mon, we need to get you back to the others." He lifted her off his lap and held on to her hand until they had both stood. Her clothes were dryer in all the places she had touched him, and as she moved away from the furnace that was his body, she felt the dreary chill.

But it wasn't the same as a chill from cold, but of something else, something darker. Wendy looked over her shoulder at the surrounding woods and shuddered. Something sinister lay beyond her sight, she could almost guarantee it, but what was it? She stepped close to Jax as the cold and wet made her feel vulnerable.

"It's too steep of a climb straight up. We have to head east for a bit before we can get around. So that means quite a hike. Are you okay with that?" he asked.

A shadow came up and wrapped around her wrist, and Wendy gasped, feeling all of the shadow's terror, but it was impossible to understand what it was trying to tell her and Jax couldn't see the shadow. The shadow showed her the future. Woods, trees—not just trees, but the boughs. An image of Jax, lying on the ground, covered in blood.

Wendy couldn't get over the pressing feeling of peril and didn't answer right away. She didn't know how to describe the urgency that she was feeling in her soul—the warning of what was coming, demanding for her to take action —bubbling up out of her.

Up. Up the danger is up.

"Wendy, you're pale as a ghost. What's wrong?"

Her body was trembling, she could hardly move or respond. The forest was moving. No, not the forest. A shadow within the forest. A coldness overtook her, and she knew if they stayed, they would die.

"We need to run," she whispered and tried to give him a shove, but it was like trying to move a brick wall.

"What?" He was confused, but she continued to drive him forward.

"Run!" she screamed as a beast crashed down from the tree canopy and landed where Jax had been moments ago.

"Morphling!" Jax pushed Wendy back and reached for his brace, flicking his wrist to try to activate it. But the wand didn't come forth and the light weapon died. He attempted it a second time.

Wendy tried to activate her own brace, but it wouldn't come to life. "Jax, they won't work!"

"They must have been damaged in the fall."

A morphling in the shape of a dragon beat its massive wings, sending twigs, dust, and pebbles directly into their eyes. Wendy turned away, trying to protect her face with her hands and squinted to keep a wary eye on the monster.

The morphling roared, taking flight into the sky. It circled above the waterfall before doing a kill dive, claws opened and aiming for her.

Jax cursed under his breath, and power in the form of bright orange flames materialized in his hands. An unseen wind blew his dark hair as power gathered. With a mighty bellow, he released the fiery blast into the mouth of the morphling. Wendy cried out as it exploded outward, leaving a trail of glistening slime everywhere.

The exertion of power made him stumble for a second, but he quickly regained his footing and turned to make sure Wendy was all right.

Was she? She didn't think so. Her heart was beating frantically like a caged bird, and her arms were prickling from fear. She looked into Jax's eyes and said, "Jax, what was that? Was that a morphling?"

His brows furrowed in confusion as he looked at her. "I think so, but that was less shadow and more—"

"Real," Wendy stated. "How are they becoming real? And how come they're still chasing us when we haven't seen a Red Skull?"

"Good questions, but I suspect this morphling wasn't here because of Hook. I think it came because of Alice."

"Alice?"

Jax's cheeks turned red, and he reached up to brush the back of his neck. "I think she was trying to communicate with me, with that morphling.

Wendy gave Jax a bizarre look and flipped out her palms. "Girl wants to talk to guy, girl sends monsters after him—when a phone call would work just as well?"

"It's not like that," Jax said impatiently. "She dreams and her dreams create morphlings."

"Jax, someone has to say it. That's messed up."

"She's like you Wendy. I mean like us. Except she's trapped at Neverland."

More crashing came from the woods, and Jax placed himself in front of her protectively, fire building in his hands. The crashing grew louder as whatever was rushing through the brush drew close. Wasting no time, Jax released a fireball in the direction of the beast and heard a surprised yelp.

That was no morphling. Wendy tried to move out from behind Jax, but he kept pushing her back, keeping himself firmly in place between her and the noise. The rustling continued, but Jax stayed his hand, waiting and watching as their intruder emerged.

Not a monster, but a large Saint Bernard dog. One Wendy recognized.

"Nana?" she said in disbelief. Behind Nana, two very disheveled people staggered out as well. An older man with white hair and glasses was patting down his singed jacket, while a woman with a torn coat was untangling twigs from her dark hair.

Jax's hand dropped to his side, and he stumbled in surprise. Wendy's hand reached out to steady him as he regained his composure. "Mr. Barrie? Dr. Mee?"

Dr. Barrie brushed off his singed jacket and wagged a finger at Jax.

"Jax, my boy, what have we discussed about using your gifts without having a clear line of sight? And don't try and play it off, like I don't remember." He tapped his head. "I'm back."

"Yes, Dr. Barrie." Jax grinned.

Dr. Mee gave up on untangling the sticks and approached Jax, holding up her hands for a hug. Jax didn't hesitate but lifted the small-framed women up in the air, and her accompanying laughter made Wendy smile.

Jax took notice of her again and his smile faltered. "Dr. Mee, you remember Wendy?"

Dr. Mee looked over at Wendy and extended her hand. "Yes, unfortunately she was much younger when I last saw her, and then recently, we didn't have the time to get reacquainted." Wendy shook her hand. "I had hoped we would have met under better circumstances. A police station and a hospital are not quite the reunion I had in mind. But all will be well. We will make it so."

It took ten minutes for them to follow the path back up toward the house. And as they made their way up, gripping tight to the safety chain, Wendy hugged the wall when she came near the spot where she had slipped, noticing that Jax had done the same.

Dr. Barrie paused at the door, his hands smoothing his hair back in nervousness. "Do you think she's forgotten me?" he asked Dr. Mee. Nana was brushing against his knee.

"Nonsense, no one could ever forget you."

"I did, I have forgotten so much, but never again," Dr. Barrie said.

"Then you're ready." Dr. Mee opened it, waiting a good ten seconds before motioning for Wendy and Jax to enter first.

"What took you so long?" Tink shrieked at seeing them enter before pulling out a backpack and unzipping it, completely preoccupied with her clipboard and other contents of her bag. "It's time to get going. I've packed everything we need to take down Neverland and Hook. Rat repellant—well, not really, but I call it that—it's a mini stun gun. Also braces with the latest updates, and a full stock of . . ." Tink trailed off as Nana ran through the door and barked, her large body almost knocking Tink over as she tried to lunge up and lick her.

Then she saw who came in the door after Nana, and the clipboard fell from her hands and clattered on the tile floor. Her face scrunched up into an expression that was hard to decipher, but then her censor band went off. "#$*! #%^&!" When her cussing tirade was over, her expression shifted, not entirely readable. There was a wariness in her, but also longing as she said, "Took you long enough, Dad."

"Too long, Isabelle," he whispered.

Wendy couldn't help but grin as she watched the scene unfold between father and daughter. Tink's face pinched and was soon glistening with tears as she took the most direct path to her father, which meant jumping up and over the couch and into Dr. Barrie's arms.

-20-

PETER AWOKE WILD-EYED and terrified, strapped to a gurney in a moving medical vehicle. An EMT had used electrical paddles on him to jump-start his heart. He had thought he was dead, but a reassuring woman in a wheelchair explained that he had injured his head during a training exercise with his troops and lost his memories. That he would be back to fighting shape in no time.

Candace. That was her name. It was nice of her to explain that they were in transport to their base and that once there she would be able to reboot more of his memories. He wasn't sure what that meant exactly, but was assured she had done it before.

They took his vitals and radioed another vehicle of his progress. The caravan of trucks pulled over and he was escorted from the medical transport truck to a waiting semi in broad daylight. As he stepped out of the medical transport, guards greeted him with guns. He smiled at them but received nothing in return for his friendly efforts. Just a nod, a grunt, and orders to move and not talk.

As he passed the waiting semi, he took note of the hauling company's logo on the door. Part of the name was obscured with dirt, but he could read the word *Wonder* aside a picture of a heart and crown. He couldn't quite make out the name of the originating town. Three more semis from the same hauling company passed them on the road, shipping various cargo under large white tied-down tarps, followed by another full trailer. He didn't know how many were in the caravan or how many were ahead of the trailer he was heading toward.

They opened the back door and Peter was ushered inside, where he took an empty seat across from a different armed guard. There were two long rows of kids his age already buckled and strapped in on benches wearing the same uniform. Twenty pairs of eyes watched him closely, their faces wary. Peter swallowed nervously. Nothing about being escorted and shoved into a trailer at gunpoint seemed normal.

The guards were about to close the door when a stranger wearing civilian clothes approached them. He seemed to have appeared out of nowhere. Maybe he came out of the medical transport like he did? A few moments later, the stranger, entered the semi, briefly touched the seated guard's arm, and whispered to him before he waved for the guards to close him in.

He was tall, with long dark hair that brushed his ears and inscrutable, piercing eyes. He glanced at the open seats and sat in the one next to Peter. Peter couldn't help but notice his long curly lashes as he occupied the seat next to him. He leaned back, closed his eyes, and stretched his long legs out in front.

The brake released, and the semi pulled back onto the road. The tension in the trailer lessened as the teens began to freely talk.

"Who's he?" a young soldier asked, nodding to the newcomer in civilian clothes.

"Beats me," another answered.

Peter tried to observe the laid-back newcomer but couldn't make out much in the dimly lit trailer. He seemed to be asleep already, in the overly humid enclosed space. Or maybe he was faking.

The noise-level lowered and then died down entirely as, one by one, each of the occupants of the trailer were lulled to sleep by the rocking motion of the trailer. Peter felt drained, but he was too keyed up to sleep, trying to recall what happened to him before he woke up on that gurney. But then the newcomer slumped over in sleep so his head was near Peter's left ear, and Peter found himself going stock-still. "Hey, Peter," the newcomer whispered, keeping up the pretense of sleeping.

"Wha—"

"Shh, don't move, don't talk," he whispered. There's no way I can take on a semi full of Dusters, and neither can you in this condition."

Peter was motionless, keeping his attention straight ahead. The guard didn't even seem to notice him; he was preoccupied with a hangnail on his thumb.

"It's me, Curly," the boy said, and before Peter could ask anything else, Curly continued. "Yeah, I know you don't remember me, and maybe that's for the better, since I'm part of the reason you're here. Wasn't a fan of how you were running the Neverwood School, didn't really feel like I belonged. Had a grudge and I took it out on all of you, but I had a change of heart, and I realized that you guys were the only ones that truly cared. So I'm here to help. If I can."

Peter looked at Curly out of the side of his eyes and nodded slowly, wondering why this person wanted to help him?

Curly yawned and covered his mouth, continuing to whisper for Peter's ears only. "In short, this place is bad. Where you're going is worse. I took the time to do some digging, and I didn't like what I found. No way am I letting the boys end up there, or at least not alone."

Peter stiffened when he heard Curly's warning. Where were they going that was so bad? And what boys was he referring to?

"Look, I know I messed up, and I can tell you've panned again. I'm going to try something. I nicked it from Dr. Mee's office when we went to get her for your girl Wendy."

The name caused Peter's heart to flutter. He knew that name. "Nicked what?" Peter asked warily.

Curly's fist was wrapped around a small syringe, and he jabbed it into Peter's leg.

Peter gasped and jumped up but the seat belt held him down. He tried to unbuckle and move away from the Curly.

"Remember, Peter," he encouraged, touching him on the arm.

"What did you just do?" Peter snapped.

Alertness ripped through his mind, and he tensed as memories came flooding back and he began to view the others in the truck with new eyes. They weren't troops being sent out on a mission; they were young teenagers, and most looked scared out of their minds, all except for a few. One, a blond-haired guy, kept glowering at him with the most intense hate-filled eyes.

Jeremy.

Peter remembered him. And he knew that he meant him harm.

But with Curly's touch, the boy accidentally shared his own memories with Peter. Peter gained knowledge not only of his own past but also Curly's, and he knew it wasn't intentional. Peter was swept through Curly's own memories and learned more in those few seconds than from years of having lived with him at Neverwood.

Memories of young boys playing in a large mansion that doubled as a school, images of boys refusing to play tag or football with him for fear of being manipulated. Peter learned that even amongst a school of boys, caretakers, and teachers, Curly was always alone, always watching from a distance, never being touched. It was a lonely life.

His heart felt heavy. Peter knew that he was one of them that had hurt Curly, and one of the reasons why Curly turned traitor to Neverland. Curly had betrayed them because he'd believed that what Neverland had done to him could be reversed, that if he helped them gather up the boys, they might feel grateful enough to help him if he asked for his power to be stripped away. Only after the lost boys were captured did he learn of Hook's true plan. He was never going to help Curly, intending only to use him to control all the Dusters.

Ashamed that Hook had used him, the master manipulator, he took off and headed back to the school to find it destroyed. It was down by the river, by the fresh gravesites that Curly had his epiphany, his change of heart. He spent the night, weeping and mourning his friend Fox.

Peter reached up and felt his own cheeks glisten with Curly's tears. He was sure that he'd never meant for Peter to have full access to his memories.

"What's the plan?" Curly asked after a few minutes. "You always have a plan. Mine was just to find you."

"We don't do anything till we find the boys," Peter said gravely. "Then we bring Neverland down once and for all."

-21-

THE LIVING ROOM WAS filled with the joyful reunion of the few remaining lost boys and their famous leader and father figure Dr. Barrie. John, Michael, and Wendy found themselves hiding out in the kitchen, out of the way of the gathering. The shed tears, the hugs, and the laughter—it wasn't meant for them. It pained Wendy to think of Tink reuniting with her father while the three of them were still orphans. When John and Wendy first lost their parents, it had seemed like it would be okay, that they would always have a home at Neverwood. But with the return of an able-minded Dr. Barrie, would that still be the case? Wendy and Michael may be part of the lost boys, but John wasn't and she wouldn't stay if he wasn't welcome.

John ran his fingers along the countertop in the kitchen, tracing the pattern in the stone. She could tell he was worried. Michael couldn't help but stare at the two doctors in the other room, and whenever they would glance his way, he would quickly lean forward to disappear behind the small partition again. Wendy sat next to them and tried to put herself in Michael's shoes. He wasn't one of the lucky ones that had made it on the boat and escaped with Dr. Barrie and Dr. Mee, and she wondered how much he remembered, if he recalled the meeting with the psychologist and the doctor that oversaw their initial testing at Neverland.

It seemed that he remembered enough to be fascinated with them. If only he had been with them, then he might have grown up differently. Who knows what havoc and irreparable damage Hook did to her brother's mind?

Wendy shook herself off and told herself to stop fretting. Such thoughts were too unsettling, and didn't help anything.

This was just one more delay in their quest to find the lost boys and rescue Peter.

She glanced at Jax and she couldn't stop her thoughts from drifting to the kiss she'd inadvertently shared with him, as if she didn't have enough things to worry about. *Could she really tell who it was? Yes, it was Jax.* Peter would never be so demanding with her. *Did she enjoy it? Yes.* Wendy rubbed her face and groaned in guilt. She needed to do something.

She pushed out the chair she had been sitting on, and it scraped loudly across the tile floor. All eyes met hers and she turned, scurrying past them and up the stairs into her room. Maybe it was her guilt over the kiss with Jax that was driving her to act out, but she felt desperate and didn't see how anyone else had a quicker way to get to him.

Wendy was unwilling to let Peter pan again. She couldn't let him take that chance, in case he couldn't come back to her. But that didn't mean she couldn't go to him.

Even though she had been warned, even though Jax forbade her, Wendy did it anyway.

She called the shadows to her.

A tingling sensation ran up her arm, and she felt an invisible breeze stir her hair from around her shoulders. First one came, then more. Her hairbrush on the nightstand rattled as she continued to gather more shadows. They wrapped around her, and she had but one thought. *Take me to Peter.*

The coldness enveloped her like a second skin and a rush of air pulled her through to the shadow realm, where the bitter bite hit her like a slap. She let the shadows lead her through the darkness.

The shadows were pulling, trying to move her faster than she could run, and even moving at an unnatural speed, she heard the terrifying roar of the beast as it caught the scent of its prey.

Wendy hadn't wanted to believe Jax was right, and she ran as hard as she could, outpacing the beast. But in this other realm, her legs and limbs didn't move with the same urgency as she wanted. Like a dream, where no matter how fast she ran, it was never fast enough.

The shadows beckoned, then pointed and stopped when they came to a dark body of water. Wendy slowed and stared at the pool of water moving in toward her feet and then receding like an ocean, but instead of an aquamarine or crystal blue, this was a murky black.

Her heart dropped and she quaked in terror. Wendy hated the ocean, hated swimming, ever since she had died at sea. She couldn't do it. Didn't want to cross the water.

"I can't," Wendy whimpered as the shadows beckoned over the water. "No, I can't do it."

A squealing howl of a morphling hot on her trail brought her back to the problem at hand.

She couldn't go any farther forward, and now it seemed she couldn't go back the way she came, unless she wanted to run right into the morphling hunting her down.

"Okay!" Wendy cried out, looking over her shoulder in fear. Behind her, the colossal morphling was running straight for her.

Two shadows grasped her under her arms and lifted her into the air, flying with her up and over the water. The morphling—a nightmare beast, half-bull, half-lion—scratched angrily at the water's edge and began to pace.

Her heart was in her throat and she knew that any minute she could plummet into the ocean.

Wendy felt herself plunge slightly and looked up as the shadows became more transparent. She lost altitude, her body inching lower and lower toward the eerie black ocean.

"NO!" Wendy cried out, as the murky depths were about to swallow her.

Then one of the shadows gripping her arm disappeared with a poof, leaving behind nothing but misty black spirals.

The second shadow doubled his efforts trying to get her to their destination. She knew that in the shadow realm, they traveled much faster than in her world. But there was no way they were going to make it. The black water came closer. She pulled her knees up to her chest, but it was no use. The shadow was trying, but like the one before, he began to fade. She felt the warning tingle in her hand, and like the first one, he disappeared, and then she was falling.

Wendy didn't have time to scream before she hit the water. Her body went into shock at the cold as the water covered her head and she plunged into its murky depths. Kicking with all of her strength, she felt an unnatural pull on her body as if she was being ripped in two. The current spun her around once, twice, and she kicked and fought, searching for the watery ceiling. Then cresting through the gloom, she finally surfaced and gasped for breath.

Salt and light stung her eyes and coated her lips. She continued to tread water as she searched her surroundings.

Wendy was no longer in the shadow realm. When she had hit the water, she must have passed through to the real world.

Marine blue as far as the eye could see, and above her, clouds dotted the sky, but nowhere did she see a boat or a speck of land.

"Oh no!" Wendy cried out, and a wave sprayed salty water into her mouth, causing her to gag and cough. Trying to keep her mind and body from panicking, she slowly turned three hundred and sixty degrees and had to choke down paralyzing fear as another wave hit her shoulder, splashing water into her nose and face, and she coughed again.

Wendy called for the shadows again, and again but none answered her call.

She was alone, stranded in the middle of the ocean.

A soft whimper escaped her lips as a large wave washed over her head, sending her under.

She knew she was going to die.

-22-

"So all Peter knows is that the site was being moved again," Dr. Barrie said to the group gathered in the living room. "But he doesn't know where?"

"That's correct," Jax answered from his spot leaning against the fireplace. "Hook is too paranoid. He never stayed in one spot more than a few weeks. The Red Skulls are trained to tear down and hide all evidence and be mobile within a few hours. Only the lead driver knows the next location, and it is only texted to him when he is on the road and then deleted. The address is never entered into a GPS either. The other vehicles have their outer and rear windows tinted black, and the teams are held in secure trucks until they've arrived at their new base."

"He really does cover his bases."

"Unfortunately, yes," Jax agreed.

"Then what do we do?" Ditto asked. "We can't stay here and wait for Peter to tell us where to go. What if he doesn't remember? What if this time, he wakes up and is on their side again?"

Dr. Barrie looked to Dr. Mee and a worried look passed between them. "Jax, how far along did you say the new PX drug series is?"

"Pretty far. Last I knew, he had slowed the reaping of new recruits, but a significant percentage of those given the drugs were still experiencing burnout. He must have thought the numbers were sufficient and had turned his focus to the next stage." Jax's shoulders slumped, and he gave Dr. Barrie a disheartened look. "He wanted the rest of the first generation—the lost boys. He was culling his own Primes for their gifts when Wendy had come across his radar." Jax turned and shot a pointed look at Michael, struggling not to blame him for sending his sister's whereabouts to Hook.

Jax ran his hand through his hair and sighed. "He recognized her as one of the first group members and took a keen interest in her because he thought she could see the future."

"Can she?" Dr. Barrie asked.

Everyone waited for Wendy to answer but she remained silent.

"Where is she?" Tootles asked. "She was just here."

John spoke up. "I think she's in her room."

"I'll check her room," Slightly said, getting up from the couch and heading up the stairs and down the hall.

"I was tasked with a team to bring her back to him, and when I failed, he decided to go after the others, the rest of the lost boys," Jax explained.

"Why?" John asked.

"Because the lost boys have the strongest abilities. Think about it. Peter's ability to fly and regenerate, Tootle's teleportation ability, Ditto's cloning. After Neverland was destroyed, and so many from the group were lost, Hook has been unable to reproduce the same results, at least with the same numbers or powers. But the new PX-3 drug doesn't give the recruits special powers. It makes them more receptive when injected with our harvested DNA. It makes the transfer more likely to stick. He wanted our abilities to add to the Primes he already has. He already knew where the school was; he was just waiting for the next group of Dusters to be ready. But they weren't ready, not really. There were still issues with burnout, so I don't understand why he took them now."

"He had a deadline," Dr. Barrie stated matter-of-factly. "There's no other reason for him to produce an imperfect crop unless he needed to. I know all too well the deadlines of our benefactor."

"Who is . . . ?" Ditto asked.

Dr. Barrie shrugged. "Even I don't know. It was all very secret. I wasn't paid to know, only to do my work."

Slightly came down the hall with a worried look and passed by them to head into the kitchen and then into the back halls. A few seconds later, he came back out of breath. "Guys, I can't find Wendy."

"What do you mean?" John stood up and raced to the kitchen. "I saw her head toward her room only five minutes ago. We've been sitting here the whole time, no one left out the front door."

"I'm telling you, I checked all the rooms and Wendy is gone."

Chaos ensued as everyone got up and began to search. A few minutes later, it was obvious that she had disappeared.

"She doesn't have her bag, or any supplies. She didn't leave out the front door. Where would she have gone?" Tink said anxiously, holding up Wendy's backpack.

Jax cursed as all eyes fell on him. "I told her not to do it. I told her it wasn't safe."

John rushed to Jax, grabbing him by the lapels of his jacket. "What, Jax? What aren't you telling us?"

"I think she went after him."

"Who, Peter?" Tink asked. "Without us?"

"If you knew what she wanted to do, why didn't you stop her!" John said angrily and slammed Jax against the wall.

Jax had enough of being pushed around. He grabbed John's wrists, twisted and in seconds had him in a double wristlock. John conceded and backed away rubbing them. Jax addressed the group. "She used the shadows. Must have used them to teleport her to where Peter was."

"Well, if she could do that, then she should have taken us all with her," Ditto declared testily. Slightly and Michael nodded in agreement.

"No, she would have gone into the shadow realm. I've been there. Passed through it once when Wendy took me from the hospital to Neverwood. It's not for the living, I tell you. If you heard the sounds of the beasts and monsters on that side, then you wouldn't travel through there either. I think it's where the morphlings dwell, until called into our realm."

"You're #@&%$@# kidding me, right?" Tink said, her censor band ringing loudly.

"No, I told her to not go there again. It's too dangerous. She must not have listened."

"Well, what do we do now?" John lashed out.

Dr. Barrie gave Dr. Mee a curious look. "Do you suppose they went back?"

Dr. Mee was pensive, and she began to pick at her fingers. "Seven years is a long time. They could have easily rebuilt somewhere else."

Dr. Barrie paced the room, rubbing the back of his head as he thought. "No, no. The island was always the endgame. Why else go to the trouble of hiding it? Why do you think there were so many areas of the island we weren't given access to? I know we destroyed our research and Jax took care of the lab, but there was more to the island. It was selected for a reason."

He paused his pacing and stared off into the distance, lost in thought. He shook his head. "No, maybe it's just the delusions of a desperate old man."

He turned toward the fireplace and his shoe caught the strap of John's backpack and one of his Xbox games slid onto the floor.

Dr. Barrie stooped to pick it up and his hand froze midair as he studied the case and the logo on the box. "What is this?" he asked urgently.

John squinted at the case. "Warfare 8. It's just one of the coolest, hottest games out right now. The newest season is supposed to be wicked."

Dr. Barrie's hands trembled as he turned over the box and looked at the insignia. "It can't be."

"What is it?" Dr. Mee asked, coming to look at the case.

Dr. Barrie pointed to the logo of a heart with a crown around it. "Wonderland Games, a subdivision of Helix Corporation." He opened the case, pulling out the advertising and pamphlet. "Does this place look familiar?" He held up the pamphlet, unfolding it into a map of an island.

Dr. Mee stepped forward and spread out the map, her finger tracing along the edges, and she closed her eyes to think. "H—how can it be? It's so accurate."

Dr. Barrie turned to John. "What is this game about?"

"Well, it's a battle royale. Winner takes all. Contestants pay to log in, get dropped on an island where they randomly control an avatar, and take out as many monsters or other players as they can in one hour. But the cool stuff like guns, weapons, and special powers cost extra. But that—what you're holding—is an advertisement for the next update. It's a huge price tag that only the best gamers with big pockets will be able to download."

"Show me," Dr. Barrie demanded. He picked up a laptop and handed it to John, who with nimble fingers was able to bring up the game's website, which displayed clips of previous games. They saw a city, and teams fighting against each other. Mass chaos and shooting, explosions, grenades and all the players wore black uniforms, which were similar to those worn by the Red Skulls and Dusters. But the link for the newest update took them to a black page with just a few words—

WARFARE 8 BETA TEST
INVITATION ONLY
19:05

—and a digital countdown to when the battle royale game would begin.

"Can you hack it?" Dr. Barrie asked John.

"What do you mean?" Tink asked.

"I mean is there a way you can get an invitation to this elite game?"

"Well," John said, drawing out the word and garnering the group's attention, "I'm sure I could do it, but it might take time."

"I'll help him, Dad." Tink came forward with her laptop and set it on the table. "I'm sure between the two of us, we can find the information we need."

"No, Tink, I need you to do something else."

"What?" she asked.

He held up the pamphlet with his shaking hands. "Find me this island."

"Can't you? I mean don't you two know how to get there?"

Both Dr. Mee and Dr. Barrie shook their heads. "I only knew that at a certain time of the year at night a bright star was visible from Neverland, and if you followed it, you could reach land. But it's a lot easier to aim for the mainland than to aim for an island with no GPS coordinates. A few degrees off course traveling for an hour or two, and we could miss the island by miles. It's just not the same."

"I'll do what I can, Dad."

"What about the rest of us?" Slightly asked.

"Well, have you been to the garage yet?" Dr. Barrie asked.

"Well, yeah, it's where the four-wheelers are."

"No, I mean the lower garage."

"Lower garage?" Slightly asked, confused.

Dr. Barrie stepped over to the counter and grabbed a set of keys out of the dish, and then moved to a panel in the wall and pressed it. With a hiss, the lock unfastened, and the panel slid away, revealing hidden stairs.

"Whoa," John said, surprised.

"You like that, boy? Just wait till you see what I keep down here." Dr. Barrie chuckled.

"As long as it's not chains or dead bodies," John joked, though his face was serious.

Dr. Barrie got really quiet, which made John step back warily, far away from the door.

Tink flicked John on the back of the head, and he yelped.

"It's just the boat," she cackled. "At the bottom of the falls."

John looked at Dr. Barrie's grin and how it mirrored everyone's in the room. Ditto had covered his mouth to try to keep his snorting to a whisper.

Slightly hopped off a stool and went toward the door first, flicking a light switch on the wall, which illuminated a spiral staircase. He turned and gave John a thumbs-up, his eyes twinkling in mischief. "Hey, the decomp smell has worn off. You coming?"

John vehemently shook his head, causing his glasses to almost wiggle off his nose. "Nope, nuh-uh, I'm going to stay here and help Tink."

"Big baby," Slightly yelled and ran down the stairs. The others followed, while Tink and John stayed behind.

John took his laptop and with determined actions sat down next to Tink and began trying to find a way to hack into the Warfare 8 site.

"There's a boat down there?" he asked after a while.

Tink had gone into full hacker mode. Instead of sitting in the chair, she sat on the table, with the laptop cuddled in her lap. "Can't talk, must hack. Need sugar."

She opened a bag of Skittles and separated out the green apple flavor ones and put them on the table. Taking a handful of the others, she popped them in her mouth.

John reached for the abandoned green Skittles and Tink's hand slapped his wrist, her bright blue eyes narrowed in warning. "Don't. Those are for Peter."

Surprised at her slap, John pulled his hand back and studied the pile, wondering why she would go to the trouble of saving him skittles when he wasn't even here. He sighed and rubbed his eyes under his glasses, sensing that he would probably never be able to compete with Peter, because no matter how much he liked Tink, he wasn't sure his feelings were truly reciprocated. Even though she hid it well, he believed that deep down Tink loved Peter, but Peter had always loved Wendy even after he lost her, and he was doomed to forever love Tink.

Oh, what a tangled web, and now he was about to enter the dark web of the internet and try to save her friends. Yeah, sugar would have been nice. He removed his hand from his eyes and found Tink's open palm under his nose.

Cupped in the center was a small pile of yellow Skittles. Her gaze was still fixed on her computer screen and she shook her hand, waiting for him to accept her offering.

"Lemon," she explained. "It's my second least favorite."

"I don't understand," he began.

Tink sighed dramatically and rolled her eyes at him. "I hate the green ones and Peter didn't. Just because I don't like a certain flavor doesn't mean I'll throw it out. Not everyone's tastes are the same. Just because one person doesn't love green doesn't mean someone else can't learn to love it . . ." Her voice became choked up. "Just like some people don't like really smart, sassy techno-geek girls."

Tink wiped her nose with her right sleeve, growing impatient with John and her open offering. He finally understood her hidden message and lunged for the yellow skittles, shoving them in his mouth before she could withdraw her offering.

He chewed them earnestly, and then the flavor hit the back of his throat, surprising him, and he began to choke.

Tink rolled her eyes and grinned. “Dork,” she whispered as she went back to her laptop.

John swallowed the chewy candies and wiped at the corner of his mouth.

“Nerd,” he challenged back.

Grinning like a fool, she was about to put another Skittle in her mouth when she looked at the color, frowned, and flicked the yellow at him.

-23-

PETER HAD LOST TRACK of how long they'd been in the back of the semitrailer, but it must have been hours because at some point he'd accidentally fallen asleep despite himself. When the semi finally stopped, the squealing of the brakes jarred him awake.

The back doors of the trailer opened, letting in the sun and the undeniable scent of salt and fish. Then the ramp was dropped onto a loading dock, and one by one, the soldiers were ushered out of the semitrailers and slowly marched down an extended dock, toward an awaiting freighter ship. One moment Curly was right behind him, and the next, he'd managed to slip away. Maybe five minutes later, he reappeared again, just in time to follow Peter into the ship, wearing a uniform like the one Peter had on.

"Where did you get that?"

Curly grimaced. "Uh, there's now a very naked soldier taking a swim."

"Nice." Peter tried not to laugh.

He fell in line with the other Dusters, continually scanning the crowds looking for the lost boys. It was starting to get to him that he didn't recognize anyone.

"You're alive?" said a breathless voice from behind him.

Peter turned in surprise. Brittney stood shaking before him, her skin pale, her hands wrapped around her stomach as if to quench a burning pain.

"I'm so sorry for getting you in trouble. I didn't know that he would hurt you like that." Her voice began to rise in pitch and volume, her hands flailing about, and she didn't seem to be aware of the attention she was drawing to them.

"Shh, it's okay Brittney. I'm fine." Peter tried to calm her down.

Curly stepped in, grabbing Brittney by her elbow and whispering quietly into her ear. She nodded and turned around, getting into line, not once looking back at them.

"Even in Satan's armpit you still attract the attention of pretty girls," Curly bemoaned trying to lighten their situation.

Peter scanned the guards to see it they had noticed the disturbance. "You're welcome to take my place," he said somberly.

"Don't think I haven't tried. Heads up!" Curly motioned with his chin as they began to move again up the gangplank and across the deck. More guards lined the rails and hallways as they were taken down a flight of stairs and into a hall lined with doors.

A guard opened a door and began to usher ten to twelve Dusters into each cabin before locking them in and moving on to the next room. When it came time for Peter and Curly to enter a room, Curly hung back and briefly touched the guard's wrist, whispering to him as he closed the door.

There was no visible reaction from the guard, and Peter wondered if it hadn't worked this time, if Curly wasn't able to influence the guard, but Curly winked at him and he knew it would all work out. The door slammed and everyone listened for the deadening sound of a key turning in the lock.

A single flickering bulb in the cabin, illuminated exhausted and weary faces of the recruits.

They were trapped on a ship, like prisoners and Peter could feel the gloom begin to set in.

Wu Zan waved at Peter in surprise. "You're back?"

"I'm back," Peter answered somberly.

"Are you okay? You good?" Wu Zan asked, tapping his head, referring to his memories.

"I'm good." Peter smiled wanly as he was preoccupied with worrying.

"This one's yours," Wu Zan patted the bunk across from him, while Leroy took the bottom. A young man with fish gills along his neck passed by them as the other recruits moved farther down among the row of bunks. It was a tight squeeze but everyone settled in. Exhausted from the trip a few exchanged somber greetings.

Twenty minutes later, they felt the ship undock and head out to sea. A few of the other Dusters in the room began to groan as the motion took its toll on them. Especially Leroy, who kept swearing that he was going to see his lunch again. Wu Zan kept running his mouth, threatening to dump him in the ocean if he so much as belched.

"I'm gonna die, I tell ya!" Leroy groaned. "Tell my momma I love her."

"Relax. You're not going to die," Wu Zan grimaced, looking a little green himself.

"I was not made for water. If I was meant to swim, I would have been born with gills and fins," Leroy yowled, his face pale. Then he looked over at another of the duster farther down the row in a bunk and groaned, "No offense, Barbados."

Barbados, a kid with actual gills along his neck, waved back, showing off a fine set of thin skin between each of his fingers. "None taken, Leroy. I know it's just the crazy talking."

"I'm going to be sick," another voice called from the bunks.

"Make the rocking stop," someone groaned. It seemed quite a few were suffering from seasickness.

"Ohh," Leroy moaned and gestured for a bucket.

Curly got up from his seat and walked over and touched Leroy's forehead. "You're not going to die. You feel fine. The motion sickness is only in your head," he said gently.

Seconds after Curly's suggestive command, Leroy opened his eyes and grinned. "Man, that was some serious mojo you put on me."

"Do me next!" another seasick duster called out. Curly went to each one of them, curing them with the power of suggestion. Even the ones that weren't sick, he briefly touched as well. Giving them encouragement, a pep talk waylaying their fears like a coach or a father figure. Unlike Neverwood, where the lost boys would never touch Curly, here, the recruits begged for his help.

Peter began to feel sick. Not with the motion of the boat, but with a deep despair that sat in the pit of his stomach ever since he woke up. A foreboding of what was to come.

When Curly came back to his bunk, he noticed Peter's worried frown and asked, "Something's changed hasn't it? You're having one of your gut feelings again aren't you?"

"I don't know. I just . . ." He looked toward the door. "I need to get out of here."

Curly glanced at his watch. "Well, you're about to get your wish."

"What do you mean?" Peter asked.

"I ordered room service." Curly looked at his watch, pointed at the door, and counted down, "In three . . . two . . . one."

A key turned in the lock and the door pulled opened. The same guard from earlier stood there with a blank look on his face, holding the door for them.

"Let's go!" Curly peered around the doorframe into the hallway, then signaled for Peter to follow. They closed the door behind them but didn't lock it. No one had noticed their departure, because Curly had given them the order to not notice. Just like he gave the order for the guard to forget. Once the guard left the hall with an order to return to duty, Curly began to head farther down, looking for the lost boys.

Peter stopped dead in his tracks and turned the opposite way. He stared at the stairs that led to the upper deck. The worry wouldn't go away, but instead ate at his mind. He needed to be somewhere. To be doing something.

Peter was debating turning back to follow Curly, but then out of the corner of his eye, he saw a dark flicker of movement and a shadow beckoned Peter to follow. Peter climbed the stairs. The urgency he had felt earlier increased with each step he took. Out on the deck, the shadow flew right over to the rail and gestured out into the ocean repeatedly.

He touched the scar on his chest, rubbing the thickened white skin through his shirt, a souvenir from the past. A horrible memory that was coming back to haunt him with fervor. Why now? Why was he drawn to the sea when he should be freeing his boys?

The sea. The monster that stole Wendy all those years ago. That was the night he lost her. Lost his girl.

Peter!

Peter jerked at the sound of his name and looked around the empty deck.

The call came from the ocean. He was sure of it.

The shadow flew to him and then back out to sea, pointing.

A feeling of déjà vu began to wash over him, along with the feelings of helplessness and terror, the same feelings he had when Wendy went over and he couldn't save her. But Wendy wasn't there. She was back at Neverfalls.

He knew he should walk away and go search for the lost boys, but he couldn't. His soul ached and the feeling of dread continued to build. Peter couldn't peel his eyes away from the majestic waters. The shadow wanted him to follow it, but where would it lead him? Should he take the chance? What if he couldn't fly that far? What if he couldn't make it back?

Find her.

Peter spun around, but the deck was empty. He had heard it. The words . . . find her. He was almost sure of it—if not audibly, he'd heard it mentally.

"Peter," Curly whispered from below deck. Peter turned to see his friend's dark head peeking up from below. "What are you doing?"

"I don't know. I think I have to do something."

"Are you crazy? Get down here before you get caught!"

"Find the others, rally the boys," Peter said.

"What are you going to do?" Curly said impatiently.

Peter turned to look back over the water. "I have to find her. She's lost."

"Who?"

He closed his eyes and his feet left the deck of the ship as he floated in the air. "My girl." He grinned back at Curly. "I'm going to save her."

"There's nothing out there. It's just ocean, Peter. You're mad."

"Maybe, but I have to go."

At the sound of approaching footsteps, Curly ducked below deck and Peter flew over the side of the ship below the railing, flying alongside. A Red Skull rounded a corner and headed to the back of the ship, where he proceeded to light a cigarette and take a puff.

The shadow was urgently calling him, pointing to the ocean. Taking a deep breath, Peter pushed off from the ship and flew as fast as he could toward the shadow, his eyes scanning the water. He wasn't sure what he was looking for, but he knew that the feeling in his stomach, his intuition, was telling him that he needed to find her.

-24-

PETER! SHE CRIED OUT internally.

Wendy alternated between swimming and floating on her back. Her arms were exhausted and her muscles were starting to cramp. It was impossible to tell how long she had been in the water because her fingers had turned to prunes and her teeth wouldn't stop chattering. It looked like the sun had moved across the sky and it was nearing sunset.

She tried to suppress her panic whenever a wave washed over her, catching her off guard with mouthfuls of seawater. With each unexpected swallow, she thought she was drowning, that she wouldn't recover and would freeze up, slowly sinking down into the dark depths of the ocean.

Wendy had no illusions about surviving. She knew she was going to die out here. It wasn't the how that troubled her, but the when. For one always wishes they knew how they would die, and Wendy had accepted that the sea would be where she took her final breath.

After all, she had died at sea once before and washed ashore. That's where her adoptive parents had found her, washed up on a beach. Maybe it would happen again, she would just fall asleep and slip under the water and wake up somewhere.

But what if she didn't? What if she panned and came back to life and awoke miles under the water, only to drown over and over again. This time, the dark thoughts couldn't be held back. Wendy found herself treading water and choking up with tears. It was the second possibility that she dreaded.

Desperately she wished for a lifejacket, a plank, or anything that she could use to stay afloat so she could wrap her hands around it and just rest for a few minutes, close her eyes and dream of being elsewhere, somewhere other than adrift alone in the middle of the ocean.

Peter! She was getting sleepy.

Wendy!

I'm so tired, Peter. I can't anymore.

Don't give up. I'm coming.

Wendy choked again as she began to sink under the water and struggled to pull herself up to the surface. It was becoming harder and harder to stay focused and not drift off to sleep.

Sleep. Yes, where the ocean became her bed and the gentle rocking of the waves covered her like a quilt. It seemed so peaceful to just close her eyes and let the water take her.

No! The loud order reverberated through her head. It sounded like Peter, but it couldn't be.

She was hallucinating. That's how she knew it was the end. Because she heard the voices of her loved ones.

I love you, Peter, Wendy promised.

Her leg cramps became unbearable and Wendy whimpered, keeping her mouth closed and focusing on breathing out of her nose as she became weaker. Her strength and willpower diminished, she only wanted to dream.

I'm coming.

It's too late. I'm ready to sleep now. I'll wait for you in my dreams.

When exhaustion finally took hold and she began to sink, Wendy didn't struggle as she slipped under the water. She watched her hair fan above her like a trail of gold ribbon reaching toward the sun, her hands floating upward, her eyes closing just as a dark shadow blocked out the light.

The shadows would finally claim her. Wendy sighed, releasing a trail of bubbles from her lips as she sank lower into the ocean's dark depths.

The darkness took shape, and it cut through the water with sure strokes. Strong hands grabbed her around her waist, and then she was being propelled upward.

Could it be?

They broke through the surface, the cool air hitting her skin causing goosebumps. Her body so numb, she couldn't even feel the light kiss he placed on her forehead.

"Peter?" She still couldn't believe that he was here with her. How did he find her? Though it hurt to talk, she found her voice again. "You came for me."

"I will always come for you. Always."

Wendy laid her head on his shoulder and passed out.

-25-

TINK PUSHED A FEW buttons on the keyboard and a satellite image zoomed in on the ocean. John felt a shiver of excitement at being in the same room as this beautiful, technologically savvy girl.

"Of course there wouldn't be anything there. Neverland would have erased all evidence of it ever having been there. They probably have people working at NASA." Tink munched on a Skittle.

"What am I looking at?" John asked. "I just see a bunch of blue."

"No, look." Her fingers flew across the keyboard. "This is the satellite image of these coordinates from a year ago." A picture popped up on the screen. All blue like before. This is the same location from today."

He couldn't notice anything different between the two images. "So it looks the same."

"Exactly," Tink smirked, crossing her arms. "Although it's not."

"What do you mean?"

"Well, I've been going through all the data and written accounts and interviews of everyone that had ever been on

Neverland. I've been able to calculate a probability of a hundred-mile radius of where the island should be. But the problem is there are hundreds of islands and I've been searching and studying them all on the maps."

"And?" He looked over at her as her hands started to wave excitedly.

"I hacked into the international satellites, John. I've been watching all the islands for years, and I finally figured out that I'm not looking for an island."

"You're not?"

"No, I am, but I'm looking for nothing."

"So you're not *not* looking for an island?"

"I'm looking for a non-island. I'm looking for nothing."

"How can that be? Translation, Tink," John chuckled.

"Oh, I'll translate." An unmentionable word dropped from her lips and her censor band kicked into high gear, cutting off the cuss word with a loud ringing noise.

"Someone hacked the satellite image before me. What do you see?"

John leaned in to look at the screen, his eyes squinting. "Nothing, just the ocean."

"Well, according to the coordinates we have and the weather forecast from a year ago, this patch of ocean shouldn't even be visible through the storm front that is surrounding it. They are broadcasting a signal clear as day of the open ocean, but it shouldn't be. When I go and remove the hacked code, I can see the real-time satellite and . . ." She zoomed in the satellite's camera feed. "How about now?"

"There's an island."

"See? Something hidden behind nothing. And when I put the hacked code back in . . ." Her fingers danced across the keys, and the island disappeared, replaced by ocean.

"But how can someone do that?"

She leaned back in her chair, grabbing a chip from the open bag on the table, and took a bite, the crumbles falling down her chin and onto the keyboard. "It's hacker magic."

"Did you find it?" Dr. Barrie's deep voice bellowed from the stairwell as he came up from the lower garage. His hands were covered in grease and he was wiping them on a rag.

"I think so." Tink grinned proudly, spinning her laptop around to show him the coordinates.

"That looks like the right island. That's my girl."

"What do we do now?" John asked.

Dr. Barrie tossed the rag on the kitchen island and went to the counter. "The engine is tuned and ready to go."

He ran his fingers along the underside of the counter until he hit a button, triggering a secret panel in the wall. The panel turned, revealing an arsenal of weapons.

Dr. Barrie grabbed a gun and checked the chamber and extra magazines of ammo before handing it to John. "Now we go get our boys back."

Tink let out a squeal of happiness.

-26-

HE COULDN'T FIND THE ship. Peter tried to fly back with Wendy, but he must have strayed off course. His arms were tiring from holding her, and he was exhausted from flying. Thankfully, Wendy had immediately fallen asleep and had stayed that way since he rescued her. He could feel the rise and fall of her chest and her warm breath on his neck, so he knew she was fine. But if he didn't find a place to land soon, they might both end up in the ocean again.

Ascending even higher into the air, he tried to get a better vantage point. Slowly turning, he searched the horizon for a glimpse of a reflection, or a shadow of any kind. The sun was setting and he knew it would be harder to find the ship at night.

"C'mon," he begged. The sun cast a magnificent yellow and orange band across the sky, and he couldn't help but watch the light show as it turned red. But as the bright colors deepened his fears intensified.

"Where are you?" Peter whispered. Wendy stirred in his arms, and he pulled her closer to him, to keep her warm against the cool breeze.

He was running out of time. He had to decide. Head toward the mainland or continue his search for the ship? He knew if he couldn't find the ship now, he might never find it and the boys would be lost to him forever.

He cursed under his breath at the unfairness. He had saved Wendy, only to lose the boys, and now he might lose her again. The sun's rays played a trick on him, because just as it was setting, he saw a dark blip on the horizon that was previously hidden.

Is that . . . ?

He focused on the spot and tried to not go blind from staring at the sun. Yes, there was something small on the horizon; it could be the ship. It was obscured, blended into the dark water and the red band of the horizon, but he was sure of it. There was something there.

Taking off, he flew as fast as he could in the direction of the speck. Praying that it was their salvation. Even if it was the Red Skulls themselves, he wouldn't care as long as he could get her somewhere safe. The speck grew larger, and the sun disappeared beneath the horizon. His only choice was to stay his course and hope that the speck would pan out to be somewhere to land.

He tried to shift Wendy in his arms again, and he began to lose his grip.

"No!" he grimaced and dipped to try to reestablish control. It was just enough to relieve the weight and to feel the blood pumping through his arms. He had her again. But he didn't know if he could catch her a second time.

Peter almost shouted with joy when that small speck began to take shape, yet it wasn't the shape of a ship, but of an island. He didn't care, as long as it was a place where he could take care of Wendy properly and see to her needs. The side of the island he found didn't have a long beach, but he found a small inlet of sand at the base of the cliff, with a few sparse palm trees. His feet buckled under him as he touched down, and he nearly dumped Wendy unceremoniously on the ground. But he held it together, and carried her over to a downed palm tree. Then he laid her out on the soft sand beside a fallen palm tree and collapsed next to her. His hand reaching for hers, clasping it, he curled around her, keeping her warm.

A soft tickle brushed against her cheek, slowly waking her. Her eyes were crusted with salt water and stinging, but the pain subsided. She felt movement beside her and a touch of a hand on hers, and she opened her eyes to meet a familiar pair of emerald eyes. Just seeing him, seeing Peter alive, provoked fresh tears, helping to wash away the sting of salt and sand.

He ran his hand gently up her cheek and brushed away the single runaway tear. "Shh, no more tears. It's okay."

"I thought it was over. I thought that was the end," she whispered, her throat burning.

"Nonsense, our story isn't over." He smiled, brushing her strawberry blonde hair behind her ear. "I wouldn't let it end like that. And if it did, I would just rewrite it."

Her heart, the organ that betrayed her by stopping and starting whenever it wanted, began to pick up speed, her cheeks warming at his promise. Had it only been a few days since they had been together at Neverwood? Not including his shadow, or time in Jax's body. This was her Peter, and he was whole.

They lay together, entwined in the sand, and neither was capable of moving, both lost in the closeness and joy of being near each other. The morning sun cast a warm glow over his skin.

"How did you find me?" she asked.

"How did you get out there?" Peter simultaneously asked. They chuckled.

"You first," Wendy said.

He quickly caught her up with what had happened since he left her, recounting the story of Curly's change of heart and even how he followed the shadow to where she was. "What about you? How did you end up floating in the middle of the ocean?"

She couldn't meet his eyes. Looking down, she drew circles in the sand with her fingers. "I went into the shadow realm," Wendy answered. "I had them take me through their plane to try to get to you, but something went wrong. I was crossing a dark ocean and when I hit the water in the shadow realm, I came through in our world in the middle of the ocean."

Peter had fallen deathly silent at her confession. He stiffened, dropping his hand from her face. "Why would you have done something so foolish?"

As he pulled away, she felt the loss of his warmth, intensified by the disapproval in his voice.

Wendy sat up, pulling her knees up to her chest and leaning her back against the fallen palm tree. She began to steel herself against the heartache and the fight that she knew was coming. "Foolish? I didn't throw myself into another person's body. You didn't even know if you could get out. No, Peter, you are the foolish one. I did what I had to do to try to save you, because I love you." Her words held power, fueled by her anger.

His eyes widened in surprise at her tone, and he took a deep breath. "No, you're right. We were both foolish. I'm usually the one that makes all the rash decisions. I just wasn't expecting you to be as reckless as me." He chuckled, his eyes twinkling.

"You're in for some competition then." Wendy bit her bottom lip, trying to contain the smile that was building, relieved that what she read in his tone wasn't anger but worry. "Because I am the queen of recklessness. I don't save receipts. I frequently lose my car keys and my phone. Goodness knows where that is half the time."

Peter tossed his head back and laughed. "Oh, Wendy. I think I have you beat. I squeeze the toothpaste in the middle, and put the new roll of toilet paper on top of the old one instead of changing it."

"Oh, the horror!" Wendy mocked, putting her hand on her forehead.

"And I tear the warning labels off of mattresses and pillows." Peter's grin was full-blown.

"Okay, you rebel!" She leaned forward, and he met her with a sweet and gentle kiss. The pain from her chapped lips was minimal.

He leaned back and frowned. "We need to take care of you."

Peter stood and offered her his hands, helping her up, but instead of letting her go, he pulled her into an embrace, resting his chin comfortably on the top of her head, and sighed. "You know, I could get used to this. Maybe we should build our home on an island like this and put the new Neverwood school on, say, a different island?"

Wendy laughed. "Marooned with you? Sounds good."

He gave her a long, heated look and Wendy's cheeks burned in response. He kissed each of her blushing cheeks, and she knew he must feel the heat radiating off of them from embarrassment. But then he pressed his cheek to her forehead and his brows furrowed. "Wendy, I think you have a fever."

"Oh?" She pressed her own palms to her cheeks and felt the same heat. Maybe she wasn't feeling as great as she'd thought.

He turned, holding her hand, and began to walk along the small sandy beach. When they'd first landed on the island, high tide had brought the water up to within a few feet of where they had sought shelter by the fallen palm. But when they woke the water had receded, revealing a wider length of beach. They decided to explore, with the hope of finding something to eat, but the tide began to come in, more swiftly than seemed possible, quickly narrowing the beach so that they found themselves clambering over the rocks and boulders to stay dry. When they turned back to face the sea, the beach was gone and only water remained.

"Peter, this place gives me the creeps." There didn't seem to be anything alive on the island, except for the few birds and trees.

"It's just an island, Wendy." He kept pacing, looking back up at the cliff and then back out at sea. He motioned for her to come to him.

Wendy came. His arms wrapped around her waist and he whispered, "Ready?"

"For what?"

"We need to know where we are." He took off into the air.

"It's an island," Wendy answered. "A deserted one."

It couldn't be the same island, could it? Wendy scanned the island looking for some sort of clues, but how do you tell islands apart?

Peter's face turned to stone, unreadable and pale. He gradually flew them upward, staying close to the cliff's edge, slowly building her apprehension.

His grip tightened around her waist, and Wendy's stomach dropped the higher they flew until gradually they crested the top of the cliff and she let out a sigh of relief. There was nothing there, just trees and shrubs. No visible structures were present, so it couldn't have been the same island where they had been held captive. This wasn't the same cliff that he had jumped off of years ago and flown for the first time.

Her sigh of relief must have eased Peter's tension because his grip lessened.

"It's just an island," Wendy reiterated. "It doesn't mean it's the same island."

Peter continued their ascent beyond the top of the cliff. He wanted to see more of the island, get a scope of the land.

"Just an island," he repeated with a sigh.

They abruptly stopped midflight, and Wendy squeaked in surprise. They held absolutely still as movement rustled in the bushes below them.

Hugging Peter tightly to her, all her muscles clenched with foreboding, Wendy peered down to the cliff's edge, nearly twenty feet, and inhaled a sharp breath at the sight. A Red Skull now stood looking over the edge of the cliff, his AK-47 strapped to his back. He walked directly below them as he scanned the cliff's edge, looking over to where they were only minutes ago. What if he had seen them? He would have shot them out of the sky, like clay targets.

Flying slowly, Peter backed them away and out of sight until they were well hidden behind the palm branches.

"Red Skulls," Wendy whispered. "Why are they here?"

"I don't think this is just an island, Wendy."

"What?" she whispered, terror rushing through her body as horrible memories of her childhood came flooding back to her. The locked rooms, the experiments, the Red Skulls taking kids away only to never return.

"We're back."

"No, no, no, no, no!" she chanted over and over, her voice rising in uncontrolled panic, followed by a relentless trembling. She could feel her body break out in sweat, and she began to flail, alerting the Red Skull to their presence.

"Shh, Wendy," Peter warned gently, trying to keep her still and quiet.

But quiet was the last thing her brain wanted. She had stayed silent for so long, hiding the deep, dark secrets and repressing the feelings, and now she was face-to-face with their abuser. The island that started it all. Her frantic cries became louder and the Red Skull began to rush toward them.

He burst through the underbrush, a look of surprise on his face, then aimed the gun on them.

A grim look covered Peter's face, he set Wendy down on the ground, turned and flew straight at the Red Skull, knocking him in the chest. Swinging the strap around to his back so that he couldn't immediately reach the rifle. Peter grabbed his uniform and flew right to the cliff's edge and out of view.

A series of gunshots echoed over the edge of the cliff. Birds scattered into the air, their black bodies looking like pepper sprayed across the table. They cawed and twittered in warning, but Wendy didn't hear anything. As soon as the shots went off, her world went silent. Her mouth opened in a scream of terror, but no sound came forth. She rushed through the brush, tripping over vines and sliding on rocks as she dropped to her knees at the edge and looked over, expecting to see two bodies splayed across the rocks below. One form clad in black was bent at an odd angle, unmoving.

Her breathing was ragged, and she worked to control the panic. One. There's only one body. Not two. One. And it was too big to be Peter. Sound returned in a flash, overwhelming her—the noise of the water crashing against the rocks, the wind in the trees, the birds and the ocean—it was all too loud. The birds and the ocean became too loud. Her own frantic breathing drowned her senses.

"Wendy," said a voice from behind her, and she spun around on her knees, the rocks scratching through her jeans. He alit right behind her, his feet touching down, his eyes not meeting hers. He wasn't going anywhere near the cliff. He didn't want to see what he'd had to do.

Her face scrunched up with emotion, and he held out his arms. Wendy stood up, and with three long purposeful steps, she threw herself into his embrace and let the fear out.

"I know," he soothed. "I never expected this. Never thought we would ever set foot here again. It's changed so much, I barely recognized it."

"I don't want to be here, Peter. We need to go," she begged.

"We can't go, Wendy," he explained. "I saw them. Hook is here. The boys are here."

"Oh, Peter," she hiccupped, and tried to swallow her fear. She knew she would have to face Hook again, wanted to get the boys back, but she never expected in a million years to walk back onto the set of her childhood nightmare. The final battle would take place where her trauma began.

"Well, we're here. Let's go ring the doorbell," Peter said with a grin.

-27-

THE WAVES WERE choppy, but the motor yacht cut through the surf with ease as they followed the river out to the ocean. John seemed thrilled to be at the helm next to Dr. Barrie, who was steering. His look of contentment and joy mirrored that of a dog with his head out the window.

Tootles and Michael were sitting next to Tink, who kept checking to see that neither boy loosened nor removed their life jackets. Every time she would turn her head, she would catch one of the boys taking a turn pretending to undo a strap or loosening it. She would whip her head around so fast, and the impish boys would turn into angels, their halos glowing so bright that one would need glasses. Tink continued the game to keep them occupied and to distract them from the fact they were chasing down an army of Red Skulls, powerful Dusters, and their lost boys. The odds weren't in their favor, and this after they had barely survived the attack on Neverwood on their own turf, with home field advantage. How would they survive on Neverland's death trap?

That's what Jax referred to the island as—a death trap. John had hacked the website and found a backdoor to a second hidden website not accessible to the public. He traced that IP address and was able to get a location. Everyone had gathered around his computer at the house when he did a reverse trace. When the location was found. Jax looked up at Dr. Barrie, and shook his head in disbelief.

The boys slowly turned to each other, understanding dawning on their surprised faces.

"No way," Ditto said.

"Can't be," Slightly chewed on his thumb nervously.

It happened to be the exact coordinates of Tink's non-island.

Dr. Barrie solemnly confirmed. "Looks like we're going back, boys. Back to Neverland."

They had loaded the motor yacht and set off an hour later.

Jax cursed and punched the bench seat before heading below deck to speak with Ditto and Slightly. Their somber faces mirrored his own. Nana was sprawled on the floor sleeping, oblivious to the world.

"Are you sure it's the same place?" Ditto asked nervously, his hand subconsciously going to his midsection, covering his wound. Whether from pain, or an intuitive motion to protect that, which is vulnerable, he didn't know.

"Positive," Jax stated.

"But didn't you destroy it?" Ditto continued.

"Fire doesn't destroy stone, not unless it's hot enough, and since we never went back, who knows what's hiding there, or what they've built over the years."

Slightly had taken to chewing on the side of his thumb, something he only did when he was under severe stress. Jax knew this was definitely one of those times. Neverland was the epitome of all of their nightmares combined. He had a right to be stressed. They all were.

"What do you think is there?" Slightly took his thumb out of his mouth to ask.

"Monsters," Jax answered. Ditto scoffed and Jax glared his way. "You think I'm joking, but I'm not. What do you think they've been doing all of these years? Creating super soldiers and what else? Morphlings. Do you really think that after getting their hands on morphlings that they stopped and only focused on the D.U.S.T program? No, they continued their work, and I'm fearful of what else they've done. Look what they've done to us." Jax flicked his hand and a ball of flame danced in his palm.

"You know this for sure, Jax?" Ditto asked, crossing his arms to hide the slight tremor, but Jax saw it.

"Not exactly. I've seen what they do, how they train their Dusters and how they treat the Primes, their strongest soldiers. They pit each of them against each other, not encouraging comradery, their futures hanging in the balance each day. I always thought we would end up sold as mercenaries. But now I'm not so sure." He stood up and moved to look out the porthole, shoving his hands in his pants pockets.

"There's this girl," Jax said.

"Wooo," Ditto singsonged. "Did you get her number—"

Jax's glare cut him off and he never finished his sentence. "I don't know where she came from. Beautiful, angelic, but her mind is a broken and fragile thing."

"Isn't that all girls?" Ditto started but cowered a second time at Jax's threatening glare.

"This is why you'll forever be single, Ditto." Jax said.

"Okay, I get it." Ditto waved his hands in defeat.

"You know he only jokes when he's nervous," Slightly defended Ditto.

"Hey, I don't need you to explain," Ditto added.

"Stop!" Jax barked at both of them. Both boys calmed down and looked his way. "You don't understand. This girl is special."

Ditto opened his mouth for another retort and Slightly's hand promptly muffled it.

"She is Neverland's greatest weapon. She's kept in a pod, though not a harvesting pod. Hers is constructed different. I . . . I believe that Alice creates the morphlings."

"Whoa!" Slightly said aloud.

"Mmoh," Ditto muttered through Slightly's hand.

"How is that possible?" Slightly's scientific mind began to work, and he moved away from Ditto, releasing his mouth, and then Ditto stretched his jaw comically. Slightly opened a drawer, grabbed a pad and pencil, and began to write down calculations. "The morphlings are not from our world. I've been able to break down their genetic material, and it is unlike anything anywhere. How is she able to?"

"I don't think she is from our world either," Jax muttered and immediately regretted it. He had been thinking it for months, but to finally voice his own thoughts aloud suddenly solidified them, cementing them into his mind.

"Jax has the hots for E.T.," Ditto snickered and immediately yelped as Jax launched himself across the table, knocking Ditto to the floor of the boat. Both boys began to spar mercilessly. Slightly, ignored the commotion as he began to scribble out formulas.

"Uncle!" Ditto cried out, and Jax finally stood up, releasing him from the headlock.

"Jax, you've described the harvesting pods to me before, and how they are used to extract our DNA to turn into a serum. Can you describe her pod to me? I think I'd like to try to figure out the mechanics of it."

Jax felt a surge of relief. If anyone could figure out how to get Alice out of the pod, it would be Slightly. Maybe Candace was wrong. Maybe there was a way for her to survive outside the machine. He diligently began to describe every inch of her containment unit. The size, switches, levers, even the static screens that showed images of her dreams. Slightly's mouth would drop open in awe at the detail Jax was able to provide.

"You've seen her a lot," he said quietly so Ditto couldn't overhear and chime in with another diatribe.

"Almost every night. My friend Candace would let me in to see her, but only for a few moments."

"Why?"

"Because I didn't want her to feel alone in a place like that. She needed a friend. Even one that isn't a good friend is better than none." Jax lowered his eyes.

Slightly tapped his pencil against his lip and didn't say anything else but continued to write. "We're going to be traveling through the night. We'll get there in the morning. Hopefully by then we will have a plan."

Jax was relieved that someone else was thinking of how to take down Neverland beside himself. He placed a lot of pressure on himself, now that Peter wasn't here. He was worried the last few remaining lost boys wouldn't follow him into battle after he betrayed them and worked for Neverland. They might never understand why he did it. Or maybe they would, if he would take the time to explain. He sighed, sat back on the bench in the galley, and leaned his head back against the wall.

Rest sounded good. He didn't know when he'd last had a peaceful night's sleep. It might have been years ago. Jax left Slightly to his doodling and Ditto to his shenanigans as he spun a quarter on the table, and closed his eyes.

Whhhrrrrr . . . clatter.

Whhhrrr . . . clatter.

Ditto picked up the quarter again and spun it. Jax followed the sound with his ears as the coin moved across the table.

Whhrrrrrr.

His hand shot out and slapped the quarter flat on the table, never even opening his eyes. Jax picked up the quarter, the heat intensifying in his hands, until he felt the metal melt into a pool in his palm. He uncurled his pinky, then ring finger, letting the melted quarter drip onto the table.

"Hey!" Ditto whined. "You smelted my quarter." He snorted at his own pun.

"Better than your brain," he warned and tried to stifle the smile from his lips as he imagined Ditto's discouraged face.

Silence filled the cabin, and Jax breathed out in relief.

Then he heard it again.

Double *whhhirrrrss.*

He opened one eye and saw Ditto had replicated into two, and now each one sat on either side of him, flipping and spinning the coins as loud as they could, their impish grins identical. Jax swore under his breath and reached for the coins, but both Dittos moved out of his reach. Seconds later, more coins began spinning on the table, and Jax opened his eyes to see that Slightly had joined in as well. Three coins were spinning, taunting and clattering to the table.

Jax groaned and began to wish he had melted Ditto's brain instead. But he was glad they were momentarily distracted from the fear of what's to come when they reach the island.

-28-

THIS DOESN'T LOOK good," Peter said. They had begun walking away from the cliff and discovered the ruins of the old Neverland facility. Wendy gazed upon the torn-down brick and half walls—all that remained of the building. They didn't immediately recognize it, because the six-story building was now only one, the heat from the blaze made the brick walls cave in. The whole building had collapsed in on itself, and Wendy marveled at the damage done by a simple fire.

"Dr. Barrie did this?" Wendy asked. "To destroy his work?"

Peter shook his head and hopped over a wall, turning to help Wendy over. "No, this was done by someone else."

"Hook?" she asked.

"No. Jax. That night long ago."

Wendy looked around at the damage with new eyes. Most of the walls had collapsed because the heat had been too much for the structure, but there were parts where it had melted, like lava, and the fauna overgrowth took care of the rest.

"He was that powerful, even as a child?"

"Yes, this was done by his hatred," Peter said softly. "He's never been the same since that night. He murdered Red Skulls to save us, and who knows how many more he killed destroying this place. At a very young age, he was forced to become a murderer. No one should have to endure something like that, especially so young."

"He didn't have a choice. Neverland did this to him. And to us," she added.

Peter nodded, agreeing. "Jax's anger never fully receded. It's always there just beneath the surface, waiting to bubble over and burn someone. He swore to never use his gift again, and hadn't until you came along. That's why he was so good at fighting and weapons—he had to be so he wouldn't have to use his special power. It's why he was able to stay under the radar at Neverland. He made them think he didn't have any gifts. That he was immune to the treatments, but was still genetically viable. So Hook kept trying to treat him with new PX drugs, but Jax's immune system would burn it off."

"Hook never suspected?"

"Who knows what Hook thought? I'm not sure how much he actually knew about him."

Wendy stopped when she came to the remains of the stairwell. Here was the place where she had chased the shadow up the stairs seven years ago. She had thought she was going crazy, seeing things. Seeing shadows. No one knew then what she knew now, that she was seeing souls of those that died on the island.

She shivered.

"Are you okay?" he asked.

"I will be when we save the boys and never step foot on this island again."

"Really? I was thinking we could put the couch over there." He gestured to a fake wall. "The kitchen could go over here, and the espresso machine right here." He went over to a dilapidated half wall and pretended to make her a shot of espresso. Turning to her, he took a sip with his pinky up in the air.

Wendy laughed. He was doing it. Being the *Boy* again, keeping her spirits high and her fears at bay with his antics. Her joy was coming back.

"And the crib over here," she teased, pointing right next to the imaginary espresso machine. Knowing that the thought of bringing up children should wake anyone up from their daydream.

But Peter knew how to play along. "Of course, that's why we have the espresso machine, because we have *sooo* many kids," he said dramatically, swinging his hands out wide.

"And a puppy," she giggled.

"Of course."

"But not for a while," Wendy corrected, her heart soaring at his admission.

"No, not for a while. We already have a lot of kids we have to watch over and make sure are grown before we have our own." He paused and became really still. "That is, if you think we should have kids. What with our uniqueness and all, is it something we would really want to pass down to them?" Peter cleared his throat and leaned against the half wall, looking down at his feet. "Yes, flying is great. What boy wouldn't want to grow up and fly?"

He pulled his heavy gaze from the ground and looked up into her eyes, and she saw him truly—he wasn't hiding behind his sarcasm and boyish charm. She saw his fear—and the contempt he held for himself.

"But our other gift is really more of a curse, and I'm not sure we should play God with those odds," he said softly.

Wendy had never thought of her future in those terms because she only recently relearned that she was unique. She always assumed she would go to college, get married, have kids. But she remembered what it was like growing up in an out of psychiatric wards and hospitals because she saw the dead, and how much medication she was on, to keep the visions at bay. But now with the knowledge of their DNA, and what their kids could be like, they would all have to make that decision. Her heart ached at her own lost future, and she could see the same heartache in Peter's face.

She lifted her hands, and he reached for them. Clasping them between hers, she looked into Peter's wet, glistening eyes. "Peter, what if we can't even have kids? What if what they did to us makes it impossible? We don't even know. . . But I know that what I saw at Neverwood was a family. Boys of all backgrounds, gifts, and talents. Shapeshifters, teleporters, all of them unique in their own way, and all of them loved by you. I would be proud to have any of them as our kids . . . except I don't want any—"

"Dittos!" Peter cut in and Wendy laughed.

"Yes, I'm not sure I could handle a child that can replicate and run circles around me and cry in stereo."

"He was a handful growing up, but still he was a great kid."

"They all are, Peter, all the Neverwood boys. I love them and would love to raise any of them. There should be more like them in the world."

Peter sucked in his breath at her admission, caught off guard. He looked up at the sky, his eyes tearing up again, and he pulled her into his arms, whispering into her hair. "Thank you. You don't understand how much I needed to hear that. That someone could love me, love us, despite our defects. That's it, Wendy, it is our duty to get married and to create more defects to love."

"Peter, you're not a defect," Wendy laughed, pulling away from him and slapping him playfully on the arm.

"Just wait, I don't clean toilets." He winked and pulled her closer so he could brush his lips against her.

"That's it. You are defective," she whispered back, giving him another peck.

The cocking of a gun pulled them out of their bubble. They looked up into the dark eyes of another Red Skull.

-29-

"DON'T MOVE," THE Red Skull growled. He was scruffier than any of the other soldiers they had seen on the mainland. His uniform was snug, stained, and did little to hide his beer belly. He must have been stationed on this island for a long time to be so slovenly.

Peter and Wendy raised their hands above their heads.

"How did you get here?" he asked. "No one is supposed to be on the island. It's off-limits."

"We were given a day pass," Peter said.

"They don't give out those." His face scrunched up, and rapidly blinked his eyes. They were bloodshot, and he seemed to be a bit inebriated. "How'd you get here?"

Peter coughed. "We flew." He gave Wendy a wink.

"Don't get cocky with me, boy," the soldier said.

"No, never. Wouldn't dream of it."

Wendy's nerves were getting the better of her, as Peter was not taking their situation seriously. She met his gaze and he tilted his head and gestured. *Oh, he was distracting the guard, so she could escape.*

"I'll ask you again, and you answer me straight this time, or—"

"You'll buy me a present," Peter interrupted, completely throwing their captor off guard.

"What? No."

Wendy took a tentative step to the side, but the Red Skull zeroed in on her movement and she stepped back closer to Peter.

"Phew, I'm glad, because it would be really awkward to get a gift from you. I mean, we only just met."

"What's wrong with you, boy?" The soldier slurred his words.

"Nothing's wrong," Peter answered and stood up tall, puffing out his chest. "I'm supposed to be here. Was given orders to run this Prime to the cliff as punishment." His voice was clipped, filled with authority.

The Red Skull swayed, his eyes blinking fast as he focused on Peter's uniform, his flushed face turning even redder as he realized his blunder.

"S—sorry. My mistake. Must not have heard the radio call. Dearborn hasn't been answering his radio."

Peter stepped in front of Wendy, blocking her with his body. "Yeah, that sounds like Dearborn, blowing off his work. Probably out sunbathing on the rocks or something."

Wendy elbowed Peter, and she heard his silent guffaw. That was below the belt for his humor.

Peter took a step backward, pushing Wendy even farther away. "Well"—he leaned forward to read the Red

Skull's name—"Biers, if you decide to take a break, I will cover for you with the others."

Biers had already sat down on the half wall and was reaching for his flask. "Why, thank you, that is mighty fine of y'all. I may just take you up on that." He gave Peter a salute with the silver flask and lifted it to his lips, drinking greedily, a dribble of the contents trailing down his unshaved chin.

Peter turned, pulling Wendy by her arm, and hastened into the woods. "We need to hurry. I don't want to be anywhere near here if he decides to look over the cliff," he whispered.

"He looks like he's been here a long time," Wendy murmured. "There's bound to be others, but why would there be *any* soldiers guarding ruins? Just a pile of rubble unless . . ." She trailed off, and Peter nodded his head.

"There's more than just ruins. There's something else hidden here."

They traveled farther inland, the trees and undergrowth becoming denser and harder to navigate a straight path. They kept getting turned around, finding themselves inadvertently returning to the same vine-covered wall, only to turn back the way they came. Wendy heard a soft underlying hum but wrote it off as her imagination. Flying would make it easier to scope out the island but they feared that someone would see them, and would sound the alarm and shoot them down. Even if it were possible that they could be mistaken for a large bird high up in the sky, the tree canopy was too thick to be able to see any Red Skulls down below with any real advance warning.

After another hour of traipsing through the underbrush, Wendy heard the sound again.

"Do you hear that noise? A humming sound?"

Peter shrugged his shoulders. "I don't hear anything."

Wendy became frustrated at her obvious hallucinations and lack of direction. "We aren't making any headway. I don't remember this being here before."

"We were in the main facility on the south side of the island. I briefly had flown around the island, but that was years ago. A lot of the landscape is different. It's changed, grown, and feels darker."

Wendy shuddered. "The sun's rays don't reach the forest floor. I have a bad feeling about this place. Listen, even the birds have stopped singing. As if they, too, know what lies beyond is perilous." Wendy turned to Peter and pointed up. "You need to fly."

"I don't want to leave you alone," Peter responded.

"I'm fine, but we can make better headway if you just find out where we're going. We're so deep in the undergrowth, we don't even know if we're heading north." She planted her hands on her hips. "I'll stay here. Look—" She plopped down on a large rock. "I'll sit here till you return."

He didn't seem convinced, but Wendy was exhausted and hungry and knew that time was of the essence. "Go! I will be right here."

"All right. I'll be back in five minutes. I promise."

"Good, I need the rest," she lied. Wendy wanted to go with him as well but knew he would probably balk at the idea. She watched his lithe form fly up through the trees, silent as a mouse, and then he was gone. Promises were meant to be kept, but Wendy had no intention of sitting on the rock and waiting uselessly. She hopped up and went over to a sheer cliff that they had been skirting for the last few minutes. There was something about its location and shape that wasn't sitting right with her.

From a distance, the jagged rock looked real, overgrown and covered with vines. Some areas of the cliff even had rivulets of water running down it. She wouldn't have given it a second thought if it weren't for the silence of the birds—or rather, what had taken the place of their singing.

While they had gone conspicuously silent, the forest wasn't completely devoid of sound. She heard it again and this time didn't dismiss it. It was not her imagination. Then the hum became louder, though still masked by the sound of the wind and trees.

It wasn't her imagination. She turned her head, and moved to another outcropping, knowing the sound grew louder the closer she drew. Grasping the vines and testing her weight, she decided to climb the cliff. It wasn't that steep, maybe thirty feet, and she had been rock climbing with her brother and friends loads of times. She would just have to focus on using the rock outcroppings for her support and use the vines as backup. A few minutes later, Wendy had crested the cliff. She wanted to cheer and scream but instead pulled herself into a sitting position and looked around. Ten feet in front of her the ground dropped suddenly down into a valley, so Wendy tried to stay away from the edge as she explored.

The humming was definitely louder and was coming from an overgrown bush. Wendy scanned the sky for Peter, but she didn't see him, or anyone else patrolling. She approached the overgrown bush and began to pull at the branches, until she could see that there was some sort of metal object underneath A few more minutes of breaking and pulling off branches, and then the hair on the back of her arms rose as she felt an adrenaline rush at the discovery. It was a satellite dish, and it wasn't the only one. A hundred paces over was another satellite dish hidden under bushes.

What in the world is going on?

Wendy went to investigate the other dish when her path narrowed to only a few feet wide and was loose beneath her sneakers. She was about to give up and turn back, when the ground caved in beneath her causing a landslide.

Wendy stumbled unable to get her footing as the earth gave way, and she slid along the cascading dirt and rock on her belly. A yelp of surprise escaped her lips, and she desperately tried to grab hold of branches, roots, and trees to slow her descent. She rolled, tumbled, and landed face up in the bottom of the valley and looked up at the cliff she had just fallen from. She had only climbed thirty feet but had fallen down close to a hundred. Scratches littered her arms and neck and her pants were torn. Wendy tasted blood in the corner of her mouth. She must have bitten her lip. Her head was pounding and she touched her forehead and her fingers came away sticky with blood.

Sitting up, she grimaced in pain. She must have bruised a rib or two. Squinting, she looked back up at the top of the cliff and could easily spot the dish she uncovered. Turning full circle, Wendy realized that she was in a dirt filled basin of sorts, with nothing more than a large hill and palm fronds. The satellite dishes were situated around the lip of the basin.

Her back and joints ached as she stood up and dusted the debris from her pants and hair, knocking a pebble to the ground, which clinked when it encountered . . . glass?

Confused at the sound, Wendy kneeled brushing away the dirt on the hill, revealing a glass panel. Grabbing a few palm fronds, Wendy constructed a makeshift broom and dusted off an area, revealing more glass panels. But they were sloped like a dome and when she had fallen in the landslide, she'd tumbled onto the edge of a dome.

Cupping her hands around her eyes, she looked into the dome and was surprised to see a small town, with buildings, a park, billboards, restaurants and cafés and even the glistening reflection of a lake. It had to encompass most of the rocky island. How could this be real?

Wendy searched the city for movement, but while the streetlights worked, no cars passed through any of the intersections. The flag on the flag pole didn't wave in the wind. It was a ghost town.

Why would Neverland go to all the trouble to create another city hidden within an island?

From the corner of her eye, she caught some movement within the dome. Wendy pressed her face to the glass again, looking for the source of the movement, thinking she'd seen it down an alley behind a brick building. She held her breath, trying to discern if anyone down there was alive. Friend or foe? Red Skull or a lost boy?

It was neither.

Wendy shook in fear and her breath caught in her throat as the unmistakable shape of a morphling glided through the city and slipped into the sewer.

"No," she whispered and leaned back to stare at the dome in thought. She moved to a cleaner side of the dome unscathed by the landslide, then kneeled down to scan the city below. Lights kicked on from inside and the city came to life. Projectors lit up the sky, with a fake display of a sunny afternoon. Wendy understood then she was looking in through a two-way glass and the inside of the dome must be covered with a projection screen.

What terrified her most was the number of morphlings that scattered into the shadows, scrambling for cover against the light. There must have been twenty or more. Was this where they kept their monsters? Why did they need to be in a city? Why the multi-million-dollar movie studio setup?

After the morphlings had scattered, Wendy saw someone come out of a gray cement building near the center. Wonderland Games was lettered on the marquee, and it didn't take her long to recognize the uniform, or gait, of her hated nemesis—Hook. And he wasn't alone.

Following beside Hook as he made his way through the city was another man in a business suit talking on a cell phone. Hook pointed at the various buildings and landmarks, and his partner only nodded his head. After a few minutes of a guided tour, a morphling decided to try to come out of hiding to attack Hook and his partner.

Hook nudged his companion as if to get him to watch, and then pulled out his gun and emptied his clip into the morphling, until it collapsed to the ground. The man's mouth dropped, and his phone slipped from his fingers and clattered on the road.

They spoke, and the man loosened his tie, clearly uncomfortable from being so near the morphling. After a few moments of discussion, they shook hands.

Then with a renewed fervor, the man in the suit grabbed his phone and began to text. Hook grinned, placed his hand on the guy's back, and led him back into the building.

A black form slapped against the glass, and Wendy jumped back in surprise as a morphling had braved the light—it must have seen or sensed her on the other side of the dome. Teeth gnashed at the glass, and claws scrabbled along trying to tear through it to reach her. With each slash, more of the screen was ripped away on the inner side of the dome, and she knew in a few moments, the whole world below would be able to see her.

Terrified about being spotted, she began to toss leaves, branches, and dirt over the spot the morphling uncovered, then ducked down, praying that she wasn't discovered, that Hook hadn't seen her.

-30-

HOOK WASN'T THRILLED that Helix had made it to the island before his crew did. Helix was waiting on the dock, his hands tucked into his expensive suit pockets. A look of indifference covered his face. It angered Hook even more when Helix made a show of checking his watch and looking bored.

How dare the man insult him like that? Hook had broken down and moved the entire operation plus the Dusters onto a ship and got them to the island an hour before his designated arrival, and the man had the gall to act like Hook was late and had inconvenienced him.

He hid his contempt behind a fake smile, but chose to take his time unloading his cargo. Even when he came down the gangplank with his soldiers, directing the transportation of the various pods, he didn't acknowledge the CEO until after he saw the girl safely loaded into the back of the army surplus truck and watched his soldiers drive her down the beach to the underground garage. He knew that in a few minutes, she would be loaded onto a freight elevator and then taken into their compound and hooked up under the city for the launch.

"Hook." Helix was now tapping his foot to show his impatience.

Hook's jaw clenched uncomfortably, but he nodded and turned again, going over the manifest and giving instructions to Hans, who had been in charge of overseeing the lost boys during transit.

"Are they still under?" he asked Hans.

"Yes, sir." Hans checked his tablet, pulling up the vitals of one of them, and showed Hook the screen. "They're all still stable and thriving."

"We've got all that we need for now. Helix wants the best for tonight, so begin final preparations. Have Candace prep them in the locker room."

"Understood." Hans nodded and typed a code into his tablet. He waved to a second and third surplus truck, and they slowly drove down the ramp and headed to the underground garage. On the long truck bed were eight to ten pods, with an unconscious person floating in stasis inside each pod.

Hook whistled and his Red Skulls began to march the Dusters and recruits down the ramp next. He finally decided now was a good time to give his attention to President Helix, who looked like he was ready to pop. His face had turned three shades of red, and the vein in his forehead was bulging. It was hard for Hook to hide just how much inconveniencing the president tickled him.

"Hook!" Helix barked again.

In an imitation of a very Southern drawl, Hook put his hands in his pockets and slowly gave his full attention. "Yes, Helix," he replied.

"Are we ready?" He checked his watch again.

"What do you think I've been doing?" Hook was careful to keep his temper in check. Years of work were coming down to this, tonight's test launch. And he wasn't ready to blow the deal and money because he couldn't hold his tongue. "I just did the impossible, moved everything up by weeks so you could launch tonight. No one else would have gotten you the results like I have."

"And I appreciate it. I do. But I need to see for myself that it's ready. I want a tour before the buyers arrive in a few hours."

"I've sent you the schematics so you can walk through the tour yourself."

"That's not what I'm paying you for. I want to hear it from your own lips so that I can judge for myself whether you are lying or holding something back." Helix licked his lips. "Because that would be a shame, if I found out that you lied to me."

Hook exhaled, a growl of displeasure rumbling out. "As you wish," he snapped and marched down the beach, not slowing his step. President Helix had to run a few steps to keep pace with him.

Out of the corner of his eye, Hook spotted the soldiers running down the beach, each of them greeting him with a salute as they ran past.

"Captain."

"Cap."

Each one addressing him and ignoring the president of the company next to him. Hook couldn't help but smile until, amongst all the greetings, Hook swore he heard another name slip out.

"Cap'n."

"Captain."

"Codfish."

Hook's head swung around and he studied the backs of the retreating boys, surveying each of them, wondering who it was that dared to call him a codfish. They were paces away and disappearing around the bend. His fingers itched for the knife at his belt. He wanted to slit the gullet of the one who dared to insult him. Even as the soldiers moved farther away, he unbuckled the strap around the base of the knife.

Not a single head turned back to look at him. No one stood out among the group. He couldn't be sure he could get the right boy, and killing him now would disrupt the boys and work against the timeline he had put in place.

Sighing, he snapped the strap. Then he continued striding toward the garage with a renewed vigor, chuckling, as Helix was now huffing to keep up with him.

They entered the garage, and once inside, Hook pointed out the red button on the wall on their right. "The garage, the only entrance, is underwater most of the day except for low tide. This button seals up the entrance so that it is hidden below the waterline. Even at low tide, it is camouflaged and barely discernible from the rock face. In fact, other than the old facility wing, most of the island has been dug out and modified to your plans. The arena, the viewing areas, and the holding cells are all part of the new addition."

As they spoke, Hook led the president through the underground tunnels. Emergency lights were strung along the walls, keeping the tunnels well lit. Signs warning of high voltage and electrical shock hazard were posted every ten feet, the danger emphasized by the persistent hum of electricity.

"Is this . . . ?" President Helix pointed to the cables inside the tunnels running along the walls and up into the ceiling.

"What's holding the morphlings captive? Yes," Hook answered.

"And the girl is still controlling them?"

"Not so much controlling them, but creating them. Her nightmares are so terrible that they become a reality in the shape of the morphlings."

"Incredible," Helix muttered. "I knew as soon as I heard about her gift that she'd be the future of my company. What about the others? You mentioned two other originals you were picking up. One that is immortal and another that can see the future? A girl, I believe."

Hook clenched his hand tightly around the door handle and took a deep breath. "I acquired the boy who doesn't die. He's been incorporated into our program. Although, there have been a few glitches with jump-starting his memory. The girl, we have not been as lucky."

"Pity," Helix said condescendingly. Hook wanted to curl his hands around his neck, but instead pushed open the handle on the door and went up three flights of stairs, then stopped on a landing. He reached into a breaker box and flipped lights on in the compound.

"What are you doing?" Helix asked.

"Bringing the city to life. You don't want to see it in the dark. Plus, it disperses the morphlings." He turned to another Y-shaped lever with a green light above it. "And this stops the electrical current around the door." Hook pulled the lever down and seconds later, the light above the switch turned red. "Now it's safe to enter the building."

Hook felt a trickle of sweat drip down his neck as he waited an extra two or three seconds to touch the handle. In the early days, he had watched one of his soldiers disarm the door and then touch it too soon, frying himself on the spot. A darkened imprint in the shape of a hand was still visible on the handle.

Helix didn't have Hook's common sense and pushed open the door, saving Hook from having to do the deed himself. He was almost sad when President Helix wasn't promptly electrocuted.

They took an elevator up to the ground floor of an office building designed as a smaller version of Wonderland Games. Couches, chairs, and large TV screens lined the wall, and on each screen was displayed the same digital countdown timer with only hours to go until it reached zero.

As soon as they came to the ground floor of the main building, Helix's cell phone rang. "Finally," he said, opening his phone. "Yes, you're on your way? Good. Bring your checkbook—heck, bring your wife's as well. You are going to love what we got."

Hook exited the elevator and walked through the lobby to the front door. It looked like a normal door, but it was reinforced glass. In fact, the whole central building was designed to withstand fire, earthquakes, storms, and pretty much anything someone could throw at it. They learned after last time, when their research had gone up in flames so fast. Unlike the other buildings in their city, this one was made to stand. The others were just very expensive models with real-life special effects. They spared no expense.

Hook hit the code, and the door opened. Both men walked into the street, and he grinned.

"This is . . . a perfect reconstruction of Hollow City from your game," Hook boomed with undisguised pride, spreading his arms wide. "But I call this one Hollow Dome." He pointed up at the dome ceiling.

"Nice. Nice." Helix said looking around in awe, before making another call.

It looked perfect. Hook wrinkled his nose. Well, almost perfect.

The only thing they couldn't quite replicate was the smell of the outdoors. Instead, the city had a faint musky odor, but that was virtually unavoidable given the unconventional location of the city. They had dug out the rocky island and built this city deep underground, with the glass-reinforced dome only visible from inside the basin, and even that was carefully camouflaged, invisible to any plane, or helicopter. The satellite dishes were a bit harder to hide, but they did their best. They had spent ten years building the underground sanctuary. Seven years in research and development and the last two spent culling, training, and recruiting those for the program. They were ready.

Hook had pulled off a masterpiece. But Helix, focused solely on the money to be made, seemed disturbingly oblivious to how truly amazing this place really was. There was a school, a hospital, a park, and a library. Even the new car lots had the latest models available. The cafés had actual working soda machines, fryers, and were stocked with food. The landscape, grass, trees, and bushes were real, all watered with automated sprinkler systems and timed rainfalls, and of course, there were real working sewers. It was a perfect fully developed community. The only thing it lacked was souls.

Hook stared at the listless flagpole and made a mental note to check on the wind machine, to ensure it would move. They had turned it off when the birds kept getting in through the turbines and were being killed by the morphlings. Now that the birds couldn't find a way in, the city was only populated with the unliving. The morphlings that hadn't been destroyed by the lost boys, were still alive and now held here. Waiting. Watching. Hunting.

Even with the lights on, and the city fully armed, Hook was always wary.

Hook pointed to the mural painted on the side of the grocery store with the words, *Welcome to Hollow Dome* in decorative font above a silhouette of the city.

The president's request that the fake city be designed after his most popular video game stuck in his craw, even more so when the man barely gave the grand reveal a nod.

He was still too preoccupied with whoever was on the other line with him.

Hook's hand was inching back toward the knife in his belt again when he saw the shadow move from behind a parked Mini Cooper. He saw it, was prepared for it, but decided to see how far the morphling was willing to go.

The morphling slunk back into the shadows and moved along the wall to cross the street. Being as they were, trapped in the city and surrounded by electricity, they were blocked from escaping. The longer they were trapped here, the more they solidified into something more corporal, affected not just by lights and electricity, but by actual weapons.

This morphling looked about as solid as any living thing, its shape having taken on the form of a gigantic rabid raccoon, and Hook stepped to the side, leaving the president completely open and vulnerable.

The morphling rushed Helix, letting out a high-pitched squeal. Helix, seeing the approaching monster for the first time, screamed aloud and dropped his phone. Hook quickly stepped in front of Helix and pulled out his Glock, emptying it into the morphling. With physical weapons, creatures didn't explode outward into goo, but instead would turn to ash. Yet another example of how they were changing.

"I'm always impressed by these creatures," Helix said in awe.

"Impressed enough to give me more shares in the company?" Hook's slow smile was pure evil.

President Helix loosened his tie around his neck and wiped the perspiration from his brow. "It's true I'm impressed, but I can't give you any more shares. You still need funding, though, and I'm willing to make you an offer you can't refuse." He explained the details of his offer and Hook whistled at the amount.

Helix held out his hand, and Hook's firm grip made him wince.

Once the deal was done, Helix searched for his phone, making sure it wasn't damaged, and then began to send out a group text.

Distracted, Helix paused his texting and looked up. A black mass had moved out of the shadows and crawled up the faux wall, in pursuit of something. Helix eyed the morphling warily, but kept talking. "Maybe we should talk again inside and go over our launch plans. Our guests will be arriving any minute."

Hook was pleased with the way this meeting went. He clapped Helix roughly on the back and guided him toward the building. He knew the mega-billionaire would be writing him even more checks before nightfall.

He dangled the carrot and now just had to wait.

A high-pitch morphling scream echoed in the arena, and Hook looked up and saw a morphling scratching furiously at the film on the underside of the dome. Why would it be attracted to the ceiling? There's nothing—

The scrim began to peel away, and he could see daylight streaming from outside, and movement. Something or someone was outside the dome. He saw the trickle of light, and then it went dark as dirt and branches covered it.

Who?

His soldiers wouldn't dare come near his Hollow City dome. He ushered Helix inside and locked the door, activating the electric lock. He pulled out his radio and called for the Red Skulls to grab a few Dusters and search the island for the intruder. Morphlings didn't react that way to animals. Yes, they hunted down humans and killed them, but they never went that crazy unless they found someone with the PX gene.

He cursed under his breath. He would bet his entire operation that there was someone from Neverwood out there. One of Barrie's brats. The timing could not be any more inconvenient.

Well, he'd just have to hunt them down and put them in the simulation. "You want to play, do you?" Hook muttered as he gazed up at the retreating shadow of their intruder as it ran across the outside of the hollow dome. Helix was back on his phone and didn't hear him. "Well, that can be arranged."

-31-

PETER HAD ONLY meant to be gone a few minutes, but in his search of the island, he'd found the small inlet as well as the freighter ship, docked and already in the midst of unloading. He hovered over the top of the closest palm tree as he tried to scope out the lay of the land.

Had Curly found the lost boys? Were they free, or had he been caught? Peter shook his head at that thought. No one could catch Curly. He could take care of himself. He wasn't invincible, but he could talk himself out of any situation.

An engine roared to life, and he saw a truck drive down the ramp with a few of the pods on it. He recognized Onyx's unconscious form inside one of the pods, and a couple of the other boys, Craft, Torque, Rash and Nibs. He bit his lip and watched the truck drive down the beach and into an underground garage. That seemed to be the only way inside, as he couldn't see any other opening or door.

Another truck followed the first, and Peter's heart broke over the decision he was about to make. He had to go after the boys and leave Wendy to fend for herself. If he didn't, they might never break into this mountain fortress.

"Sorry, Wendy," Peter mumbled and punched his fist into his thigh. He took a deep breath, then shot off to the far left of the ship, out of view of the trucks driving into the garage, and came up around the back side of the ship, alighting on the deck just as the Dusters began to march up from below deck. He didn't see Curly, but he fell into line behind Wu Zan and Leroy as they marched down the ramp.

Peter stiffened when he saw Hook on the beach with a companion. All the feelings of resentment and contempt came rushing back, but then he realized Hook still thought he was a brain-dead dimwit. Peter quickly suppressed his grin when they ran past the captain. The other soldiers were saluting and greeting him with a formal address.

"Cap'n," Leroy said.

"Captain," Wu Zan said stiffly.

Peter couldn't help the cough that came out, and he muttered, "Codfish."

He heard the unmistakable sound of Wu Zan snort, but no one turned around or acknowledged Peter's comeback. They wouldn't dare. Peter's grin spread from ear to ear as they ran down the beach and into the underground garage. The boys slowed and Peter followed suit as he took in what he was seeing. There was so much more than just a garage built into the cliff. This was the headquarters, built deep underground.

A grinding echoed through the cavernous garage, and Peter glanced back over his shoulder. Hook had followed them inside and was closing up the door. The lower ramp cranked up, creating a halo of light around the door until it met with the top, sealing them inside in pitch black. They stopped marching. His mouth went dry. Then the darkness was diminished as lights clicked on and down the tunnels.

He heard Hook speaking to his companion about the high tides and the entrance being closed off for most of the day. His stomach plummeted even more. He was now trapped inside, and Wendy was alone outside.

"Way to go, Peter," he chastised himself and once again prayed that Wendy would have the common sense to stay put and wait for him. Then he scrunched up his face in realization. Who was he kidding? That was not at all like Wendy. He could almost guarantee that she was in some kind of trouble already. If she wasn't the cause of it, then it would most certainly seek her out.

"Hey, Peter," Leroy whispered. "Where did you go on the ship with the other boy?"

"I needed to help a friend out. In fact, we are still trying to help them."

Wu Zan crossed his arms over his chest and stared down Peter. "You're trying to break out the others, aren't you?" he accused. "The new ones."

Peter didn't have time to lie or dance around the truth. "Yes, I am. They're my family."

"Neverland is our family," Wu Zan spoke indignantly.

Peter shook his head, "No, it's not. This place is built on broken dreams and promises. I've been here before." He pointed up aboveground. "Seven years ago, we were taken, all kids ranging from infants to twelve years old. We were in a psychiatric hospital as they tested us, treated us for this imaginary disease. When we weren't taking to the treatments fast enough, Neverland ordered us to be destroyed, but instead, we destroyed Neverland. Or so we thought. This new drug, this PX-3 or whatever number they're on now? It's still bad news. What if they get tired of you and decide to order you destroyed as well?"

Wu Zan's face paled and Leroy looked disturbed by the news.

Peter laughed dryly. "I guess they forgot to put that in the recruitment pamphlet."

He turned to leave, but Wu Zan's hand shot out and grabbed Peter's elbow painfully.

"We should report you," Wu Zan hissed. He looked around to wave down a guard.

Leroy stepped between the two boys, blocking Wu Zan from Peter. Leroy's brown eyes were filled with worry. "Are you saying we're going to die? That the drug doesn't work, right?"

"I don't know, but ask yourself, how many burned out? How many have you watched die unnecessarily?"

"We should stop him!" Wu Zan snapped. "Make him stay with us."

"No." Leroy's deep voice made Wu Zan wince. "You will do no such thing. Let him go. Let him save his friends.

If it was you Zan, if you got into trouble, I would do everything I could to save you."

Wu Zan's mouth opened to spew an even louder tirade, but Leroy clasped his hands over Wu Zan's mouth, hushing him.

"Go, brother," Leroy said sadly. "Save your family, and I will take care of mine." He nodded to Wu Zan, who was vibrating and kicking violently, but not enough to hurt his friend.

Peter reached out and touched Leroy's arm. "When we rebuild our home, you are always welcome there."

There was a resigned sadness in Leroy's face. His lips turned up in a smile, but it never reached his eyes. "Thank you."

He turned, his hand still clamped over Wu Zan's mouth, and faced the front with the other soldiers, pulling Wu Zan along with him. The larger boy leaned down and whispered something in Wu Zan's ear, and he finally settled down, only casting one or two heated looks back over his shoulder at Peter, who was scoping out the idling truck parked on the side.

Slipping over to the truck bed, he swung his leg over the side and crawled into the back. Hands grabbed hold of him from behind and pulled him onto the truck bed with a thump. Peter began to fight, but Curly reached a hand out to calm him.

Peter felt the cool rush of peace wash over him, and then he punched Curly. "Don't use your magic on me," he snapped.

"Sorry, but you needed to get down fast," Curly whispered.

The sounds of the Dusters marching down a tunnel echoed back, and Peter imagined his friends with them. Louder footsteps came as they drew near, and then they heard the driver door open. Seconds later, the truck began moving.

"I heard Hook say something about taking them to the locker room. Do you know where that is?"

Peter shook his head.

"What is this place?" Curly asked.

"It's the island. We're back."

"I don't remember this area."

"We're underground. Remember when the kids would disappear from the hospital? We passed through here, but it wasn't finished then. I remember lots of construction and tarps and security."

Curly lay on the truck bed on his back, his knees pulled up because there wasn't much room to stay low. "It's been here all this time."

"I don't think they ever stopped building it," Peter mused. He was stuck between two other pods, lying uncomfortably on his side.

"I'm sorry again, Peter, for—"

"Don't. Curly. You said your peace. Let it rest. Don't drag up the past." Peter lifted his head to see Curly. "Prove to me your loyalty by helping me shut down Neverland for good."

Curly's mouth turned down. It was obvious that he was still carrying a heavy burden that he wanted to get off his chest, but Peter needed him clearheaded and focused.

The truck came to a stop, and Curly and Peter slipped over the side closest to the wall, then kneeled by the truck's tires.

"We can't just break them out of there," Peter warned in a low voice. "There has to be a way to safely unplug them."

"Got it," Curly nodded.

More Red Skulls arrived, and Peter and Curly rolled under the truck, lying on their backs looking up at the undercarriage.

"Well, this is fun," Curly murmured, frowning, as if sneaking around Neverland should be a blast.

"You could make it fun." Peter wiggled his eyebrows, and a slow smile crept up Curly's face. He gently reached out a hand and brushed it across the boot of the nearest soldier.

The soldier paused and then continued working to unload the pods, but now he was quietly singing show tunes.

"Hey Potts, cut it out with the singing."

Potts paused, and then broke out singing at the top of his lungs, "Don't stop believing!"

Other Red Skulls groaned and made fun of him and then just begged him to stop, and Potts responded to all of them—but in song, growing louder and louder, his voice a little off-key from disuse, but unforgettable to say the least, and with a bit of vibrato to it. Curly was now cackling silently, his knees pulled up to his chest, rocking in undisguised mirth.

Peter knew, because Curly had only brushed his hand across the soldier's boot, that his compulsion would only last a minute or so. If he had managed to touch skin, he would be singing tunes for hours.

"I'm warning you, Potts," a third soldier grumbled. "At least sing something with a beat."

The soldier no longer needed the compulsion of Curly's gift and began to sing and throw some shade as he switched to beatboxing. The other soldiers hollered encouragement, while continuing to unload the pods, making a few trips. Within a few minutes, the pods were all unloaded onto pallet jacks and while the Red Skulls were well distracted, the boys slipped out from under the truck, keeping care to keep a moving pod between them and any Red Skulls.

When they got into a freight elevator with three Red Skulls, Curly touched the closest Red Skull and whispered, "You don't see us."

They both hugged the corner and tried to stay out of sight. The Red Skull nearest them was the last out of the elevator pulling the pod on the pallet jack, and they followed him down the hall where he deposited the last pod into a large warehouse. Peter and Curly slipped inside and ducked behind a row of metal lockers and benches. There seemed to be three large lifts in the middle of the room. Peter did a quick count and realized there was one pod missing. One from the trucks hadn't been brought here.

When all the soldiers had exited, and the warehouse was cleared, they moved over to the pods and began to inspect them.

"Where's the instruction manual?" Curly joked as he ran his hands over the pod, looking for hidden panels.

"In here," a female voice spoke up from behind them.

The boys turned around and were greeted by Candace, who was pointing to her head. Her right hand was tucked by her thigh.

Curly took two steps toward her, and she yelled, "Stop!" aiming a gun at both of them. "I know what you can do. You will stay over there where I can see you. If you come any closer to me, I will shoot. And it won't be the one who comes back to life."

"Candace," Peter pleaded. "I just want to help the boys. You know what they're doing here is wrong."

Candace's hand shook as she held the pistol. Curly tried to take a step to the left, but she followed him. He moved to the right and the barrel of the gun kept pace. He frowned, thoroughly displeased at his inability to step out of the line of sight.

"No, we're helping people," she whispered.

"Who?" Peter tried to calm her down. "Because all I've seen is this company hurting people."

After several tense moments, the gun lowered to her lap and Curly sighed. Peter moved to kneel by Candace. "Good intentions can easily be clouded. Especially by family."

Curly's head shot up in surprise.

Candace nodded. "How did you know?"

Peter sighed. "It was an educated guess. With how much Hook prizes soldiers, athleticism, and perfection, it seemed odd that—"

"That I would be here." She wiped at the corner of her eyes. "Because I'm crippled."

Peter winced. "Don't call yourself that. You're in a wheelchair, but you're not . . . that." He inhaled deeply, trying to keep from getting distracted by the tears welling in Candace's eyes. "But yes, why else would Hook allow you to stay here with a disability if you weren't family?" He tried to soften the words by speaking gently, but really there was no getting around the cruelty of them.

Candace's face scrunched up in tears. "He's never shown me any concern, never called me daughter. He's a stranger to me. I hate him."

"And yet, you are here working on one of his top projects. I don't think Hook knows how to love," Peter said thoughtfully. "But he is a greedy pirate, and he does keep things that belong to him close."

The words had opened a floodgate of tears, and she was using her sleeve to wipe them away. But both Peter and Curly were still standing at an awkward distance, at an impasse.

"Can you help us?" Curly asked.

Candace chewed the inside of her cheek. "I'll do what I can. But I have to warn you. Not everyone survives being unplugged. Why do you think there are so few Primes left? It wrecks their systems and sometimes there's nothing left but husks."

She rolled her wheelchair over to the nearest pod, which happened to contain Onyx.

She pulled a tablet out of the pouch on the side of her wheelchair and began to type in a code.

"We have to do this slowly. They've all been heavily medicated, and they're going to be a bit loopy. Do you understand?"

Both of them nodded and Candace sighed. "Okay, stand back."

She typed into her keyboard and the pod lit up. Then water began to drain from the pod onto the floor and flowed to the middle of the room and into a drain.

"I've stopped his medication and have begun to wake him up."

Inside, Onyx crumpled against the glass and slowly slid to the bottom, his mask still attached to his face. Peter rushed to the pod, but Candace called him back.

"No. If you open the pod, he could hurt you. He needs a few minutes for the drugs to make their way out of his system naturally."

Just as she had warned them, Onyx's eyes opened and turned black, and then the pod began to vibrate, and Peter turned and looked away. Inside, Onyx was fighting the mask, writhing against the glass. Unaware of what was going on, he was attacking everything.

"Onyx," Peter called through the glass, keeping his eyes closed. "Buddy, I'm here for you. We're here to get you out, okay?"

Not daring to look, he heard the lost boy settle down, the thrashing coming to a halt, and then a gasping breath.

"P-e-t-e-r," Onyx croaked out a response.

"Yes, it's me." He opened his eyes and was relieved that his friend was okay. "We'll get you out." He searched the side of the pod for the release. "How do I open the door?"

"He is still dangerous," she warned.

"Open it!" Peter demanded, and Candace pointed to the metal panel on the side of the pod and made a gesture for him to lift it. He pried the panel open with his fingertips, revealing a hidden release switch, and then with the heel of his palm, he flipped the lever, and the pod swung open with a hiss.

Peter reached in and, grabbing Onyx under the arms, pulled him out of the pod and across the floor.

"Pe—ter." Onyx coughed and raised his hand weakly to touch his face. "You're late."

Peter's head fell back and a deep laugh rumbled from his chest. "Nah, you know I just like to make an entrance," he teased.

Onyx was trembling as his body was fighting the drugs, and his mind tried to control his limbs to move. He stuttered, "S—such a d—diva."

This time it was Curly who snorted from across the room, followed by a hushed giggle from Candace.

"I tried to stop them," Onyx whispered. "I tried."

"Shush, don't talk. Just focus on regaining your strength. Because we're back at Neverland, and I'm going to need you to help me tear this place apart."

Onyx's eyes turned dark, and Peter looked away for fear of being turned to stone, but Onyx was able to get his fear under control.

Peter held on to him, speaking quietly, comforting him until Onyx had stopped shaking and seemed to be on the mend, with his breathing even and color back in his cheeks.

Curly was looking at the vitals of the other boys, and he didn't look hopeful. "Peter, they're not doing well."

Peter observed all the others and wondered if it would be like this with each of the boys? Onyx was strong and was struggling to come out from what he had undergone. There were so many young ones, weaker ones than Onyx. Could they all make it? He didn't have a choice, though. He couldn't leave them in the pods and under Neverland's control one second longer. He needed to free them.

Even if freeing them meant from this life.

He could feel the sting of tears at the corners of his eyes, and he knew this is what they would have wanted. They'd want to be free.

Peter turned to Candace, his eyes filled with anger. "Begin draining the other pods now. I won't let them be in there a minute longer."

-32-

THIS WASN'T HER IDEA of fun or an adventure. Wendy was running hard through the underbrush, her nerves raw as she was assaulted by a flashback of running from the Red Skulls in the middle of the night. Her breathing was coming in gasps and the stitch in her side wasn't letting up. She really should have spent more time practicing running long distance.

Her prayers about hopefully not being spotted had gone unanswered. Because not even five minutes after spooking the morphling, more Red Skulls appeared around the dome and were hunting her down. She had only barely been able to avoid them. Once because she had fallen and slipped down an embankment, and another because she had doubled back and tried to come up behind them.

But she didn't have any special powers or guns to fight them. The shadows had abandoned her once she stepped foot on the island. It was as if they knew what was living below the earth and how much they wanted to hunt and destroy them.

Pop! A gunshot went off, and she shrieked, ducking and staying low to the ground.

Think! Wendy, think! she kept chastising herself. What would Peter do?

Obviously, he would do something really heroic, have something extremely witty to say, and then fly them over a cliff and drop them into the ocean.

Okay, she could maybe pull off one of the three, but with how much her brain was fried from running and adrenaline, she didn't think she could come up with anything witty.

She saw a path and began to run like crazy, making sure to zig and zag.

Ping! Another shot whizzed by her ear.

"Hey, you almost shot me!" Wendy snapped, and covered her mouth.

A husky laugh resonated from the forest behind her. "That's kind of the point."

Okay, spouting off to the Red Skull hunting her was not a good idea. She couldn't do any of the three things Peter would do. She'd have to rethink her strategy.

Wendy jumped over a small ditch and, misjudging the distance, missed her landing. She slipped and fell, hitting her chin on the hill. Sucking in her breath between her teeth, she grunted in pain and continued to run, but not before looking over her shoulder.

Jeremy?

How, what, and why questions plagued her. Why was he chasing her down? The last she heard, he had been . . . taken by the morphlings.

Wendy grunted and changed directions last minute when she realized she had been running in a straight line for too long. Her instinct proved correct as another bullet whizzed by. Maybe she could foresee the future without the shadows, but then she would have foreseen this.

Nope, she would not have expected her high school crush—who she had dumped after a bad date—to be shooting at her on a hidden island in the middle of the ocean. Wendy wished she had one of Tink's censor bands, because she had some very choice words for him.

So preoccupied with her thoughts of telling off Jeremy that she almost ran right off the edge of a cliff. Wendy stopped, her arms pinwheeling to keep her balance. Looking over the edge caused the world to spin, and she fell back onto the ground. *Ground was safe. She liked the ground.* Funny how she had no problems flying through the air with Peter, but stepping close to an edge by herself was a different matter. She really hated heights.

"Wendy?" Jeremy spoke in surprise as he emerged from the tree line.

"Hey." She waved nonchalantly and then put her hands in her pockets. "What are you doing here?" she asked, all the while eyeing his Red Skull uniform with contempt. Seeing the frown on his face, she quickly rearranged her expression to show doe-eyed innocence.

"Wrong question. What are you doing here?" He still had his weapon aimed at her.

"I'm not really sure," she quipped and produced her own greatest weapon, her smile and charm. "I signed up for a three hour cruise on the tour ship called the Minnow and—"

"Not funny, Wendy," he snapped.

Wendy let out a small giggle and flipped her hair over her shoulder. "Of course it was funny." She wanted to stab herself in the eye, but she forced herself to reach up and swirl her finger around her hair.

Jeremy paused, and Wendy knew the moment her ploy to convince him she was unthreatening had worked, because he holstered the gun. He was probably confident in his ability to bring her in without the use of force. To Wendy, this was the perfect opportunity, even though she wanted to gag on a spoon.

In the blondest voice she could muster, she batted her eyelashes. "A big shadowy monster thing grabbed me in the alley and took me to some lab. Where they said I had some special gene. I don't remember much, except, I was on a boat and then I woke up here," she lied, trying to feed him enough facts about his own kidnapping and what she knew happened once Neverland got ahold of you.

"I would have seen you at the training facility," he accused. "You weren't there." He took a step toward her and Wendy panicked, wanting to move farther away from the cliff's edge, but she moved closer to Jeremy.

"I was there. I was in a separate room."

"I don't believe you." He stepped closer, his eyes running over her face and resting on her lips.

Inwardly, she shuddered in revulsion at his appraisal. She hated that he was so handsome on the outside but completely rotten to the core on the inside. He was a junkie and only interested in two things, and she was willing to give him neither.

She held still as Jeremy approached and walked around her, looking her over. "Where's your uniform?" he asked.

"I don't need one." She stood tall and followed him with her eyes.

"All recruits are given one," he challenged.

"Do you have one of these?" Wendy asked, pulling the neck of her shirt and lifting her hair to expose the small mark with her serial number that deemed her an experiment of Neverland.

Jeremy stilled when he saw the mark, his eyes widening in disgust. "You're a Prime."

Prime? Wendy hadn't heard the term before, but she went with it. Locking eyes with the beast before her, she refused to back down.

"Yes, and you're not!" she challenged back, throwing it in his face.

Apparently, that was the wrong thing to do, because he smiled cruelly. "Hook only wants the strongest. He weeds out the weak, and I don't think he would mind me culling you from the pack."

"What?" Wendy asked and was surprised when Jeremy launched himself at her. She fell backwards, his one hundred eighty-pound frame pinning her to the ground.

"C'mon, fight me, Wendy." He pinned her arms painfully, and she screamed. "If you're an original, you should be stronger than this. I swore that I would kill a Prime to prove myself to Hook. Funny that it's going to be you."

She had a flashback of her training with Jax, when he told her this might happen.

Wendy brought her knee up, but Jeremy was prepared.

He moved to sitting on her torso, his weight crushing her chest, her lungs unable to expand and contract. "You're pathetic. I want a fight."

She kicked but was unable to get enough breath to scream for help.

Jeremy opened up his pocket and pulled out an injector pen. "This should help even the playing field, Wendy. Stole it from the lab myself. I wonder what it does."

His fist rose and Wendy lurched, trying to move just as it came down. She felt the injector hit her in the chest, heard the crack of the plastic applicator, and jerked as it pierced her.

The pain was excruciating. Her body shook, and then she went still, her mouth opening and shutting as he moved off of her. Air filled her lungs, and she cried out and rolled into a ball, the pen still sticking out of her chest.

Grunting with pain, she wrapped her left hand around the injector and carefully pulled it out, marveling that he had used enough force that he broke the casing around the tip and sent the needle in farther than it was designed to go.

Dropping the pen, she lay on the ground, her body quivering and shaking as she fought the adrenaline that rushed through her. Never before had she felt such excruciating agony, and she could only close her eyes and pray for it to pass.

"Get up!" he snapped, and when she didn't move, he kicked her in the stomach. Wendy curled into a ball to protect herself. "Move." He was drawing his foot back to kick her again when a shadow rushed out of the woods and dove through Jeremy. The cold shock of the invisible mass sent him spinning.

"What was that?" He spun, his hands waving off an invisible threat. He couldn't see the shadow, but it didn't mean that he couldn't feel its presence. When one of them passed through a human, it left them cold and disoriented.

Jeremy's chest was heaving, his eyes wild, but he could not see his shadow assailant and moved toward Wendy again.

Her veins felt like fire was pulsing through them, but she had to pull it together, needed to get up and get away from Jeremy. She pulled herself to her knees and started to crawl away. A few steps later, she was wobbling but made it to her feet.

"Where do you think you're going?" Jeremy grabbed Wendy by the back of the hair, and she yelped as he spun her around.

The shadow was back, skirting along the ground and in an animal form. Unlike the ones that usually followed Wendy, this was one-third the size. She looked to the shadow, and it zigzagged across the field and leaped, passing through Jeremy a second time.

"What the—?" He spun and clutched his chest again. "Am I having a heart attack?"

Wendy could only assume that's what it felt like, and she wondered if these other shadows were able to take over and share a body, like Peter had, or was that only because of his gifts? Wishing desperately for a weapon, or a bracer that hadn't been destroyed by ocean water, Wendy searched for a way to defeat Jeremy and came to a horrible conclusion. She didn't think she could. He was hyped-up on the PX drugs, made stronger than humanly possible. Even his physique had changed, and he was more muscular than he was days ago.

The shadow jumped out of Jeremy's body, and Wendy clearly saw the distinct shape of a fox. Her heart fluttered with joy, and she knew then that she wasn't truly alone on the cliff.

Jeremy confronted her again, his eyes even more crazed with fury than before.

"What is that thing? What are you doing to me?" he accused.

He could see the shadow, without specs. Did that mean he died like her? Wendy became worried. "I'm not doing anything. The shadow, on the other hand . . ." She waved in the direction of the fox. "He doesn't like what you're doing to me, so I would suggest you stop."

"That thing is nothing compared to the morphlings. I wonder what would happen if I radioed in for one to be released?"

"Jeremy," Wendy said calmly. "You've seen the morphlings, and what they can do. You don't mess with them. They can't be controlled."

"Neverland controls them. I've seen footage."

"No one can really control them, just like no one can control a rampant river. You can redirect the flow, but not stop the force."

He continued to step closer, and Wendy was now on the edge of the cliff, her heel skirting it dangerously, knocking rocks over the edge.

"Come on, Wendy. All I wanted was a shot."

She was confused by the change of subject. Was he referring to their date?

"But you had to dump me for him—for Peter. And it turns out that he's a Prime too. What is it with you two? What makes you so special?"

Her mouth went dry, and she tensed. He was talking like someone at the edge of his rope, with nothing left to lose.

"I can beat a Prime, though, I know I can. I will. That'll change everything. Then I'll get respect. Everybody will know my name. I'm sorry it has to be this way, but I have to stay—I belong here—I'm staying. And if that means I have to kill you, then so be it. Besides, my orders were to eliminate the intruder on the island. Even if we know each other, it's still my orders. No hard feelings, okay?" He turned, his mouth curling into a cruel smile as he unhurriedly unbuttoned and rolled up his left sleeve, then proceeded to roll up the right.

"You're quick, but you're not fast enough for me." In a dramatic show of force, Jeremy threw his weight and punched a rock, splitting it in two.

Out of the corner of her eye, Wendy saw the shadow move to help her again, but she shook her head. She needed to deal with this once and for all.

Jeremy rushed her, his fist drawing back for a punch, and she sidestepped and ducked, spinning away so now Jeremy was the one standing on the edge of the cliff.

He slowed his momentum and turned, bouncing on the balls of his feet, like a boxer getting ready for a bout. He took a few more practice punches. "Come on, Wendy, show me what you got."

The fox shadow ran toward her, followed by two more shadows. A jolt of cold air passed through her, followed by a second and third. Her eyes rolled into the back of her head as a vision came of the future. She saw it clearly.

She was falling, and Jeremy was falling as well.

Wendy glanced over Jeremy's shoulder to the cliff's edge, her heart thumping faster with fear. She knew what she would have to do. Take him over the cliff, no matter the consequences. Was she prepared? *Yes.* Could she do it? *No.*

This is where she wasn't like Peter. She didn't want to kill, especially not Jeremy, whose bravado and cold heart she knew were just symptoms of his insecurities. He was uncertain and depressed. How lonely he must be, how very lost, to look to the Red Skulls and to drugs for a sense of comfort and acceptance This was not his future, not if she had a choice.

She hesitated too long in her vision as his fist connected with her face, and she stumbled backwards. Wendy's cheek quickly swelled, and she tasted blood on her lip. She wiped it off with the back of her hand and turned away, giving him her back.

"No!" Jeremy called after her. "Come back here!"

She kept walking, ignoring Jeremy's cursing, but the moment she heard him chasing her down, she called for help.

Closing her eyes, she stopped where she stood and turned her face up to the sky, she called to the shadows. And just like that, three shadows rushed in to join her. From where they came, she wasn't sure, but she was grateful for their assistance. Would they be enough? She hoped so.

She threw open her arms and jumped into the air. Letting the three shadows wrap around her, in a flash she disappeared and reappeared one hundred feet away in the underbrush. After her last experience teleporting with the shadows, Wendy didn't dare travel farther, not with a city full of morphlings underground, dying to hunt down the shadows.

She crouched down in the underbrush and pressed her cheek to the ground, trying to slow her breathing. Jeremy was screaming her name, chasing her down, and stopped in the spot where she disappeared. Through the brush, she saw him turn full circle, studying the grass and then looking up in the air and surrounding trees. He looked right at her—no, not at her, beyond her. He cursed, and she smiled, silently congratulating herself for not killing him and for proving the future wrong. She didn't fall from the cliff.

She was safe . . . for now.

Then she felt the barrel of a gun press against the back of her head.

"Don't move, Wendy," said a familiar feminine voice.

"Hi, Lily," Wendy said calmly without turning around, knowing the Red Skull with Tiger-like features had found her in the underbrush.

"Fancy meeting you here," Lily said snidely.

"I know, right?" Wendy held very still, calculating her odds of getting out of here alive. It wasn't looking good. "I was hoping we'd get a chance to reconnect sometime. Maybe we can start over? We used to be friends, at one time."

A sharp blow across the side of her face was her answer to that question.

-33-

"I'M SORRY, PETER," Onyx whispered as he placed his hand on Peter's shaking shoulders. They had freed twenty of the lost boys, but two of them—Torque and Rash—didn't awaken from their drug-induced comas. Their vitals were stable, but there was no brain activity on the monitors.

"Is there nothing we can do?" Peter asked Candace.

Seeing Torque and Rash laid out on the floor attached to the machines, lifeless and nonresponsive, seemed to have an adverse effect on Candace. She had become withdrawn, sullen and depressed.

"No," she sniffed, her eyes red from holding back tears. Her fingers flew over the tablet and she looked up at Peter confused. "They're gone. We've never been able to account for why some wake up and others don't."

"Maybe it's too much for their hearts to handle?" Nibs said. He, like the other lost boys, had found a towel and wrapped it around his torso. "It was awful, like being trapped in a nightmare that you can't wake up from. Your mind screams and screams and screams, but no one hears you." Nib's brown hair was still wet and trickling down his face, masking his own tears and grief.

Onyx came over and gave Nib's a hug. "It's okay, little brother. Maybe they were needed somewhere else."

Nibs nodded and wiped at his eyes. The boys turned to stare at the other unopened pods, where girls in silver swimsuits floated in the water. Peter didn't recognize any of them. Is this what would have happened to Wendy if she hadn't escaped? He looked away, anger and bile rising in his throat.

"Who are they?" Nibs asked.

"The lost girls," Peter answered. "The ones we left behind all those years ago."

"Correct," Candace said, nodding in agreement. "These were the ones that refused to fight or didn't have abilities that Hook found useful so they were kept here in stasis. But most of the girls and the few boys left behind that survived harvesting are in the program."

"Well, let's free them." Nibs was shaking, his lower lip trembling from the cold. "No one should be left in there."

"Wait!" Onyx shifted uncomfortably, holding the towel around his waist. "We're barely dressed."

Candace nodded over to the lockers. "You'll find clothes and uniforms in there. Boys on the left."

It was night and day, what wearing clothes and being warm and dry did for a boy's confidence.

After they were dressed they felt stronger and now were able to refocus on saving the rest. But they recognized it was risky to continue opening the stasis pods, after having lost Torque and Rash. Did they really have the right to unplug them from their life support, to risk their lives just on the hope that they might be aware enough to breathe on their own?

Peter was the leader of the boys. They would have trusted him to make this decision for them. But he didn't know these girls.

No, he should have known them. They should have grown up with them at Neverwood. They shouldn't have left them on the island in the first place. Dr. Barrie should have gone back for them, and he wasn't about to leave them on the island any longer. He wouldn't dare make the same mistake twice.

"Open them," Peter declared decisively.

Onyx walked over to the closest pod, which held a girl with black wavy hair, and waited for Candace to begin the drain. Each boy took up a position outside of one of the girls' pods, and when the doors swung open, they were there to help, to encourage, and to wrap them in towels.

"Shhh, you're safe," Onyx spoke, wrapping the towel around the dark-haired girl's shoulder. She was shivering and looking about with wildly with forest-green eyes. "We won't harm you." Her eyes turned even darker and her face paled when she spotted what he was wearing.

"Now, I know we look like the enemy wearing these uniforms. But we're not. We're just like you. I'm just like you. More than you realize. I'm going to help you up, okay?"

She nodded.

"I'm Onyx."

"Jade." She looked around at the girls from the other pods waking up.

Curly placed his hand on Peter's shoulder and pulled him over to an opened pod. One of the newly released girls with honey brown hair was holding a girl in her lap and was calmly stroking her wet curls as she was convulsing. "It's okay, Vivi, you're safe. You can wake up now."

Vivi let out a soft wail of distress and clawed the air, as if to ward off monsters in her sleep. Seconds later, she stopped breathing. Her body went limp in the other girl's arms.

Cries littered the warehouse floor as the girls gathered together and hugged each other. Two more nameless girls didn't survive the removal.

"Listen up," Peter spoke loudly to the girls. "You're safe and out of the pods, but it doesn't mean the danger is over. We are back on the island, back at Neverland." Wails of grief came from the recently released girls, and the boys, who'd had time to adjust to the news, did their best to comfort them. "But we won't leave you. We will get off the island together."

Questions came at him as the girls tried to piece together what had happened.

"Follow me, girls," Candace called out when the room had calmed, and led them over to the backside of the lockers, where they had privacy to change and get dressed.

Peter let out a long sigh and rubbed the back of his neck in worry.

"Are you okay?" Curly asked.

Peter shook his head. "The guilt is weighing heavily on me. We all knew there were others there with us, that night."

"But we didn't know they'd still be here."

"I know. But don't tell me you didn't have nightmares about being left behind. Or waking up still there."

"Every night for two years," Curly answered.

"For them, they never woke up. The girls still lived the nightmare. Now tell me that wouldn't mess with your head."

Curly's face reddened. "Yeah, it would."

Jade was the first to come back around the locker wall, wearing a gray uniform, and her wet hair was pulled back into a neat braid. By all appearances, she was ready to go. But she seemed twitchy, unable to stand still, and she kept looking at the ground and averting her eyes.

While her behavior was probably understandable, Peter began to feel a rising panic at the thought of what would happen if Jade and the others, who had only just been released from these cruel pods, were confronted with combat.

"Are you ready?" he asked Jade.

She looked up at him and nodded, then averted her eyes and shivered. Finally she said, "I don't know."

Peter bit his tongue and waited to hear her out.

"I don't know if I can fight. I couldn't, before. I didn't want to be a weapon," Jade began. "I refused to do what Hook asked of me. We all did, and because of that we were punished."

"You should always have a choice. You will never be forced to do that again. But we may have to fight to get out of here. Can you do that?" Peter asked. "I'm not asking you to kill, but can you fight for your freedom?"

The girl with honey brown hair came forward and draped her arm over Jade's shoulder. "I'm Ash. We may have not wanted to fight for Hook, but it doesn't mean we aren't up for revenge." She squeezed Jade's shoulder and her eyes lit up.

"Now, that I can do," Jade said firmly.

The other girls streamed out from behind the lockers, each one with a determined face. Gone where the wide-eyed lambs they rescued. Standing in front of them was a pack of lionesses.

Peter nodded, his grin spreading across his face. He had an army.

He guided them toward the exit when suddenly an alarm broadcasted in the room. Everyone turned in surprise as the overhead lights turned red, and then they heard the very distinguishable sound of a heavy deadbolt sliding across the door, locking them inside. Peter scanned the room in alarm, prepared to fight, but it was empty other than a wall of lockers, the pods, and the lifts.

"Welcome back to Neverland," Hook's voice blared over the loudspeaker. The overhead lights continued to flash red and white, red and white. A TV, hung on the far wall, flickered on and Hook's face appeared on the screen.

Onyx and Craft ran toward the closest exit.

"Candace?" Peter asked.

"It's a live feed," she answered, pointing to the speakers that hung from the ceiling.

Hook's ugly mug grinned back at them. "Don't try to escape. The room is sealed, and if you touch the door, you will be electrocuted."

"Craft," Peter warned just as the boy reached for the handle. Onyx's reflexes were quicker, and he pulled the boy back just as his fingertip touched the metal. A spark of light flashed, the red pulsating lights flickered once, and Craft fell backwards onto the cold, hard cement.

Onyx checked his pulse.

"Is he okay?" Peter asked, running toward the boy.

Onyx leaned back on his heels. "He has a pulse. Just out cold."

"What was that?" Peter asked Candace accusingly.

But Candace wasn't paying attention, and neither were the other boys, as they all stared up in revulsion at Hook's delighted expression.

"Oh, did one of you touch it? What happened? Did he die?" he asked eagerly.

"Can he see us?" Peter asked.

"And hear you," Candace mouthed with a nod, then motioned her head to the corner, being careful to not move too much.

Peter eyed the corner where she'd gestured and spotted the small blinking red light of a camera that had been virtually invisible before, having blended into the dark ceiling while it was off.

Hook leaned back in his chair. "Well, never mind. Let this be a lesson to you that you can't escape. It's time to play the game."

"Game? What game?" Peter stepped away from the boys and tried to draw all the attention onto him.

"You again? Why are you here and not with the other Dusters?" He slammed his fist onto the table.

"Obviously, I'm loyal to a fault, despite your attempts to reprogram me."

Hook glowered menacingly at the camera. "Well, too late. I tried to put you on the winning team. But now it's out of my hands."

"What's out of your hands?" Peter asked, but Hook had stepped away from the screen, and the man in the business suit from the beach appeared, taking his place. He was older, white-haired, but he had an air of quiet authority.

"That's right. It's in my hands. I'm President Helix of Wonderland Games."

"Why are we here?" Peter asked him.

Helix laughed. "Why, Hook, you're right, he is spunky. What is your name, young man?"

"Peter."

Helix leaned back and spoke to Hook for confirmation. "This is the one . . . right?"

Hook mumbled something off-screen, but it must have been an affirmation, because Helix's face beamed in delight.

"Well, Peter. You were identified, as our answer to the future of Virtual Reality Games. We've been developing the software for years, and more recently we've had a breakthrough as to how to make the reality even more real."

Onyx leaned over and whispered to Curly, "Hey, isn't that the multibillion-dollar online game designer?"

"That would be a question for Ditto and Slightly. But I think you're right." Curly observed the room cautiously.

"They haven't been able to stop playing the online co-op game for months."

"The problem with video games is that they become predictable. The avatars are programmed with a limited set of moves, and if you play them long enough, you can see the pattern. Even if you are able to randomly generate an infinite number of moves, they always have a weakness. I have found a way to rid the world of the humdrum monotony of video games. I've made it personal and more live-action based than ever before," Helix announced.

"Better graphics?" Onyx snorted.

"You won't get more 4-D than this. The newest expansion and world update is being beta tested live in one hour, and I can't wait to hear what you think." Helix sounded pleased, but he was the only one. He didn't seem to care about the grim faces looking back at him.

"If you survive that is," Helix laughed sinisterly.

The screen went blank and everyone spoke at once.

"What is he talking about?" Jade asked.

"I don't understand why we're here," Ash said.

"A video game unveiling doesn't sound so bad," Nibs added.

Peter walked over to Candace, and grabbing the back of her wheelchair, he leaned down and said, "Explain fast. I don't care how nonchalant he is being. There's always a catch."

Candace swallowed nervously, playing with the watch on her wrist.

"There is. You're the game."

-34-

"I CAN'T DO IT," John mumbled in defeat. He leaned his head back to look at the crew of hopefuls that had gathered in the yachts galley. "It looks like I need a password to get past the next stage to the instructions. I never received an invite, so I don't have the user-generated code."

Tink had given up long ago and laid her head on the table, and now began banging her forehead on it in frustration.

Michael was sitting in the corner, his hands white-knuckled around his knees. "Can I try?" he whispered.

Tink's head snapped up and she looked at the young boy. "Why didn't I think of that? Let the kid with the computer brain go at it."

"I did," John said and moved to sit next to Michael. "I didn't want to put him through it, if I could do it myself." He ruffled the young boy's hair. "Do you really think you want to do this? I mean, it's syncing up with Neverland's computers again. What if they get inside your head again?"

Michael blinked through the goggles at them. "Let them try. I've always focused on keeping them out of my head, but now it's my turn to break in." A mischievous smirk crossed his face, and John swept out his hand toward the computer.

"Be my guest."

The young boy gave a shy smile to Tink, then hopped over to the bench and sat in front of the computer, leaning forward. At first he didn't seem to be doing anything.

Tink nudged John. "Look at the screen," she whispered.

Michael didn't even need to touch the keys. His brain started opening pages on the computer as he searched without using a mouse. He found whatever backdoor he was looking for, and they watched in awe as code began to scroll across the screen.

"Look at him go!" John clenched his fists and Tink put her arm around John's waist as they leaned close to watch him.

"He's amazing!" Tink cheered.

Michael's grin grew bigger, but then his tongue stuck out as he encountered a slight hitch. His brows furrowed and he closed his eyes. His hands went to his temples and he grunted in pain.

"Hit a firewall," he mumbled. "Trying to get through." Sweat beaded across his forehead. He sucked in his breath and gasped in pain, his small hands pressing to his temples as if to alleviate the pressure building.

"Look at his eyes," Tink murmured. John stepped back when he saw it—the computer screen showed one thing, but reflected out of Michael's eyes and amplified by the goggles was computer code—all ones and zeros.

"That's how he's communicating. It's so fascinating." Tink pressed closer, but John pulled her back and shook his head, giving the young boy space.

"We're in," Michael crowed before collapsing on the table, his head cocked to the side, his mouth slightly opened.

"Is he okay?" John asked, but Tink had already rushed to check on him.

"He's breathing, and I think . . ." She leaned forward and smiled. "He's asleep. Must have tuckered him out. Let's call the others and give him a few minutes to recover."

It didn't take long for the news to spread, and everyone gathered in the galley for news. Thankfully, Michael was back in tip-top shape after a five-minute nap.

"We got in," John told the group. "Thanks to Michael."

Michael grinned as he dug his spoon into a package of freeze-dried ice cream.

"And you won't believe what he found," Tink added, spinning the laptop so Dr. Barrie and Jax could see.

Jax leaned over the table, and John clicked on the link. A black screen with the words Warfare 8 appeared, but then the 8 shifted and turned sideways.

The countdown clock listed sixty-five minutes left.

"Warfare Infinity, that sounds awesome!" Ditto said a little too enthusiastically. He read the byline of the game.

A Division of the Unnatural and Supernatural Teams have infiltrated Hollow Dome. Your mission is to defend the city from the ever-increasing shades.

"Okay, now shades sound lame," Ditto added. "Who came up with that name?"

John began to read aloud. "Real time, real video, real explosions. It's all real and so are the stakes. High-end gamers log on and pay money to link to a specially designed D.U.S.T. avatar for the combat. Upgrades and special abilities are extra."

"I don't get how they could make money off of this?" Jax asked.

Dr. Mee shook her head. "I have no idea."

John was biting his thumb and kept clicking through the screen. "Guys, this is bad."

"What?" Slightly asked.

"It's Peter." John pointed out a 3-D rendering of Peter. "Look at this. Stats, weaknesses, and special abilities: flight and regeneration."

Tink leaned over John's shoulder and gasped. "Not only that, but Onyx, Nibs, Craft, and the others. Who are they? I don't recognize them at all."

"They're what's left of the Primes and the new generation of Dusters. I'd be more worried about the upgrades."

Tink's and John's heads bonked each other as they tried to read more of the screen.

"So to go to the beta test live, the buy-in is one million. Who has this kind of money?"

"Celebrities, millionaires with nothing to spend their money on," Jax said. "Video games are the future, and when you have the best setup, you can spend your money on it."

"Today's the trial run," John sighed, reading the fine print. "Think of it as preseason in football. It's the game launch for future investors and game owners. The site says a buy-in of a million gets one of us in the viewing room, to watch the first battle royal. We'd get the first-round draft pick, and before it goes live to the public next month."

"One of us needs to get in there," Tink said, tapping the screen.

"Oh, Tink, I think you're too big to fit in the computer," Ditto joked.

"Don't be a dork! You know what I mean. We're in my dad's yacht. We have a hacked invitation. One of us can get inside the friggin' building."

Dr. Barrie looked around at the group with a hopeless expression. "Well, it's not going to be me. I know nothing about virtual reality or video games."

"They know me." Jax held up his hands.

"I can go," Tink answered.

Slightly chuckled and rubbed the bridge of his nose. "Tink, I don't think they'd buy it. You may be a hacker, but your mouth will get you in trouble."

"It can't be Isabelle. They know who she is as well. They've bugged Dr. Barrie's bookstore; I suspect they've watched it as well. It has to be someone they don't know."

All eyes turned to John. His face was pensive as he studied the screen, and then when he realized the scrutiny he was under, he jumped up from the seat. "Hey, guys, I'm flattered. Really. But I'm the wrong person."

"He's perfect," Tink said. "They don't know him. Does he match any of the profiles of the investors that Hook contacted?" She glanced at Michael.

"There's a few in their twenties. With the right attitude he could pull it off. I just need to go in there and change a few things, send the wrong coordinates to one of the other investors, and get John in—we'd be golden," Michael said.

"Dr. Mee?" Dr. Barrie called out.

"Yes?"

"Take young John into my room, and see what is in the closets. We need to make him look like a million bucks." Dr. Barrie clasped his hands together.

Tink snorted. "Might as well make that three million."

"Now, you two, make him believable on this thing," he said, gesturing to the computer, and Michael grinned.

"You mean on the internet?"

"Yes, you know what I mean, you rascal." Dr. Barrie motioned for Jax to come over to him. "Now, son."

"I'm not your son," Jax snapped.

"I know that, but do you remember what happened when we left the island last time?"

"How could I forget?" Jax growled out, his arms crossed over his chest.

"I want to say I'm sorry," Dr. Barrie sighed, then pulled out a chair and sat down. "I shouldn't have asked you to use your powers like that all those years ago."

"No, you shouldn't have. I was a boy."

"Yes, I made you a murderer, and for that I am deeply sorry. But we are about to walk into a situation again, and I want to know if—"

"I'll kill for you again?" Jax said, his face guarded.

"No, I . . ." He sighed sadly. "I regret what happened that day, but I want you to know that I'm not asking you to fight for us. It's your choice only."

"What you don't understand"—Jax pounded his fist to his chest—"is that it's always been my fight. You asked me, and I agreed. I swore never to use my powers like that again. When the guilt weighed too heavily on me, I ended up joining them freely. But then I had to use them again to save my friends, and I realized I can't run from my gifts and what was done to me. This is my fight, today, tomorrow, and the next day, and I will only ever fight for what I believe, and I choose to be here." He slammed his fist onto the table.

Both Tink and Michael stared at Jax's red flaming hand, and when he lifted it, a burned knuckle pattern remained on the table.

Dr. Barrie didn't flinch, didn't back down, but in a calm voice, stated, "From what I hear, there are a lot of young misguided youths that are under Neverland's control. Do what you can, but show mercy."

"And there are a lot of misguided Red Skulls," Jax countered.

"You can't right the past, but we can always change our future."

"Whatever, old man," Jax called out and stormed up the stairs to the deck.

John came out of the bedroom; his normally slicked-back hair was stylistically messed up. He wore a gray slim jacket over his own white T-shirt. His jeans were cuffed over white boat shoes, and on his wrist was a Rolex.

"Nice," Tink whistled. "You look young, reckless, and loaded."

John pulled his pockets inside out. "But I don't. Broke, unless they take personal checks."

Dr. Barrie went into the back room and came back with a briefcase. "Here you go."

"What is it?" John asked.

"The buy-in," Dr. Barrie said. "I keep money in a hidden safe, enough to start over again if we have to."

"Is there more?" Tootles piped up and teleported into the back bedroom. Seconds later, he was back with the group, and then he teleported back in search of the hidden safe.

"That will keep him busy for a while," Tink chuckled.

"What about the rest of us?" Slightly asked. "They're going to search the ship, right? Then how do we get off?"

"I have a hidden room, though it will be a tight fit for most of you. Dr. Mee will be John's personal chef. I will be the valet, and after John is safe inside Neverland, Tootles can teleport you inside."

"I can't teleport where I haven't been or seen," Tootles spoke up nervously. "I can get stuck in a wall."

"You will be able to see," Tink reassured him. She pulled out a small button camera and attached it to John's glasses. "What John sees."

The computer screen displayed Tink's zoomed-in face as she adjusted the camera.

"Yes! I can do that!" Tootles exclaimed.

Jax came running down the stairs. "I can see the island and they're trying to radio us. Michael, were there any instructions about docking the boat?"

He slapped his forehead. "Yeah, I forgot."

"Isabelle, in the closet in the stateroom, there's a trap door. Get everyone down below. John, you come with me. We will radio the island with Michael's help. Dr. Mee, start cooking."

Dr. Mee wrung her hands nervously and tucked her hair behind her ear. "Did you see what's in the fridge? It's empty. All we have are rations. There isn't any fresh food to cook. What do you want me to do? Boil water?"

"Yeah, and put on an apron," he chuckled. "Well, guys. We're here. Not under the best circumstances, but let's get our boys back." He gave them a salute, and with a nod, Tink pulled Tootles toward the stateroom, her face scrunched up with emotion as she tried to keep the tears from flowing.

Jax was about to follow them when Dr. Barrie grabbed his arm and spoke softly. "Jax, I did my best to protect them. It's up to you. It's always been you. You and Peter have done more for them than I ever could. I'm proud of you."

His speech nearly undid Jax, his stony exterior crumbling, and he reached for the older man, giving him a long, hard hug.

"I will protect them," Jax promised.

"I know you will. Do a better job than me, okay?"

Tears filled Jax's eyes. He didn't know it before this moment, but he had longed for a father figure so much and didn't realize how much he'd missed Dr. Barrie until now.

-35-

THE SCREEN HAD flickered on again and Hook was staring at them with an unpleasant grin. "It's time."

"We're not doing it." Peter approached the screen and the room full of lost boys and girls gathered behind him. He looked over his shoulder and was pleased to see their faces grim, full of distrust. Tense and ready for battle. "You can't make us play your sick and twisted game, Hook."

"I thought you would say that, which is why I have made it more interesting. Do you see this?" The screen flickered and the broadcast changed to a live feed from inside the hollow dome. A lone Red Skull was tying up someone to a light pole outside of the city's main square. When the Red Skull moved away, he could see her clearly.

"Wendy!" Peter rushed forward, but Onyx held him back.

"Yes, I happened to have found her outside of the dome. Now, how did she get on the island, Peter? Was it you? Did you bring the cavalry? Don't worry, I have all incoming ships being searched as we speak. We will find the others, and we will kill them on the spot. Or I may save them to be next week's motivation to fight."

"Let her go!" Peter demanded.

"Play, Peter. Play the game and I might just do that. Go out into the world we created for you. Fight the monsters you've been fighting your whole life. Give us a good show. They paid good money to watch," Hook sneered. "You like games, remember?"

"I like games, but I hardly follow rules." Peter's arms crossed over his chest and he gave a wry, mocking smile in return.

Hook's brows furrowed. "Don't worry, in three minutes I'm going to release a toxic gas into this chamber. The only way to escape is to go up to the Hollow Dome. Let's see how you'll do then."

The screen went black except for a red digital countdown clock ticking down from three minutes.

"Where are the lifts?" Nibs asked as he tentatively made his way to what he assumed to be the lifts.

"That's them." Candace pointed to the three daises on the floor with handrails.

"And where do they go?" Craft asked. He woke up a few minutes after his shock, with a nice burn on his hand, but still raring to go.

"The Hollow Dome." Candace wheeled her chair over to the group, her eyes scanning the clock worriedly.

"Well, let's do it," Jade said. "Let's stop wasting time waiting for that maniac to come back. Let's go."

"The helmets," Candace said, pointing to the helmets above the lockers. "They will help you. Trust me."

"Nibs," Peter ordered, pointing. "Helmets . . . Go!"

In the blink of an eye, Nibs had made it across the room, grabbed the black and gray helmets, and deposited them in four of the girls' hands.

"Whoa," Jade said in surprise.

Nibs winked at her, and in seconds had distributed another round of helmets.

"It's not that simple," Candace warned. "There's morphlings up there."

Onyx snorted and flexed his muscles. "We can handle morphlings."

"We don't have our light bracers." Craft held up his bare arm. "And what about the morphling venom?"

"We'll just have to fight our way out." Onyx held up his fist. "We can do that."

The others nodded and headed over to the lifts. Peter and Curly were the last to step on the dais.

"Are you sure about this?" Curly asked.

Peter shook his head. "No, I have a bad feeling about this, but I don't see another way out. If President Helix and Hook want us to play the game, we'll play. But as soon as we see a way out, we bail. With everyone. No one left behind."

"Got it," Curly agreed.

The timer had wound down to two minutes fifteen seconds.

"Remember. Whatever is up there? We will handle it together!" Peter called out as the group tried to cram on the three different lifts.

There were a lot of scared faces mixed in with the determined ones. There wasn't another way out, and with the room charged to electrocute everyone if they touched the door and a poisonous gas about to be released in the room they were in, he didn't see a way to extradite them except through the lifts, but he couldn't find a way to operate them.

"Where are the controls?" Peter asked and glanced up to find Candace had wheeled herself over to the lift controls by the far wall.

"Candace," Peter called. "Get over here. Quickly."

"Can't." She shook her head sadly. "Someone has to stay and manually operate the lifts. They won't work unless someone is holding the buttons down."

"No, you can't stay. If you do, you'll be poisoned," Peter tried to reason with her.

A look of resignation crossed her face. "I have to stay. It's all part of Hook's sick game. He made it to operate this way. I admit, I was supposed to wake you all, then get out of the room before it locked everyone in. I'm not even supposed to be here," she cried from her chair. "That was my mistake, and my salvation in one. But I doubt Hook will even know I'm gone." She wiped at the tears in her eyes. "I'm sorry, Peter, for everything I did to you. Even when I was helping you, I hindered your progress—withheld certain memories, tried to manipulate you into a tool for Neverland. It doesn't matter what anyone says, I'm not a good person. I'm still a Red Skull." She sniffed and wiped her nose on her sleeve.

"Candace, you are a good person. Come with us. We will find a way." He flew from the dais and looked at the control pad. There were three different touchpad controls, labeled Lift One through Lift Three. She was right—there wasn't a way to weigh them down.

"What if Hook was lying about the gas?" Curly called out and motioned for Candace to come to them. "What if he was lying? He does that a lot."

The clock hit zero, and from the pipes above, gas began to pour into the room. Peter covered his mouth as the gas burned his eyes, and the lost boys began to cough. Screams of terror came from the lifts.

"Go," Candace whispered, her eyes clear and glistening with tears. "Let me do this. Let me try to save you. I couldn't save all of them"—she nodded to the still forms of the ones who didn't wake from the pods laid out next to each other—"But let me try and save you." She held the three buttons down and they began to lift into the air.

"I can't let you do this." Peter grabbed her arm, then tried to lift her from the wheelchair. When her hands left the buttons, the lifts ground to a halt and he could hear the cries of fear from the others.

"Don't you dare!" she hissed. "Leave me." Candace began to cough and tried to wave him away. "I'm not worth risking the lives of the others for. I told you, I'm not your friend. Go!" She pushed him roughly, then hit the three buttons again, and the lifts moved upward.

Peter was torn, his heart hurting. He looked at the still forms of his two lost boys and the girls, and into the determined eyes of Candace, then back up to a frantically waving Onyx and Curly.

He leaned down and gave her a hug. "Thank you, and yes, you are my friend."

He felt her shoulders shake from emotion as she leaned her head into him in affirmation. She didn't dare release the buttons.

Peter let go and flew up to the lifts, but when they were nearly to the top, they ground to a halt again. Their lungs burned and most of them were using their uniforms to protect their noses and mouths, while some had already collapsed to their knees.

Why had the lift stopped?

Candace had collapsed on the console, her head wobbling from side to side.

"Candace!" Peter cried. "Candace, wake up!"

She stirred, her coughing becoming worse, and she weakly reached up to continue holding the buttons. The lifts shuddered upward again, and just when they thought they would crash into the ceiling, it slid open and they were through.

Peter couldn't pull his eyes away from Candace as the moving floor began to close around the lift. Once they were through, she released the buttons. Peter watched in horror as she fell out of her wheelchair to the floor. Seconds later, the floor had closed beneath them, hiding Candace from view and sealing them inside the Hollow Dome.

"Everyone all right?" Peter called out, running to the different lifts, checking to see that no one had any permanent damage from the poisonous gas.

"Yeah," Nibs coughed. "My chest hurts, but we'll survive."

"Onyx, Curly, Craft." He sounded off their names, waiting for their responses.

"We're good," Onyx answered, his arms wrapped around a younger teen girl named Piper who had collapsed on the ground. "I'm not sure about her though. I wish Slightly was here."

Peter mumbled his agreement, but was trying to focus on the immediate danger. He turned to scan the area, searching the shadows where the morphlings could hide, and struggled to get his bearings in the Hollow Dome. Wendy was in here. He had to get to Wendy.

Peter rushed across the street and looked into a dummy coffee shop. "Onyx, take the injured to the coffee shop. Secure the entrance. I'm going to find Wendy."

He didn't wait but immediately flew into the air, searching for the main square and the light pole. But in a city that looked to stretch a few miles, it could take a bit.

It amazed him, how believable and detailed the city was, and through the visor on the helmet it took on an amber hue.

"Identify," an automated voice spoke in his ear. Peter lost altitude as the voice startled him.

"Identify," the voice came again.

"Peter," he said aloud, unsure of what was going on or how to identify himself.

"Identity confirmed. Welcome, Peter, to Warfare Infinity."

His visor lit up, displaying a band of text along the top, but this time he didn't stray off course He quickly read the instructions and discerned it was much like a video game screen, displaying health stats and—what he found most impressive—a map icon. And when he focused on it with his eyes, a gold map of the city appeared across the whole visor.

"Sweet," he murmured as he searched for the main square. Also appearing on the map as little gold triangles was what he assumed to be the lost boys and girls, and they were gathered in one large group by the café.

After studying the map, Peter corrected his course and flew to the main square, where he believed she was held.

"Wendy!" he yelled as he came around the corner and slowed. Landing on the ground, he ran to a light post, but there was no Wendy. Where was she? Did Hook lie? He was sure it was this light post. "Wendy!" he called out again, but there was no reply. He surveyed the ground around the post, searching for clues, and picked up a frayed rope covered in fresh blood.

She had been here, and was in trouble.

"Wendy!" he screamed, his heart breaking as he realized he was too late.

A morphling answered his call and rushed at him from out of the post office.

Was this the morphling that hurt Wendy?

Fueled by rage at the loss of Wendy, his lost boys, and Candace, Peter roared in challenge and met the morphling head-on.

-36-

WENDY GRIMACED AT her predicament. Tied up and left as morphling bait. This was not how she thought her trip back to Neverland to save the boys would go.

Her old friend Lily was taking great pleasure in lashing her hands behind her back around a light post until they hurt and were going numb. She made a valiant attempt to find compassion for the girl who had been left on the island when the others had escaped. Wendy knew that if she hadn't snuck out of her room that night to chase a shadow, she could very well be on the other side of this coin. It could be Wendy that had ended up brainwashed and in servitude to Neverland.

"You know, I don't hold it against you," Wendy said, then winced as Lily pulled to tighten the rope.

"Save the pretty words for your gravestone," Lily sneered. "Oh wait, you won't get one."

"You don't have to do this," Wendy tried again. "You can be your own person. Your future doesn't have to end with Neverland."

Lily's tiger-shaped irises stared at Wendy unblinkingly. Her hands shifted into long claws, and she rubbed one under Wendy's chin, digging in just until it hurt. "You're right. My future doesn't end here, but yours does."

An electronic tone sounded within the city, and Lily's face lit up with glee. "It's about to start. You're not going to want to miss this . . . Well, that is if you live that long." She scoured the ground for a rock, and after testing its weight, she tossed it at the bulb above Wendy's head, breaking it. Glass rained down on Wendy and so did darkness.

"Just making you more appetizing for the morphlings." Lily laughed and tossed the rock away. "Now I'm off to hunt down your boyfriend and the others." At Wendy's look of confusion, Lily laughed with glee. "What, you hadn't heard? Oh, we got what we needed from him—his DNA. And he keeps turning into more of a liability than an asset to our program." She sighed dramatically. "We thought you could see the future. If you could, then you would have seen this outcome. But, Wendy, you didn't see this, did you?" Lily grabbed her chin and gestured to the Hollow Dome. "Could you ever have seen this place?"

Wendy stayed strong, using all of her control to not wince at the pain, and gathered her courage and will, keeping her face immobile as she tried to think of a plan. But all of her plans involved controlling the shadows, and that would bring the morphlings down on her like syrup on hotcakes.

"Hook agrees with me—you just aren't worth the time and effort anymore. Wendy, you aren't worth it."

"You underestimate me, Lily," Wendy breathed out.

"Prove it," Lily challenged, holding her hands wide and backing away. "Show me what you got. Oh, that's right. You can't." She winked at her. "I'd love to stay and watch you get eaten, but I need to lead my team to victory." Lily blew Wendy a kiss and waved goodbye before putting on a black helmet and running off down the road.

Wendy thumped her head against the post, and then looked up at the broken bulb in defeat. There was still glass in her hair, so she shook her head and heard a chunk fall to the pavement. That was it. Wriggling her body down to the ground, Wendy was able to sit on the ground and pick up a piece of the glass.

"Ouch." It nicked her, but she didn't have time to worry. Pinching the piece of glass between her fingers, she began to hack and saw the rope, unfortunately also hacking at her hands. Warm blood trickled down her palms, coating her fingers, making the glass difficult to grip.

"Come on," she gritted between clenched teeth, her focus straight ahead at the dark alley across from her and the movement in the shadows.

She sucked in her breath as she painfully sliced her hand again. This wasn't working. She was cutting herself more than the rope. Another warning tone blared over the speakers, drawing her attention up to the top of the dome, where a countdown timer was displayed across the ceiling scrim. Countdown to what? Whatever it was, she'd only have to wait one more minute for it.

A loud thud in the alley startled Wendy into momentary stillness. Something was definitely lurking in the dark, and she was positive it was a morphling. With renewed vigor, Wendy hacked at the rope—and sadly her wrists too—until her hands came free. Rising to her feet, she saw stars and had to grab the post for balance. She had lost a lot of blood and needed to stop the bleeding.

Cupping her hands to her chest, she took off running in the opposite direction of the alley, her senses on high alert.

The tone sounded again, this time a higher ear-piercing pitch, nearly knocking Wendy off her feet with no time to recover before a chorus of shrieks echoed through the dome as every morphling simultaneously screamed in pain. There had to be hundreds of them crying out, filling the dome with deafening screeches. Wendy had to cover her ears, trembling, her senses overwhelmed.

The tone, whatever it was, had riled up the morphlings. The shadows themselves look like they were moving, vibrating, coming alive.

Shaking from fear, she pressed her back against the wall of a bodega and tried to gauge the location of the closest morphling. With a bloodied hand, she reached for the doorknob, trying to grip it, and slipping.

A shrill cry came again as a bulky morphling stalked down the street, its pronounced wolf head swinging side to side, shaking its head in pain, as if still reeling from the effects of the tone that had finally stopped.

Wendy looked up at the clock as it had reached zero, and Wendy didn't want to be on the street for whatever came next.

Using two hands, she was able to grip the knob and it turned. Her eyes still watching the street, she slipped into the store and closed the door, locking it behind her. Then she collapsed to her knees and fought off tears She needed to keep it together and find a way out.

She should have waited for Jax, Ditto, and the others. She was so impatient, desperate to get back to Peter, that she might have done more harm than good.

Get yourself together, Wendy, she told herself. You can still help the others.

Scanning the room, she found it was sparsely stocked. But the front window had T-shirts on display, and that was all she needed to bandage her hands.

A dark silhouette moved toward her in the window, and Wendy flailed instinctively to fight off the morphling, knocking over a mannequin, to reveal one of the shadows floating behind it.

Wendy smiled sheepishly.

The shadow motioned for her to follow it to the back room and she did. She was becoming better at identifying the different shadows and knew this was a female.

The shadow reached out to touch her hand and Wendy let her memories speak to her. Unlike the other shadows who showed her scattered memories because they were confused and didn't understand what was going on, this shadow was calm and able to communicate with her in clear images. Wendy saw the pods, recognized Peter in one of them. Then Jax in his Red Skull uniform, laughing and joking with the person whose memories she was seeing. He then was talking quietly to a young woman floating in a pod. Wendy could tell by his posture and the way he spoke and looked at her that he was in love.

This is Alice, Wendy realized.

The shadow showed the Hollow Dome being constructed, and Wendy was in awe of the whole inner workings of the city within the island, and the rooms underneath. There was a maze under the city, where the morphlings lived in the darkness and traveled up through the sewers.

There were a series of images depicting Dusters, troops putting on uniforms, training to fight with virtual equipment, then fighting each other. She saw an office for Wonderland Games. And the more the shadow shared, the more she understood.

"It's a game."

The images stopped and the shadow guided her over to a mirror and saw her own reflection, her way of telling Wendy who she was. A young woman with sad eyes hidden behind colorful glasses. Her legs were thin from disuse, but her arms were strong as they wheeled her around in her wheelchair. Wendy saw the woman's fingers fly across the keyboard of her computer and understood she was involved with everything.

"You're with Neverland," Wendy said in surprise. "You're one of them." Wendy pulled her hand away and didn't want anything to do with the shadow. This was the enemy.

The shadow reached for her again and Wendy backed away. "No, I don't trust you. You did this to us."

The shadow wasn't going to take no for an answer and dove for Wendy, inserting herself right into Wendy's body, and she jerked as the shadow relayed her final piece of information.

The morphlings.

Everything there was to know about them, the shadow gave her, filling up her mind, downloading the information about the shadows, morphlings, and the plane they came from. It was exhilarating and terrifying at the same time.

The images came to a sudden halt and the shadow left Wendy's body and hovered a few feet away. Wendy grabbed on to the counter to steady herself. The information she gave her was the key to stopping Neverland.

Wendy now knew how to stop the morphlings.

She hoped.

"Thank you, Candace," Wendy said breathlessly after having learned her name from the memories. "I'm not sure why you want to help, but I am grateful."

The shadow bobbed her head.

"I can also see that you're free," Wendy added, pointing to her legs that were no longer bound by a wheelchair. "But you can't stay here. The morphlings eat the shadows. They will hunt your soul. Please, go. Stay safe."

The shadow refused to leave, sticking close to her. Wendy had no choice but to let her follow her.

Infused with knowledge of the layout of Hollow Dome and the power it gave her, Wendy walked confidently to the back of the store and opened up a closet door, then grinned when she saw the medkit inside, with a uniform and helmet.

Candace had showed her that Hollow Dome mirrored Warfare 8's Hollow City, but in real time, with real players. Wendy had watched her brother John play the game enough to know that meant that each store, once searched, held goods for the player who was lucky enough to stumble upon it.

Opening the medkit revealed bandages, disinfectant, and the Hail Mary of medicine—a gold vial filled with the antidote to morphling venom. Quickly, she bandaged her hands, changed into the suit, and took the injector gun and vial and pocketed them in the side pouch on her hip. She was about to leave when Candace gestured to the helmet.

"No, not really my thing," Wendy said. But the shadow was adamant.

"Fine." She grabbed the helmet, and continued to tear the back room apart looking for any other loot, spoils, and some kind of weapon. Giving up on finding a weapon, she placed the helmet on her head. The visor lit up across the top, but she ignored the words and searched the last room, to no avail.

This store had been looted. There wasn't anything left to take, so she'd have to brave the streets and search another structure. But she had to get past the morphlings.

She suspected it would not be easy, and unlike anything she'd faced before. The morphlings here on Neverland were corporeal forms, more solid than light and shade when they had attacked at her school or town. Back then, they had been farther from their source, stretched on their tether, and the farther they got, the more ethereal and weaker they became. But now they were close to their source, and they were strong. Which is why Wendy needed a gun. She didn't think she'd have time to try and fry a morphling with construction lamps again. This was like fighting a whole new enemy.

The word *SOLD* appeared across her visor, and Wendy frowned but otherwise ignored the blinking text— until a map pulled down over her eyes, forcing her attention, first to the blinking light over what appeared to be this building, apparently marking her location. Then she became excited, as a little icon of a gun lit up over the sporting good store right next door.

"Well, that's handy."

Wendy tiptoed to the door and scanned the streets for movement. It was empty. Giving herself a mental countdown, she opened the door and rushed to the next shop over. Unfortunately, the sporting good store was locked.

Grabbing a decorated pot, Wendy smashed through the decaled glass window and stepped through into the dim interior, heading passed the counter into the back room. Boxes. The room was filled with hundreds of boxes.

"You've got to be kidding me," she groaned, kicking them over, knocking them aside, until she felt one that was weighted. Looking inside, she found her first weapon. A bat.

If John could see her now, no doubt he'd advise her to level up her weapon ASAP. She would have to keep searching. The gun icon was still blinking, so she hadn't found her target yet.

-37-

JOHN'S HANDS WERE sweating as the Red Skulls searched the motor yacht. He'd been escorted at gunpoint to the end of the dock as they thoroughly searched the ship. They must not have found Dr. Mee or Dr. Barrie particularly threatening, because when the Red Skulls were done, the two of them were ordered back onto the yacht with instructions to take her back out to sea and stay within two miles of the island. If they came any closer, they would be shot down.

Beads of cold perspiration pooled down his neck and he carefully wiped them away and looked at his Rolex in pretend irritation. "I'm going to be late," he huffed.

"Hold your horses," the Red Skull growled. "What's your name again?"

John took a deep breath and spelled out the code name and handle he had taken from the email—*Dealbr8kr42.*

The Red Skull found his name and checked it off the list. "You're the last one. Trying to make an entrance, are you?"

"Trying to get fired, are you?" John snapped back. "Nothing irritates me more than waiting."

The Red Skull glared at him and motioned for him to be escorted to the War Room.

"Got here any later, and you wouldn't have been able to get in," the Red Skull chastised as they drove into an underground garage that was half submerged in water. They parked the truck and John hopped out. Water sloshed in his shoes, but he ran up to an area that wasn't submerged in water and watched as the door was sealed behind him.

John was careful to turn his head slowly side to side, recording as much of the layout as he could, hopefully giving Tootles enough information for him to teleport inside. The problem was that it was dark and hard to see once the door was closed. Two Red Skulls escorted John away from the tunnels, where they passed parked surplus trucks and a freight elevator.

Together they walked up a few flight of stairs, and through an armed door, that had to be deactivated, into an office building. From there he was taken into a smaller elevator, where the Red Skull punched in a code using the five floor buttons. The doors closed and they went up to the top floor of a five-story building. When the doors opened, he was shoved out into a square room with windows on all sides filled with men of all ages.

John swallowed nervously but kept his head held high as he studied the other investors. Luckily, he wasn't overdressed or underdressed. Some of the big-name gamers—two he even recognized—came in wearing T-shirts and jeans.

"The buy-in," a gravelly voice greeted him. John turned and saw Hook. He had heard much about him, had seen him on the computer screen, but had never met the man face-to-face.

"Uh, here." John held up the briefcase and watched as Hook laid it on a table and snapped it open, turning the case to show a gray-haired man reclining in a chair.

"Good, good." The man rose from the chair, came over and shook his hand. "I'm President Helix. Welcome to the unveiling of Warfare Infinity." He gestured to the group to come before a large TV screen.

"In ten minutes, you will be seeing the first ever live-action Warfare Infinity. You know my games create billions in revenue. Warfare has been the hottest game series for the last ten years, and I've always, always been the first to monopolize when the time is right. Well, gentlemen and gamers, I bring you the first ever live battle royale."

Helix pointed to a screen, where a video began playing, describing the Hollow Dome, the real version of the game that is played online. "We matched it building for building, created new levels and traps, and of course as the gamer, you have the option of participating. Select your real-life avatar."

A selection of teenage avatars like the ones shown online appeared on the screen. John had seen them already, the very real replicas of Peter and the others.

"Each of them have already been battle tested and have a special ability. Additional abilities or upgrades can be purchased for a fee, and we will take them out of the game and adjust them accordingly to what you purchase. But remember, like any game, there's a slight chance that your avatar won't adapt to a new ability."

Grumblings came from the investors, and Helix grinned. "Those are the chances you take."

"So why video games? You've got the troops. Why not mercenaries for hire?" Diego asked.

"War and politics are messy and unpredictable. Soldiers for hire are only profitable during wars in countries of unrest. In video games, there's profit to be made twenty-four hours a day, every day of the year, all over the world. It's guaranteed money", Helix glanced over to Hook, and rubbed his hands together. "Are they ready?"

Hook looked at his watch and down at his tablet. He frowned at what he saw on the screen. "I will go motivate them."

Hook stepped out of the room and John was about to follow him when Helix turned and looked at him. John froze in his tracks.

"Now, where were we? Oh yes, you can play as one of the new Dusters, or play as the bad guys and select a shade, then unleash one on your opponents," Helix said, his voice rising in excitement.

John's head snapped up as an index of morphlings scrolled across the screen, all different animal-like shapes. There were hundreds. His hands began to sweat again, and he rubbed them on his pants.

"If your shade is killed, no worries, regenerate a new one for a fee."

A celebrity gamer, with gold chains and his hat on backwards, who John recognized as Killz4realz, or Killz for short, spoke up, "So we don't actually control these avatars? Is that what I'm hearing? That sounds lame."

Helix shook his head. "No, you don't need to. They have a life of their own, or should I say, your own. You pay for them. They're yours. You become their owner. Think of it like this—I'm giving you the chance to be an owner of an NFL player of video games. Your avatar needs medicine. Well, you can buy it and an icon will appear in their visor and lead them to a medkit hidden in the world. If they need a real-life doctor, well, that's going to cost you too. We have staff on hand for this sort of thing. You see what the avatars see through their visors and through their suit cameras. If you want to upgrade their weapons, you purchase the upgrade and their visor will lead them to where it is hidden in the world map."

"And what's in it for us? We're the ones spending the money and what do we get out of it?"

"Royalties, stock options, book deals—think of what your player could make you. But once the timer clock starts, the game never ends. It is perfect for the twenty-four-hour gamer. The stakes get more interesting because these avatars are real humans, with their own choices, and you never know what they will do. They eat, breath, sleep, and you can choose to lead them to where there's food and help, or ignore your player and they may perish while you take a nap or run to the restroom."

Helix handed out a computer tablet to an investor and touched a button on the screen. "Each of them is wearing a helmet, which allows you to see in first person what they are seeing.

"But what if my avatar chucks his helmet?" Killz asked.

Helix grinned smugly. "Click here"—he tapped the map on the tablet—"and you can switch to one of Hollow Dome's many cameras."

"I want one of those," one of the older men spoke up, and Helix obliged, handing out the tablets. Soon every single person had one and was scrolling through their options and playing with the Hollow's cameras.

"This is real?" Killz asked.

"Look out the window below," Helix answered. "You are in the Hollow Dome as we speak, in a fully secured building, where you can watch the action below." The group moved to the window, from where they had a full view of the city.

John recognized it from the Warfare 8 game he played online. It was a perfect replica, and what's more, John knew this game, knew how to play it, except for the morphlings. This was a new feature, both brilliant and terrifying.

John adjusted his glasses and tried to take in the surrounding city. He inwardly cussed and backed away from the glass. What if Tootles couldn't teleport into the garage and used the city he'd just glanced at as a collection point. He would be teleporting Jax and the others right into the middle of the war game.

John moved farther and farther away until he was in a corner sitting and staring at the wall, his hands over his glasses. What should he do? He didn't have a way to communicate with the others on the yacht.

"Ah, they've arrived." Helix pointed to the street, and the group moved to the windows to look. John looked on his tablet and clicked the Wonderland Games building, and the camera zoomed in, allowing him to observe the inside of the dome remotely. The floor slowly opened, and through the wide gap, three lifts rose up from below, carrying at least thirty players all dressed in black, who John knew to be Red Skulls. Immediately, they scattered, each running in pairs or teams down different roads. A few went off by themselves.

Helix clapped his hands together and pointed to the men in the room. "Which one of you will lose to the other first? I've taken your buy-in and loaded the money as in-game credits on your tablet. If that's not enough, link up your credit cards."

Some, already feeling the pressure, pulled out their wallets and began to load their credit cards, which of course he didn't have.

Helix was feeding a gambling and video game addiction in one. Killz began scrolling furiously through the screen. Others had picked up their tablets and had begun the selection.

"This, my friends, is the experience you will only get from us. That's where the risk is and the biggest gamble. Do you yourself dare to eat, sleep, or nap? What will happen if you leave for one second?"

John's heart thudded in his chest at the excitement and adrenaline that was coursing through him. His gamer's competitiveness was kicking in—he understood the opportunity he was being presented. It was empowering and pure genius, and he began to scroll through the avatars a little closer. Intuitively, he began to weed through ones that he didn't like, their powers not conducive to taking out morphlings, but then he saw that they were cheaper. The Dusters were each tagged with a price according to their strengths and abilities.

"Sixty thousand for a guy with super speed?" one investor whined.

"If you don't want him, Diego, I will buy him," Killz taunted. "Done, Wu Zan is mine. Take that. You'll never catch me now. You think you got me beat online, well, let's see who has deeper pockets."

"Oh yeah, well, I just got one named Pilot. We will see whose super speed is more super," Diego teased. Diego and Killz began to taunt each other mercilessly.

An acidic fire burned deep in John's stomach as he realized how sick and twisted the video gaming world was becoming and how easily he could be swept up in it if he had money. Wait, he did.

John held the tablet in his hand and scrolled through the avatars quickly, searching for the lost boys. Maybe he didn't have to buy them—maybe he could use his credits to help them.

His brows furrowed as he searched but couldn't find the one he was looking for. Peter. He scrolled and scrolled. And then he saw Peter's avatar, with the word sold on it.

John sighed. He was too late. Someone else had grabbed him up. Under Peter's avatar was the gamer's name spinning in a circle. Helix.

He glanced up at President Helix and studied the older man. It looked like he had a horse in this race, having known ahead of time who to bet on. Buy the guy that can regenerate. John grumbled at the unfairness and continued to search for a player.

"Attention everyone," Helix announced excitedly. "The last group has arrived in the Hollow Dome. Let's get started, shall we?" Helix pushed a button on his tablet and a loud muffled tone rang out through the city. The investors could hear the shriek of the morphlings down below.

"That should wake them up. So, who's ready to play?" Helix asked.

John continued to search through the players, more or less scoping out the competition. Neverland had done well creating a wide range of soldiers. Speed, shapeshifting, strength, agility, but none were as unique and strong as Peter and the lost boys. He didn't see anyone with abilities like Jax, Ditto, or Tootles, and a confident smile crossed his lips. Then he saw someone he recognized.

"Brittney?" John muttered and couldn't believe the missing girl from his high school was here and alive. He pulled up her stats and quickly read over them and was surprised at her results.

"See anything you like?" Helix had come over and leaned on his chair, looking at his screen. "Oh, you like this one, do you?" he asked, pointing out Brittney.

"Oh, I don't know. It's hard to choose." John turned the tablet away and began ramble on like an expert gamer. "Do I choose agility over strength and rely on upgrades, or do I invest now and buy an upper-tier player and hope that over the long run they make me back money with endorsements and winning the battle royales and mini competitions?" John had read enough on the website to understand that there would be mini games held throughout the seasons.

Helix arched a brow, clearly impressed with his use of gaming lingo.

"Wow, you really have given this a lot of thought." Helix gave John's arm a squeeze. "But don't take too long deciding. The others have already snatched up the good ones."

"I know, but I don't want to be a reckless buyer. I like to check under the hood. I may watch them in action for a bit before I invest."

"Suit yourself, but don't forget about upgrades." He winked knowingly.

"Yes," John laughed uncomfortably and waited for Helix to leave him before he went back to the screen.

What to do?

What looked like a glitch on the screen became real when a blank avatar popped up on the roster. John tapped on the avatar and watched as it slowly began to download and appear on the screen. A new player? There were zero stats listed. He clicked on the suit cam and saw that whoever the newcomer was in the Hollow Dome was putting on a suit. They walked past a mirror and John saw the familiar blonde head of his sister, right before she put on the helmet visor.

As soon as she did, the visor scanned her and the rest of her avatar appeared on the screen, without a name and with a base price of thirty thousand.

Thank goodness she was alive, but for crying out loud, she was in the Hollow Dome!

"Oh crud, Wendy," John muttered. "Forgive me." He clicked buy on Wendy and immediately she was his. He didn't know what else to do except try and help her with the other credits he had. The only good thing going is that he knew he couldn't kill her. Well, not really. He hoped.

But first things first. He needed to get her armed. He opened the map and noticed the closest weapons were in the sporting goods store one building over. John felt a thrill of excitement as he pulled down the map and clicked on the icon of the weapon. Praying, hoping his sister would see it.

He fist-pumped the air when he watched her break into the building next door.

She had seen the weapon icon, and he groaned the same time she did when she stumbled into a room full of boxes.

"Start breaking them down," he encouraged, and Wendy began to knock them out of the way, secretly cheering her on and laughing out loud when she found a bat.

"No, keep going," he murmured. Looking up, he was dismayed to see just as many other investors and gamers equally engrossed, managing their own avatars. John realized just how dangerous a game he was playing.

-38-

"GOT ANYTHING?" Jax asked anxiously as he paced back and forth in the galley.

They were on the yacht a few miles from shore along with the other boats and investors' yachts, a situation that had ramped up their anxiety levels tenfold. Initially, they'd thought fate was on their side, when the Red Skulls searched their yacht and managed to overlook the hidden compartment. But they hadn't counted on Neverland keeping them this far from shore. So now, as they waited nervously for John to find a spot for Tootles to teleport them into Neverland, Jax worried it may very well be too far away.

Tink had the computer out and was watching John's hidden camera with Tootles. She pointed to the underground area and he shook his head. It was too dark.

Tink's censor band went off, and she cupped her hand over her mouth and tried to focus on other locations to teleport, clicking, freezing, and dragging the camera images into a larger focus for Tootles to study.

"No, nothing that has a large enough view. We want to get inside the building, not end up on the beach, and so far, we have an elevator," Tink mumbled. A few minutes later, she yelled, "Yes!"

Slightly, Ditto, and Michael had gathered together and Tink pointed to what appeared to be a full-fledged city inside Neverland.

"Is that inside the island?" Ditto asked.

"Looks like it," Tink answered. "That looks like the best place to teleport too, but now we have a problem." She looked around at everyone and counted heads. "Who's going to go? Tootles took three of us last time the same distance and it knocked him out. There's no way he can get us all there. Maybe he could take four, but that's pushing it."

Jax had forgotten about that. He looked at Tink's stubborn face and knew there was an argument waiting to happen. Dr. Mee, Dr. Barrie, Slightly, Ditto, Tink, Michael, and him included made seven. Over half of them would have to stay back.

"Okay, Tootles will take me, Ditto, and Slightly," Jax announced.

"No way," Tink argued. "I want to go. John is there and I won't leave him. He is going to get into all sorts of trouble if I'm not there."

"No, Tink," Jax ordered. "You will stay here with your father. You just got each other back, don't waste it." Tink opened her mouth but promptly closed it.

"I'm going." Michael got up and stood next to Tootles. "Someone needs to take down Neverland's security system and I can do that." He pointed to his head. "But I need to be closer. I can't do it from here."

Jax had to rethink his strategy now. Michael had a point—he would prove to be an asset if they had to crash the system. "Okay, Slightly, Michael, and I. That's final."

A quiet look passed between Ditto and Slightly, and Jax almost missed it. Tootles came over and grabbed hands with Jax and Michael. Slightly pretended to lean forward and reach for Tootles' shoulder, but at the last minute, Ditto replaced him.

In a flash they were inside the city, a few blocks from Wonderland Games. Tootles had teleported them to the spot Tink had targeted with a screen capture. A loud tone echoed through the air and a wailing scream followed. Tootles shrieked and cowered in fear, and Michael pulled the boy into a doorway of a hair salon.

"What was that?" Tootles asked, his breathing ragged, as his head fell back on Michael's shoulder and he passed out.

"Well, at least he got us here," Ditto said and helped prop Tootles up against the door, brushing the boy's hair to the side.

"What are you doing here, Ditto?" Jax growled. "You're injured. I told you to stay put."

"Slightly and I had already discussed this outcome. We knew Tootles couldn't teleport us all, and he agreed that I should be the one to come," Ditto answered.

Jax didn't have time to argue as a morphling crawled out of the sewer and ran across the road to them, its long tentacle arms waving threateningly in the air.

Maintaining eye contact with Ditto, Jax raised one arm and blasted the morphling with a fireball into air, across the street and through a building, where it decimated into a pile of ash.

"Now is not the time to test my patience, Ditto," Jax growled out.

Ditto's mouth fell open and he did a double take between the ash and Jax's hand still engulfed in flames. "Yes, sir, I mean no, I . . . just want to make up for my stupidity in the woods."

"This is war, not the time to make amends. You want to prove to me you're capable of fighting? Protect Tootles," Jax snapped. He needed to find the others.

"But I know this place," Ditto insisted. "It's just like Hollow City in the games, I'm almost sure of it. And Slightly and I agreed, if this is anything like the game, I'm your best chance at survival." He jogged into the street and looked down the road. "Like down Woodland Avenue is a rest station." He turned and pointed the other way. "Two blocks over is the Workman's Guns and Ammo shop." He grinned cheekily at Jax. "Now who's mad I came?"

Jax shook his head. "Well, get to it. Take care of Tootles and Michael. I will meet you over there in a bit."

Ditto split into two. One picked up Tootles and headed to the nearest bench, Michael following behind him; the other gave Jax a salute and headed toward the gun shop. Jax watched them go, his eyes taking in the Clip N Go Salon.

He hadn't said anything to the others when he'd watched John interact with the other investors. He had recognized Helix and Hook and didn't want to alarm them. He knew they were a few blocks away, laughing, eating and playing the game in their impregnable building. Just they wait until he brought the building down around them.

But first, he needed to find the lost boys.

"What is this appearing on my visor?" Craft asked. "I keep getting messages and prompts for ammo and supplies—should I follow it?"

Peter had only received one or two prompts, but he was too busy searching for Wendy to notice what they said, or any of their instructions. "Yes, take two others with you, though. The morphlings keep increasing in numbers, and we'll need more than our powers to take them down."

He was angry that he hadn't found Wendy, and was preparing to lead a group of the boys back to the main square to find her. His boys had been training for years to fight the Red Skulls and the morphlings. These girls, however, had spent the last seven years in stasis and likely had never even thrown a punch. They were hardly prepared to take on well-trained Red Skulls and deadly morphlings. He owed it to them to protect them as well as his own, but having this many of them in one area kept drawing the morphlings to them as well.

"Incoming!" Nibs yelled as a morphling crawled down the side of a three story building and leapt toward Jade.

Onyx jumped in front of her placing himself in the line of fire, his eyes flashing and trapping the morphling in his deadly gaze, turning it into black stone. Glistening as it fell, the morphling cracked and shattered into pieces.

"That was impressive." Jade tucked her hair behind her ear. "But I didn't need your help." A second morphling was coming down following the first. Jade's eyes turned dark, her hands lifted into the air, and vines shot up from the ground, wrapping themselves around the morphling over and over until the dark mass was covered with green.

Jade's lips curled up, her teeth bared, as she controlled the living vines until the morphling couldn't move anymore and was mummified.

"Very nice." Onyx high-fived her.

Curly rolled his eyes. "Stop it, you two."

"Behind you!" Peter called out as a large morphling with horns like a bull ambushed them from a blind alley, steering right down the middle of their group.

They scattered, trying to dive behind cars and buildings as the morphling bowled right into the side of a car, denting the door and setting off the car alarm.

It turned again and seemed to be considering its next target, pausing as it eyed the largest gathering of their group. Then it scraped the ground with its shadowy hoof like a real bull and charged. Surprised by the speed and aggressiveness of the bull, their group splintered. Four more bull morphlings appeared and banded together to charge at a group trying to stand their ground, causing mass chaos and confusion as one of the boys was gored by the morphling horn in the leg and tossed across the street to land on the hood of a car. Whenever anyone stopped to fight, they were immediately run down, making defense impossible, leaving them no choice but to run, until they were all racing, running to distance themselves from the herd of monstrous bulls.

Explosions and flying debris littered the street as they fought for their lives.

"Move!" Peter commanded. "Keep moving!"

Craft returned, leaping over a fire hydrant with a bag of weapons, as he ran alongside them. Not enough, though, and the few guns they had were nothing like the light brace he was used too.

"Curly, report," Peter called, and Curly came running up, sporting a bruise on his cheek, his lip bleeding. "It's bad, Peter. We're cut off from the others. I saw one group run north. Dillinger went south and we're east."

"They drove right through us on purpose," Peter said dismayed. "They thinned the herd, hoping to pick us off one by one instead of attacking all at once."

"Who knew morphlings could be so smart?" Onyx grumbled. "They weren't this sophisticated when we fought them before."

"Everything's different," Peter said.

A close roar took Peter's group by surprise. They spun around, and once again, they faced another morphling bull. It opened its mouth, and an otherworldly scream erupted from between its gaping jaws.

"Onyx, can you take him?"

"Not when he's moving, Peter. His eyes are on the side. I can't maintain eye contact."

"Craft?" Peter called over his shoulder, not needing to look.

Craft held out his arm, and a metal spear appeared out of his hand, crafted from thin air. The boy was a metallurgist and could create any form of metal object.

"On it, Peter." Craft stood boldly in the middle of the street, gripping his spear much like a matador. "Although, I've only ever seen this done in movies," he joked, laughing nervously, clearly uneasy facing down a bull of this size.

The bull bowed and gave Craft a hard stare, then charged. Craft ran to meet it, pulling his arm back to launch the spear, and let it fly, then rolled to the right, and missed being trampled to death by mere inches. The spear jabbed the morphling, but it only enraged the beast further. It grew in size, and additional horns appeared out of his massive head, and from its back end developed two spiked tails.

"What in the world?" Craft said in awe. He thrust his hands out and two more spears appeared—one for each head—but he was tired, and limping.

"Craft, don't," Peter called, changing his mind. Trying to call his boy back.

"Run, Peter, get the girls out of here," Craft yelled, waving his arms to get the bull's attention again. "I'll draw him off."

The bull charged again and Craft launched another spear, but it missed. The second spear, he held tight and was going to drive it into the bull's neck, but Peter knew he would be trampled. He took off flying toward the boy, but a ball of fire beat him.

Screams of pain erupted from the bull's mouth as another fireball followed the first. They burned so hot the flames were white, and then there was nothing but a pile of ash.

"I knew I couldn't leave you alone," Jax said smugly, making his way to Peter, he clapped him on the shoulder.

"What? No. You were just scared I would take out all of the morphlings myself and forget to leave you any," Peter joked.

Jax's smile disappeared as he glanced from face to face. "Where is she? Where's Wendy?"

"I lost her," Peter sighed.

"Again?" Jax turned and looked for her, not seeing her among the small group. "Don't worry, you'll find her. She always comes back to you."

"How did you get here?" Peter asked, and grinned when Ditto came running over to them, carrying a sleeping Tootles, Michael right on his heels.

"Same way you did. Boat." Jax counted, his lips moving, and his frowned deepened. "Where are the others? There should be more of the boys."

"We were separated," Peter answered.

Jax's jaw clenched. "Looks like you really need your second in command."

"I've never said otherwise," Peter admitted.

"Where did you get those cool helmets and uniforms? Can I get one?" Ditto asked, handing Tootles over to

Jake, another of the lost boys. "They're just like my character wears in the video game." He kept running his hand over Onyx's helmet and even flipped up the visor to scope out the make and model.

"It is just like the game. Even the screen controls are the same."

"We're in a game," Peter said. "Although, not one I've played much."

"Don't worry, I have." Ditto grinned.

Screaming caught them off guard, and Peter whipped around—Ash had fallen to the ground and was being dragged by a morphling toward the sewers, its jaws clamped around her leg.

"Help me!" Ash cried out. Curly was the first to her side, reaching out and grasping the morphling's head as he tried to control the beast's thoughts, but nothing came of it. It didn't work. Then Craft slammed the spear into the morphling's skull. It squealed in pain and retreated into the sewer.

"Peter, she's been bitten!" Jade cried as she helped Ash to her feet. Her leg was bleeding profusely and covered in inky black poison. They needed the cure, but where in the city were they going to find the antidote?

"Craft, help carry her. We need to find a hospital."

"No, you need to find a medical storage locker. It will have the antidote. Or at least it does in the game," Ditto corrected, tapping Peter's head. "Use the visor."

Peter, feeling dumb for ignoring it for so long, finally paid attention to his visor. Pulling down the map, he discovered the city drawn out in gold lines and was easily able to find his own location. An envelope pinged in the corner of his visor, and he saw it was a message. A glance with his eyes centered the message on his visor.

Medical storage locker on right.

Peter turned and sought out the corner grocery store that matched the description. It was so close. Craft was right behind him carrying Ash. Everyone else had spread out in a circle to watch his back.

He hurried over to it and with a swift kick, he broke into the grocery, and in the front by the register sat the red and white lockers. How in the world did the game know? He ran to the locker and tried to open it, but it was locked with a digital keypad and sensor box.

"It won't open," he grunted and punched the locker.

"Does anyone have any credits?" Ditto asked. "Check your upper left treasure box."

Silence ensued as the group searched for the correct icon in their visors.

"No," Jade groaned.

"Nope," Craft added with a sigh.

"I do," Onyx breathed out and ran to place his palm on the pad. A buzzer sounded and it opened, revealing two gold vials and injector tube. He loaded the injector and handed it to Jade, who immediately administered the dose to Ash.

"Ditto," Peter laughed. "I will never make fun of you for playing video games again."

"I'll hold you to it," Ditto said, grinning. "But really, this is so cool. We're living and breathing Hollow City in Warfare Infinity." Unable to contain his glee, Ditto kept jumping up and down, and went back out to the street to explore the block. "This is where I took down General Hag in Warfare 8." He pressed his hands to his head and spun with excitement. "This is amazing."

The group came and joined him on the street.

"Ditto," Peter called out repeatedly until he settled down.

"Sorry, Peter." Ditto was shoving his hands into his pockets to try and tame his enthusiasm when his doppelganger appeared pushing a shopping cart full of weapons. Guns, machetes, and knives—he had hauled a full arsenal.

"The cavalry has arrived," both Dittos said at the same time, something that happened whenever they were within hearing range of each other. The Dittos began to hand out the weapons freely.

"Good job." Peter turned to Jax. "We need to find the others, our boys and the kidnapped girls and get them out of here fast. Then we burn this place to the ground for good."

Jax wouldn't meet his gaze. He seemed distracted and asked, "What about you?"

"I'm going to find Wendy and then Hook. This ends today." Movement in the upper corner of his visor gave Peter pause. "Oh no," Peter muttered. "Look at the map. Do you see what I see?"

"What is it?" Curly asked, and Peter waited for him to see the same thing he did. He let out a slow whistle. "We're going to need reinforcements."

Each of them were marked as gold triangles on the map, and a small mass of purple dots surrounded them from all sides. He could only assume that the purple dots were the enemy.

"Prepare for incoming!" Peter yelled as a morphling crashed through the window of a shop and rolled into the street. A scorpion-like tail swung out and stabbed Jake in the leg. More came up from under the river's bridge and stalked them. Peter took an unclaimed short sword from the shopping cart and took to the air. Landing on the back of the beast, he shoved his blade into the back of its neck. Dark poisonous blood oozed out, and Peter took off into the air before it could touch his skin.

A stream of morphlings ran past Peter followed by a flurry of activity with bodies moving and fighting, everything blurring in the chaos, as the lost boys dispatched morphlings left and right. But for everyone they killed, two more took its place.

Two Dusters in black uniforms came around the corner. One stopped and a pickup truck flew through the air, pinning a morphling against a building. It moved once and then died. The second duster, in a stream of black lightning had cut down three morphlings.

When the wave of morphlings was either incapacitated or dead, Peter looked at the two Dusters who had come to their aid.

"Wu Zan? Leroy?" Peter called out in disbelief when he saw his friends.

Both of the Dusters gave each other a high five and then jogged over to him.

"We pinged your location and saw that you needed some help, newby."

"Wu Zan?" Jax came over and both of Peter's roommates saluted their commander. "You know each other?" Jax asked in disbelief. "They were part of my team."

Peter couldn't contain his grin, placing his hands on his hips. "Well, now they're part of my team."

"Boys, boys," Wu Zan teased. "There's plenty of me to go around . . . for the right price."

"Zan," Leroy warned softly.

"I'm teasing," Wu Zan said. "Can't you see that? We came, didn't we? We're here, because we don't leave our teammates behind." He turned and held his hands up. "I can't help it if my owner is paying me tons of credits for every morphling I bag."

"Craft, get Jake the second vial of antivenom," Peter commanded, pointing to his injured boy. That was it. They were now out of antivenom and would have to find more.

As they continued to move toward the main square, Wu Zan and Leroy quickly filled in Peter and Jax on what they knew and had learned about the Hollow Dome and Warfare Infinity. The Dusters were given more information than Peter's crew.

"I've even been given an upgrade." Wu Zan held up an empty injector pen. "Picked it up at the last locker station. I could get used to this kind of treatment." He rubbed his knuckles on his shirt. "Who knew that all those video training simulations would lead to this?"

Gamers purchased half of the kids here already and those that hadn't would be in the next few weeks. A gamer named Killz purchased craft and Wu Zan. Leroy was owned by Diego.

Peter frowned when he saw his owner was Helix.

"How do we end the game?" Peter asked.

"You don't," Wu Zan's said, the confident smile falling from his face. "From what I can tell, Infinity is the updated version of Warfare 8. They're very similar games but not when it comes to the length of gameplay, which for Infinity . . . you can look to its title for a clue. Unlike Warfare 8 that only had an hour timeline, this game never ends."

"No, there has to be a way out."

"We haven't found one yet," Leroy said. "The best thing to do right now is to find a base and set up defenses. Then we will send out teams to bring back food and weapons."

Peter shook his head. "Sorry, guys, I don't plan on being here that long. We're going to bust out of here."

Wu Zan's eyes dropped and he looked over at Leroy. Both of them shifted uncomfortably. He was missing something.

"What's wrong?" Peter asked.

"Don't you understand? We *can't* leave. We need a continual supply of the PX injections or we burn out and die." Wu Zan was becoming upset and paced back and forth.

There it was, the final piece. It made sense now, why so many of the Dusters never tried to leave, even the decent, peace-loving ones like Wu Zan and Leroy. They didn't choose to stay—they *had* to stay, and wouldn't dare leave. They chose to train and fight for a chance at survival, because the alternative was certain death. The signs were all there—he just hadn't seen it.

This is how Neverland controlled their kidnapped victims and turned them willingly into supernatural combat soldiers. They had been experimenting with time-delay drugs for years, and apparently it had paid off. The only wrench in their grand plan was the loss of so many originals, who didn't need the constant supply of PX injections to survive.

"We've lost too many friends who tried to quit taking the drug, or escape Neverland and they died. I didn't want that for you. We didn't know this is where we would all end up, but since we're together. Why not go out like champions?" Wu Zan explained.

"I understand," Peter said. And he did. "But it doesn't mean I'm not going to try and find a way to stop Neverland and save you."

Both boys nodded and Jax quickly looked away, refusing to meet his gaze.

That's when it hit him. Jax knew that if they destroyed Neverland, it meant destroying all of the Dusters with it. Anger rushed through him and his hands curled into fists. He wanted to hit Jax. No, beat him to a pulp like they did whenever they had a dispute.

"You knew, Jax." Peter felt betrayed. "You knew the whole time that they couldn't leave." He pushed Jax in the shoulders, trying to provoke him into a fight, needing a way to vent his anger at the situation, at losing Wendy, at losing his friends.

"I knew," Jax said softly. "There was nothing I could do."

"You know how I feel about leaving people behind, and yet you said nothing," Peter growled, shoving Jax again. "What were you going to do, just leave them? Not tell me?"

Jax finally snapped and shoved Peter back, but he didn't fall, instead floating in the air. "I hadn't thought that far ahead, okay?" Jax yelled, waving his hands. "I'm making this up as I go."

"We'll help you," Leroy said, stepping between Peter and Jax, his large body tantamount to a wall, and Peter had to drop his fist or risk punching Leroy in the mouth.

"To escape, I mean. Tell us what you want us to do and we'll do it." He tapped his visor camera, warning, "But don't forget, they're always watching us."

The reminder was a wakeup call for Peter, and he let himself sink back to the ground, running his hands through his hair. He paced, hands on his head, then over his mouth. Each round of pacing, his posture and mood changed as he contemplated their situation. Then he froze when he saw Michael sitting on a curb, staring up at him through his goggles. Peter snapped his fingers and knew what they had to do.

Peter pointed to the cameras and gave a signal to Michael and the boy lit up and nodded. He closed his eyes, scrunched up his face. A few seconds later, the visors blinked and turned off as well as the suit cameras. "We good?" Peter asked and waited for a signal.

Michael gave a thumbs-up. "Were good, but not for long or they will suspect something. I also can't take out all of the cameras."

"How long?" Peter asked.

"I can probably give you five minutes," Michael answered.

"Okay, when I give the signal, take out the cameras. But we need to find the headquarters."

"I can take you to it," Jax interrupted. "John's in there now. We teleported a few blocks from the building."

"Great, we attack that building, get in, grab Helix and Hook and force them to let us out. If they're in that building inside the Hollow Dome, then there must be an exit."

"That building will be heavily secured," Wu Zan cautioned.

"And you can bet that once they figure out what we're doing, they're going to send every single morphling after us. Not to mention the other Dusters," Jax said.

"Leave the other Dusters to us." Leroy touched his fist to his chest in a salute.

"Then we need to find a way to stop the morphlings first. There has to be a way that Neverland is controlling them," Peter said.

Jax stepped back from the group and Peter noticed. "Jax, what is it?"

He frowned. "There is. It's a girl, Peter."

"A girl," he asked, confused, but there wasn't time for explanations. "Can you stop her?"

He shook his head. "She's not awake. She's dreaming, trapped inside of a pod."

"Then wake her up, Jax," Peter ordered.

Jax's stiffened. "I can't. She'll die."

Peter flinched. "Jax, we may all die. You have to take that chance. You weren't there, when we lost Torque and Rash, but isn't it better to die free than to die enslaved?"

"No, Peter," Jax said tightly, his eye twitching, his hands curling into fists. "Not all of us die." Jax turned and stalked off.

"Jax, wait!" Peter called, but when he tried to follow him, a circle of flames erupted around Peter trapping him in a cone of fire. When the flames died down, he flew out of them to confront Jax.

"You have an order!" Peter growled out, knocking Jax down to the ground, holding him by the front of his shirt.

"Yeah, well, you know me," Jax challenged. "I'm not great at following orders."

"You're choosing her over us?" Peter asked quietly so that only the two of them could hear. "One life over all of ours?"

All the tension left Jax's body, and he went slack in Peter's arms. His face contorted to one of pain and longing.

"Yes, Peter." Jax's head dropped back to the cement. "And you would do the same for Wendy."

Jax's dilemma became Peter's, as it mirrored his own predicament. He was trying to save her at the peril of his boys, and Jax was disobeying an order for the same reason.

Peter huffed with frustration then he shoved Jax back to the ground and stood up to address the group. He had to lead by example. Save the boys, then save Wendy.

Pain exploded in Peter's chest, and he looked down at the splash of red across his uniform. Blood seeped through and spread out, covering his palm. His body was going numb, cold. Peter scanned the rooftops, and spotted the shooter on top of an apartment building over a block, the rifle in his hands as he stood up and waved cheerily at him.

"Hook." Peter gurgled blood and collapsed to his knees.

"No," Jax cried out, grabbing Peter, before he fell face-first to the cement. His breathing became shallow and then stopped altogether. The lost boys cried out rushed for cover. Ditto tried to come to Peter's aide but was stopped by Jax.

Jax held his friend in his arms and bright flames erupted around the two friends, but neither one of them burned in the fiery inferno. He swung his head around to the apartment roof where he last saw Hook, and he knew it was time to end it.

Jax left Peter's body where it lay. Walking slowly and with purpose, he headed toward Hook. He knew that when he was done, only one of them would be left standing.

-39-

WENDY PRESSED AGAINST the walls as she sidestepped down the streets, the pistol resting gently against her hip and a machete in her hand—spoils from looting the sporting good store. The female shadow had left her as soon as Wendy was armed. She couldn't help but feel a bit like Lara Croft in *Tomb Raider* when she also found a medkit, two grenades, and a smoke bomb. Whoever was typing commands into her visor seemed to be trying to help her, if all the weapons she'd been guided to were any proof. But she still felt odd following commands from an unknown source, not knowing where she was being led. She noticed that there were more gold triangles moving her way. Wendy ducked into a storefront alcove and waited as three Dusters came down the street.

They were showing off their accuracy by shooting at the road signs. Wendy rolled her eyes in exasperation, as only an idiot would waste ammunition like that in a life or death situation. She was content to lie quietly in wait as they passed, but a morphling from inside the store slammed into the storefront door, shattering it, and sending Wendy careening into the street and in the path of the Dusters.

Her gun raised, she quickly took out the morphling with three shots to the head, but by doing so, she gave away her position. Wendy lifted her visor and tried to keep her face neutral as she stared into the furious face of Lily, Jeremy, and a third Duster.

"You!" Lily shrieked. "You should be dead."

"I told you, I'm not that easily killed," Wendy taunted back, holding her gun up and keeping Lily in her sights.

Jeremy ignored the gun and sauntered over to Wendy, flicking his hair back like he did in high school, trying to ooze charm.

Had he already forgotten their encounter a few hours ago? He reached for her gun, but she shot at his feet, forcing him to jump back. His face contorted in rage and his veins bulged along his neck and cheeks. He reached out again and this time grabbed the barrel of her gun, twisting the barrel like it was a wet noodle. Wendy pulled the trigger, but the gun backfired, knocking her to the ground.

Jeremy leaned over Wendy and grabbed her by the front of her uniform, tossing her against the building like she weighed nothing.

Dazed and confused, Wendy tried to get up but slid to the ground, her head throbbing.

"She's still not dead?" Lily said, aghast. "I guess I will just have to kill you myself." She growled low in her throat as she shifted into her half-tiger form, then pulled back her long claw-like hands preparing to slice Wendy's throat.

A threatening scream from a real mountain lion had Jeremy and Lily looking up in terror just before a blurred, furry figure pounced, knocking Lily to the ground. Wendy cowered, covering her face as the mountain lion attacked the Duster. A few powerful swipes later, and Lily was stilled on the pavement.

The mountain lion's gaze came to rest on Jeremy, who had tried to sneak away, but she gave chase. Even with his super strength, he wouldn't stay to be mauled by a ferocious mountain lion. Jeremy ran, the mountain lion on his tail as he turned a corner. Wendy heard his painful scream as he was caught.

Wendy struggled to her feet, and stepped around the still body of Lily. That could have been her, if Wendy had stayed and not escaped, but she didn't have time to mourn, she needed to get away. Wendy half walked, half stumbled down the road, stopping when the mountain lion came back. The great golden cat sauntered slowly, dropping its head as it neared Wendy. The cat looked injured, but Wendy couldn't see any physical injuries. A low whine came from the mountain cat's throat, and then its fur shimmered and shifted into a young woman who lifted up her visor and promptly collapsed on the ground.

"Brittney!" Wendy cried, running and gathering her friend in her arms.

"Hey, you," Brittney sniffed, tears running down her face. "I'm sorry."

"Shhh, it will be okay. I promise."

Brittney shook her head, "No, I'm sorry. We used to be so close. But lately I haven't been that great of a friend to you. I know that." She trembled in Wendy's arms, though her skin wasn't cold but burning hot like a glowing coal. "But I think I made up for it." She smiled weakly. "In the end."

She let out a sigh, her head dropping back as she went limp in Wendy's arms.

"No, no, no, no!" Wendy cried. Gathering Brittney closer, she rocked her friend and mourned.

A dark shadow stood over her as Wendy wiped at her tears with the sleeve of her uniform, her heart breaking in two again when she recognized his shadow.

Peter.

"No, Peter. Not you too?" A loud moan escaped her followed by a howl of grief at the fear that he may not return. That she hadn't been there for him.

She was sick of it. Death. Senseless death. Her parents, the lost boys, Peter, and now her oldest friend. She was done. No more.

Wendy kissed Brittney's forehead and laid her in the soft grass. Then she picked a flower from a flower pot and placed it between her hands.

She would embrace the gift she was given, the one she had tried to put off because of fear of what the word meant when she looked it up.

Necromancer.

But Wendy pushed down that fear, and raised her hands and called them. It was time for Neverland to pay for all the death they'd dealt, and she was here to collect.

Dark shadowy tattoos appeared on her skin and wafted around her fingertips. For Wendy was the queen of the shadows and it was time for her to reign.

-40-

JOHN HAD BEEN A silent watcher and player, trying not to freak out his sister and let her know he was the one helping her by sending commands and directions. If his sister knew he was in the Hollow Dome, it would distract her and she'd become reckless trying to save him.

Keeping one ear open to the rest of the room, he heard the shouts of victory and the cries of loss as the gamers' avatars either thrived or died. One investor named Merrill declared he was investing in generating morphlings and sending them to rain down on Killz's team as revenge.

As long as their plans weren't an immediate threat to Wendy and his friends, he didn't care what they did. It was all he could do not to rage at what was happening to Wendy. He was helpless when Jeremy and the tiger lady attacked Wendy, and he'd thought that was it for his sister, until the unthinkable happened. Brittney appeared, transformed into a mountain lion and saved his sister. A tear slid down his face and he tried to wipe it away as he watched Brittney's death. He hadn't believed it when he read *shifter* in Brittney's profile, but now he did.

Clearing his throat, he knew it was time to stop playing and figure out a way to bring down Neverland from the inside. He picked up his tablet and moved to the door that Hook had exited.

"Where are you going?" Helix asked suspiciously.

"I need a restroom." John waved the tablet around, and said, "I don't dare leave this behind."

This must have been the correct thing to say because Helix clapped enthusiastically. "I knew it. I knew that once you had a taste, you wouldn't be able to stop. Here, let me show you where it's at." He opened a different door and pointed down the hall. "On the left."

"Thank you." John saluted with two fingers, and headed into the restroom. He waited to make sure that no one was following him, then glanced down at the screen to check on his sister and was startled by what he saw—her hair moving, blown by an unseen force, her face glowing, her eyes dark with vengeance.

"Uh-oh," he muttered, then ran out of the restroom and began to search all of the rooms on the floor, looking for a control room, looking for an exit besides the coded and locked elevator. He needed to help the others, but all of the windows were reinforced, the doors locked with digital codes and fingerprints sensors.

He was trapped inside the building. But if he could get the lost boys to his location in the Wonderland Games building, and get Helix's tablet to Michael. They could bring the whole system down. But they would have to not get caught or seen.

One step at a time. John took a deep breath and headed back to the game room.

A trail of ash followed Jax's wake as he destroyed every obstacle in his way. He blasted through the front doors, raced up the stairwell, and met Hook, who was on the way down. A look of surprise flashed across his face.

"Well, if it isn't the prodigal son," Hook sneered, grasping the rifle in front of him. "Are you here to teach me a lesson?"

"No, I'm here to kill you," Jax said solemnly.

"Can you? I don't think you can. I've trained you, taught you everything, even let you run back to the boys, but you always came back, and you know why? Because of the anger that resides deep inside of you. The hate that was unmatched, searching for another until you met me. We are the same."

"We are nothing alike," Jax grunted out, his hand resting lightly on the railing, sending a smoldering heat into the metal and burning an outline of his hand.

Hook tried to smile and moved away from the railing. "I'm the only one who knows the real you. Even though you try to be loyal to Peter, you're jealous of him. I understand the resentment you harbor toward him, and the nagging guilt. It's why you left and came to me. I know the truth about why you stayed with us, why you came back. It's because of her."

Jax tried to hide his shock; he thought he'd been discreet, that no one other than Candace knew about his secret obsession with Alice.

"Would you like to know more about her? Would you like to see her again?"

Jax couldn't suppress his intake of breath, and Hook grinned.

"Yes, I see you do." With a smug certainty, Hook shouldered the rifle and stepped past Jax, then headed down the stairs, pausing to look up at him. "C'mon, boy, you won't get this offer again."

Knowing that it could very well end up being a trick, Jax followed, back out onto the street and through the melted door, across three city blocks. They arrived at the building with the Wonderland Games marquee. Hook disarmed the door and ushered Jax inside and into an elevator.

Once inside, Hook punched in a code and the elevator headed down a few levels.

Looking straight ahead, but aware of every move and glance Hook made, Jax asked, "Why did you shoot Peter?"

Hook chuckled. "Because he was getting on my nerves. Keeps coming back to life, and I give him an opportunity to try and follow me, and at every turn he betrays me." Hook gave him the side-eye. "Kind of like you. Except Peter, I can vent my anger on, because he always shows up. But I think his time has run out. He's not coming back this time."

"Why do you say that?" Jax asked, his heart thudding in his chest in fear.

"Just intuition, you know. He's always been more reckless than the others because of his ability. What's he at, seven pans now? You know what they say about a cat having nine lives. Curly told me a lot about him, and I've figured it out. Peter has spent his lives. He takes longer to regenerate each time, and the longer his body goes between pans, it dies a little more. I had his body preserved in a pod, kept my medical team with him for his last two pans, and it was going on twenty-four hours before he came back. I saved him. Who is going to preserve his body now and keep it from rotting on the ground in the dome while it waits for his return? No one, I tell you."

"His soul—"

"Is having problems reentering his body," Hook interrupted. "That's why it's taking longer between each of his resurrections."

Jax's stomach rolled, his mouth going dry, and he instinctively touched his own chest as he remembered Peter sharing his body. That's why the others became lost shadows. They couldn't reenter their bodies because they were well and truly dead, unlike Peter, who could slowly heal and regenerate himself, but even his body was slowing down.

His eyes burned with unshed tears and Jax blinked them away, keeping his feelings at bay. He had to, if he was going to stop Hook and Neverland, but now he wasn't sure if he could.

The doors opened and Hook waited for Jax to enter the room first. It was empty other than her pod that was clipped into a stand suspended three feet in the air. Above her were larger empty glass pods, similar to the ones they used to transport the morphlings on missions. The glass egg was the only thing that could contain them, the only surface they couldn't slip through.

A single technician monitored her stats at a compact rolling computer desk. He didn't see Candace and her wheelchair anywhere.

"Who is she?" Jax asked, unable to peel his eyes away from her. She looked at peace floating in a one-piece suit, her hair a crown of gold. She was beautiful.

"I don't know. I found her."

"I don't believe you," Jax snapped. "You took her, like you took all the rest of us."

"No, I'm telling you the truth." Hook walked around the pod, slowly explaining as he went. "We found her washed up on our shore seven years ago. She's been in this perpetual dreaming state ever since. This machine"—he patted the pod—"is the only thing keeping her alive. At first, we didn't understand what was happening when these monsters started appearing, but it didn't take us long to make the connection and learn to harness them. Of course, what do you do when you have an unlimited supply of monsters? Use them as video game fodder. As you can see, our soft launch has been an instant success. We've made millions in the last few hours alone. Just wait until we go wide. There will be no stopping us." Hook walked around the pod.

A lump formed in his throat. "How do you not know who she is?"

"It was unlikely she was one of you," Hook said with a shrug. "She didn't have a number tattooed on her neck like the rest of you experiments. Normally we might have tried to match her up to one of the numbered experiments in our records, but of course"—he turned, looking at Jax point-blank, his features darkening with his recollection—"our records were destroyed that night."

Hook moved to stand behind Jax. He leaned over and whispered, "Do you want to see how it's done?"

"How what's done?" Jax asked.

"Why, the morphlings of course," he said, sounding giddy.

"Sir," the technician interrupted. "We have another order for a morphling."

"Perfect timing! Any particular target?" Hook asked.

"Yes, someone is sending it after Pilot."

Hook chuckled, shooing away the technician and then took his place. Leaning into a small mic, he whispered an inaudible command and the girl inside the pod stirred. An image appeared on the screen, flickering black-and-white snow, and every few seconds the image appeared and disappeared.

"Watch." Hook pointed as the stats changed and a dark mass appeared in the glass pod on the ceiling, starting out as purple shadowy mass that began to solidify into something more corporeal.

"It's a morphling," Jax breathed out. He'd suspected this is how they were made, but to see it in person was a different matter.

Hook stepped back and let Jax observe Alice in the pod. Jax touched the glass. The girl stirred, but her eyes never opened. She knew he was near her.

"My dreamer," he whispered. "What I wouldn't give to know your real name."

She stirred again as if trying to wake up to answer. Her finger on her right hand spasmed, and he watched in awe as it twitched again, voluntarily.

"She's waking up!" Jax said excitedly.

"We can't have that, now can we?" Hook growled, and Jax heard the audible click of the slide on a semiautomatic pistol.

He turned and looked into the barrel. Hook motioned for him to move away from the pod.

With the gun aimed at Jax, Hook spoke quietly into the mic, but Jax only made out a couple words.

All dead.

She stirred and an influx of morphlings began to materialize in the glass orbs above. As soon as one was formed and its pod filled, a conveyer belt took it away to release it into the streets above. He could only assume the target was the boys. One after another, like an assembly line, they were created and sent out into the dome.

His heart lurched his mouth went dry as he imagined young Tootles, Michael, and the others trying to fight off the army without him or Peter to lead them.

"No!" Jax snapped. "Don't do this. You just said that they were making you money."

"Relax, that's why I have my Dusters. We got what we needed from your group of boys. Besides, my Dusters are loyal they follow directions. Unlike you."

Jax had tried to move closer to the pod, his hand reaching for a switch, hoping to turn it off.

The gun rose toward his head and he froze, swallowing nervously.

"She needs to stay asleep," Hook warned. "I'm not stupid—I know you've tried this with her before. I saw the irregularities in her stats that kept popping up late at night. I watched the video footage of you sneaking in the lab. I put two and two together, figured out that Candace was lying to me. Well, she always had a soft spot for you and Peter, but she's paid for her treason. And so will you."

Alice's eyes opened in the pod, and her hand hit the glass with a thud, startling Hook.

Hook's eyes widened as he watched Alice coming to life in the Pod.

Jax took advantage of the distraction and lunged for the gun, trying to wrestle it from Hook's hands. Jax knocked Hook into the pod, and pulled the gun down.

They fought, in desperation, both clawing at the trigger and it went off with a bang.

Hook stumbled back, his hands clenching his stomach as blood gushed between his fingers.

"Well played." Hook grinned, blood coating his teeth. "Well played." He fell to the ground and his breath escaped his lips as he died.

Jax dropped the gun and fell to his knees, shock running through him. The technician ran out of the room as soon as the gun went off, and now he was on his own.

He looked at Hook's still form, and waited for the feelings of grief or guilt to follow. It never came. "It's over," Jax said calmly. "You will never hurt another person again."

He looked up at Alice, who had dropped off to sleep again, her eyes closed as she floated listlessly.

Had he imagined her intervention? He swore she helped him, but she continued to float in the fluid, her nightmares materializing and sent out to hunt his friends.

Jax moved to the technicians seat and grabbed the mic. "Stop," Jax said and waited for the dreams to stop appearing on the screen.

"No more morphlings," he commanded, but he didn't receive any response from her. Another glass pod filled with smoke and shadow and formed into a long slithering snake with wings. He moved over to stand in front of Alice's pod, eyeing the morphling forming in horror. It wasn't working. The snake monster was lifted up into the floor above, and another empty glass orb replaced it.

Snakes? Why snakes? Tootles hated snakes. Jax slammed his fist against the glass and yelled, trying to wake her up. "Stop, please stop," Jax cried out, pressing his forehead to the glass. "Please, I need to save them."

Tears fell down his cheeks as he came to terms with what he would have to do. To save his friends, he would have to kill Alice. Kill his true love.

-41-

TOOTLES SCREAMED IN terror and ran as a snake morphling lunged for him. The separated groups of lost boys and girls and fought their way back to the main group. The girls were doing their best with makeshift weapons to help protect the injured. Those that couldn't fight sought shelter in a circle of the stronger fighters. Both Dittos, already in battle, tried to fight their way to Tootles' aid, but their hands were full. Tootles tried to teleport but kept flickering in and out. He had not yet regained enough strength.

"Tootles!" the Dittos cried out, realizing they were too far away, both of them locked in combat with morphlings. With a mighty howl of desperation and pain, Ditto forced his body to replicate a second time.

Two more Dittos appeared next to the other two.

"I'm coming, Tootles," four mouths spoke at once as the third Ditto doppelganger ran to snatch up Tootles and the fourth picked up a gun and shot the morphling in the mouth, drawing it away, but the bullets didn't do anything more than bounce off and annoy the snake. It turned and lunged.

"Ditto!" Tootles cried out when the snake struck, catching the fourth Ditto around his middle.

All Dittos froze up, their four shapes flickering in and out before being pulled back into one very limp and still body, collapsing as one unit to the ground.

"DITTO!" Tootles screamed.

"They're just not stopping," Leroy yelled, catching a stray morphling by the jaws, and with a quick snap, he broke the jaw of the monster and it died, turning to ash.

Wu Zan pulled down his visor and looked at all of the purple dots that were racing toward them. "This isn't good."

The team gathered in a circle facing outwards, preparing for the onslaught.

The morphlings rushed in all at once. Wu Zan became a blur of motion as he raced into the oncoming mob of morphlings. Knife in hand, he slashed and stabbed and destroyed a morphling in seconds, but his burst of speed was short-lived, and he doubled over, winded.

"I can't keep this up," Wu Zan said breathlessly, but there was no time to recover. Not seconds later, he was back at it, attacking another morphling. He was doing his best to keep the morphlings at a distance, but he was slowing down.

A second blur shot by and mirrored Wu Zan's attacks. Then the runner slowed, revealing himself to be Pilot, who paused midstride to give Wu Zan a wry salute and then joined in on the attack.

"It's the Primes," Wu Zan shouted in excitement. Out of the corner of his eye he saw a rhinoceros charge a morphling, knocking it into a car.

"And the Dusters," Leroy called out, giving a whoop as the rhinoceros shifted into the young duster girl—Slip.

One by one, the other Dusters—for safety or out of loyalty—joined with the lost boys and girls and fought as one unit.

"Never thought I'd be seeing this," Onyx whistled, and then a message appeared on his visor. "Hey, it's John. We've got location of Wonderland Games and a plan to shut the system down. Michael, are you ready to take out the cameras?"

Michael nodded. "Ready." His face scrunched up in concentration and a bead of sweat appeared across his forehead.

Onyx waved for the others to follow him. "Let's go. Let's blind them."

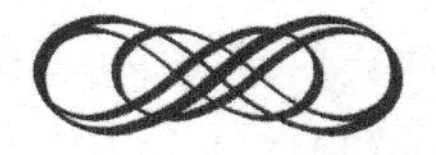

"What is the meaning of this?" Killz screamed at his tablet as he stood up and pointed at Merrill. "Why are you sending so many of those shades after my guys?"

Merrill wiped the sweat from his brow, looking worried as he scrolled his screen, searching through his history. "That's not me. I don't know where those other ones are coming from."

Killz tossed his tablet onto a couch cushion and turned on Diego, making a show of rolling up his sleeves as he sauntered over to him. "If you have a problem, you should settle it here now."

"Calm down, Killz," Diego said dismissively. He continued to type instructions into his tablet. "I didn't send them either. Look, I sent my player to help yours. Safety in numbers. But they're picking us off one by one. Our avatars are falling like flies. What's going on? I thought this game was supposed to last longer than a few hours." He glared up at President Helix.

Helix was frowning at his own tablet, confused as to why his own avatar, Peter, was down and not regenerating. He cleared his throat. "Gentleman, I'm sure there is an explanation. But I can guarantee that this will be looked into and taken care of now. Just give me a few minutes as I make some calls."

He laid his tablet down and stepped into the hall to make a call, and John took action, casually slipping over and picking up the abandoned tablet. Helix had left so abruptly, the tablet hadn't gone into sleep mode and John didn't need a password to get in.

John went back to his corner chair and sat down, scrolling through the president's tablet, looking for secrets, backdoors, and security measures.

What he saw instead was Peter. Dead.

"No," he whispered, knowing that would be enough to send Wendy on a rampage. He found the security access and quickly turned off all of Wonderland Games locks, disabling the elevator code as well. Now, if they acted quickly enough, all they had to do was survive long enough to make it to this building and down the same elevator he had come up on. John quickly swiped through the rest of Helix's team, searching for an in-game ally. Luckily, Helix had also bought Onyx.

John typed instructions into the tablet and prayed that Onyx would relay the message in time.

Take out cameras. Main headquarters location Wonderland Games pinged on your map. Escape elevator in building. Bring Michael.

John knew that by taking down the building's defense, he was also opening it up for morphlings to enter and they would be hot on the boys' tail.

"And now the cameras aren't working," A third investor complained, clicking on his screen. "I've got nothing. The screen is blank."

John grinned, knowing that Onyx and Michael got the message.

-42-

WENDY WAS LIVID, her heart aching with sorrow while on fire with revenge, because of Peter. She had promised the shadows vengeance, and she planned to deal the hand of justice, but she wasn't blind. Wendy stormed through the middle of the park, not bothering to duck or hide.

Peter reached for Wendy, wrapping his shadowy hand around hers. A vision burst into her mind—an underground room, brightly lit. And right in middle of the room next to a pod—Hook. She saw Hook. . . and Jax.

Instinctively, she ripped her hand away and turned, traveling in the opposite direction. He'd tried to share his thoughts and memories with her, but she rebelled.

He panicked and lunged in front of her, his shadowy hands reaching for her shoulders. She froze in place as he leaned in and hugged her.

Through the embrace, he showed her the past. Them laughing and playing on a rug together at Neverland. Lost in dreams and games. She saw her thimble, and his acorn. He showed her the night he met her again, how she looked on the park bench defending herself from the shadows of the night. She saw herself asleep in his arms in the rain outside of the church. Their kiss.

"What is this?" Wendy asked, confused. Why would he show her these things now? "What are you doing? What are you trying to tell me?"

He showed her the memory of him flying her to her bedroom and leaving her on her bed to wake up safe and sound with no memory of ever meeting him. She watched through his eyes as her bedroom window became smaller and smaller as he flew away.

Peter's shadow pulled away from her and she felt cold at his absence.

"No!" she gasped. "No, I won't let you."

He was saying goodbye.

"You can't. You promised me that you would always be here. That you would always come back to me," she screamed, not caring if the whole world heard her. "You pan right now, and I will come to you. I will find you and help you remember me."

Peter's shadow placed his hands on his hips and shook his head. She knew that posture, knew he was telling her no.

"It's not fair!" she cried. "Then let me come with you!"

This idea seemed to distress Peter because he flew up in the air.

"No, wait, I'm sorry. That's not what I meant," she said regretfully. "We're supposed to be together, grow old together, go on adventures together."

His shadow drifted down and settled inches in front of her. Wendy held her hand up and he pressed his shadow hand to hers. With their hands clasped, he leaned in close and kissed her lips gently, and through his touch—his hand, his mouth against hers—she heard his words in her mind, clear as a bell.

You are my greatest adventure.

When she opened her eyes, he was gone.

No, she couldn't lose him again. Wendy closed her eyes and focused on that instinct. Raising her hands, she called the shadows, and eagerly they came, wrapping themselves around her like a gossamer veil. She wouldn't let this happen. She would fight for Peter, even if it meant going to hell and getting his soul back.

Deep in the throes of the shadows, she heard the otherworldly scream—the painful echo—as the morphlings changed direction. She knew by the purple dots on her visor, they were closing in. So many of them, they nearly looked like a solid mass. So be it.

She set aside all her fears, as if the morphlings weren't even there, and she refocused, centering her every thought on Peter. On his laugh, his mischievous green eyes, and before she knew it, the shadows had pulled her into their realm. They didn't travel far, and as she went into the nightmare realm, she was surprised to discover it wasn't as scary as she remembered it. The noises the morphlings made didn't seem as horrendous, but more like a painful cry.

Then she was out, back on the physical plane, landing on the ground, amidst a battle of Dusters, lost boys, and morphlings.

"Wendy?" Michael cried out, running out from behind a car, when he saw her, wrapping his arms around her waist. She looked at his scared, young eyes and saw the bruise that was forming on his cheek. Patting his head, she gently unhooked his arms and moved through the streets, ignoring the morphlings and fighting and focusing on the still body of Peter on the makeshift stretcher outside of the Wonderland Games building.

The fighting had become so thick he had been forgotten. She kneeled next to him and placed her hand on his chest. His body was still warm, but growing colder by the second.

Come, she commanded. *Peter, come.*

His shadow came at her bidding, and she tried to direct him into his physical form. Peter's shadow tried but was unable, his shadow skating off of his old body, like he was covered in slippery soap.

Try again.

Again and again he tried, but each attempt was just as unsuccessful.

Tears flowed and her lower lip trembled. He was gone. Stuck in this shadow form.

A morphling rushed toward them bent on devouring Peter's shadow. Wendy spun on her heels, thrusting her hand out instinctively to the beast and it stopped mid-lunge. She was taken aback, shocked that the morphling stopped, though she didn't know why.

"I am not scared of the shadows!" Wendy yelled, and the morphling took a step back as the ground heated and bubbled underneath Wendy and Peter, the road buckling like waves as the tarmac gurgled up and churned as if something living was pushing through.

Fire and molten rock spewed forth and then sank inward as a hole expanded, leaving a great gap and expanse. Looking down into the hole, she could see Jax down below, inside some sort of lab, his body surrounded by flames, scorching, melting everything around him. With his hands held aloft, he fired an endless stream of flames at what was left of the ceiling above him, torching it into cinders and dripping asphalt from the street above down into the lab, and sent glass orbs crashing down around him.

Wendy could just make out the shape of a morphling burning inside one of the glass chambers still dangling from the remains of the lab's ceiling.

One escaped the glass and roared as it flung its arms out to grab the road and try to pull itself up, but Jax's fire engulfed it and it fell back into the hole, crashing into a pile of ash.

"Wendy?" Jax called out, surprised at seeing her. "Help me." His eyes were red from crying, his face blackened from soot. "I can't do it."

She knew what had to be done, and why Jax struggled. She glanced around her as the lost boys made a mad dash to the Wonderland Games building.

"Inside," Onyx called out as he got to the front door and opened it, ushering the lost boys and girls inside. Jade,

Leroy, Wu Zan, Pilot, Slip, and Onyx hung back and kept up a line of defense against the advancing morphlings. The others ran inside and were met in the lobby by President Helix, who was having a mental breakdown.

"How'd you get in here? This door is supposed to be secured. Are you crazy? You're bringing those morphlings right down on us."

John stepped out of the elevator and grabbed Helix by the shoulder, spinning him around. His fist connected with the game designer's jaw with a crunch. Helix fell to the ground, out cold.

"John!" Michael hugged him in joy.

John hugged him back. "Hey, here's the signal for the system. Shut it down, little brother." He handed Michael the tablet, and the boy quickly began to eradicate the gaming program.

With her brothers safe for now, Wendy held Peter close and used the shadows to move them both into the lower underground level where Jax was pacing.

The room had a partial sixty-foot ceiling, covered with half melted glass orbs. The floor was covered with pools of melted and broken glass. The air smelled like a kiln, a mix of coal and heat. Just beyond the pod, Hook lay prostrate on the floor, deadly still. Wendy quickly turned away in alarm. "Is he?" she asked breathlessly holding Peter close to her as she sat on the floor.

"Dead? Yes," Jax answered. His face fell when he saw Peter. "Is he still?" he asked, mirroring her question.

"Yes. I've tried to send his soul back into his body, but he's not panning. It's not working."

"We'll save him," Jax promised. "I promised he'll come back to you."

Wendy nodded, unsure of whether to believe him or not. She looked past Jax to the pod behind him that still held an occupant—Alice, the one who Jax loved. A twinge twisted her heart, and she clutched her chest. Was it jealousy? Why should she care?

Scanning the ceiling, she saw the glass orbs that the morphlings were created in and understood why Jax had tried to destroy them, but that didn't seem to stop them. Alice was still dreaming, her eyes twitching, and the morphlings were still forming, just outside of the glass orbs, their shadowy forms collecting in the corners where they would slither up into the street, right into the lost boys.

"Open it," Wendy demanded.

"I can't," Jax cried, touching the glass. "If I do, she'll die."

"You've never met her," Wendy argued. "She doesn't even know you're alive. What if she doesn't return your affections?" Even as she said it, she knew it was a lie. How, she wasn't sure.

Wendy took a deep breath, carefully laid Peter out and ran for the tablet, then using the information the shadow had shared with her, she punched in the code and watched as the pod began to drain slowly.

"How did you know?" Jax said, his face a mix of pain and relief.

"Candace told me," Wendy answered, but draining the pod was taking too long. The girl was still dreaming inside.

Screams rang out from above—another duster injured by a morphling—and Wendy bellowed, "Jax, they're dying."

Jax closed his eyes and took a strengthening breath. Then he flicked out his hand, setting it alight so that it glowed with power, and he reached for the glass pod as if to melt it, then abruptly whipped his hand back in disgust.

There was another scream from above—this time, Michael's. She couldn't wait for Jax to gather his courage. Her brother was in danger and Wendy wouldn't abandon him a second time. She picked up Hook's pistol, cocked the slide, and shot into the glass pod, aiming low and away.

The glass shattered and the rest of the fluid rushed out. Alice crumpled to the ground, her oxygen mask still over her face.

Jax knocked down the glass around the edges, desperate to help Alice. He lifted her soaking wet form from the pod and carried her to the floor. Prying the breathing mask from her mouth, he stilled in disbelief when he saw her whole face for the first time.

Her skin was pale as snow. Her blonde hair had a reddish hue. Jax looked over at Wendy in confusion and then back at Alice.

"How can it be?" he muttered. "It's impossible."

Wendy leaned close to Jax to get a better look and collapsed to the ground in disbelief. Jax reached out to steady her as she stared at the person in his arms with recognition.

"How?" Jax sobbed out, rocking the dying Alice in his arms.

More screaming erupted from above, pulling Wendy's attention upward, where she saw a spider-shaped morphling crawling up the side of the Wonderland building. With the electric security system down, it had no problem throwing its body against the glass, trying to break into the top floor. She had to stop them, had to stop the nightmares.

Then it came to her.

"It never happened," Wendy said aloud and reached out to touch Alice's limp hand, which felt cold and lifeless between her warm one, and was instantly taken back to the hallway outside Dr. Mee's office seven years ago, where she'd rocked herself in a chair. "It's just a dream," she said softly, and looked up in fear.

The spider morphling squealed and then began to dissipate, and with a poof, it disappeared into the air, a stream of dark smoke in its wake.

"I made it all up," she continued, chanting the mantra she'd used to repeat as a child to calm herself.

The sleeping Wendy's eyes began to flutter as she struggled to come awake.

"Don't go there, concentrate on better things. Think happy thoughts," she encouraged herself. Finally, leaning down, she brushed her lips against her own forehead. For the girl in Jax's arms was Wendy herself, or a part of her.

"Wake up, Wendy. Wake up!"

The sleeping Wendy gasped, her head falling back, and her eyes opened for the first time in years, but her eyes were black, not blue like her own.

"It's just a dream," both of them spoke in unison. With their words, an invisible command filled the air, soaring through the sky, and with it, the power to dispel the nightmares. Hundreds of morphlings dissipated and floated away like seeds from a dandelion.

Cheers of victory rained down from above as the morphlings disappeared.

Wendy held her other half, her shadow, her soul, and cried. All the years she thought she was crazy, imagining shadows, but the shadow she was seeing was herself. She had unlocked her own room that night and led herself to the rooftop years ago. It was her own nightmares that plagued the world, and all she had to do was wake up.

It was her gift, her power over death that allowed her to live without her other half, her shadow.

It was surreal to be beside her soul, but the longer she was out of the pod the more ethereal she became, her skin becoming colder, translucent. Jax sucked in his breath and touched Alice's arm.

Wendy could feel his warm hand touching her own arm, and she looked down in disbelief.

Her shadow reached for Jax, gently grazing his cheek, and whispered, "I believe." Then she faded away and a shadow bearing Wendy's silhouette took her place.

Scared, nervous and filled with anticipation, Wendy felt her shadow slip inside her body and she became whole. Joy, love and laughter bubbled up within her and a confidence that comes from knowledge. She wasn't scared anymore.

Led by her shadow, Wendy turned and kneeled next to Peter's body. Alone, she hadn't been strong enough to make him whole again, but Wendy was no longer missing her other half. Now, with the power of dreams and shadows, she might be able to.

Laying her hand over Peter's chest wound, she breathed out the words, "I believe."

Her hands grew warm, and she opened her eyes to see shadows glimmering and becoming corporeal. Her eyes glistened with tears as Wendy recognized her parents, George and Mary, kneeling by her, and behind them, Fox, Brittney and Candace. The room was filled with hundreds of souls bathed in a warm glow of celestial light, all of them touching each other, and touching the shadow in front until it culminated into her parent's hands overlapping hers.

"I believe," Wendy whispered again with passion.

"I believe," she heard her parents say.

"I believe," came the chorus of shadows.

"I believe." Jax laid his hand on top of Wendy's, his eyes focused on Peter.

"We believe," Wendy cried out, and almost jumped when Peter's chest began to move underneath her hands.

She screamed in delight when his green eyes opened, his cheek dimpling when he smiled. "I believe too," he groaned and winced at the pain.

"You remember?" she asked hopefully.

"I remember everything." He tried to sit up, and Jax extended his arm to assist him. "You saved me." Peter reached out and cupped her cheek, pressing his forehead to hers, his lips parting as he breathed in deep. "You didn't give up on me, even when I did."

"I figured it was time to return the favor." She grinned, blushing. "I will never give up on you. You promised me an espresso machine, and a puppy."

He chuckled. "It sure doesn't take much to make you happy."

"All it takes is you," she whispered, her heart quickening.

Peter sighed and pulled her in for a kiss. Their lips touched gently as they rediscovered each other, their hearts searching and finding the one that completes them. When they parted, they sighed.

Then she turned to thank her parents and the other shadows, and they waved.

"We love you," Mary said. "Give John our love."

"We are so proud of you." George grinned, his arm wrapped around Mary's waist.

Like a dial being turned down, their voices slowly muted and their bodies faded back into their shadow forms. She couldn't help but cry as her parents blew kisses and waved goodbye.

"Thank you," Wendy spoke, then blew a kiss and waved goodbye again. "Thank you all," she said, addressing the other shadows. She was grateful, for whatever power allowed them to band together and save Peter.

"Can you see them?" Wendy asked in disbelief, reaching to clasp Peter's hands in hers. Her heart ached at seeing her adoptive parents, at getting to say goodbye.

"I see them." He brought her hand up to his mouth and kissed the top of her knuckles.

"How touching," a gravelly voice interjected. "Don't you love unexpected reunions? Especially when they come back from the dead."

-43-

HOOK STOOD OVER THEM, the bullet hole in his chest healed, his head cocked to the side in triumph. His gun pointed right between her eyes, before swinging it to point at Peter.

He must have panned. It's the only way he could have survived, and he was able to see the shadows, like Wendy. But somehow he had kept his memories intact.

"How is it possible?" Jax asked.

His mouth turned up into a sinister grin, laughter rumbling loud and deep in his throat. "Fools. Such foolish little children, to think you could take on someone like me. Me—*Captain Hook.* I have contingency plans for my contingency plans. We've spent years studying you. I own you and your abilities. I wasn't going to pass up on eternal life. I had to try it on myself."

Hook moaned happily. "It's good to be alive." He turned to Peter, tossing an empty injector pen to the ground. "You should have told me how great it feels to regenerate. Even if there are a few unfortunate side effects."

He sucked in his breath and grasped his chest in pain. "It was worth it," he muttered, wobbling, his hand trembling, unable to keep the gun trained at any one of them.

"Hook, something's not right," Jax said.

"I'm not sick, I feel great." The veins bulged in his forehead and his face turned red, sweat beading across his brow.

"You don't carry the PX gene," Peter warned. "Your body won't be able to adapt. You're burning out."

"I wasn't about to let immortality slip by me," Hook said irritably. "And it seems only the Primes lose their memories. Lucky me." He stumbled forward, and a blister formed on his cheek, followed by another on his forehead.

"It's not taking," Peter said softly. "You're going to burn out."

"What do you know? Worthless brats. You thought you destroyed me before, but look at this place! Look what I created! No. No, you don't get to win. I'm sick of you interfering with my plans. It's time for you all to die." He swung the gun between the three of them. "You might regenerate, but this one can't," he said, leveling the gun directly on Jax.

"No!" Wendy cried, and with a rage born of pain and too much loss, she thrust her hands into the air and called on the shadows to help her one more time. The shadow tattoos merged at her fingertips as a dark cloud rolled across the floor, gathering to encircle Hook's feet like a moving sea.

"What's going on?" he cried out as the shadowy waves surged and rolled, flowing like water, up to his knees to spread across the whole room.

She wasn't done with Hook and his machinations. Her soul cried out for revenge, and Wendy heeded her cry, letting her other half take control. A dark mass weaved its way through the shadow waves and bumped Hook's leg, startling him. It circled slowly around Hook, propelling itself with its powerful tail, just enough above the surface to display the ridges on its back.

Terrified at what was swimming within the shadows around him, Hook randomly shot at the black mass, missing the morphling that was hunting him in the fog. Wherever he ran, the waves followed him, until he climbed up on a table to get out of the darkness.

"Tick. Tock. Tick. Tock," Wendy chanted. "Your time is running out, Captain. It's time for you to leave." She raised her arms and slapped her palms together as a giant crocodile sprang out of the shadows behind Hook, snapped him between his jaws, and dragged him into the shadowy sea.

-44-

"WHERE DID HE go?" Jax asked, spinning in a circle, looking for signs of Hook.

"Where the shadows live," Wendy answered. "He may or may not find a way out, if he indeed can live forever. But I wouldn't count on it being anytime soon."

"That's my girl!" Peter crowed, picking her up and spinning her around. Wendy's laughter filled the room as they flew into the air. Their spinning slowed as they floated high in the underground room, looking into her eyes, he kissed her nose, her cheeks, and his eyes lingered on her lips until she blushed again.

"I will never stop hungering for your kisses," he whispered and pressed his lips to hers, the kiss so deep it left her breathless.

"Are you guys done kissing or what?" Tootles blew a raspberry at them from the street.

Peter and Wendy glanced up and he grinned sheepishly. "Never." His green eyes met hers and twinkled mischievously. "Are you okay with that?"

"You promising to never stop kissing me? Yes." Her laughter rang out like bells in the air.

No, not her laughter.

Tink's censor band. *Tink was here!*

"What the heck is taking you so long? Do we have to do all the work for you?" Tink snapped, softening her words. "Get your bahoobahaber up here." Slightly and Tootles stood next to Tink and waved down at them.

Tootles teleported down to the floor next to Jax, grabbed his hand, and seconds later, he was on the street with the rest. Peter flew up through the hole with Wendy, and what greeted them was a sight to behold as the Wonderland Games building's front windows were blown out. Shattered glass, ash, and the gooey slime of morphling remains coated the street. Everyone left of the Dusters, and lost boys and girls had made their way to the street outside of Wonderland Games.

Peter went to speak with Onyx. Both of their faces were solemn as Onyx pointed to the casualties laid out along the sidewalk, covered with curtains and sheets. There were at least four wearing the gray uniforms of the lost boys and girls, and five wearing the black uniforms of the Dusters.

"Hey, Slightly, you made it," Jax clapped him on the back.

"Yeah, Tootles was strong enough. He came and got us," Slightly chuckled. "Looks like you had a blast without me."

"Dad and Dr. Mee are on their way to us now. They had to wait to dock the boat. Michael was able to override their security system and unlock all of the doors. Slightly has set up a makeshift clinic in the Physical Therapy Clinic." She pointed to the white building to the left of Wonderland Games. The Dusters are bringing in the injured now. Hey, you!" Tink screeched at President Helix, who was trying to sneak away. "Get back in line. No one said you could move your lazy butt off that sidewalk."

Wendy smiled with tender affection, as Tink's censor band didn't go off. She was learning to tame her words. Maybe there was hope after all.

All of the investors were standing outside the building, obviously upset and terrified by the events that had just transpired. One or two looked mad enough to spit, but the Dusters had taken up guard duty.

"You're going to hear from my lawyer," Killz spat out, pointing a finger at President Helix.

"Now, now, this was just a beta test. I'm sure this can all be worked out in the second relaunch," Helix said, trying to calm the crowd.

"You don't seem to get it," Peter said, addressing Helix. "It's over."

"The only relaunch that is happening," Curly said, rolling up his sleeves, "is you." He touched Helix's temple and a slack expression moved over Helix's face, followed by a giggle.

"What just happened?" Diego looked terrified at the instant transformation of Helix, his hands covering his cheeks. "Why does he look like a happy baby?"

"Because he no longer has a care in the world. I've made him forget everything," Curly answered and moved toward Diego.

Diego squealed like a piglet and backed away, tripping over a fire hydrant. "Don't you do any mind-mojo on me!"

"I'll pay you a hundred thousand to do it to him," Killz laughed, taking off his hat and slapping his knee.

Curly touched Diego's temple and the man's face went slack as well.

"What's going on?" Wendy asked Onyx.

"When we got to the top floor of the building, John had them pretty much under control. It seems having the morphlings trying to tear down the building while they were in it was all the motivation they needed to pull the plug on investing in the new game."

John came out of the building and gave Wendy a side hug. "Hey, I always tried to get you to play Warfare 8 with me, and now you have. You kicked butt, especially against the room of boxes."

Wendy groaned in embarrassment. "You saw?"

"Hey, I was there. I led you to it. We make a great team." He held his palm up for a high five, and she rolled her eyes in response, then turned back to the group on the sidewalk. John cleared his throat and gestured to them. "So, like Onyx said, I don't think they know too much, and it was my idea to have Curly use his gift of persuasion to adjust their memories."

Onyx nodded. "We decided the safest course of action is to make them forget the last few days and this island.

We're going to send them home with a command to never tell anyone or come back."

"What about the Red Skulls?" Peter asked, placing his hand around Wendy, pulling her close.

"We made President Helix make an announcement to have all troops meet at the beach. Pilot and Nibs are gathering up the stragglers. We're going to do the same thing. Mind-wipe them and take them back to the mainland. But we haven't found Hook."

"And you won't." Jax grinned. "Wendy took care of him."

Heat rose to her cheeks and she blushed. Onyx lifted his fist for a fist bump. "Way to go!"

She raised her fist and bumped back, to John's mock horror. "He gets a fist bump and I get dissed?"

Gently slapping her palm to John's head, she laughed. "Is that better?"

His crooked grin was her answer.

"Wendy, I'd like you to meet my friends, Wu Zan, and Leroy." Peter proudly introduced two of the Dusters to her, and she couldn't help but grin and shake their hands—Wu Zan's shake was quick and brisk, Leroy's shake firm and long.

"Nice to meet you," Wendy said.

Dr. Barrie and Dr. Mee came rushing out of the building into the street. Dr. Barrie's face filled with worry as he searched through the sea of faces. "Peter, Craft, Onyx!" He called each one out as he recognized them.

Hearing his familiar voice, the Neverwood boys turned as a unit and ran to him, embracing him with a hug, patting his back. Their father was home.

Dr. Barrie's face glistened with tears. "My boys! My boys, you're okay. I'm sorry that I forgot you. It will be okay now. I'm here. I promise."

Peter was the one who had to break the news to Dr. Barrie. "Not all of them made it. We lost a few of the boys today. Torque, Rash, and Dillinger. "

Dr. Barrie was stricken, his mouth pulled down in a frown as he patted his heart as if to console himself. Tink came over and leaned her head on his arm.

Lifting his glasses, he wiped away his tears and took in the hopeful gazes of the Dusters. "But it looks like we gained a few additions to our family. What's your name?" he asked the young woman next to him, who was pulling on the ends of her hair.

"Jade."

"Jade, I'm Dr. Barrie, or Mr. Barrie, or Dad—any work for me. Welcome to our family."

Jade grinned and gave him a hug. "I remember you," she whispered. "You were always kind to us."

"And I strive to always be, but I'm sorry that I couldn't save you back then. It seems like all of you have saved yourselves." His eyes rested on Jax, and Dr. Barrie held out his hand. Jax grinned and took it. "Good job, my boy." He looked around and nodded. "Didn't burn it down too bad."

Jax threw his head back and laughed. "Just wait. I will burn the island down to dust this time, as soon as everyone is off of it."

"Oh, really? It's kind of growing on me. I have a mind to vacation here. What say you, Dr. Mee?"

Dr. Mee was asking about Ditto's wound as she came out of the Physical Therapy Clinic. Without looking, she retorted, "Not on my life. I'm going to head back to the school when it's rebuilt."

"Bet you thought you got rid of me," Ditto called out to Jax and winced as Dr. Mee checked the bandage on his midsection. Not only had he reopened his earlier wound but also had two more punctures from the morphling's bite. They were lucky he survived; it seemed that replicating might have been what saved his life. It turned out that because only one of his four doppelgangers was bitten, the morphling's poison was only a quarter of its normal strength when he merged back into one.

"I'll have to try harder next time," Jax said without emotion.

"I'm like a cockroach," Ditto grinned. "Impossible to kill."

"And always multiplying," Jax added, unable to hold back the snort that turned into a full belly laugh.

Ditto laughed hard, causing Dr. Mee to frown, but he seemed okay, so she moved into the clinic to help the others. "You're always welcome to be on my team, any day," Ditto added. "You didn't do so bad for not being a gamer."

"I'm a fast learner," Jax agreed.

Onyx, still wearing his visor, got a message from Nibs. "Hey, guys. Looks like they need help gathering up the soldiers. They're running into some resistance."

"Go," Peter said, directing Wu Zan, Jax, and Onyx to help. "We'll take care of things down here."

Peter took Wendy's hand in his, and together they turned to assess the full damage inside the dome. There was an awkwardness between the Dusters and the lost girls as they introduced themselves. A few held back and were more aloof than the others. A few chuckles came when the teens began to show off for each other when they met.

Wendy was thrilled to see that most had survived the morphling invasion. But the sight of all the losses dampened the joy. Lily, Brittney, Torque, Rash, and the others she hadn't met yet. Plus, there were still many injured to deal with. Michael, Ash, Craft, Ditto all had wounds that would heal.

Peter brushed Wendy's arm to get her attention and pointing to the makeshift clinic. Slightly and Dr. Mee were busy inside, tending to the injured. "Don't worry. We'll fix them all."

Not all of them. Not the dead. But Wendy forced herself to smile and they began to undo what was done. But she was also worried about the wounds you couldn't see. The emotional ones. First things first. The visors, helmets, and guns were dumped in a pile by the trash can. No more weapons, no more war.

"What's going to happen now?" Wendy asked, looking at the size of their group.

"We live," Peter said simply, reaching for her hand. "One day at a time. We live, we survive."

Wendy watched the cleanup take place, the bandaging, and the hustle to right all that was destroyed. Wendy unzipped her uniform and shed the top, then made her way to the makeshift clinic to help Dr. Mee, knowing she could make herself useful there. But through all the people coming and going, and those in the clinic and the dead laid out on the street she had yet to see Jeremy. In fact, no one had seen him or could account for his whereabouts. *What happened to him? Did he get killed?*

Wendy hoped that wherever he was, that he had survived his encounter with Brittney.

-45-

SO MUCH HAD happened the last few days, it was difficult to process it all. A week had passed since they had defeated Hook and taken down Neverland and, by way of association, Wonderland Games. And in that time, there had been a lot of decisions to make, people to take care of, and futures to plan—and yet so little time to make such life-altering choices.

There was no doubt that Neverwood would rise again, this time bigger and better. But there were more of them now. They would need more space.

And here they had a whole hidden island at their disposal. It seemed a shame to burn it all to the ground now. It would not turn back time, or bring back those they had lost. But they could make something good of it. Rise from the ashes to make something beautiful.

It didn't take long to come to the consensus to turn Hollow Dome into something real, something lasting. It could be made into a haven. A home.

So they decided Neverland would rebuild here inside the dome, and they would keep the Neverwood school on the mainland for a vacation home. Why settle for one school building when you could have an island?

Dr. Barrie demanded that Helix sign his gaming empire over to them, which he did. All the income from future sales of any Wonderland games would be reinvested for the upkeep of the Hollow Dome. Slightly, John, Tink and Ditto had become obsessed and were now helping run, design, and launch future updates to bring in a steady income, just not to the 4-D extent that Helix had been planning.

John and Tink had become adorably inseparable since their reunion. They were the brains behind the new Wonderland Games, and John dubbed her his Queen of hearts, and bestowed upon her bags of Skittles with all of the yellow and green ones picked out.

Curly had spent hours erasing the minds of the investors and they had all gone home on their yachts, and Michael had been monitoring their computers and phone usage ever since. It had become his job to protect the lost boys, girls and Dusters and to erase any digital footprint of the island that he could find.

When it came to the Red Skulls, it took a little bit more work to reprogram since they were dedicated mercenaries, not to Neverland but to Hook himself. Without their leader, they were eager to go back to work for hire. Curly couldn't let that happen, so they became blank slates. With the help of Dr. Mee's psychiatric evaluations, they were able to rewrite their futures without the influence of the darkness in their pasts. In this group of mercenaries, they uncovered men and women with a passion to be teachers, florists, mechanics, nurses, and doctors. Everything they needed to keep their city going.

Curly persuaded most of the techs to continue their work on the island creating the PX dosages that the Dusters needed to stay alive under the guidance of Dr. Barrie.

Most of the Dusters, like Wu Zan and Leroy, chose to stay on the island with Dr. Barrie and live in the Hollow Dome. Not just because they may not have a home to go to, but because they didn't know how to go home. And those that could remember, fear of what they had become, and of having to explain to their families, where they had been the last few years or how they achieved their new powers made going home seem too daunting. In short, they were still imprisoned, but their leash was longer. Now there was a place they can call home, even if it wasn't perfect.

Wendy sat on the half wall of the ruins and looked out to sea. She had spent days staring out at the aquamarine water, praying to go home, to go anywhere but here. She wasn't sure if she was meant to stay on this island, if it would ever feel like home. Her hand brushed her heart and she felt it quicken.

She knew he was near her. Ever since she was made whole again, she always knew where he was, and when he was close by.

"Hello, Jax," Wendy whispered without turning around.

Silent as ever, he came and stood next to her. He had spent the last week avoiding her, and it hurt every time she saw him run away. A heaviness came over her as she stood, seeing her pain mirrored in his eyes. She could tell he had questions.

"Is she gone?" Jax's gray eyes dropped to focus on his feet. He meant Alice, of course.

"No." She reached for his hand and placed it on her heart. "We're here. I'm here."

His eyes glistened with unshed tears and he blinked them away. Looking up at the sky, he sighed. "I think I always knew."

"How could you have known? When I didn't even know that I lost a part of myself. But I think I figured it out."

"What do you mean?" Jax asked.

"Dr. Mee believes my powers were so strong as a child that I was unconsciously locking the power away in a corner of my mind, telling myself that it was a dream, that none of it was real. That the monsters or shadows I created while asleep were only a shadow, a figment of my imagination.

When I panned, I must have split my own soul in two. Locking away my consciousness and the power that terrified me. I refused to allow that part of my consciousness back in, therefore leaving behind part of my soul, an echo of my shadow."

"That figures. I can't fall for you, so I fall for a shadow of you."

"Jax, I—" Wendy began, but he cut her off.

"No, I don't want to hear it. I've known all my life that you and Peter . . . you belonged to each other. You two always gravitated to one another. He was in tune with your moods, he always knew when you were sad, and exactly the right thing to say to cheer you up. When you were scared, nothing anyone else said or did could help, but when he walked in the room, he chased away the darkness. You two are destined to be together. You share something special, but I feel—" He kicked at a pebble, averting his gaze. "I don't like what I feel."

She opened her mouth to respond, but he shook his head. "Please know that I never hated you. I was mean to you to keep you from getting close to me. I was scared I would fall for you, and I did. But I'm not a good person, Wendy, not yet."

He rushed to her, his hand cupping behind her neck, pulling her close into an embrace, and he leaned down and whispered into her ear, "I promise that I will guard you, and watch over you, because within you, you hold what is most dear to me."

He pulled back just enough to kiss her on her forehead.

"What is going on, Jax?" Peter snapped, flying in and landing on the ground. He pulled Wendy out of his arms. "I turn away for one second . . ."

"It's not what you think, Peter. I was saying goodbye," Jax growled, and Wendy's heart thudded in fear. Although it wasn't her fear, but her shadow's, at the thought of losing Jax.

"Well, I'm not a fan of how you say goodbye," Peter said, his voice deepening. His hands clenched. Jax's fists and temper mirrored Peters.

"No!" Wendy stepped between the two, glaring at Peter. "I will love you for all eternity, you know that, but I don't love you with all my heart."

"W—what?" Peter stumbled, taken aback by her admission.

"It's the truth. I love you, but a part of my heart belongs to Jax. It's a small part, but one that must be recognized." Wendy bit her lip and looked into Peter's deep green eyes. "Do you trust me?"

"Yes," he said emphatically.

"Thank you." She grinned. "Jax, come with me." She held out her hand and he took it while watching Peter warily. Holding on to Jax, Wendy called the shadows, and together they passed into the shadow realm.

This time, it wasn't dark, creepy or cold, but filled with colors, a warm wind, and the smell of ocean. It was a mirror image of the island, except the colors were brighter, the wind not as crisp, and the sound of the ocean more pleasant.

"Where are we?" Jax asked.

"My dreams," Wendy smiled. "It's not the shadow realm, Jax. It never was. This is the plane where unconscious thought and consciousness collide. See?" She pointed and a fox came running over to them and yipped at Jax's heels before taking off into the jungle, chasing a bird. Jax grinned when he recognized their old friend Fox.

She took his hand and walked along the cliff, then down a path to the beach, where her parents were having a picnic under an umbrella. They waved at her, and Mary went back to reading a book aloud to George.

Two girls were playing with a beach ball farther out, and she pointed out the other lost boys.

"How is this possible?" he breathed out as a beach ball rolled over to his foot. He picked it up as Brittney ran over to get it from him.

"Thanks," she giggled and ran back toward Lily.

"My dreams are powerful Jax. You should know that more than anyone, and it was only because my dreams scared me that the shadow world looked the way it did. But I've slowly been recreating it to be more of a haven for lost souls, instead of the dark and scary nightmare it was before."

He scanned the island and listened to the soft sound of the ocean. Everything was more muted and pleasant. "This is heaven."

"No, that's the big guy's job, I would never dare to try and recreate his masterpiece, and I assume that after a while, the lost souls will leave my dreams and go where they belong. But for now, as long as I dream it, they exist."

"Why did you bring me here?" His voice sounded pained and he looked at her with accusation.

"I hoped it would make you happy being here," Wendy said softly. "Maybe ease the pain of losing Alice."

"You mean losing you," he said angrily.

"You never had me, Jax," Wendy corrected softly. "You only had a small part of me." She sighed. "I dreamed of Peter, but my shadow dreamed of you. Ironic, isn't it? After seven years apart, I thought my shadow and I would fit back together like a glove, but we don't. The glove is too tight. Her heart has grown so much that we can't coincide together anymore." Wendy touched her chest. "It gets confusing."

"What do you mean?" Jax asked.

She closed her eyes, her lashes fluttering against her cheeks. A soft sigh escaped, and then she opened her blue eyes and grinned. "I'm surprised you haven't noticed yet."

"Noticed what?" Jax growled out. "The trees, the ocean, the beach. What do you want me to notice?"

"Alice," Wendy said with a chuckle and pointed.

Jax spun so hard on his heels that he lost his balance. He focused on where Wendy pointed, and he couldn't believe he hadn't noticed her right away. She was walking along the beach in a white sundress, her sandals held in her hand as she watched the sunset.

"How?"

"Like I said, I created her long ago, and our power combined is frightening. Every time I saw you, my heart would beat like crazy, and I knew that she was pining for you. But I can't have my heart betraying me like that. It's too confusing. So my shadow is here. It's safer if we part. No one should be able to wield that much power over life and death."

"She's real."

"She's real as long as I live," Wendy breathed out. "With all of the other shadows. And I will bring you here, Jax. To visit a few hours a day, if you like. But you must remember to live. Out there, in the real world."

"Does she remember me?" he whispered.

Wendy touched her chest and felt her own heart quicken when Alice turned and spotted them. "She remembers."

He took off his shoes and walked toward her. His hands were sweating, and he rubbed them on his khakis. When he got to the water's edge, she held out her hand. He took it and felt her palm slide into his. A perfect fit. He looked into her eyes that were a dark gray, almost black, so unlike Wendy's. He didn't care.

"I dreamed of you," Wendy's shadow spoke and her voice soothed his soul.

"And I dreamed of you," he breathed out and looked in awe at their hands clasped together. "What should I call you? Do you go by Wendy, Wendy's shadow?"

She laughed and shook her head. "I like the name you call me. Alice."

"Alice," Jax confirmed.

"Will you visit me often?" Alice asked.

"Every time I dream," Jax promised.

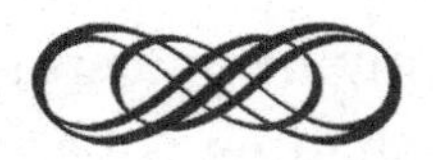

Wendy watched their reunion on the beach and felt her own heart rate pick up, an echo of what her soul was feeling. She still couldn't believe that she had lived so long without a part of her soul that her soul dreamed itself into reality—a reality so real her shadow had become corporeal enough for Hook to find it, and yet not real enough to wake without fading out. That is why they had kept her shadow in a constant sleep.

Time could easily slip away in this realm, and Wendy wanted to get back to Peter, but first she needed to check on someone. Not needing the shadow's help anymore to navigate her dreams, Wendy materialized on the deck of an old pirate ship in the sky and found Hook exactly where she had left him the last time she was here, and where he would remain for good—running back and forth, trying to raise the sails and steer the ship among the clouds.

When she'd first found Hook, after she'd cast him into the shadow realm, he'd been hunched in a shadowy corner, muttering and alone, the drugs having burned out his mind. Soon after, she'd begun to reshape her dreams, and decided she couldn't just leave Hook as he was. Instead, she created a ship for Hook to sail among the clouds, a ship that could never land. And keeping him always on the move was his own personal nightmare. For following in his ship's wake, always in pursuit of the mean old man, was a crocodile desperate to catch him.

"Tick, Tock," Hook mumbled as he wound the rope, and as he tightened the sails. He looked in fear over the side of the flying ship and saw the crocodile swimming among the clouds. "Out of time, must keep moving or he'll get me," Hook muttered, ignoring Wendy completely. She left him to continue his sailing adventure.

She passed through back to the physical plane.

Peter was exactly where she had left him.

He looked around. "Where's Jax? Did you drop him off a cliff? I hope you dropped him off a cliff."

Wendy came and wrapped her arms around him. "No, I gave him his dream."

"What do you mean?" Peter said nuzzling her neck. "You mean he's happy?"

"Yes," Wendy confirmed, kissing him on the lips. "I will explain later, but I thought it only fair that he gets a happily-ever-after."

"Speaking of happily-ever-afters . . ." Peter kissed her on the lips. "I made you a promise when we were younger."

"You promised me a lot of things," she whispered and led him over to the edge of the cliff. "Like you promised me a puppy—"

"And an espresso machine." He grinned, but she backed up to the edge, and he frowned, trying to pull her back to him. "Wendy, what are you doing?"

"This is the exact spot where you fell off the ledge seven years ago. It was here where you promised to take me away, buy all the ice cream in the world, build me a tree house."

Her foot dangled dangerously over the edge. "You once promised me that I could fly, if I just believed." She swept her arm out into an arc over the cliff.

Peter's brows furrowed and he tried to pull her back from the edge, but she wagged her finger at him.

"Ah, ah, ah. It's my turn." Wendy held her hand out to him and said, "Come with me, Peter. I won't let you fall," her smile sparkling with mischief.

He reached for her hand and Wendy took off up into the air without him.

"What?" His hands covered his head in wonder. "You can fly? You never cease to amaze me." In two steps Peter launched into the air and flew with Wendy in the clouds. "You are something. When did this happen?"

"I don't know. I can only assume I got an upgrade.

"Or you dreamed it," Peter said, laughing.

"Yes, this could all be a dream," she giggled. "My dreams do have a habit of coming true."

He stilled and wrapped his hands around her waist. Her cheeks flushed as he leaned in, cupping her cheek.

Hundreds of feet above Neverland, on an island in the middle of the ocean, he asked her, "Promise you will always be mine. Promise you'll dream of us forever."

Peter flew a circle around Wendy and she got dizzy trying to keep him in sight.

"I promise," she whispered huskily.

His lips pressed against hers, and she knew her heart would always be his.

-EPILOGUE-

JEREMY SAT IN the hold of a fishing boat. The stinking nets and swells of water sloshing against his boots was enough to make him sick. He had stolen off the island in one of the Red Skull's boats as soon as Peter and his crew had taken control. He'd heard in passing about Hook's death at the hands of a morphling, and mourned his leader. Now he didn't know where he was going and the speed boat's navigation was messed up. Not long after he departed, it had run out of gas and was left drifting with the current. After drifting for days with very little supplies, he had begun to hallucinate.

"Neverland—Peter pans—Hook."

He was delirious by the time he was picked up by a passing fishing boat and nursed back to health by two fishermen who didn't speak his language.

But Jeremy hadn't left empty-handed. Next to him on the floor of the boat sat three crates filled with enough of the stolen PX drug to last him a few years if he used it sparingly. The fishing boat captain noticed the crates and assumed they were important to him and hauled them on the boat.

Jeremy left his precious cargo and made it to the head to wash his hands and check the bandage that covered the right half of his face. He needed to change the dressing and without any proper medical care other than what the fisherman had supplied, it looked like it would scar. Jeremy carefully pulled off the bandage to gaze at his face and the damage that the mountain lion had done. He never expected Brittney, little Miss Priss Brittney, to have it in her to turn on him, much less to shapeshift into a mountain lion. Her parting gift was a long scar that ran up length of his right cheek.

One of the fishermen found him in the bathroom and handed him a bowl of soup, then gestured to his face.

"H—hook," the fisherman said.

"What?" Jeremy snapped and his heart beat erratically as he waited in fear for his captain to barge into the head and yell at him.

"Hook," the fisherman repeated in a heavy accent. "Look like . . . hook." He imitated the shape of a hook by crooking his finger. Then he trudged back up top and Jeremy was left staring at the scar on his face in disbelief.

"Yes, it does look like a hook."

His ran his hand along his Red Skull uniform, and his resentment toward Peter only grew. He belonged with the Red Skulls. Neverland was his home. As soon as he stepped foot off that island, he had known he would be back. He vowed to seek revenge, even if it took him years. Jeremy would gather a crew, go back and find Neverland, and destroy Peter and his boys, if it was the last thing he ever did.

"Hook," Jeremy repeated, running a finger over his scar. His mouth turned up into the most sinister of grins, stretching the painful scar and making his once handsome and debonair face look cruel.

"That's Captain Hook to you."

Chanda Hahn is a NYT & USA Today Bestselling author of Reign and Forever. She uses her experience as a children's pastor, children's librarian and bookseller to write compelling and popular fiction for teens. She was born in Seattle, Washington, grew up in Nebraska, and currently resides in Wisconsin with her husband and their twin children.

Visit Chanda Hahn’s website to learn more about her other forthcoming books. **www.chandahahn.com**

Made in the USA
Monee, IL
18 September 2019